Michael Fontaine is a career not-for-profit professional who works in Washington D. C. He is working on a master's degree in public administration, and spends his spare time writing fiction, playing the French horn, composing music for chamber ensembles and has also published another novel, *Tawsi Melek Meets the Dragon Prince*.

He lives alone in Washington, D. C.

The Rage of Ganumede is dedicated to all of us who got swept away by the unexpected appearance of utter, total beauty, and during its disappearance.

Michael Fontaine

The Rage of Ganumede

Austin Macauley Publishers™
London * Cambridge * New York * Sharjah

This is a work of fiction. Names, characters, businesses, places, events, locales, and incidents are either the products of the author's imagination or used in a fictitious manner. Any resemblance to actual persons, living or dead, or actual events is purely coincidental.

Ordering Information
Quantity sales: Special discounts are available on quantity purchases by corporations, associations, and others. For details, contact the publisher at the address below.

Publisher's Cataloging-in-Publication data
Fontaine, Michael
The Rage of Ganumede

ISBN 9781643783987 (Paperback)
ISBN 9781643783994 (Hardback)
ISBN 9781645367697 (ePub e-book)

Library of Congress Control Number: 2020922051

www.austinmacauley.com/us

First Published (2021)
Austin Macauley Publishers LLC
40 Wall Street, 33rd Floor, Suite 3302
New York, NY 10005
USA

mail-usa@austinmacauley.com
+1 (646) 5125767

Thanks to Stefen, who gave me the time, the place, and the confidence to tell this story.

Description

The Rage of Ganumede follows two characters: Ganumede, the Prince of Troy, and the Demigod Attis, his cousin.

Ganumede, the 'Most Beautiful Mortal of Myth,' desired by mortals, raped by the gods, had wants and needs of his own. Specifially, those embodied by his cousin, Attis, the son of the Goddess Isis.

Everyone from High Olmypus to the Underworld and in between has other plans for both of them. The secrets of the gods and the other young men that fell prey to seduction and abduction are revealed after Ganumede is taken by Zeus to be the new Cupbearer of the Gods.

After Ganumede disappears; Attis, stricken with sadness, pursues his plan to save the world from the notorious King Midas and his daughter, Zoe, the Golden Girl, whom he is forced to marry by the evil King.

Before the marriage takes place, Rhea, Zeus's mother, abducts Attis in hopes of creating a new race of Titans to overthrow her son.

A brutal fight takes place at Zeus's table when Rhea tries to enter the Abode of the Gods with Attis at her side. Zeus, indomitable, shrugs off Rhea's assault and she and Attis are cast from Olympus.

Defeated and castrated, Attis, and Rhea, then, search for the Phallus of Osiris, believing it to be the key to ending Zeus's reign.

After Ganumede recovers from Zeus's abuse, he learns that Attis is not the first or only boy-toys of the gods.

With the help of the Holy Trinity of Goddesses, Ganumede escapes Olympus and returns, armed with the might of the Storm Soldiers and the secret of the most important mystery of them all: Who God and the gods are and the destiny of all things.

Attis, newly equipped with the Phallus of Osiris, continues Rhea's plan for cosmic domination simultaneous to Ganumede's plan to rescue him from certain and absolute corruption.

The second half details the quest of a council of goddesses banded together to defeat the Final Emperor, Marcus Prefect, AKA the God Yahweh, reborn in a new guise who intends to settle His old scores with a rebellious creation.

Category

LGBTQ/Fantasy/Sci-Fi Interest

1. **The Rage of Ganumede**

Introduction: The Preludes

Establishes the main characters: Attis, Zoe, the goddess, Nana, Osiris, Horus and the protagonist, Ganumede, his brother, Tithonus, and, parents, The King and Queen of Troy. This is done by Hekate, the Goddess of Children, Witchcraft, and Murder.

Chapter 1 – Eos, the Goddess of the Dawn

Eos and Phoebus Apollo, brother and sister, share an interest: boys. They also share a profound lack of frustration tolerance for the other character flaw they have in common: nymphomania.

Chapter 2 – Bombs from Heaven

Ganumede fails to find a suitor and becomes ostracized. The only person who wants to be his friend is not a person but the Demigod Attis, who is betrothed to the sociopath Zoe, daughter of King Midas.

Attis wants an ally in his plans to free the world from his crazy girlfriend and bring unity to the world, Ganumede wants the only person he thinks is worthy of his affections. No ordinary boy will do!

Chapter 3 – Ganumede Takes a Lover!

Unwilling to wait for Attis to figure it out, Ganumede seeks the help of Eros, the god of desire and attempts to win the god's favors in a legendary game of chance. If he wins, Eros will make Attis change his evil ways and love Ganumede. If he loses, he becomes Eros's special friend for all eternity.

Chapter 4 – The Lost Boys

The Titaness of the moon helped Zeus overthrow his father, aunts, and uncles and all that fighting made her horny. She cuts a deal with Zeus. In exchange for Her loyalties against Kronus, Zeus agrees to turn Her lover, the mortal Endymion, into an immortal that will never, ever turn Her down or forsake Her for another.

Phoebe makes a booty call to the boudoir one day to discover something is missing. Endymion's penis. A tense discussion with the god Horus, the god of the sun, sheds some light on the matter.

Mid-chapter we meet Hyakinthos and Daphne, office mates, who share a lover, Phoebus Apollo. They are never heard from again.

Chapter 5 – Doors, Roads, and Gateways

We've met and heard quite a lot from Hekate but know very little about her motives or agenda. They must remain mysterious or Witches' Honor will be violated.

Ganumede's mother, the Queen of Witches, disagrees completely. When Ganumede, far too smitten with the god Attis, for his own good, heads out into the night on the back of an otherworldly gold motorcycle, the Queen and goddess of witches decide to intervene.

Chapter 6 – Tapers, Torches, and Conflagrations

Dissatisfied with their attempts to rid her son of the ungodly influence of Attis and marry him to suitable partner, the King and Queen of Troy arrange his marriage.

This draws the attention of Zeus, the King of the Gods, who has no intentions of letting the Most Beautiful Flower *Ever* to be plucked from his garden. Ganumede disappears.

The goddess Eos, engorged with lust, takes a page out of Zeus's book and Ganumede's twin, the studly Tithonus, disappears.

Interludes

Bereft over the loss of his sons, Tros arms and aims two aconite missiles at Olympus. Zeus, knowing he will need Troy's favor in the future, sends Hermes to the mysterious realm of the Storm Soldiers to retrieve two storm-footed horses as compensation for the mourning king's losses.

Simultaneously, to celebrate the end of the Trojan legacy, King Midas throws a wedding for Attis and Zoe.

The Queen of Troy, deeply angry and bitter over the deaths of her twins prays to Rhea, the Mother of Titans, and begs her to intervene in the unholy union.

The loop closes.

Chapter 7 – Boys on Fire

An unlikely and inconvenient reunion between Rhea, Attis, Eos, and Tithonus and Ganumede takes place in Olympus. The fight nearly tears Heaven from the skies but Zeus reigns supreme.

Attis vows revenge, Eos vows revenge, Ganumede serves the wine.

Chapter 8 – As Above So Below

Ganumede gets acquainted with the gods of Olympus on High and hears their stories. They haven't had anyone to talk to in a long time that cares to listen.

Attis and Rhea journey to Duat, the Underworld River of the Egyptian gods, in search of the Phallus of Osiris. The disenfranchised souls of the Duat, like the gods in heaven, have also not had an ear to fill with their entreaties and a deal is struck.

Attis, the newly ordained Father of Titans, leaves the Duat to get allies from Tartarus.

Ganumede finally gets some action. If only he could remember it…

Interlude 2

The goddess of the Dawn does the unthinkable and unspeakable and once more, someone is having a baby.

Meanwhile, the battle at the Tartarus gate between the gods of Heliopolis and Attis for the Phallus of Osiris goes poorly for the forces of light, and back in Olympus the Holy Trinity of Goddesses think it's time for something new.

Chapter 9 – Forms and Formlessness

Hermes restores Ganumede's memories and finds Zeus' porn hub that he's been building using all of Ganumede's sexual adventures in Olympus.

Worse, Ganumede learns he has a brother who is trapped in the dungeons of the Labyrinth.

Ganumede attacks Zeus.

Zeus is indomitable and uninterested in the Rage of Ganumede. Even the combined forces of Olympus are not enough to help him, the Cupbearer of the Gods, and the Most Beautiful Mortal is discarded; thrown over the wall of Olympus into the Ether like a leftover gizzard.

Chapter 10 – The Secret of the Storm Captain

Hermes sends Ganumede on an errand to fetch the one thing that can usurp Zeus's power; Soma, the Beverage of the very horny Storm Soldiers, the keepers of the Storm-Footed Horses.

There, he meets Marici, the Storm Captain, who reveals a secret.

Then it's back to Olympus one last time.

Chapter 11 – The Seventh House

Attis divides his forces as another secret, the Seventh House enters the battle for the future of creation.

The long-awaited confrontation between Attis and Zeus, Ganumede and Zeus, the Divine Mothers and Zeus, the Storm Army and Zeus takes place.

Olympus falters and the Storm Army and the Forces of the Seventh House are left with one last objective; to restore Order by recovering the Phallus of Osiris, stolen by Attis.

Pace Nightclub

Hestia, the House Mother, delivers an innovative solution to everyone's troubles.

The Seventh House

Attis and Ganumede rekindle their friendship and there is a happy ending it seems, until Ganumede's nephew, Nefertem, the god the dawn, arrives to take up the role of Eos, his mother.

If he can take his eyes off of Attis. Like Father, like son.

2. The Absolution of Attis

I. Before

Orion, the son of Poseidon was raped by Zeus. Scandalized, ostracized, and exiled to the stars, he serves as the Steward of the Happy Hunting Grounds for Medicine Woman, who adopted him.

There, they both witness something damned peculiar…a bunch of dead sacred animals and a white rabbit with a penchant for sex with men.

II. Rabbit on the Run

Jezebel the legendary whore meets her old lover, Marcus Prefect in hell. Once again, the goddesses and gay boys of creation must contend with a self-righteous God, back to enforce His will on a self-determined creation.

III. The Absolution of Attis Begins

Jezebel, tells her side of the story. Threatened, cursed, and finally sent to hell because she had a mind of her own, Jezebel, apparently joins forces with Yahweh in his new guise as Marcus Prefect in hopes of understanding and thwarting His Plans instead.

In the Seventh House, Attis is ready to fit Nefertem with a muzzle and a chastity belt. With his mother, Isis's, help, he comes up with a plan: To host a cotillion and marry him off to one of many irresistible suitors.

Unlike his uncle, for whom an arranged marriage was unappealing, Nefertem is overjoyed.

IV. Hunting for Sport

There are assholes and buttholes and, then, there's *the Four Sportsmen.* Orion and Spanx, the Brass Dragon/Shinx hybrid, find them piling up bodies, or what is left of them, of the sacred animals which Medicine Woman gave sanctuary.

V. Fembots!

Marcus Prefect has a way into the Cotillion and the Seventh House; a miscreant god who wants Nefertem's hand in marriage. Jezebel builds a vampire lesbian robot army for him to help out and help herself into a position where she can get revenge on Isis for abandoning her in ancient Babylon.\

VI. Cotillion

The attack of the Fembots and Marcus Prefect on the Seventh House results in the addition of Jezebel as its newest resident, and the loss of Nefertem, the god of the dawn to the clutches of Tezcatlipoca, the god of Deception.

Jezebel explains who and what Marcus Prefect is and a rescue effort for Nefertem departs.

Meanwhile, the Four Sportsmen attack the Happy Hunting Grounds again.

VII. The Death of Attis

The Fembot attack left Attis drained of blood and near dying. The goddesses submerge him in the womb of the goddess Branwen, the Lady of the Lake, and hope for his return.

VIII. What Can be Seen?

Jezebel reveals she has been cursed with a *hollow,* a baby without a soul, levied upon her by the cruel and vicious God Yahweh, who now calls Himself Marcus Prefect, the Last Emperor.

The Seventh House rallies around her and decides to give Marcus what he wants: War, one last time.

Marcus gears up by reuniting Himself with what remains of old friends: Edith, Lot's Wife, Saphira, Job, Adam, and Tantalus, each given a special role in helping the world to do God's Will.

IX. She's Having a Baby! Everyone Is!

Marcus and the Administrators enact their plans to poison the oceans, start wars, and proliferate weapons. Chief amongst His plans to make hell on earth is overpopulation and Job, bitter against the world, eager to see how it handles its suffering, is ready to help.

The Goddesses of the Seventh House identify a solution for Jezebel's unborn child. Ishtar, also called Isis, asks the gay angel Cerviel, the lover of Daniel the Prophet, for help. And surprise…it's a boy!

The other goddesses come up with an equally innovative solution for the Fembot Lesbian Vampires…which is good because the new Pope Tantalus, releases his blood drinking Hierarchy, the Vultures on the world.

X. The Cave of the Heart

Orion, Ganumede, and Spanx go searching for Nefertem, who is being held prisoner as the love slave of the Smoking Mirror, Tezcatlipoca in the cavern of Talocan, the Aztec Hell, along with Xochipilli, the Prince of Flowers and Power Bottom Extraordinaire.

The rescue seems doomed to failure but for the appearance of the mysterious Ace of Swords.

XI. The Riddle of the Heart

The Four Sportsmen and the Five Tops prepare for war.

XII. Nine Plus Nine

War between the House and the Administration begins.

XIII. Medicine House

The war with Marcus Prefect concludes. Leading the way to…

XIV. The One True Abomination

What is the one True Abomination? Can it be defeated?

Author's Notes

I got the idea for this novel after I saw the painting *the Rape of Ganymede* in a museum. I did some research and discovered the subject was beloved by pederasts, viewed with suspicion by others. It is thought to have been invented by Socratic philosphers to justify man/boy love, and some of us appreciate this, others not so much. We bury the myth today, but it remained a part of Greek Myth Canon because of the aura of Zeus Himself: he was the King of the Gods was able to do what he wanted. He did it quite a lot, in fact.

Greek philosophers loved to use his example as point and counterpoint in arguing the question, "Are we better than the gods or not?" Goddesses were not exempt from the argument.

It might seem erotic to think of a very hot young man as the target for randy encounter with an older man or woman and these things certainly happened, but whether or not they made a lasting good impression depended on the situation. Rape fantasies being the subject of many a young man's life, they don't always turn out.

I wrote the *Rage of Ganumede* to discredit the idea that Ganumede would appreciate being raped mid-air over the City of Troy by an eagle that held him tight in its razor-sharp talons.

Rape and sexual abuse change their victims. I wanted to know more about what Ganumede's life was like prior to the loss of his innocence. I wondered who and what he left behind once he was deified as a consequence.

Ganumede, Prince of Troy was called the Most Beautiful Mortal. When you are good looking, you are everyone's property…or they want to be yours. We simply must know what such creatures want and need from us, hoping they can be captured, stowed, and prized in private. They don't need feelings, dreams, or desires of their own, or do they?

I wrote the character deliberately oblivious of all this drama, even dissociative from himself. He never uses his looks in a devious or manipulative way; is shy about their impact on others. He knows he's good-looking but he wants to *actually feel attractive* through actual another boy's affection.

I avoided depicting or describing the character in any way. I do not put him in any sexually convoluted or compromised positions because I have no idea what the most beautiful boy in the world actually looks like, or what *you* would do with him if you could. Moreso, *I just wasn't attracted to him*. It's too hard to be attracted to myself!

I wasn't raped or abducted but had an experience as a young person that changed my life. The incident is in this story, subtly shaded and cloaked in metaphor, but please be aware I made sure to tell Ganumede's story and not my own.

Introduction

The Preludes

From *Hekate's Cahier*
Written by Triune Hekate, the Goddess of Witches, Children, and Murder
The Wedding of Attis and Zoe
The Temple of Rhea
Mideaum, Capital City of the Phrygian Empire

Osiris reattached Nana's head back to her body. The roar of lions mixed with the screams of men and women, the sound of breaking dishes, blaring trumpets, and the drum roll of feet pounding the temple floor as people stampeded to get away.

Blood pooled on the floor and trickled down the walls. The odor of a slaughterhouse mingled with the scent of incense and orchids.

A Midean soldier stood apart from the mob and stared up. His mouth gaped open and he pulled his pants down. He grabbed his genitals in his hand, forming a mini guillotine between his knuckles and his sack, drew his sword, and hacked away.

"Ouch!" Osiris said, and sheltered the little goddess with his body so she wouldn't be splattered with more blood or get stepped on as the crowd ran about.

When the way was clear, Osiris grabbed Nana under her arms and pulled her to safety behind an overturned table. He nearly tripped over the body of another young man who lay there, hands clasped over his crotch, fingers locked together over the open gash where his rooster used to be.

Nana's eyes moved beneath her eyelids which were shaded the color of the sky. Her hands twitched and moved to her neck. She inhaled and more of her syrupy gold blood spilled over her lips and chin.

Osiris grabbed a linen napkin that was embroidered with *Attis and Zoe* in gold thread and wiped her mouth. As he settled Nana across his lap, one more body fell backwards over the upturned table. Another wedding guest, blood sprayed from the hole that he tore in his groin using a butter knife from one of the place settings.

Nana's eyes opened; saw the carnage, the green man holding her, and recoiled. She coughed up more blood when she attempted to cry out.

"Hello," the green guy said. "Do not worry, I will protect you."

"Who are you?" Nana's rewoven vocal chords squeaked, "Where is Attis, and where is my husband…?"

"I am Osiris of the Western Land. I do not know where your boy is," Osiris looked around, "I lost sight of him after Rhea attacked."

"She's not still here, is she?" Nana tried to sit up but Osiris shook his head.

"She is pursuing her prey," Osiris peeked over the edge of the table. "Such a mess."

"I need to get to my husband," Nana freed herself from Osiris's arms. "And find Attis before that bitch gets to him."

"I'm sorry Innana," Osiris stared for a moment. "Silenus, the Prophet, is gone, Rhea…is come."

"Yes. I suppose I knew that already," Nana covered her eyes. "He said this would happen, all of it. My father…"

"Also gone, back to his stream bed," Osiris pets her jet-colored hair. "The price of challenging the Mother of Titans. I have to take you away from here. If Rhea senses you are not dead, she may consider her vengeance incomplete and return to finish the job."

Nana stood, "No. I have to get to Attis before Rhea does or her vengeance against me will be the least of our problems. All of creation will suffer!"

"There is no risk of that," Osiris kept hold of her hand, his deep green eyes were sad. "Zeus's curse has ensured Rhea will not able to use your son's parts to regain any of her former power."

Nana knew what that meant. "Oh no!" Nana fell back to the floor of the temple, its expansive marble floor blotted with black blood as if from some massive overturned ink well, "I can't bear it! This was his wedding day!"

"I wish I could have saved him for you." The green eyes panned around the devastated temple, "But even the Hathors said his fate could not be averted. Only yours, Great Mother."

“Did the Hathors design my fate to be *this* then?” Nana flapped her hands at what had become of the wedding ceremony of her son, “Mother of…mass murder?”

“You have not spilled one drop of blood in your life, Nana. You never shall.” Osiris held her in his arms, “The Hathors told me I would save you and take you away with me to the Western Land and you would fall in love with me.”

Nana shivered inside the green biceps, veined deep green like a banyan trunk, “How could you fall in love with me? Look what I’ve done. All these innocent people that are dead becausee of me…”

“Of course not!” Osiris caressed her bruised and bloodied cheek. “You tried to save them. Someday all in the universe will know how hard you tried to protect them and they will love you forever for it. I will see to it.”

“Are you kidding me?” Nana shook her head and she began to cry again. “If my name is ever spoken again, Rhea will find me. And, then, no one will be able to protect me.”

“The gods of the Western Land will watch over you,” Osiris said. “We will call you Isis and she will never find you or trouble you again. This, I promise, in the name of Ra.”

The calamity subsided to weeping and wailing, the roar of lions was distant. A few survivors wandered about, most of them women trying to get assistance for their sons, friends, fathers, and brothers that maimed themselves.

Nothing could be done. Nana left with Osiris and joined Him in His House.

The Death and Resurrection, from the Great Hymn

Lord Osiris, The Lord of Love, King of the Living and the Dead, took a liking to Nepthys, his brother Seth’s sister-wife.

While Lord Set, the god of the Night Wind, was out rabble rousing with the scorpions and jackals, Lord Osiris seduced Nepthys. They were discovered together upon Set’s return at sunrise.

Set was outraged and hurled insults at Lord Osiris. Osiris kicked Set in the shin and Set vowed vengeance for the violation of his wife and person.

Upon his return with Mother Isis from Phrygia, Lord Osiris and his new bride lay together to celebrate their union and a wild bull broke into their bedchamber. The creature had eyes like a red desert sunset and roared like a sandstorm. It took Osiris by its horns and threw him into the air.

Osiris landed beside the Nile, where many crocodiles tore him into bits and pieces.

By the time Isis discovered the whereabouts of her husband, his parts were spread out widely across the land.

The Nile began to overflow its banks from the many tears Mother Isis wept at the murder of her beloved. Nepthys, sorry for what happened, offered to help her find Osiris' scattered remains and put him back together.

They sent a flock of kites to search far and wide with their keen eyes in order to find where the Lord's vestiges had been scattered.

Some were washed into the Nile, others sank into the marshes. One was eaten by an oxyrhynchus fish.

Isis traveled the land, sometimes disguised as an old hag, gathering up her murdered husband's remnants. She was able to find all of them but one, his phallus.

Isis and Nepthys carefully reassembled Osiris and wrapped him in the usual ceremonial dressings of bright white. Because they were unable to locate his manhood, Isis asked Divine Pitah to fashion a replacement of gold and inserted it into his body like the final piece of a jigsaw puzzle.

Isis and Nepthys cast a healing spell over the body but Osiris lay still and did not move. All the gods were very sad and lost all hope the Lord of the Living would ever rise again.

Falcon Headed Ra, Father of Order, heard their cries of lament and descended from Heliopolis in the Night Boat to offer his assistance.

"I heard you weeping," the Lord of the Sun Kingdom said. "Why are you sad?"

"Great King of the gods," Nepthys said, "we are sad because Osiris was killed by my husband Set and we cannot return him to life with all of our power."

"It is not Maat that good Osiris should be slain in such a way," Ra placed his hand over Osiris's heart. "And he is my friend."

The Great God Ra issued a commandment, "Rise, Osiris, now crowned King of the Living and the Dead."

Osiris returned to life and sat up, for no man or god or beast or any creature can disobey the Word of Ra, for it is Maat.

As the gods celebrated the return of Osiris to life, Ra also said, "Hereafter, the dead shall be embalmed, just as was done with Great Osiris. He, along with Mother Isis, will await them in the Western Land, so they will have no fear in life or in death."

And Ra declared, "This also is Maat."

Before Ra turned to return to his barge, which was now the Day Boat, Isis knelt before him and prayed, "O King of the gods, I bless you and pay homage to you for your gift of eternal life. Were that Osiris being complete, so I could bear children who could also sing your praises."

"I bless you in return, Divine Mother," Ra said. "For before Osiris was murdered, you conceived a son. He will be known as *Ra-Horakhty*, Ra, who is Horus of the Horizon, the god of hope, and the Savior of the World."

With that, Ra returned to Heliopolis. The sun rose and the gods celebrated. The phallus of Osiris remained lost.

Hekate, the Goddess of Witchcraft, Children, and Murder She's having a baby
Bitch is crazy
She's having another, his twin brother!

The truth is, I lie. Not all the time but sometimes. When I do, I do it quite well. All you haver to do is convince a beleiver that the hint you're about to give them is everything you have. Leave the rest be, they might figure it out on their own. It is a stitch to see what they will believe, and what they'll do next. They'll think you've revealed something fundamental to the rules of existence and all you did was ad lib! Gods love doing this. It entertains them.

I do it out of necesssity.

Here is a rule I follow, however, and it is one to which I suggest you pay close attention. No matter what she does, never, ever lie to a witch. I am *the witch* and even I don't lie to a sister or even a brother that acts like one.

Don't ask a witch for a love spell, we hate that, and being tasked with making babies makes us downright ornery. Unless it's one of us. Then, we try and, unfortunately, it never works out. The Fates forbid a person of our faith and power from becoming too numerous or too powerful.

Even still, I was once asked by a very dear friend, Callirhoe, the First Queen of Troy, who was a very powerful witch and the Queen of Nymphs to help her have a baby with a mortal. That is absolutely off limits. The offspring of a Royal Witch, a Nymph Queen, and a mortal would cause the universe to be horny, horny, horny. And it did.

As the Goddess of the Three Roads however, I had no reason to worry about boundaries and rules, so I agreed to help her. She was my best friend and there was no way I was going to tell her no.

So, I told her yes. Twice!

Now, remember I told you that making god babies was not wise. I employed the necessary spells to give Callirhoe a son and I made women unlikable to him, so he would never philander and create a bunch of Demigods. I knew that would put him at a disadvantage, in some ways, and I had my pride, so I made him quite a dish. The dishiest, in fact. The result of my work, I, Hekate, the Mother of Daughters made, was called the World's Most Beautiful Mortal.

Then, I saw that caused a bit of a problem: Royal grandchildren. So I made another one just like him and made him breed-able, hoping this might, at least, give the Queen grandbabies and her husband an heir to the Crown he could be proud of. *And what a stud he turned out to be*!

But this also was a problem. I did mention making children was problematic, didn't I? Most people can't even raise a normal child, much less a god, and don't get me started on parents that treat the ordinary ones like gods. *Cripes!*

It was not my intention to cause grief or harm but even though I know what I know, I still do what I do. I am a Goddess of Witches, and that means my good intentions will never win anyone over. I must cause mischief in the lives of others in spite of the fact I know of the grief it will cause well in advance.

Listen in while I try, really try, to be a good friend and explain all this to the Queen, hoping it will make a difference if I try to warn her as much as I am willing:

"A god is going to take your son from you," I told Callirhoe.

"Excuse me?" Callirhoe, the only frigid Nymph in all mythology was quite irritable toward disagreeable news.

"But not the other one."

"The other what?"

"The other son."

"*What* other son?"

I did my best to not look away with any of my faces. “You’re having twins, my dear.”

“Shut up.”

“And one of them will be taken from you by a god.”

“I don’t understand.”

I hated this part.

“He’s a boy lover. And a god will take him from you.”

“A god?” Callirhoe smiled, her green lips and moss green eyes blazed. “Well That’s wonderful! Of course, a cute little god will come along and…”

I gently shook my head, “No…not quite like that. There are no gay weddings in your future, dear, I’m afraid. The god that comes for him will take him far, far away from you and you will never see him again. This is the just way that it is going to happen.”

The look in her eyes, “Still. Can something be done? Since I am forewarned?”

She knew not to ask any further. Another aspect of ‘Witches Honor’: never ask for more than what you are told.

“*Something* can always be done,” I said. This was one of my better true lies.

“What about the other one?” Callirhoe asked.

“Him? No god will not take him from you,” I said. “Both will be handsome, beautiful beyond comparison, and all will adore them.”

“So what will I tell Tros, my husband, about his sons?”

Women! Always worried about how their stupid husbands will react to finding out that fucking isn’t just for sex.

“Tell him he has twins on the way. What else would you tell him?”

Callirhoe resigned herself to that- the worst part of having children and then the second, “What will I call them?”

On this, I told the full truth, “Ganumede and Tithonus, Joyous and Gregarious.”

Penis from Heaven, Mother is Leavin’ the Earth is Heavin’

Zeus told Rhea no.

“I’m not leaving,” she said.

"Yes, you are," Zeus said. "You were told never to come here. No one is even supposed to know you are alive. I spared you on the condition you remained out of sight."

"I'm lonely," Rhea tried to reach out for him, "I have no one. And here you sit on High Olympus where I helped to seat you, surrounded by your sisters and brothers, lovers, children and grandchildren. Everyone but me. Allow me to enter and I will serve at your feet."

"You should go," Zeus took her by the arm and led her forcefully to the edge of the Aerie, Zeus's Loft from where he observed all the activities taking place in the Ether, the Sky Between the Worlds.

Rhea pulled away. Her amethyst eyes burned ultraviolet, "I am the Mother of Titans! You will not touch me!"

"Mother," Zeus said. "Please just leave."

Rhea refused, called upon her full providence and stood tall before Zeus, her youngest son, and said, "*I will go, Zeus. And I will make more Titans and return with an army of gods*! We will force you from this Aerie into Tartarus to rot forever as punishment for your blasphemy against me! See!" Rhea revealed her penis, erect and throbbing, and thrust it in his direction. "*I am potent with more than outrage at your disrepsect*!"

"You will do no such thing, Mother, for it is not Até."

Rhea laughed and began to sublimate away, "I am the Mother of Titans and will do as I will. Até can fuck itself."

"Mother, I said no," Zeus summoned his mighty *vajra,* the cosmic lightning and the symbol of his authority, from the firmament over Olympus and struck Rhea with it.

Rhea fell.

And so did her penis!

The Birth of Attis
The Second Most Handsome
So much trouble, and then some!
Hekate Watches as Kingdom Comes!

It's me again. I had nothing to do with this one, I just watched. I knew the departure of Rhea from Olympus was a big deal, and her detachable penis was even bigger. In order for you to understand how free-range dicks affected my dish, Ganumede, you need to be privy to what happened after Zeus castrated his mum and created the first of them: Attis, the Father and Son of the Titans.

Zeus appeared to Sangarius, the Titan of the River Sangarius, and said "There's a penis falling to earth."

"*So go and catch it*," Sangarius, shaped like a giant frog, belched. "Flying penises aren't exactly my thing, old man."

"I could easily make you into a catcher's mit," Zeus smiled. "But that would be an act of utter impropriety. It belongs to my mother."

"Holy shit," Sangarius's big frog eyes bulged. "What the fuck happened?"

Zeus explained, "So, as you can see, I need your help."

"My help?" Sangarius bleated. "Again? More help again? *Zeus Blunderer! Always needing help*!"

"I can't be seen handling this, else my siblings would know I am aware of Rhea's presence. And I can't take her phallus to Olympus as that would also be the cause of too many questions. In any case she mustn't be allowed to use it, so I-we- have to do something about it, or all that work we did ridding creation of the Titans will end up being for nothng."

"You are such an idiot!" Sangarius roared. "What the hell am I supposed to do with it? And what if she finds out I've got it? I am no match for her!"

"She will never suspect you, and neither will anyone else."

"You employ me to help you and then claim I am insignificant?"

"Sangarius. It's entering the stratosphere," Zeus said. "Rhea is recovering from her wounds. She will soon sense its whereabouts and close in on it. You don't have much time. And I have to be elsewhere now."

Zeus left.

Sangarius splashed and flopped about on the surface of his river, "Fuck! Fuck! God, I hate that guy!" and "How the mother fucking goddamn am I supposed to suck a penis out of the sky?"

Then, he knew how. Nana, his daughter, the Winged Goddess, the Night Star, she knew all about penises! She wold surely know what to do with one. "Nana! *Nana!* Hurry! Daddy needs you!"

The Birth of Attis

Nana saves us Saints preserve us

"What am I supposed to do with it?" Nana asked, rainbow feathered wings spread, ready to lift her into air and speed her towards the penis that was plunging into the atmosphere like a genuine pocket rocket.

"We'll figure that out later! *Just keep that bitch from getting her hands on that cock!*"

Nana smirked, "I'm actually quite good at that, so please stop yelling at me! I'll be right back!"

On the way, Nana called to her lover, the time-surfing satyr Silenus, and explained.

"I have seen that we know what to do." Silenus, a powerful prognosticator said, "Here is how we successfully deal with the matter of this displaced dick."

Nana, who was adorned with plumage in bright colors flew into the air and intercepted the Phallus of Rhea. She snatched it out of the air began her return descent to where Silenus waited.

"Nana, honey," Silenus said calmly. "You are pursued."

There was a bright purple streak behind her. The earth groaned in its wake, fishtailed dirt and wrenched trees and rocks out of the ground wherever Rhea's careening took her.

"She's not well," Nana said, "That's for sure. I can feel her agony. Should I try to comfort her?"

"Not one bit. Her pain is nothing compared to the havoc she will wreak, if she couples with herself. Should she ever, Heaven will be corrupted by a brood of miscreant gods," Silenus said. "Meet me in the apricot grove as I suggested. Do not tarry."

"I'm almost there," Nana said.

Nana presented the Phallus of Rhea to Silenus, the Satyr. "She's almost here."

He placed the phallus under his tunic.

"Lay back as I instructed."

"I thought you'd never ask!" Nana said.

"Yes, and can you do as I have suggested, Adorable One?"

"I am Divine Mother," Nana said. "Let's get it on!"

Silenus fucked Nana with the Phallus of Rhea, who touched down near them.

"*Who are you two and what the hell are you doing here in this apricot grove*?" Rhea's voice caused the ground to reverberate.

“I am Ishtar,” Nana said, “The goddess of fertility and this is Tammuz, my lover. And we are performing in our prescribed roles. Why do you ask?”

“I’m looking for an amputated penis.” Rhea asked, “Mine.”

Nana laughed and pointed towards her snatch, “I have only seen one penis so far tonight and it is firmly in place!” She giggled like a child, “I do know a place that sells randy men and boys, if you want to know where to find a replacement for the one that left you…some of them are into older women, too! For a price, of course.”

Rhea scowled, “*You petulant sow*! When I get my phallus back I will surely deal with you.”

“Hmph!” Nana shrugged, “I wouldn’t want that. Now, if you promise to let me get back to climaxing, I promise to keep my vision keen for should any wandering phalluses pass by. If one does, I will surely call for you.”

“Me, too,” Silenus said.

“I suppose that’s as much kindness as I can expect.” Rhea’s shoulders sagged, and she left.

“That was close,” Nana said.

“You didn’t climax?” Silenus asked.

“Yes,” Nana laughed, “I did and it was super! I was afraid for a moment there it wouldn’t happen, but I made it! How about you?”

“Our plan worked.” Silenus said, “The phallus gave up its final seed to you. You are with child.”

“Just like you planned!” Nana was glad.

“Like we planned!” Silenus said.

The child she gave birth to was called Attis. He was the Second Most Handsome Mortal ever born.

Naturally, Ganumede had to have him. Who else could catch his eye instead?

And Attis was conveniently also Ganumede’s cousin because Callirhoe, the Daughter of the River Titan Scamander and the Wife of Tros, the King of Troy, was Nana’s cousin first.

Chapter 1 – Ganumede Gets a Sweetheart

Everyone was always looking at me. For the right reasons, of course. Of that, I made sure, and my mother helped. She told me my whole life that the men and boys appreciated certain things and helped me cultivate a dignified and dainty little style all my own!

"Just remember, Ganumede," she'd say. "Men want the whole hole, not half."

"Huh?"

"Don't give yourself away to just anybody. You're the Prince! No one likes a stingy prince. You need to look like you belong to everybody! Here," she'd say as we spent time together in her Boudoir, "shave between your eyebrows. Why are you wearing that shirt? Wear the ones I bought you. Your brother wears boxers; those things you wear are three times as expensive, show them off! Try these drop waist jeans. What are these…panties? Work out in these jogging shorts like I said! And let your hair grow longer. It's the style."

My answers to her never changed, "Not my style, Your Highness, but thanks for the un-fabulous fashion tips, just the same."

I once overheard her telling His Highness, my father how my appearance would attract the wrong kind of man to me and wanted me to butch it up a bit.

"Don't take yoga class this year, try out for wrestling instead," she said during breakfast before the first day of my senior year.

Tithonus, twin, spewed his strawberry guava juice all over himself. "Ma, that's hardly the way to keep him away from the mens you know."

"I'm not trying to keep him away from anyone, but attracting a someone. Someone on the top of their game so to speak."

"It's not quite a game, Ma." Ti said.

I wonder if my brother knew my mother was trying to get my ass ruined before it was too late? At the time, I had no idea why and *my own ideas* about that and it wasn't something I wanted to experience on a wrestling mat.

"Nope." I said. "Just got a new yoga mat, mat case, and pants from Lala Limone. And the patterns all match! I simply must pose in them."

"I guess I'd better take kickboxing class, so I can protect you then," Tithonus said. "They're going to be all over those fancy pants, I can just see it."

"Take deodorant class first."

"Wha'?" then he actually smelled himself. *"Gah."*

"Yeah!" I said and got up to get ready. I gave the Queen my usual "you're not the boss of me" scowl.

They waited till I left before they started arguing…again…about who, how, and what kind of boy was going to get a crack at me. And when I was going to just give in and give it up.

Fantasize for me all you wanted, the answer, given the raw material I had to choose from was *never*.

Later: Troy Finishing School

I hurried through *savasana* in yoga class so I could change clothes privately before lunch. Unfortunately, the Javelin team finished tossing off early and stampeded into the locker room. I was just about ready to step out of my outfit and in came the sweat hogs.

There was no way to hide in my Lala Limone ©Hibiscus Heat Conserving Yoga Shorts. As I mentioned, every aspect of the ensemble was eye-catching, color coordinated, and tastefully planned. So what happened was not unexpected.

"*Lookin' good in the neighborhood*, Ganumede!" Travis Interstate, the captain the Javelin team said.

"Hey, yeah, Ganumede, that mussy is steaming!" Justin Thyme added. "Hot, hot, hot!"

"Excuse me?" I narrowed an eye and asked, quite innocently, "Is there something I can help you losers with?"

"Yeah, baby, I'd like a piece of that sweet, sweet mussy!" Justin used that…*word* again.

"What. Is. That?" I acted unconcerned and focused on re-rolling my mat.

"What's what word?"

"A mussy."

"You don't know what a *mussy* is, Ganumede?" Justin laughed and checked with his buddies, who all feigned a degree of perplexity that you'd have to be really stupid in order to accomplish. Somehow, they managed.

"Come on, man, surely you've been *grabbed by the mussy*!" This prematurely swarthy kid named Peter Paisley asked, making lobster claw gestures at me, inched them toward my bottom.

"Peter," I said, smacking at it. "What have I said about that?"

"Fisting is like eating your vegetables? Being forced to eat them when you're little makes you lose your appetite for them when you grow up?"

"Um, yeah, Peter, that's what I said!"

"Dude, that's just gross," Brian Boron said. "Besides, with Paisley's oven mits, you're gonna need a bigger butt!"

"Oh my gods!" I blushed. "You guys are such pubes."

"Seriously, Gee," Justin asked one more time. "Can I just get a little taste of that...*sweet and savory mussy*? Just a sample?"

"Yeah, come on, Ganumede! Pass that *mussy* around, don't be so selfish!"

"Yeah! Selfish people are *low class*, not like us! We'll share that mussy!"

The team couldn't stop laughing at itself. Or grabbing themselves; fondling their hairy bellybuttons with their fingertips like woodpeckers, trying to catch woolly caterpillars in their beaks.

"All right!" I yelled, "What the fuck is a mussy anyway, you assholes?"

There was this pause as Travis, the leader of that very impressive phallocracy, revealed his latest penile proclamation, "Mussy: Man pussy! Get it? Man plus pussy equals..."

I am sure I turned the color of my outfit, "*Jerks*!"

I gathered my things and went to change in the girl's locker room.

That's when I saw him; my golden god, Attis, the son of the Sky Mother, Nana, and some goat. Some things you don't ask about. And frankly, I don't care how he was made, boy was he stacked!

He had that unruly kind of hair that all straight guys possess, His bronze skin was as smooth as polished river stones, and his eyes, a deep reddish brown that sparkled like they had copper glitter sprinkled in them.

It was unusual for us to have a real demigod in our school. There weren't that many to begin with and those that surfaced usually died in military service before they could finish or even start their education.

I'd heard of this one because his mother, Nana, was a distant cousin of my mother's. She had so many weird relatives I lost track of which was which, and didn't pay attention, but this one—*Attis*—we'd been told was way off limits. I was told it was religious and political and the few times I'd overheard anything about him made him sound worse than Polyphemus.

There was a reason for that. Nana and Attis were worshipped by the people of Mideaum, ruled by the Tyrant King Midas, and we, of course, served Zeus by proxy through my father Tros, the King of Troy. Both cities hated each other and that meant our gods did too. That made relations between Nana, her son, my mother and thus our families rather strained.

Attis was betrothed at an early age to King Midas' daughter Zoe, who attended Troy Finishing School like Ti and I, like all the kids and progeny of the wealthy and powerful in the region did. This made making war, more money, more marriages and more babies make more sense to some. I was a weirdo. As of my senior year there, I had guaranteed no one I would contribute to the royal coffers, uteruses, or hairams of any of the sons of the rich and powerful and I knew how that made people feel about me.

I was sort of friendly with Zoe, even though it was considered improper. She'd done nothing to me, was alwayss nice to me and so I was as nice to her. It was easy for both of us. She was obviously not a threat to my social order nor was I to hers. No one saw the potential of this…no one but King Midas himself.

Attis' sudden appearance at my school was clearly a power move by King Midas and thereby also Zoe's way of marking her territory to the rest of us and claiming her future. She, like me, did not want to marry an ordinary boy and she proved she didn't have to. I was not about to let her outdo me.

Attis was gorgeous, a motorcycle dude that oozed cool. He wore gold tipped boots, jeans with gold threads in them, around his waist he wore a belt with a huge gold belt buckle in the shape of a winged circle, the symbol of Nana, his mother, and the part that still makes me squirm, a huge gold zipper that ran down the center of his fly.

He almost always wore a black t-shirt and made up his eyes with kohl along the corners in the tradition of his mother's priests and priestesses.

Attis smelled like cedar. He left a trail of it behind him that was warm and spicy, very much unlike the orgeano and garlic odor of the locker room. I know how Attis smelled because I smelled him! Obviously!

I'd just changed out of my yoga togs and was planning to make a sprint to my car when I went splat! against him and my books and gear exploded into the air and landed in a pile around me.

Attis waited for it to all settle, then he knelt by me, "Why were you running out of the girl's locker room? Shouldn't it be the other one?"

"Yes!" I laughed. "I did! Right out and into this one. They weren't about to follow me there."

"I think I get it." Attis said. "Here, let me help you with this."

The bell rang, and when everyone crowded into the halls, they saw Attis helping me to my feet.

"Hey, Sweet Cheeks!" Zoe came along and she, too, helped me pack all of my things back up.

"Hi Zoe." I said.

"Hey, Prince," she said to Attis. That sound straight boys and girls make when they smooch…they made it.

"Ready to eat?" Zoe asked him. Before he answered, she said to me, "Join us?"

I said yes. No one else asked me that day, and Tithonus, whom I normally ate with, didn't even bother to text me to tell me why not.

Zoe was ready to be the Queen of Mideaum. She explained this to me as we got our trays and sat down.

"Our people don't get along, Ganumede, but Alliances between neighbors are important to me, so I thought we should talk."

That made me feel important and useful so Zoe, Attis and I talked.

When she heard about it, the Queen of Troy dumped a pumpkin about it, too.

The Queen gets Mean; Why, It Does Not Seem

"Ganumede had lunch with Attis today," Tithonus said.

Queen Callirhoe, my mother, lost it. Her eyes turned black and bright green rings replaced her irises, her black nails grew long like blackthorn briars, and the dinner table shook, plates and silverware rattled and the water in the glasses and pitchers sloshed back and forth.

Tithonus was never scared of that like I was. He continued:

"And with Zoe. She's been telling everyone they're getting married and they want Gee to be the best man or something."

The dinner table tempest intensified.

My father, King Tros, came running. "Oh dear. What the hell did you do now?" he asked me.

"And…" Tithonus said, "he ran out of the boys' locker room during a very important moment in his high-school career. Ran out! Right into the girls' changing room."

Callirhoe turned down the Maleficent routine and carefully repeated him, "Consorting with an enemy Demigod and his whorelet. Then…*what*? You started chasing girls? *What has gotten into you*?"

"I was not chasing girls! They wanted to grab the mussy!" I shrieked.

"The what?" my father made this horrified face.

Tithonus rolled his eyes, "No, no, they didn't want to grab the mussy…they were trying to make friends with you. They like you! They think you would be asset to their team."

"See! See! *Mussy*!"

"They didn't want the mussy!" Ti said, "And they're my friends, they wouldn't dare do anything silly to you!"

"Oh yeah? Do you want to know what they said? What they were threatening to do to me?"

"I heard everything, Gee!" Ti said, "I'm the fucking Prince, I know everything about everyone!"

Tros and Callirhoe were obviously at a loss. While Tithonus and I argued the details of what happened in the locker room, my mother started crying and ran from the table.

My father went after her, and after a few paces came back to point his finger at me, "No more mussy at the dinner table! Got it? It upsets your mother."

Tithonus said sternly, "And don't hang out with that Attis guy. People don't like it."

"So what?" I said.

"*So stop it*! They're using you! I knew the second I heard you went out with Attis and Zoe what was going on. You're being duped, fooled, and manipulated into the plutonian schemes of a foreign power and I need you for mine. *Whoops*."

"Yeah. Kinda."

"Sorry." Ti said, "Just don't do it again. Gee—stay away from him, I mean it."

"*No I will not*! I never met anyone like him."

"HE IS STRAIGHT!" Ti said, "And there is no point in meeting anyone like him Gee! Plenty of nice boys are interested in you, spend time with one of them!"

Tithonus struggled with that. My brother may have looked like me but in every other way, he was someone else.

"Don't want to." I said.

"Ganumede!" Ti yelled, "He has a girlfriend," he said. "A fiancée! They kiss each other!"

"It's gross I know."

"He won't love you like you need."

"*I know!*"

"Stop this now. Trust me."

"I can't. Ti, he's a god." I said. "And he said he wants to know me."

"Yes, Ganumede, he is, but he's not our god. And to other people, you're pretty darn close. Find someone who will treat you like one and complete your life. It won't be Attis. I guarantee it. I'm saying this to help you."

That made me nauseous. "No, you're not."

"Yes, I am."

"Why would you want to help me?"

"You're my best friend." Ti said. "So," he said at last, "about that scene in the locker room. I think you misunderstood."

"I don't want to talk about this," I said.

He didn't stop talking. "They didn't mean to piss you off. Everyone likes you and they think you're so cute! But you won't give anyone the time of day. You should open up a little. Stop being so aloof. Try going out with one or two of them."

"All right, Ti." I said, "Who am I being set up with?"

"Trajan Grande."

“That fine blond boy?” I asked. “For reals?”

“Yes!” Tithonus reached for his phone, “Let me give you his phone number.”

“No,” I said, “I have plans already.”

“Gee…he’s a very nice guy. He comes from a prominent family; lots of money, he’s intelligent, his dad works with the Prime Minister…”

“Tell Trajan and the Prime Minister I’m very flattered but I’m not available.”

“Please, just go out with him and see what happens! Just once! For me?”

“I thought this all supposed to be for me!”

“It is! But it’s for me too! It’s very important!”

It was the first time Tithonus asked me to invest in his future as the King of Troy and all he was whoring me out.

I had been told since I was born I had my place and to play my part, and when would I learn doing it would make my life easier?

“Sure. I’ll text him,” I said.

“Awesome. Don’t worry about it though, becausee I already did. You’re going bowling on Friday night.”

Shriek! “BOWLING?”

“Yeah!” Tithonus said. “Tray is the Captain of the Team, and you’re going to be his Cheerleader.”

“A *bowling team*? But…I don’t know even how to bowl! And I can’t cheer, I got Cheersmacked! Remember? How could you humiliate me like this?”

“Easy,” he said.

Ganumede vs. the Whole Team. Again

Trajan was a beautiful kid. He had pale blue eyes, hair so blond it took on the color of anything near it, and smooth skin that shimmered when he sweat. He wasn’t anyone special in the social hierarchy like Travis, Justin, or the other doofuses but politically, he was the one to know. His father had and spent lots of money and all the alliances the Grands made paid off very well. He apparently thought doing the same with would return a handsome profit and he was probably right.

Except that was why I couldn't stand him, no matter how hot or nice to me he was. Yes, everyone, I was a doosh. But that was okay because Attis, *a real god*, liked me.

Trajan's smile, with those lips that were pink like bubble gum revealed sparkly white teeth when he smiled, and he smiled very well. His face brightened genuinely when he saw me, and even Apollo would have looked at him more than once.

But not me.

I kind of felt like an asshole after I finally called him and he sounded so excited and I truly was apathetic.

"Perfect," he said "I'll come get you at 6, we strike at 7."

"I can't. I just remembered. I don't have a uniform. What a shame, maybe next time!"

"Wait!" Trajan cut me off when I tried to sashay away, "Ti said you could wear one of his extras."

"We. Don't. Wear. Each. Other's. Clothes." I said. "And I don't have a bowling outfit because I have no idea how to bowl, and I promise you this is going to suck!"

"Ganumede," I could hear Trajan licking his pink lips, "I really like you. I'm very excited you agreed to go out with me. Don't worry about not being any good at bowling. I'll teach you how. *And Ti will provide you with a Team Shirt*. Thanks."

***

My parents were in on it, too, of course. Trajan came over, looking quite like a boy in his Hoplite Bowling Team jersey, the maroon and gold making him look like he was blushing or sunburned more than usual. He'd parted his hair on the side and gelled it, even still a few feathers fell over the tops of his ears.

The shirt was unbuttoned too far and I could see this ridiculously heavy pendant, a lion made of gold with red enameil on a gold chain around his neck, which matched his class ring, a gigantic *thing* with a red gemstone in the center and roaring lions on either side of it.

The ring I wanted to toss; the pendant looked like it was trying to repel down the cleft of his fabulously hair-free pecs. I wanted to fish it out.

"Hi," I said and made myself smile. I learned how to do that from my mother, who never meant it either, "I need to go change, then I'll be right down. What time are we teeing off again?"

Trajan laughed and so did their majesties, "We *bowl* at 7:30."

"Fuck! I only have to wait an hour? I'll try to hurry so we make it!"

"What are you wearing?" Tithonus barked. "You can't wear that. They'll think you're being a dork. Or…a wuss!"

"I'm not joining the Blowing Team, Ti."

"You look like you're going to the opera. Take that stuff off. Here, wear this." He handed me a brand-new Bowling Team shirt, still in its shrink-wrapped package. "Like we told you to!"

Weary of arguing and accepting of my fate, I turned to leave and put it on.

"Gee!" he barked. "I've seen you naked before, you know? We don't have time! Put it on!"

"No!"

"Yes!"

I turned my back, took my shirt off, and wiggled into the bowling shirt.

"Turn around, so I can see!" he said.

"No!" I said.

"YES!" Ti said. "I've seen your armpits! I don't care how hairy they are!"

"SHUT UP TITHONUS!"

"And here!" Tithonus said. "It's cold out."

He took his Troy Finishing School hoodie off and handed it to me.

"GAH! It smells like you've been having sex with an Empusa."

"What the hell is that?"

"A lesbian vampire that has a brass leg and the foot of a donkey."

"Not that I'm aware of," he said. "Now go downstairs so I can get ready."

I held the sweatshirt in front of me. I'd never worn school paraphernalia before. I was afraid it would make me look like I belonged there.

After I put it on, covered myself in more of that Sword N Shield stuff (AKA Axe Men's Extra Strength Stank) that Tithonus, frankly, needed to become a bit more generous with after his exploits, and went to face my parents and my future husband if they had their way.

On the way, I stopped one last time to look at myself in one of the many mirrors, some of them magical, that hung on the walls of the palace.

Please don't judge me but the sight my reflection in that sweatshirt made me feel attracted to myself. It wasn't vanity. It was a curse.

What I saw was all the more reason to fall in love with someone I felt was more beautiful than I. I made it so easy for them didn't I? I was surrounded, not only by beautiful boys, but *truly beautiful* boys and none them were attractive to me. Just the one. With that in mind, I descended to the ground floor.

"He's building up his treasury, for sure," Trajan said to my father.

"And he's got that advanced warning system," Tros said back. "I think I can get you more information on that," Trajan said.

"Hi," I said. "How do I look?"

"Hold me back!" Trajan announced when he saw me. "All set?"

"Yes," I said. Many times later in my afterlife, I wondered what would have happened to me if I'd just gone with the flow. A nice guy with a future and a car came calling and I might have had one too if I wasn't so determined to have the love of the gods instead.

Undress You Up!

Trajan had a red convertible *Pegasus* roadster. He put the top down. It was chilly out, so he cranked the heat up for me and turned the heated seats on. Still, the roar of the wind was loud, and it messed my hair up, and that annoyed me out of trying to be infatuated.

Then, I heard it.

"*What are you doing*?" I asked, my voice arcing into soprano range.

"Singing," he said, "*You're the Prince...that's what all the boys say...purple sheets and underwear, let me undress you, I'll take your breath away...*"

"I really don't think this is an appropriate song for right now," I said and I really preferred hearing *Mantona* sing it without Trajan's hideous backup vocals.

"*Gonna undress you up in my love! Oh! OH*!"

"Charming," I folded my arms over my chest and waited. The song wouldn't last forever, but the night was just starting. I needed to conserve my strength.

"Sing along with me," Trajan grabbed my knee. "Come on, Prince. Loosen up."

Gods forgive me but I was speeding along the road in a bright red sports-car with a blond jock that was 17 years old. I sang along. It had to be done.

Undress You Up vocals by Mantona.

You're the prince, that's what all the boys say! Purple sheets and underwear so fine, don't make me wait in line!

Let me undress you

Let me treat you like the king, I'll take your breath away

Gonna undress you up in my love oh, oh, oh! (Repeat)

Some guys like it when other boys wear dresses!

Then be my queen, you're the one for me! Oh yeah! What you've got, it still impresses,

And your birthday suit's the only one you need! Gonna undress you up in my love oh, oh, oh!

Interlude

"Have you seen me?
Orion, the Hunter, son of Poseidon Earth-shaker has gone missing.
Please contact the Poseidonic Temple if you have seen or heard from him please. There is a reward being offered for any details that lead to his safe return."

Back to the Bowling Alley

I should have let Trajan handle everything. Instead of hanging back with the guys to talk about balls, bowling balls, shot-put balls, soccer balls, tennis balls, golf balls, and ball bearings, I got in line with him to get shoes. I never, ever, let anyone pick out my shoes for me.

I know some guys think wearing some other guy's shoes is hot, I think *that is so nasty*, and so when the cashier asked me to pay for my rentals I, without hesitation, reached into my sweatshirt pocket to get my wallet and pulled out instead, a handful of extra-large *Achaen's* glow in the dark flavored condoms in every color of the rainbow.

I was surely going to be one of a kind when I got home *because I was going to positively kill my twin brother*.

"Hot dog!" Justin Thyme whistled, "Ganumede's gonna give us the trophy tonight, boys!"

"Winner, winner, chicken dinner!" Craig Overnight said.

"Finger lickin' good!" George Underpass contributed.

"Are these your real names?" I don't know why it took me so long to ask!

"Rush the frat, li'l bro, and find out," Calgary Slingshot raised his eyebrows up and down.

"Hey! Are you going to help me pick these up?" Trajan came over and snatched the condoms off the ground, "They could be dangerous if they fell into the wrong hands."

"Aren't condom supposed to make it less dangerous? And they don't go on your hands, do they?" I often said the wrong things in an attempt to have the last word.

"If you're into that, they sure can Sugar Baby!!"

Then someone called out, "Hey, Ganumede, are you a top or a bottom?"

There was no way for me to win by answering that, so I said, "Is Poseidon's ass water tight?"

"Yes! It is!"

"'Xactly."

"Hey, Prince," Eli B'neath threw his hat in the ring. "I'm bi, I'd take that off the floor for a test drive!"

"Would you really do that, Eli?"

"*Vroom!*" he said.

"Let's not get *too* friendly here, Ganumede," Trajan said. "There'll be time for that later. Besides, we need to get warmed up."

"Yeah, sure," I was glad I bought my own shoes. The smell of that stuff they were spraying into the rented ones smelled like FDS.

So, just like Trajan said, we started warming up. Not the kind with stretching and shadow boxing, but the *do-re-mi kind.*

"Um, Tray, I'm a little confused about what's going on. How does humming make it easier to bowl?"

"Oh, didn't I tell you? It's kind of an Olympics."

"Bowling?"

Then, he explained. I'd been asked out to join in on some sort of teenage variety show.

"Let me get this straight, so to speak. You're the javelin team, bowling team, and you're also the glee club?"

"Yes!! Watch!"

They started singing 'Along Comes Harry' by The Royal Consorts. And dancing. And doing cartwheels and backflips.

Along Comes Harry
The Royal Consorts

Sometimes, I think that I'm the only bee that needs some honey,
But you're the flower that blooms for me, hey daisy,
They tell me not to waste my time,
Find a bee with a big stinger, don't be crazy...
And then along comes Harry,
Says he wants to marry, be my good fairy,
Give me some nectar, Hector,
And we'll see, come along and sting me... Harryyyyyy!
Wasn't sure, but got a text, then we met,
Profile's true Harry' as fine as they get!
When bees need some sugar baby, they call on me
They say I'm sick, but I'm sweeter than a holiday,
A masked ball with the boy next door,
he'll never get free I've got some time, call me right away
Come along Harry, whaddaya say, hey, Harry?
He wasn't sure so he had a beer,
Have another, Harry, never fear!
Shriek!

The music stopped, and the guys wound up the number in formation, precisely in rhythm and time.

"So!" Trajan and the others, proud of themselves and basking in the well-deserved adulation of the other bowling teams in the alley came over to get my flattery as well.

"Trajan. Did you just sing me a song about teen boy bondage?"

"Sorta."

I was truly a gander in the gans haus. And this goose was not getting gilded in a bowling alley in front of a bunch of girls. I ran. I ran like Hades.

As I bolted, I heard them chanting, *"That's not all right, that's not okay! Sweetheart just ran away!"*

"Sorry fellas, *Sweetheart busy today*!"

I ran and ran but I was no match for a track and field stud like Tray Grand.

"Ganumede, wait! What's wrong?"

My chest burned and my legs wouldn't take me further. Trajan grabbed me by my arms and held me, not roughly and I sensed a terrible mistake had been made but I wasn't sure by whom.

"Why did you run away like that? What's the matter with you?"

"You, and those…guys just wanted to humiliate me, didn't you? Like you always do in the locker room in the hallways, after school! I hate all of you!"

Trajan's eyes watered, "What the fuck? Humiliate you? Why would we do that? We're crazy about you! I'm crazy about you!"

"Huh?"

"It was all in fun, Ganumede! Has anyone of us done anything, anything at all, to hurt you or fuck with you?"

"Um. Sorta? What was with all that mussy stuff and the lewd dancing?"

"Bitch! We rehearsed for days to get that serenade ready for you! They were helping me ask you out! You're supposed to be my Sweetheart."

"Oh fuck."

"Yeah! Cunt."

"So?"

I know, I was an idiot. "Tray," I said, "please just take me home would you?"

The ride home was swift and the radio played something I can't remember. I was the earth's most handsome boy ever, wealthy, in good health, intelligent much of the time, and I failed to muster at my culture's most important rite of passage; the honor of having my person appealed to by the best-looking, most talented, and socially gracious young men in town.

I was ostracized as much as someone of my station could be. I was beloved and then scorned by them, and because I was in the line of succession, feared by them as well. I had no idea how to cope with any of that.

My parents weren't particularly happy with my fuck up either. My father wanted to brag I was the It Boy with the dudes and my mother…I don't know. All she said was, "That's a shame. He seemed like a nice boy."

Like I'd died instead of losing my chance at a good reputation. The former would have been preferable if you grew up where I did.

I didn't know who to be angry at and I certainly wasn't going to choose myself, so I replied, "*You sold me, didn't you*? Buying me back is going to be very expensive! I promise you!" and went to my room.

Ti followed me and tried to convince me to make amends but I him to fuck off. In doing so I told everyone to do it too, and that meant I was in big trouble and no one was going to help me out after that: I flunked out of society and there was no way back in. Except for one.

Chapter 2 – Bombs From Heaven

Eos the Goddess of the Dawn, sees a stud and then it's on!

The goddess of the dawn held a pivotal, if dull, job: to oversee the transition between Nyx's ownership of the skies at night, and her brother, Apollo's, over the day. She was a kind of a swing shift worker, important, necessary, but not given a lot of recognition or reward for her dependability.

All she saw when she showed up for work were dark windows, empty streets with traffic signals practicing for morning traffic jams, security guards yawning at the end of their shifts, bleary eyed bus drivers and train operators beginning theirs.

No one liked the dawn. It meant alarm clocks, sitting up, remembering what kept you up the night before, screaming kids, starched shirts, and high heels, the rush to the office.

Rousing so many tired, annoyed people was exasperating.

Most of the time, Eos was lonely and bored to death. Her only company were those infuriating larks that never gave her a moment's peace when she turned up the lights. She was never nearly as excited to see them as they were over her. She fantasized about treating the universe like it did her; roll over, turn the alarm off, and just sleep in.

Then, one morning, she saw Prince Tithonus of Troy jogging.

The youth was shirtless, the early light caused a glistening sheen of sweat on his back, a brilliant trickle from under his arms and across his chest. Eos couldn't tear her gaze from the up and down rhythm of his calves, the flexing biceps as they pumped at his sides.

"Hello?" Apollo blew hot air into her ear. "Wake up!"

"Stop!" Eos shoved her brother and returned to her staring at Tithonus' buttocks, which were unfortunately obscured by a pair of jogging shorts.

"What is your problem?" Apollo said annoyingly. "Why are you…oh."

Then, he saw. "*Oh my*! Cut me some of that!"

"No. Who is that?" Eos asked.

"You don't know?" Apollo shook his head. "That's the Crown Prince Tithonus, Heir to the throne of Troy, Father's pet city."

"Oh yes!" Eos pinched a pink fingernail between her teeth. "He's the one that likes girls, right? Say yes!"

"Unfortunately," Apollo sneered, "or I'd have had him already."

"Well, you still could," Eos laughed like a lark. "In fact, I'm surprised you haven't."

"No, thanks. I don't like it when they aren't utterly smitten by me," Apollo glared hotly at the jogging prince. "I don't like that at all."

"So, go after the other one," Eos suggested. "We can each have one!"

"Nope!" Apollo gasped, "No way. Father said *he's* off limits."

"But not this one?" Eos nibbled her nail again.

"Didn't say anything about him," Apollo watched the sweat soaking Tithonus' shorts, making them cling to his butt crack, "Anyway, thanks for the opening act as usual, sis, but it's time for the main feature."

"When I've seen the main feature, Phoebus, you'll be the first to know!" Eos tipped her head toward the boy on the ground.

And Eos returned to the Temple of Dawn to think.

Classics Class, don't sell your ass in order to pass!

I saw Attis the Monday following my demotion from life in the Classics class we shared. No one at home was talking to me and if they tried, I said nothing back.

Everyone in school was cold. They avoided me, made fun of me. I preferred the sexual innuendo over being called a stuck-up prick, frigid bitch, a tease. A loser.

Attis was the only one left I could talk to expecting something civil to happen. "Hello, Ganumede," he said. "How was your weekend?"

"Surely you heard?" I asked.

"No. In case you haven't noticed, no one speaks to me."

"No one but me," I scooted my desk closer to his. "And Zoe."

"*You* can talk to her if you want," Attis said and his eyes transitioned from deep red to deep purple.

"You don't...like her?"

"*Do I act like I like her*?"

"Well, yeah."

"Good," he said.

"You don't like her?" I frowned.

"She's just a girl." Attis laughed and clapped me on the back. It made every bone in my body rattle.

"Hey," I said, "I'm not a girl but I'm still delicate."

"That is correct, Attis!" A strange voice said, "Isn't keeping your hands to yourself something we learned a decade ago?"

Attis and I both turned to front of the classroom and saw this gigantic man in a suit with a neatly trimmed beard and these creepy blue eyes. "As for the rest of you, who are hopefully able to show adult decorum, please allow me to introduce myself. I am Mr. Diaz, your new Classics professor. Mrs. Thoreau has retired. I will now be instructing the class full time."

"Great," Attis said.

"Yeah!" I said. "*Greeeat*!"

"*See me after class,*" Mr. Diaz said. "Both of you."

When I stayed after class as directed, I was subjected to more intimidation from our new 'teacher.'

Mr. Diaz erased Socrates quotes from the blackboard, "I hope you understand the immense privilege you have been given to be allowed to attend this school."

"I do." I said.

"I'm as deserving as any," Attis said.

"Not as deserving as King Tros' boy," Mr. Diaz turned around, "and I won't have you distracting him or involving yourself with his...affairs."

"Distracting?" Attis swallowed loudly. "Involving? I think you misunderstand. Very much so."

"I don't ever...misunderstand," Mr. Diaz's bearded lips curved into a bloodied sickle of a smile. "And neither should you."

He took a step toward Attis and something told him to take one back.

Still, He was Attis, and the other, a lowly philosopher.

"I think you're the one that's interested in the prince's...affairs, sir," Attis said. "But I'll do my best to make sure I'm not too much of a distraction going forward."

He walked away.

"And you will also deliver a comprehensive paper on the teachings of Socrates to my utter satisfaction," Mr. Diaz said. "By the end of the week."

"Your satisfaction is not my problem." Attis dared to talk back, and added, "Find someone your own age."

"Attis." Diaz hissed, "I want that paper, or there will be consequences."

"I get you the paper." Attis groaned.

"Gee," Attis said in the hallway. "Help me out."

"Definitely!" Woof!

Then that blond doosh, Trajan, walked past us and bumped into me *hard.*

"Hey!"

Attis grabbed him by his shoulder and spun him around, "Behave."

"Fuck you. And you too, Ganumede! Asshole!"

Attis zapped a zit on his chin with a spark from his eye.

"Peep!" Trajan, my Big Blond Stud, squeaked like a parakeet and ran away.

"Holy shit!" I said. "What was that?"

"I don't like bullies," he said.

"Want to come to my house after school?" I said, "I can help you write your paper."

"Sure." He said.

Squeal!

Interlude:

The Tale of the Golden Collar

King Midas, a slight, nebbish, bent over old crone of a man wanted to conceive. And he wanted money. And power. And immortality. Like all tyrants, he wanted, wanted, wanted, and didn't want to earn.

He'd heard of this Satyr that could change that. Satyrs were easy to find; they loved wines and whores and went wherever those things were easily provided.

Midas decided to trap one. He had a party by the Fount of Sequana and made sure there was plenty of ripe whores and the booze flowed freely.

Sure enough, a man with a head and feet like a goat came ambling along and availed himself of both.

When at last, he was very drunk and satisfied, Midas dismissed his other guests and put a leash around the satyr's neck.

"Now, you beast, you will tell me the way to ultimate power!"

"Do you want to know my name first?" the creature asked, unconcerned with the situation he found himself in.

"Will it grant me more power over you?"

"Definitely." Silenus never lied. He had no need. "I am Silenus, the Father of Dionysus. And power is indeed mine to give, O King of Appetites. Please tell what piques your interest today."

"I want a child. A daughter that will be like me and revere Mother Rhea with all her heart. No matter the trials she endures, she must never lose faith."

"Easy."

"I want wealth never ending and I want no man, woman, child, or god to be able to take it from me."

"Piece of cake," Silenus said.

"And I want you to be my advisor. To tell me of all the omens and portents and things to come and the things that might."

Silenus said, “This shall happen but not yet. Later.”

Midas, “Swear to me you will enter my service before I set you free.”

Silenus sighed. The drink and his satisfaction were wearing off and he needed refreshing, “I swear.”

Midas was skeptical. Tyrants, men who are without honor, always are. Lacking truth and dignity in themselves, their appearances in others are evasive to them, “I do not believe you. Swear again to serve me.”

“We all serve Até, King Midas. So, yes, I swear.”

King Midas conceived a daughter, Zoe, a psychopath with too much gold in her brain and not enough in her heart. Her mother died upon her birth.

After she was made, King Midas developed the Golden Touch. Everything he touched turned to the purest gold, including food, water, and other people.

Even though he was able to fill Midaeum’s coffers with gold coins and with its revenues, finance one of the largest militaries in the world, big enough to challenge Troy itself, he was not able to feed or console himself.

Furious and insane with grief, he tried to invoke the mercy of Rhea and revoke the curses Silenus had inflicted upon him but she never came to his aid.

He sent an army to the house of Silenus to retrieve him. He and Nana were themselves attending to a baby but even still, the soldiers put a collar around Silenus’s neck and locked it and through it, strung a leash, so they could take him to Mideaum to see the king.

“Let him go,” Nana said, and flapped her wings at them.

“It’s all right, Dear. I promised,” Silenus said, “I will be back.”

Nana always listened to Silenus and let the soldiers take him.

“You cursed me!” Midas said to the Satyr and pulled hard on the chain and collar around his neck.

“You asked me to,” Silenus said.

“Undo it,” Midas commanded.

“I am unable.” Silenus said, “It is Até.”

Midas knew this was so, “I want another boon to make amends for the first two then.”

“Yes?” Silenus asked.

“I want your son, who is no doubt a god to be promised to my daughter, to secure the future of Mideaum.”

Silenus laughed, “Why would I promise you such a thing?”

“Because, otherwise, I will never take that collar off.”

And he touched the collar around Silenus' neck and turned it gold, fused it to itself, forever. He held up the key, "On the day of their wedding, I will remove the collar and release you from service."

"Why would you do that?" Silenus asked, "And why should I be complicit?"

"With a god to watch over my daughter and kingdom, I would have no need of your soothsaying," Midas spat at the Satyr. "And you knowingly took my wife from me, your son is the least I should demand of you. You should be grateful my offer is this generous. Do you agree?"

Silenus nodded, "I agree."

Thereafter, Silenus served the court of Mideaum with strategic intelligence and stock market tips. Nana never forgave him for promising Attis to Zoe, who as mentioned, was not a nice girl.

Silenus never told Nana why she had no reason to worry about Zoe. It would have only troubled her.

Homework with Attis! Ganumede's the Gladdest Cuz He's the Baddest!

I met Attis after school as we agreed.

"Where's Zoe?"

"Ballet class."

"Oh. Cool."

"Yes. Here," Attis said and handed me a gold helmet.

"What's that for?"

"That," Attis pointed to a motorcycle plated in gold and jet. "Get on," he said and mounted it.

"Yes, but…"

"I have a car. And I don't want a broken arm or back or leg…" and I wanted to get on that bike with him more than anything I had wanted in my life. And I was not used to wanting stuff.

"They can follow you in that. You have a marker in your car."

"Well yeah, I'm the prince but…oh."

"Yeah. Now get on."

"We're sneaking away?"

"Yes!"

I was so excited!

"Sneaking where?" Tithonus asked.

"We're going to do homework," I said.

"Nuh-uh," he said, "Attis, get lost."

"You aren't the king yet, asshole," I said "and no one tells my friend what to do!"

Attis wasn't a muscle head but he obviously had a formidable presence. He dismounted without urgency, "Like he said. No one tells me what to do, either Tithonus."

"I'm telling *him* then. Gee- get in your car and drive home."

"Piss off," I said and walked away.

"Ganumede, I know you think it's really cool to be rebellious and act like an outsider, but you're making a big mistake. You need to go home!"

"I will. Later."

"It's not like I've hired a bunch of my friends to rape him." Attis said, "I'll bring him home in time for dinner."

Attis mounted the magnificent motorcycle, picked me up and slapped me down right behind him. "Gaumede…the helmet please?"

I put the helmet on and lowered the visor.

Attis kicked the engine and it throbbed, like a choir of horns playing.

"Hang on," he said. That I did. We streaked from the parking lot in a fanfare of sound and light.

Midaeum, the Temple of Nana

"*Young beauties are worse than scorpions,"* I read out loud. *"A scorpion must touch you to do harm, but a beauty can do it from a distance, when all you do is contemplate him.*"

"What the hell?" Attis cried out, "I have to write a paper about that?" He made tea prior to our sitting down and his voice made the cups rattle.

"I can write this one for you easy," I said, contemplatively.

"I can write it," Attis said.

"You can?" I laughed, "When was the last time a young beauty threatened to sting *your* ass?"

"Okay." Attis raised his eyebrow, "you write it,"

I couldn't help but look around. The Temple of Nana was so different from the Palace.

It was all alabaster and lapis, mosaic tile floors, filled with potted trees and fountains were ubiquitous. Much of it was open to the sky and colored light filtered through skylights, and the wind came through in refreshing breezes.

The Palace was closed up and closed in, a bunch of boxes and cylinders connected by a maze of staircases and narrow hallways. Statues of the gods and paintings of their adventures were all over the place…I think there was one palm tree in a pot by the front door in the foyer.

When I asked why there were so many silk plants in the house instead of real ones, my mother said, "Plants have dirt."

"What is it?" Attis asked.

"I guess I've never seen how gods live. On earth, that is. I've seen all the bas reliefs and stuff in the Temples, but I didn't really know what to expect of the real thing."

"Disappointed?"

"No. It's beautiful, but what about your mom? Isn't it…weird for her to be here?"

"She…de-sublimates to do it," Attis explained.

"What about you? Do you…de-sublimate? Is it bad to ask?"

"You can ask me anything you want, I'm not going to hit you or anything!"

The conversation had me nervous. I was in the presence of a god just like I wanted to be and I was infatuated and feeling totally out of control. Not like that time in the bowling alley or the locker room where I didn't care what a bunch of bumblefucks thought about me, but really truly nervous about how likable and attractive I was to someone else.

"My father is an earth bound magical being," he went on, "And so he doesn't move between the worlds. My mother is one of the oldest goddesses in existence and is, herself a kind of map of creation, and she's trying to teach me how to move around, but so far I can't make it happen. It might not be possible, we don't know."

The thought of Attis sublimating away from me so soon, at any time, was more than I could handle.

"Oh. Well I'm glad you're here and I think you should just stay."

"It's okay," he said. "It's a good place to start anyway, now I want to tell you why I really wanted to get to know you. Zoe is not what she appears to be," Attis said. "She's a curse. On you, on me, on all that lives."

"What do you mean?" I shuddered, "I've known her or of her my whole life. We've gone to school together, I've seen her at diplomatic 'exchanges', parties, holidays and celebrity galas and she's never acted anything like a curse."

"Well she is."

"So tell me why you would say that about her? She's your fiancée."

"I have to marry her. I don't want to."

Attis told me the Tale of the Golden Leash.

"I play along," he said, "and so does she and her motherfucker of a father. They have no intention of taking that collar off my father. And it's sealed by Até, and so is my father's agreement to help King Midas make Mideaum a world power. Not even I can break it."

"Won't Até force Midas to take it off?" I asked. "He promised he would! Isn't breaking a promise a violation of Até?"

"It is, but Midas just won't," Attis went on, "and once Zoe and I are married, he thinks my father and I are going to help him conquer the world; *starting with Troy*."

My clothes became drenched all at once and my hard dick nearly bust through my shorts. "Are you going to hurt me Attis?"

He laughed. "Not you, idiot!" Attis shoved me playfully and grabbed the chairback when he realized I was going to topple, "Gods! I want you to help me stop all of this craziness!"

"Me? How? Attis, I'm…nobody. I can't do anything like that. Tithonus is your man; he's getting all the military training and everything. I'm just supposed to look pretty, write poetry, sew buttons on cute little baby outfits, and fuck his friends. As much as I'd like to help you, moral support isn't going to do you any good. You really need to talk to Ti."

"If I approached your brother war would certainly break out and millions of people would die. Zoe and her father are too powerful for your people. You're the obvious choice for what I have planned because they already think I'm helping to conquer your countrymen."

"They do?" I said, "Who does?"

"Zoe and Midas!"

"How are you doing that?"

"Right now!" Attis couldn't stop laughing, "Right now, you are being seduced. I have you right where I want you and you're a fool for me."

"*I. am. game,*" I said. "Tell me what you want me to do."

"I want you to kill Zoe," Attis said.

When Attis took me back to school to pick up my car, I saw Nana, like a hummingbird vibrating with every color of the spectrum, de-sublimating back into her temple.

She waved, and I knew I had to help Attis. Somehow.

Shame and Blame is the Name of the Game

"He went off with Attis," Tithonus said.

"Is this true?" my father, King Tros of Troy, asked.

"I came home," I said. "I'm okay though, thanks for asking."

"Why did you not come here after school like you know you are supposed to?" Her Highness was unusually collected. No wicked witch signs at all.

"Attis needed my help with some homework," I said.

"Attis has all the resources required for help with his homework," Callirhoe, the Queen, said, supreme and full of confidence. "Why did he ask *you* for help?"

"I was teaching him how to be seductive." I said, "Or he was teaching me. It really depends."

"Ganumede, please leave the table," she said.

"*I'm not done eating,*" I said back.

Tros held his hands up, one in front of either of us, "Sarcasm aside, why did you get on a motorcycle, which is a very dangerous thing to do, and go into an an ever more unsafe situation? One that could have involved me or your mother or brother, or even caused a national emergency?"

My father was the King first because he said that made him a good example to Tithonus and me. I often wished I had a father instead.

"I was with a god." I answered. "There was no safer place for me to be,"

"Unless you count being surrounded by the entire army," Tithonus said. "Which is what it would have taken to rescue you! You should have come home like I told you."

"'Cept I didn't," I said. "Haha! *And as you can see*...I came home without the help of the army."

"*And I can see you are an incredible bitch*!" Tithonus said.

"Ti," my father said, "Gee..." Smiled. "I understand why you are drawn to Attis. He's a very handsome fellow and obviously has some...assets that would be advantageous for us to have access too, but...this is not my preference for how we'd make that happen."

"Oh really? Well even though it might be my preference, Dad, I promise. He's just my friend," I said firmly. "*And he's a god.* And the friendship of the gods is a rare blessing and not an asset."

"Leave The Table!" the Queen said. The news reported that the bitchquake she caused with her temper was felt within a hundred miles of the palace.

Everyone in town knew when I was in trouble, but no one, least of all me, really knew why.

Callirhoe the Queen of Troy talks to the Goddess of Witches! Wants to know how to make it work without any glitches!

I went to my secret place, the Temple of Hekate, deep in the palace foundation.

From there, I could radiate my influence over the happenings and goings-on above more effectively.

I kept it hidden inside a labyrinth with walls that randomly changed position, and the actual entrance required a rune that I would alight from behind my left eye and shine into its mirror image, a glyph on the wall shaped like an inverted Eye of Ra, where the actual door was located.

Once I shined the rune on the appropriate sigil, the ward was lifted and I passed straight through the bricks, which were obsidian, slick, shining, and shimmering with the blood-colored light that shined from briars that lined the passageway.

I checked behind me to be sure I was alone. Anyone foolish enough to follow me wouldn't live long enough to talk about it, but still I kept watch. I addition to needing my privacy, reverence of the Witch Goddess was strictly forbidden in Troy, and punishable by death.

Upon confirmation I was alone, I lit the twin torches on the altar. And *She* appeared.

"Hello sister!" Hekate's voices were cordial. "Blessed Be!"

I was never into that *Blessed Be* shit, and got right down to business.

"Is Attis the god that is going to take Ganumede away from me?"

"He has already," Hekate said. "And returned him to you."

"I'm not fucking around with you today! Is Attis the one?"

"It is true, Queen, the Dish is quite taken by Attis."

"I knew it! I knew the second Nana lost her fucking mind and registered that…thing at the Finishing School, it was trouble and turns out it is worse than anyone could ever guess!

"I told Tros we should have nuked Mideaum when Rheas fuck-pole landed there. Gods Dammit!"

"But as always, Queen, he obeys the will of Zeus on High, which is never unwise," Hekate said. "Zeus is watching. Surely things will be fine."

"Zeus can fuck himself, you stupid bitch! Tell me, what is Attis going to do to my son and when?"

"Sister Queen, I see in the Three Times, but Attis is a god. He moves between them. What happens next where he is concerned is not completely clear to me."

Hekate could be so full of shit sometimes. All she had to do was tell me she wasn't willing to answer me!

"Is there anything I can do to keep Attis away from my son then? Before it's too late?" I humbled myself, truly. "Tell me something to console me, please? Anything!"

"Don't worry, Callirhoe, my dearest friend. Someone will come between your son and this god. And, as with all things mortal, nothing happens too soon or too late. Fare you well."

The torches dimmed and went out on their own.

Hekate really was my dearest friend, but sometimes, I really hated Her. Especially when we talked about Ganumede.

Tros, the King of Troy, talks to Zeus

"Attis is at the same school as the boys?" Tros asked the Oracle.

"Yes. Nana is taking the 'hide in plain sight' approach," it said.

"Attis is an enemy of Troy. I worry he is trying to manipulate Ganumede and gain an advantage over the Court. I am especially nervous over the fact he is marrying Midas's daughter. I didn't see that one coming at all when we agreed how this…situation would be dealt with."

"It is unexpected." The Oracle brought a hand up to its holographic hood and rubbed an invisible chin inside its shadows, "And Attis has no romantic designs on your son, you've confirmed this, correct?"

"Ganumede is quite taken with him," Tros said. "But I don't think Attis feels romantically toward him. At least that's what Tithonus said."

"Even still, it is wise to be vigilant." the Oracle said. "Your son, the Prince of Troy, is *the most desirable*. Who would *want* to resist him?"

"He's cute, yes." Tros said, "And I'm not dense. We're trying to find a suitable partner for Ganumede and I wasn't the least bit concernted about that, except now we military threat from Mideaum because my worst enemy and that crazy bitch daughter of his think my son is vulnerable? Zoe is crazier than a nymph and Attis…he's nigh unstoppable!

"And what if all of this drama ends up in open warfare, betrays our secret, and Rhea figures out what we've done?"

"What message would you like me to relay to the Aerie and Your Lord, Zeus, the Most High, Your Majesty, the King of Troy?"

"Tell him all of this has me most discomfited and *I wish he would let me act and just kill Midas and those abominations now*."

The Oracle was silent; the only sound was the hum and crackle of the static around the projector. Finally it said, "I remain in agreement with Nana's plan. It was the best way to keep Rhea's potency from her and pretending that all is well is the best way to keep her suspicions from being aroused.

"A military solution would not kill Attis and then Rhea would know she's been deluded and all creation would pay for our deception of her."

"*Well that's just not fucking fine*!" Tros ranted. "So what do you want me to do? Ganumede has no idea what he's involved in, and he doesn't want to choose from the boys we think are good for him. He's detached and impossible to talk to…I can't keep punishing him for having an adolescent crush, and I can't tell him the truth, and *we are losing him*!"

"Follow tradition," the Oracle said. "You are the king and he's a prince, and he's going to have to accept this. Assign a consort to him. Make him obey."

Tros sighed again and nodded, "I will start looking for one immediately. He's not going to be very happy about this."

The Oracle began to sublimate back to Olympus, “Find one that is skilled in making a young man of his sort happy then.”

Chapter 3

Ganumede Takes a Lover!

Everyone run for cover

Introduction by Yours Untruly, Hekate, the Goddess of Witchcraft, Children, and Murder

In a moment I am going to tell you a story. Another story. First I am going to tell you one about myself. Before I relay it, you should know that none of the stories about the Twinkies in this epic have a cream center. They are all doomed. There was no way around that. If there is One Thing that gets me to act, it is when a child is in danger, even if it's futile to try.

The ruin of children makes *even me* cry real tears of sadness. I do it no other time. *Otherwise I laugh*! Espectially at boys. They are so stupid! How they try to ruin themselves…!

You can only do so much.

Ganumede Prays to Eros
Who plays a game that scares us
Never fear, Love is always near us…

I saw myself in the mirror without Attis. I slept without Attis in my bed. I ate without him, each minute I didn't spend with him was cold and thorny and filled with dread that the next time I saw him, he would pretend he didn't know me. I needed him in my life- no one else looked or spoke to me, and I returned the favor. Without Attis I was completely alone.

Even when Attis told me to make sure to always find him at school, no matter what, so he could keep Zoe from fawning, fondling, and flaunting herself to him, I was still nervous.

Every time she got that look on her face and put her mouth on his and made that disgusting smack-y sound which I called the goldfish, I wanted to rip her tongue out and feed it to the Kraken, followed quickly by the rest of her. She was still a virgin, after all. Attis promised. That meant he was too! There was hope!

And if I had my way, virgins were going to be in short supply around him, all except for one in particular me!

I went to my father's Aerie and hacked my way into the Oracle. I'm not a silly straight boy with IT skills, so don't think I have a capability that I don't. My mother was the Queen of Witches and she taught me a few things when were weren't trying to rip each other's nipples off.

I activated the interface and typed this incantation:

Hail, winged one, Lord of Love!
We do not always welcome you
Into our busy lives as we should,
For you have no regard for
Our convenience, our rules,
But simply see each of us
As another target for love.
Sometimes, when you come, we rejoice.
Sometimes, when you come, we weep.
Yet, even when your arrows
Are painful and agonizing,
Even when we lie awake at night
Aching from the wounds you have dealt us,
We must remember that all love
Is truly a blessing, no matter
Where it starts or ends,
No matter what its path or means,
No matter whether it must live unsung
And die unborn in our hearts
Or whether it can run freely
Hand in hand with the love of another.
Bless us with your wounds, winged one,
As you have endured love,

And made mistakes, so you will
Have patience with us as we
Fumble our way through your maze.

"That's just tedious," Eros said, and he truly and fully embodied from behind me. "All you had to do was call my name, Sweet-cheeks. So, now they I'm here, how can I help you?"

"I want Attis to fall in love with me," I said.

Introducing Eros

First of all, I am not that twit Cupid. He and anyone else who thinks that 'love' should be depicted as a creature that needs its diaper changed has already made the choice between heaven and hell.

Seriously.

I look and behave like I should. A man boy with fully developed parts and the know how to go with them. Reproduction, babies, pampers, and those slings that men wear across their stomachs to carry their burdens in while their wives do yoga: *not my thing*. No dad bods, "football builds", beer farts or chili cheese fries for me…these things cause shrinkage.

I'm not being hetero-phobic, I do love to watch mixed gender couples get all wet and wild for each other but, let's face it, the most beautiful mortal ever was a boy and as the god of desire, he's the one I wanted. The sad part was I think I actually wanted him to like me back.

I find myself having to deal with those kinds of contradictions due my pedigree…my mother felt the need to shag Ares, the most fetching god of war, *and had to conceive me*. I am, therefore, the mysterious and delicious result of the union of love and war. In other words, I have no shame.

When Ganumede prayed to me, me and not Zeus, for my help with Attis, there was no way in hell I was going to refuse to answer.

And a word of advice to all you boys and girls and girly boys; never, ever pray to a god and ask for help getting laid. You might just get what you ask for.

"Now, explain to me why I should do this for you," Eros said. "And it's okay to check me out. I'm hardly going to be offended."

“Okay,” I said and looked. Eros always looked the way you wanted. To me, he was tall, slender but busting with muscles, had an unruly shock of glistening black hair, golden brown eyes, and wherever I wanted there to be hair, there was, where I didn’t…nada!

Eros retracted his wings, put a skirt on, and sat down at my father’s conference room table.

“Am I attractive you, Ganumede?” he asked.

“*Attis*.” I said. “I want Attis.”

“It’s a yes or no question. And I can tell you are.” He ran his hand along my thigh, “So tell me the truth.”

“I don’t even know you.”

“I came here so you could know me, Ganumede. Don’t be such a woman. Say you find me ravishing and let’s neck!”

“I’m not a woman, Eros! And I don’t want to neck! So never mind. I’ll find another way to get Attis to like me.”

Eros didn’t flinch. “What do you say we figure out a way for you to like me? I’m available, Attis is not, and once you agree with me, boy we could really get it on!”

“Eros, people think I’m an idiot, but I know a few things,” I said. “People who love you are cursed.”

“So why seek *my* help in influencing someone else to love you?” Eros asked, his eyes blazed with fury at me, “If I am such a curse to deal with?”

Eros stood and came across the room. Then, in a one of a kind act of fealty, the god of love knelt before me, “*Let me love you, Ganumede!* I promise you will not regret it.”

He wrapped his arms around my waist, laid his head in my lap, “Worship me by letting me worship you.” His cheek pressed my hard dick against my leg and a hot wet stain spread inside my pants. I tried to back away to get the gooey feeling under my belly button to stop. Eros wouldn’t let me.

“I’m a devious creature, untrustworthy, but I promise, my words are sincere.”

There was a shudder; a tremor shook the room. Eros stood and backed away, “Summon me again tomorrow night. Light a red candle when the night is quiet and remember me. I’ll come to you!”

Eros began to fade away.

"I've loved many boys, Ganumede," he said, "I can make any and every fantasy you could ever conceive of better than reality; larger than life, worth dying for. How many others can offer that?"

"I don't know," I said. "I just want Attis."

"You need to find out. Either way light the candle tomorrow when the night is silent. Will you do that?"

"Yes," I said.

Then Eros was gone, sublimated back into the Ether.

From Hekate's Cahier: Introducing Aphrodite

Aphrodite, the goddess of love, is one the universe's absolutes.

Even I should probably pay homage to her, but if you don't acquire an experience of love, then you don't have to worry about its loss. I was born knowing this.

The rest of the gods and all mortals are born the opposite; all of them have to trifle with it, stab themselves in the heart with it, let the questions about its nature drain the joy from their lives.

What Aphrodite represents is scary, even to me.

The goddess herself was one of the first – she manifested even before Zeus. She came into existence when Kronus went on *his* parent killing spree and castrated his father, Uranos. Zeus had a blueprint for his paricide only a goddess of love wasn't a biproduct.

Aphrodite emerged from a puddle of blood and celestial seed left over from the First Deicide, a fully formed being, lovely, horrible, lawless, and a law unto herself. Like love itself.

Her role in this story is small but its implications are expansive. She never revealed whose side she was on and for a moment, I actually think she wanted to help.

Love is strange like that. It can hurt as much as heal, strengthen and weaken one's resolve. When it is absent, the world can end.

Love is...unpredictable
A Game of Dice
Twice as Nice
Not Sugar and Spice

I didn't know what I'd agreed to with Eros but I was committed to why. I stole some of my mother's magic candles and did as he said. If there was any chance Eros could help me win Attis over, spare me the need to kill Zoe and save the Empire, I would take it.

I waited till everyone was asleep and the house was quiet as Eros instructed. I could hear the wind outside and the fire burning in the hearth in my room.

We'd had another family melee that night about my hanging out with Attis at school, Tithonus warning me people were talking like I was an enemy of the state and a traitor, my mother pretended to feed the dog the whole time so she didn't have to participate in the conversation.

My father farted out platitudes like, "Now Ti, Ganumede's not a traitor, he's just doing his own thing. And that's okay. Maybe he'll want to help everyone else someday. That's his decision. Either way, we should respect it."

I was just dying to say, "Yeah, like not trying to stop Zoe from conquering Troy after flattening it with mass drivers that fire gold shot-puts, provoking a war with us, forcing Attis to defend Midaeum!"

I lit the candles, which were red, and dressed- etched with weird symbols I couldn't read.

"Hallo," Eros said from my desk chair. "How was your day, darling?"

He was dressed tastefully all in black silk pajamas, his hair neatly styled, and he was barefoot. He crossed his legs, and his slender fingers teased the hair on his toes and ankle while I answered.

"Exhausting," I said. "Everyone keeps telling me what to do and they don't understand! I have important things to accomplish and I can't tell anyone!"

"I, too, exist in a world of Hunty Bees," Eros said. "Always trying to kill your buzz. Now, you wanted to see me?"

"Yes, Eros! *Like we talked about!*"

"Awesomeness." He uncrossed his legs and leaned forward. "I was quite glad you summoned me, after last night I wasn't sure you would. And I could have made you do it, you know."

"Thanks, but like I said, I was hoping we could talk about Attis."

Eros sighed loudly, "So, what about Attis shall we talk, Ganumede?"

"It's very important that you make Attis fall in love me, so we can be married and save the planet from a world war."

"And because you want him to shag your lights out, let's not forget that part," Eros smirked in that super trashy James Franco kind of way, "Am I right?"

"I don't know what you mean by that."

"Sweet," That time in the ultra-nasty David Franco way.

"Whatever," I persisted, "so can you do that for me or not?"

"How does it benefit me if I do?" Eros asked, "I have my love interests, too, you know," he winked; James again.

"Why, Eros?" I moaned. "Why? Why can't you just be nice and help me?"

Eros turned his head to the side, "Ganumede. Everyone who has seen you, wants you. If it can see and it's male, it notices you and then it boils. Has that fact ever occurred to you? No one wants to help you…*they want to help themselves to you*."

"Someone will want to get to know, and his name is ATTIS if you will make him do it!"

Eros's eyes glowed with a deeper shade of onyx, "*Knowing* is generally less interesting than *having* someone that is attractive, Ganumede. And don't give me that doe-eyed look. You are fully aware of this. I find this disguise you wear to be tiresome and so did all those positively amazing and amorous boys you snubbed a few weeks ago. Quite a despicable display you gave them; artificial and ungracious, really."

"I wasn't! I'm shy," I squeaked. "I really am."

"You summoned the Titan of Love and Lust to ask for a boon. You are not shy," Eros said and it felt like I was roasting over the hearth, the heat of his temper was so hot on my skin. "And I am not practiced at holding myself back either, so let's get to it, shall we?"

"Get to what?"

"First," Eros regained his composure, his eyes dimmed a little and he did something to make me look into them, "you are attractive. You are the most attractive being that will ever be made. Even your brother lacks your luster, but he is the closest to perfect anyone will ever be. *You are it*. Can we agree to drop any pretense of ignorance you have about these things?"

"Eros…"

"*Shut up, Ganumede*. I watch you watching yourself when you're alone. I know you are deeply, impossibly attracted to yourself. You can't help it, can you?"

"I don't want to just be attracted to myself. I want someone else to, and his name is Attis! He's more beautiful to me than I am to myself. He's the most beautiful person I've ever seen!"

Eros nodded, "He's not a person, Ganumede. There's so much you don't want to understand. And am I not attractive to you?"

"You're so gorgeous, Eros, it makes me feel sick to my stomach! And you're not a person and I can't date you or go to the movies with you or marry you either, and you know this! So what gives?" I started to cry, "Please stop confusing me!"

"Empathize with how confusing it is for me then!" Eros looked desperate and it wasn't an act, "I'm the god of desire and I have never desired anything more than wanting you to seethe with passion for me. On your own, without chicanery or sorcery or some childish prank, like the other gods pull on mortals they lust for...because they have no other choices!"

He took my hand, "I can't make myself more attractive. This is the best body and appearance I can assume. I can't and wouldn't want to appear to be you to you, so please love me for who I am! Do it, and I will pledge to do the same for you, for all your days."

"Eros, it's important." I said, "I need what I asked you for."

"Very well," Eros took his hand away, slowly, and sat back. "Are you willing to negotiate?"

"How so?"

Eros opened his hand and inside were two knucklebones, "We will cast lots. If you win, I will make Attis your love slave forever. If I win..." Eros's eyes grew black, their interiors roiling with molten gold fire, "we pursue every fantasy you have ever had and I get to do the same until I tire of you. *And I will make sure things stay so very interesting.*"

"You have nothing to lose, Ganumede," Eros said when I hesitated. "One way, you get to think you're saving the world, which cannot be saved by the way, and the other, you get to escape from it. I'm an excellent lover, Ganumede...I could show you if you would like...!"

"Let's just see what happens, okay?" I said.

"*Wrong*," A voice said. "***We shall most definitely not see.***"

It was Aphrodite. She didn't look like most people thought. She wasn't an anorexic runway model nor was she a MILF. She looked healthy, handsome, full-figured. She was dressed in sea green gown, sheer enough to show off her voluptuous womanly curves, and wore jewelry made of seashells. The Goddess of Love was also not blonde and blue eyed. She had long tresses of dark hair held back in combs made of coral and pearls.

"Mother!" Eros hissed. "Be gone! This is private! *Very private*!"

"*EEP!* Momma Maia!" I said and hid my face in my arms.

Aphrodite laughed and touched my shoulder, "Oh stop that. You can look up. I have no worries you are going to look upon me with lust in your heart. This one, however, looks at everyone that way! As you are discovering! Please allow me to apologize for his rude conduct."

"Not as rude as it is going to get if you don't disengage from my affairs, Mother!"

She grabbed him by the ear, "Bluster! Now get on your feet, we have an appointment in Olympus and Ganumede has school tomorrow."

"I'm not going," Eros said, "Ganumede summoned me and that means I am allowed to conclude my business here."

"Business is usually done with some hint of integrity, sweetie boy," she looked to me. "He was going to cheat, Ganumede. Both knucklebones have been enchanted to favor him."

"Eros! You bastard!"

"I said I wanted you, Ganumede." And tears formed around his eyes. "But my heart and my intentions were true. That I also swore."

"Enough." Aphrodite said. "It's time to go, Eros,"

"But Mother…!"

"No."

"Yes!" Aphrodite said, and the god of lust was dismissed by the goddess of love.

I stared helplessly at Aphrodite, "I can't help it. I'm in love with him."

Aphrodite hugged me, "But this feeling hurts you, doesn't it?"

"Yes. A lot. Will he ever…? Is there any chance at all?"

"No, Ganumede. there isn't. Attis just wants to be your friend."

"Will I ever fall in love with someone else?"

"You might!" she said. "Get ready for bed, and dream of how lucky you are that love has passed you by this night and has every possible chance of finding you on another."

Aphrodite blew out the magic red candle I stole from my mother and took it, "*Never do this again, Ganumede*."

"I won't."

Aphrodite left and I did what she said. I bathed, handled myself as usual, pretended no one was watching. After I got dressed, I went to the hearth to turn it off.

Inside the fire was Eros, his body bathed in its gold light, "I still want you Ganumede," he said, "I haven't changed my mind about that!"

Afterward: On Olympus. Zeus, Aphrodite, and Eros in the Aerie

"Now," Zeus held Eros up in the air by his neck and shook him like a down pillow till some of his feathers fell from his carcass, "Are we now close to being of the same opinion on this matter?"

"You are the King of the Gods," Eros said. "No other opinion but yours matters to you."

"Bah!" Zeus threw Eros aside.

"Mother!" Eros looked to his mother who watched Zeus thrash him. "Please, just let me have my chance with him!"

"I have no idea what you mean." Aphrodite concluded, "I'm sorry. Now go, we will not talk of this again."

"Thank you for intervening in this matter," Zeus said to her.

"I didn't 'intervene' for you," Aphrodite said, "I did it for Até."

"As I said, thank you, my dear."

"Fuck off," Aphrodite said and began to sublimate away. "And try, if any self-control is left to you, to leave the boy for someone his own age."

"That," Zeus said, "is a most ridiculous idea."

Zeus sat back against his marble seat and stared into the Ether.

Eros, Scrying on the Aerie

"*Filthy troll!*" Eros said and spread his wings. "*I will have that hole! So Eros swears!*"

Hera, Scrying on the Aerie

"Sister?" Demeter asked Cow-Eyed Hera. "Have you seen Persephone, my daughter?"

"Let me look for you, dear," Hera said and peered back into the scrying pool, "I'm sure she's around here somewhere."

Why There are Four Seasons

Persephone went missing. She was last seen picking flowers in a meadow, but when Demeter, her mother, went looking for her, she found the flowers scattered, the basket Persephone intended for them tossed away; her precious daughter, gone.

Only one thing made Demeter, goddess of green and growing things, happier than trees, plants, and flowers, and that was her daughter.

When the child failed to return, Demeter called all of the gods to the Great Hall of Olympus to beg them for news on her whereabouts.

Only One, Hades Unseen, didn't answer her.

Hekate Herself stood silent, aloof; her three selves apparently lost in thought.

Demeter ran to her and fell at her feet, grasping at her skirts. "Great Goddess, I know you can help me find my daughter! Please, I employ you. I cannot bear to live without her!"

A snowflake fell from a graying sky over Olympus.

"Of course, I will help you!" Hekate took her by her hands and raised her up. "A mother's love for her child must be honored."

She cast a glare at Zeus, up on his marble throne.

"Go then," Zeus grumbled, "I cannot beart to see my sister so forlorn."

The King of the Gods blinked as more snow fell on his brow.

"I will return with the whereabouts of Persephone," Hekate promised.

Hekate summoned two massive, black, thorny briars into her hands. A great gold snake with ruby red eyes climbed up her sleeve, blew green fire onto the branches, and they burst into flames.

"There is no dark place too deep, no shadow too dark that my eyes cannot see through their gloomy cover!" Hekate's voices intoned, "*Draconic Fire will light the way to whence the child was taken away*!"

And Hekate, the Goddess of the Three Roads was off on her quest.

Hekate went to the meadow where Persephone was last seen, and shined he eldritch glow of the torches all around. The fire revealed what had taken place and showed her where Persephone had gone. The trail led to the Gate of the Underworld.

"I've always wanted to visit there," Hekate said to herself.

Upon arrival at the entrance to Hades' realm, she was greeted by Kerberos, the Guardian of the Gate.

"A three-headed dog!" Hekate said with delight as the thing, the size of a bull elephant, charged to the length of its chain, snapping and howling with its heads.

"Oh shush!" Hekate said, "I have three heads too, see?" she revealed her triune form and Kerberos stopped crying out.

"Can I pet you?" Hekate extended her hand and the three huge great Dane heads whined and drooled, as they considered her offer.

Finally, one head submitted and let Hekate rub under its chin and scratch behind its ears. Soon, the others got jealous and before long, all six of Hekate's hands were busy petting and scratching the beast's muzzles.

After her faces were slick from the big wet tongues lapping on her, Hekate laughed, "Does that mean you will let me pass?"

Kerberos whined with all three heads, as if in fear, but then it sat down in submission to the goddess and let her pass.

Hekate entered the Underworld.

There, she met many dead spirits and beings of unknown origin or constitution, including her dread handmaidens, the Keres, who were later thought to divert the souls of the dead on their way to see Lord Hades to Hekate instead. Through the Keres, Hekate learned more and more of the universe's secrets and about its hidden places. One of them led her to Underworld Throne, where Hades Unseen waited on a great black igneous chair. Persephone was seated next to him.

"Le jeux est finis!" Hekate said to Persephone. "You little slut!"

"I should have guessed you would find us," the Unseen said, his eyes blazed from inside his basalt helm.

"Yes," Hekate said. "You didn't speak at Demeter's council. No doubt of fear of perjuring yourself about the whereabouts of her daughter. No harm done! At least until Demeter finds out you've been getting a hot poker in your ass while she was worried sick about you! So, are you ready to go home, dear?"

"No!" Persephone cried out and grabbed onto Hades' arm, "I won't go back!"

"Be-gone from my kingdom or I will destroy you!" Hades brandished the Twin Headed Staff of the Underworld at Hekate and made it glow white hot.

"Bullshit," Hekate twittered. "You have no power of that kind. But I will go, if that's what you want."

She turned her back, "Everyone, especially her mother, will be delighted to know the girl is safe. Demeter will kvetch up a storm and Zeus himself will probably come to retrieve her."

"Let him come! I won't let her go," Hades said and the Staff hummed.

"Fine," Hekate said, "I'm sure there will be a great battle for the girl's rescue from her abductor. I'm sure Hera will get upset, and that will mean Hestia and Poseidon will get involved and then everyone else..."

"Wait, Hekate." Hades Unseen sighed, lowered the Staff. "There is no need for a rescue. I did not abduct her. Tell her, my love."

"I ran away with Lord Hades of my own accord!" Persephone wailed, "I had to get away from my mother! She smothers me! I want a life of my own!"

"Even still, you have to return to her." Hekate said.

"No. She loves me and I, her," Hades Unseen, Lord of the Underworld, confessed and clasped his hands, "My life and my kingdom, are so dark and dreary, empty of joy. Persephone gives me light and happiness. Please, Hekate, do not take her from me."

"I fear I must do something," Hekate revealed. "Demeter's distress over her daughter's absence is causing growing things to wither. The wind grows cold and dark clouds fill the sky, obscuring the sun. Even Olympus itself is being buried in snow. If Demeter is not placated, all of us will die."

"Then I have no choice," Persephone covered her face, "I have to return to Olympus."

"There might be a way for you to stay," Hekate touched a finger to her chin. "At least some of the time."

"What do you want?" Hades narrowed his eyes at her.

Hekate smiled, "What do you offer?"

After a few moments of heckling and bargaining, Hekate revealed her idea.

"I believe I have no choice but to accept the terms of your...*suggestion*, Goddess of Witches," Hades Unseen said as pleasantly as possible.

"Excellent," Hekate said and produced a persimmon from inside her robe.

Triune Hekate returned to Olympus and reported to Zeus and Demeter that Persephone had been lured into the Underworld by Lord Hades but was unwilling to permit her to return with her.

Zeus was furious and Demeter fell into an even deeper forlorn state, causing a bitter, icy wind to rake the portico of Olympus.

"I am sorry, Great Zeus," Hekate lamented, "But I lack the power to force Lord Hades to surrender the girl while on his own turf."

"Hermes," Zeus called and in spite of the snow and ice, his son, the trusted Messenger Hermes was there in an instant.

"Yes, Father?"

"Hades has the girl Persephone trapped in the Underworld with him. It is imperative that you go there and on my authority, broker a deal with him to get her back. Else," he looked at the weeping Demeter, "We are all lost."

"I will do what I can," Hermes said.

"You are the most clever of the gods, my boy," Zeus patted his shoulder. "I know you will find a way."

Hermes returned with Persephone but told Demeter, "While enjoying Hades' hospitality, the girl ate a cursed persimmon; six of its seeds. She must return to the Underworld six of twelve months or she will die."

"Is this true?" Hekate asked.

"It is." Hermes said, "It is impossible to lie to me, Divine Mother."

This made Demeter sad but she was satisfied with having her daughter's company for part of the year. And with her relief, Olympus began to grow warm again, its trees fruiting and its fields and meadows to flowering.

When the Curse of the Persimmon Seeds required Demeter to return to the Underworld, creation likewise returned to a state of cold sleep and the world above dreamed of spring.

Lord Hades was glad Persephone could continue to be Queen of the Underworld and war with Olympus was avoided. The precise nature of the pact Hekate made with Lord Hades Unseen during her visit to his realm is known only to them.

Tithonus Annoys us

What were those noises?

After Eros more or less threatened to rape me, I had trouble falling asleep.

It was, shall we say, a big night, and not just for me. Somebody down the hall from me got lucky.

"Who did you have over here last night?" I asked Tithonus the next morning. "Sounded like you were trying to circumcise each other! And for fucks' sake, dude, at least wash her off before you go to school. Ew!"

"I just came from the gymnasium and no one was here last night," he said.

"*Wash it!*" I said, "And lay off the spray tan, you look like a graham cracker instead of a saltine."

"Get bent," he said.

"Bitch," I said back.

"Cunt!"

Tithonus used the C word on me! He'd never done that. *And that was before things got really bad.*

Chapter 4
The Lost Boys

Hekate, from the Cahier!

These are stories about the missing boys, whose posters you have been seeing all over town. Get them while they're hot, I always say!

And sometimes, they were. Hot and taken both.

Not always in the same ways, not for the same reasons, but they all shared one thing. They tried to love a god or a god tried to love them. These situations *almost always* end badly.

If you can, try to love someone that acts divinely but is a mostly cute positively ordinary boy or girl. Trust me. No, don't trust me…read for yourself and see what can happen if you don't.

Phoebe Falls in Love
They Fit like Hand in Glove… Still,
She asks for Help from Olympus High Above

Introduction of the Titan of the Moon by…Hekate

This one, now she is a piece of work. If she were a god, we would call her a real stud. My term for her? *Crazy bitch.* This, from me- the goddess of murder, witchcraft and children. I would know. She was my grandmother.

Phoebe was one of the Titans, which means she was spontaneously ejected from the womb of Gaea to govern the arcane and mysterious powers of the uninformed universe. In this case, she took charge of the capricious, lusty, and busty powers of the Moon.

There are these 'glow in the dark' Madonnas they give children to help them sleep. Phoebe looked like that but she and the Virgin lack one important common attribute. Guess which one? An intact vagina! *Hello!*

Phoebe had a husband, Coeus, the Titan of the Moon, who looked like a Hipster well before his time: His hair and sideburns were neatly trimmed, his bush and beard not so much.

Like all men, he liked to whittle away the endless hours puzzling out the mysteries of the good old days back in the dorms, which weren't much different from the present, except now, when Coeus popped open a bottle of beer, it was so expensive you could pay the rent with what it cost, and he masturbated to video games instead of porn. Phoebe complained, and not just a little.

This prompted even more endless questioning Coeus had about how universe worked and what greater purpose did it all serve? And he knew that he and Phoebe were made for and with each other, but he need space and time to get it all out of his head. With her around, Coeus said, "I can't get out of my own way."

I never had the need to ask questions, all the answers were mine by my divine birthright but for Phoebe? Too much to bother with, and a husband? That wants to engage in conversations like that?

Phoebe believed, like all reasonable women, that men are so much better when you can see them when you want, and never have to hear them at all. So when her nephew Zeus recruited allies for his patricide, Phoebe was first in line.

Zeus's creation was going to be a big place and that meant there was only enough room in the sky for her and not her husband, and that would mean Phoebe could do whatever she wanted with whomever. Whether or not they wanted to do it with her? Phoebe had a philosophy about that, too.

Since where men are concernred, no means no and no means yes, the only way to be sure is not to ask. After Coeus was cast down into Tartarus, Phoebe, hornier than a toad, went on the prowl.

Endymion

Phoebe could feel his eyes on her. She was vain, even for a goddess, but that wasn't her fault. Since there was only one moon in the sky if people looked up, they had to look at her but this was different. These eyes studied her. They peered into every crater and crevasse and swept deliciously over her foothill curves and brilliant seas.

After she nearly lost it during a full moon when she could practically feel his eyelashes tickling Miss Tuesday, Phoebe found the source of the titillation, a man with a telescope.

Because Phoebe was a Titan, descending to earth took a lot of effort. That was a lot of goddess to pack into one of those human bodies. It was no surprise to her at all that Eos left scorch marks on the linoleum when she humiliated herself in front of that boy, but she knew why she went through the trouble. *Fluff that bunny up!*

Phoebe was not about to let the prospect of a hot romance with a younger man leave her behind especially since that strawberry tart was doing it, so she paid the student a visit.

Phoebe arranged herself in a pair of skinny jeans, a loose-fitting blouse also of denim, and did her best to walk on some silver shag-me pumps that all men love. Upon landing, she put her bulbous breasts in front of the telescope. "Hello handsome! What are you looking at?"

"The Sea of Tranquility," he said.

"There's nothing interesting about that," Phoebe loosened an extra button on her blouse.

"Oh I disagree completely!" the guy smiled. "Or would you prefer some other luno-graphic feature?"

He said strange things, but he was so handsome! "I'm more interested in what you would prefer, actually." She unbuttoned her blouse one more time.

"Yo! Hey! How about an introduction first?" he stood, checked to be sure his telescope was safe, and extended his hand, "I'm Endymion."

"I'm Phoebe," she said, knowing that would do it.

"Hello, Phoebe," Endymion said. "Your parents must have been nostalgic. I haven't heard that name in a long time."

"He thinks I'm old," Phoebe was crestfallen, *"Well, I am,"* she said back to herself.

"Fortunately, it's my favorite name," Endymion looked up.

Oh you gorgeous and wonderful man, Phoebe cringed with joy.

Phoebe wore the poor astronomer out. He could not satisfy her urges and it began to take its toll on him. He was further taxed by the fact he had no choice in the matter. Phoebe was a Titan and that meant she had no limits or need to respect those of others. Endymion was oversexed to the point that something had to be done. Phoebe wanted more and more and more. The more he put out, the harder it was to get him to keep up.

She put Endymion on a high protein and mineral diet, mesmerized him into visiting the gym and the track, till he was thoroughly exhausted and even hexed him so he would be more randy than a herd of Centaurs trying to outdo a gaggle of satyrs. No more of that telescope stuff, Endymion's attentions were needed elsewhere. Let's just say he became very familiar with the features of the moon, and in a lot more detail than he could ever hope with his other astronomical equipment.

Endymion began to decline from the exertion. Even when Phoebe compelled him further and further, using all the power she dared, her mortal lover began to succumb.

Phoebe became perplexed. She didn't want to make Endymion suffer; she actually liked him a little. After many millennia of existence Phoebe discovered that making love is better when you think you are in love with someone.

That made finding a way to bolster Endymion's desire and capabilities something of an emergency.

Time to Return the Favor, she wants a Lover not a Neighbor!

Zeus was in his aerie, looking grumpy as he watched Ganumede twirl his baton.

"Intriguing," Phoebe said softly. "Won't he be a stud when he grows up! What a gusher!"

Zeus averted an eye, "Yes. And why are we speaking?"

"It seems we share an interest, *my most favorite nephew*," Phoebe pointed at the boy, who was still going at it. "I mean, we both appear to like these creatures and their features."

When he realized Phoebe was not going to scold him, Zeus smiled, "They do put sizzle in my pizzle."

In spite of his mood over the Eros situation, Zeus was actually quite fond of his nasty aunt. She made him feel good about being bad. Unfortunately, that was about to change.

"I was hoping you could help me with this box o matches I have found, actually."

"Sure," Zeus said. "Who is this piece of tinder?" Zeus recovered his senses for a moment, actually tearing his eyes away from the bathing beauty. "And please, we aren't talking about freeing Coeus again. Period."

"No," Phoebe said and brightened, "I've fallen in love with another. A mortal."

Zeus turned to face her, "Phoebe, please. Don't. These January December romances never work."

Phoebe pointed to the man child in the shower, "It's more fun when it's not a spectator sport, you know? And I like him, I want to stay with him, but he keeps wearing out! He needs to eat and sleep, and do his laundry! It's very upsetting!"

"I've been around the block a few times, Auntie," Zeus said, "I get it. And I'm trying to point out you'll be happier with someone more compatible with your lifestyle. That doesn't wear out or die the second you make a misstep."

"And I'd like to propose and innovative counterpoint to your point." Phoebie explained.

"No immortality," Zeus grumbled. He hated the very idea that much. "Shag and bag if you must. There will be others. There are always others...but no immortality."

Zeus watched Ganumede trim, then decide to shave his armpits.

"I completely agree!" Phoebe said, "So I've come up with a kind of virtual immortality," Phoebe said.

"What are you talking about?" Zeus couldn't rewind this video and he didn't want to wait till Ganumede finished shaving his navel to and gave it a go again. *No, you idiot...! You're supposed to leave a little!*

Phoebe, relentless, in spite of Zeus's preoccupied state continued to explained her proposal.

"*That*!" Zeus said, "*Is absolutely bat shit crazy, and out of the question!*"

"I'm actually not asking for your opinion," Phoebe glowed like one of those lamps that gets brighter the more you turn the switch, "I am insisting on a course of action."

"No!" Zeus said, "That's vulgar. It's undignified."

"To you. As for me, I really want this."

Zeus did not like being pushed, and this was most definitely happening. “Phoebe, Auntie, we don’t do things like this. We are here to serve a purpose, perhaps to have a dalliance or two, all the while pretending we care about what happens with mankind down below. We aren’t them and they will never be us, and there must never be an attempt at even an approximation.”

“I’m not interested in your pedantic explanations of why I can’t have what I want,” Phoebe clicked up a level of brightness, casting a white glow that blurred Ganumede arranging his ruby colored underwear with the silver trim over his pelvis; one of Zeus’s favorite parts of the boy.

“I am not explaining anything to you, Phoebe. I am telling you no in a different way.”

“Well, tell me yes in a new way. *Or else*!”

Ganumede was posing in the mirror, a very flattering pose with his arms over his head. The little thing was even trying to make his thighs flex.

“Phoebe, silence!” The bedrock of Olympos jumped in response to his command.

Phoebe stepped in front of him and shook the place up a little, too, “I will not be silent! You owe me! You took my husband from me and I helped you to sit your ass down up here and watch you act ungrateful to those that put you here! And you won’t do it to me! Now, you deliver or I will find some other way!”

Zeus was Zeus and when he won the throne on High Olympus, he made it a point not to regret any aspect of it, and neither did he thank or keep any of the promises he needed to make to get himself there. Still Phoebe was a Titan and he wanted no trouble from her. Her request of him was perverse and an abomination but it was small enough.

“Fine, Phoebe. I will repay my debt to you. I hope it’s worth the price that your beloved will have to pay for being so comely.”

The Titaness of the Moon relaxed, turned down her harsh fluorescent lighting down to a soft shade of blue, “I love him, Zeus.”

“I understand. *Hermes*?” Zeus just wanted to be done with it.

“Yes, Father?” There was a breeze and the Divine Herald appeared.

“Please go to the realm of Nox and ask her if she would allow Hypnos and Thanatos to do me a favor.”

He glared at Phoebe.

“Of course,” Hermes said. Then, “And the favor is?”

Zeus explained.

He glanced at Phoebe who looked so pleased.

"I'll speak to Nox as you have requested, Father." Hermes said and was gone.

Phoebe clapped her hands like a little girl, who just got her first stuffed pony at a birthday party, "Thank you, Nephew! I am so happy!"

The Moon rose over Olympos. Zeus watched it hurtle across the Ether like a like a fly ball and descend to the earth.

The matter being settled, Zeus turned back to his scrying pond and watched Ganumede pull his pants on, one leg at a time. Shirtless, barefoot, he almost looked like a man.

The Spell is Cast, Zeus's Promise Fulfilled at Last

Thanatos and Hypnos appeared, as ordered by Zeus Thunderer, at the behest of Phoebe, the Titaness of the moon, to render one of the most handsome mortals, Endymion, into a state of eternal dreaming. Never to die, never to wake, never to be free of love's moist embrace.

Thanatos, the god of death, agreed, reluctantly, to suspend his influence whilst Hypnos the god of dreams, asserted himself fully.

The nightmarish appearance of the twins of Dream and Death startled Endymion, at first, but then he sighed, closed his eyes, his neck went limp, and his head turned and fell into the chasm of Phoebe's cleavage.

"It is finished," Hypnos declared.

"Yes," Thanatos said, "Dream and Death have exchanged their destinies for this poor soul."

Phoebe attempted to express her gratitude but the twins were not willing.

"Do not thank us, Phoebe of the Titans," they said in unison. "To interfere with life and death in this way is not Até. Never call on us again."

The pale twins returned to their realm.

Phoebe was not her nephew, King Zeus, and had no real use for Até, though it had use for her.

Phoebe took the sleeping man far away to her temple in Mount Latmos, lest her lover be vulnerable as he slumbered, and closed him in. She could then allow herself as many coital visits as she wanted and needed, regularly and often.

Later, Horus Visits Latmos

Horus alighted on the slopes of Latmos but he knew he was too late. The door had been revealed, cracked, and broken. Thrown down.

He entered the chamber and the Glow of the Horizon revealed the glitter of the broken pieces of glass, like from fluorescent lights; the remnants of the Maenads, Endymion's daughters, who watched over him while he slept.

Muffled crying came from the master cavern ahead.

There, he found many more piles of glass, and Phoebe, the Titan of the Moon, cradling the blood-soaked corpse of a young man.

"You're too late," she said, "Attis killed him. Maimed him!"

"I have nothing to say to you," Horus said. "Or any desire to listen to you."

"There is no need, if only you can save him?"

"Thanks to you, foul creature, he can't die. Now we must recover his phallus in addition to my father's and hope that we can restore Maat. Where did Attis go?"

"Horus, I am afraid he went to find my son."

"Yes," Horus knew that was true, "I will send your lover to the tender mercies of Anubis, who will ensure no further harm comes to him. If we can, we will make sure he can transpire into the afterlife and, at last, be at peace."

"No! You will bring him back!" Phoebe screamed and threw herself at Horus and was summarily tossed against the opposite end of the cave wall like a glow in the dark rag doll.

"You, the Moon, purport to touch me, *Ra of the Horizon*?"

Phoebe, sorely afraid, shook her head.

"I am not like your sort. I do not play. Never approach me again."

Horus elevated the body of Endymion into the air, taking great care to treat it gently, wrapped it in linen, and sent it to Anubis.

"I am going to find your son," Horus said. "Before Attis does. Pray I do not remember to come looking for you again, Phoebe of the Titans. You gave yourself over to your insatiable lust and a mortal paid the price. This, Ra does not permit."

Horus left and went to Thesipae. Narkissus was imprisoned there by Phoebus Apollo. If Attis wanted to steal his Ka, that is where he would go.

Narkissus Nobody Misses
Never once gave us kisses

There was a boy named Narkissus of Thesipae, who was so beautiful, even the sun could not tear his eyes from its own glimmer on the boy's skin.

From Phoebe, the Titan of the Moon, his mother, he received such a lovely iridescence that even Narkissus himself found irresistible. His favorite pastime was dreaming of ways to improve upon himself and coming up with nothing at all. His favorite *activity* after adoring himself, was allowing others to share in the fun.

All the boys in town, the men and more than a few girls, too, circled him, trying to catch a hint he might want to pay attention to them too. The through of a word, a glance, anything to indicate Narkissus noticed them was intoxicating.

He was never without a following of lovesick boys, phone calls, text messages, invitations to parties, calling cards, flower deliveries, and he had more likes on Facebook than anyone in the known world, including pets.

This was probably the result of his need to take pictures of himself in various stages of undress, in athletic costumes including swimwear, wrestling gear, football pads, and soccer uniforms, modeling the latest in underwear, pants, socks, jackets, new haircuts, shoes, flipflops, especially after he painted his toenails.

Any excuse at all to show himself off to anyone, who would watch through any sort of device or medium, that was where he wanted to be. And no one could resist: As the only son of a Titan and her sleeping sperm bank, Endymion, not only was Narkissus gorgeous, but even if he looked like the Penguin, the Danny DeVito version, people would have still fought over who got to drink his bathwater. Magical glamors overcame even the worst repulsive of flaws and curses of appearance, speech, ranges of height, weight, and proportion even better than drugs and money.

Narkissus never did anything pornographic, as that would require the presence of someone else in the pictures other than he.

The lucky ones got to see him parade through the night clubs, where he called out to each one of them by name like he knew them. Narkissus would jump up on the box at the front of the stage, take his shirt off and dance till people started to take their chances.

This usually bored him and he left before the need to say *no* became tedious.

One would think he would be hip deep in the willing, sharing himself with the best-looking people the gods made but, for all his power to attract potential lovers, Narkissus always went home alone.

One night at *Pace*, Thesipae's most fabulous danceteria, Narkissus made his way to the box located under the disco ball, hopped up, and tossed his skimpy tank top into the crowd. It landed in the hands of a rather plain looking boy, by Narkissus standards anyway, named Ameinias.

Ameinias could not believe the shiny thing had once touched Narkissus' skin. He envied its passage over Narkissus' iridescent ribcage, the rigors of being stretched over his chest, the thrill of being hiked up over Narkissus' navel whenever he raised his arms to smooth his slick dark hair away from his forehead.

When the official floor show started, some ballet-boy-rejects dressed in bright transparent silk who looked like they got a weekend pass from the harem started squirming on the stage, Narkissus stepped off the box.

"*Meh,*" he said.

Ameinias was waiting.

Narkissus tried to dodge the bespectacled dork but Ameinias maneuvered in front of him.

"I have your shirt," he presented the wadded-up piece of spandex, "if you want it back."

"Thanks," Narkissus took the tank top and wiped his face, tummy, and underarms with it.

That had the desired effect of getting many eyes off the stage, show back where it belonged; on him.

When he was done toweling himself off, Narkissus handed his shirt back to the slack-jawed boy, who could not have been more criminally boring if he'd been a straight boy.

His colorless hair lacked any styling product at all, the blue t-shirt and salmon-colored shorts were vintage Target, and he'd committed the most capital crime of them all: boat-shoes with shorty-socks.

He could have at least worn flip flops, so Narkissus could have seen his feet and hated those, too.

"What's your name?" Narkissus asked.

“Ameinias,” he said. “Are you talking to me?”

“Yes, Ameinias. You talked to me, didn’t you?” Narkissus laughed, too, because the kid was that pathetic.

“Well, yeah!” Ameinias laughed and nodded. “You don’t want your shirt?”

“Don’t you want me to keep it off?” Narkissus grinned.

“Of course, I do!” Ameinias wadded the tank top up in his hands.

“Are you leaving?”

“Yes,” Narkissus said but didn’t hurry off. “Are you staying?”

“Not if you want me to go with you,” Ameinias moved in closer. “We could go somewhere and get a coffee or something.” He prayed to Eros “*or to your place or my place, anyplace…anyplace at all…please…Eros, please!*”

Several, far more attractive, appropriately undressed guys paused to watch and listen. In a short time, a small clutch of people formed beside the dance floor, all rubbernecking to see who Narkissus was deigning to speak to.

Narkissus realized talking to the least interesting boy in the club got him more attention than he’d ever gotten! How fabulous was that?

He was curious if association with Ameinias would improve his social value, especially if everyone saw how much better he looked around the much less interesting Target mannequin.

It wouldn’t hurt Ameinias to learn a few things about being beautiful either. It would make a fascinating experiment.

“Let’s go have tea,” he said to the boy, who gave thanks to Eros.

“What do you do for a living?” Narkissus asked Ameinias at the tea house. When Ameinias reached for his glasses, Narkissus grabbed his wrist, “Do you really need to wear those?”

“I’m in real estate,” Ameinias laughed and grabbed at his rims, “and yes, I can’t see without them.”

“You’d sell more houses if you got contact lenses,” Narkissus sipped his Dragon Well. “And you’re not supposed to put sugar in green tea.”

He slapped Ameinias’s hand as it reached for a sugar shaker. He’d ordered the same kind of tea for both of them to teach Ameinias how to be civilized. It was worse than Narkissus suspected.

“Yikes!” Ameinias recoiled from the sugar like it was a scorpion. “Sorry.”

Narkissus shrugged and took a sip from his teacup. His fingers gripped the handle and balanced it, so the liquor spilled over his jam-colored lips. He could see Ameinias studying him through the few carefully placed strands of night colored hair that fell over one eye.

"Drink your tea," Narkissus said. "It's good for your skin."

"All right," Ameinias nodded and took a sip. "So, what do you do for a living?"

Narkissus revealed a smile as he lowered his teacup, "I don't work. My mother is someone...special, so I don't need to."

"Oh?" Ameinias smiled back. "Who?"

"Phoebe, The Titaness of the Moon," Narkissus said. "It's where my skin gets its sublime glow."

He framed his face with his hands.

"Right," Ameinias laughed, "I think it makes you gorgeous. Do you ever see her?"

"My mother?" Narkissus shrugged, "Not really. When she comes to earth, she usually just wants to visit my father. Not to mention, I have fifty sisters that compete for her attention too and i learned early it's best to just stay out of the fray. Do you ever work out?"

Narkissus reached across the table and pinched Ameinias's bicep.

This made Ameinias uncomfortable but he didn't pull away. "No...never. I think gyms are repulsive, and I wouldn't even know what to do in one anyway."

"You have the wrong idea about gyms." Narkissus smirked, like a razor cut a thin line between his nose and his chin. "Why don't you come with me to my gym and I'll show you how it all works. I can tell your frame will build muscle in all the right places with proper training."

"You think?" Ameinias was quite pleased with the offer and the compliment.

"I'm sure," Narkissus said.

A few days later, Ameinias met Narkissus at a small private gym near the Temple of the Moon called *Muscle Beach.*

"Welcome to Muscle Bitch," Narkissus met him in the foyer. "What are you wearing?"

Narkissus, himself wore black spandex workout pants with the compulsory matching tank top so tight not even one air molecule was between the material and his skin. For the price of his shoes, one could rent an apartment for a month.

Ameinias lowered his head and examined his cargo shorts, t-shirt, and those damned boat shoes, "This is all I really have. I said I don't work out, remember?"

"Don't be oppositional," Narkissus snapped. "We'll go shopping and get you a proper outfit. This travesty will have to do for tonight."

Once inside the gym, Ameinias surveyed the place, which had bright blue mats over every part of the floor, just like he remembered from the wrestling room at school, which he never entered as a matter of pride. Also his stark, utter terror of the place.

Ameinias felt it again upon entering the gym and of Narkissus too and wanted to run away, but just one look from Narkissus overpowered all of his other emotions and impulses.

There were racks of weights of various sizes and configurations on one side, machines that reminded Ameinias of the cranes and pile-drivers he saw building new condo-buildings all over downtown. That everyone but he seemed capable of selling.

About ten other men, all dressed in the uniform of the gym tank tops, colorful basketball or running shorts and matching brightly colored shoes operated the machines, curled barbells or dumbbells. They were all beautiful. They were all also insanely jealous of him. When Ameinias noticed this, he felt quite a lot more adequate himself.

There was a lot of noise. Some of the men grunted or cried out as they lifted heavy weights, spotters called out encouragement, the machines' pulleys, and moving parts clacked and clanged. It sounded like people were being tortured to death to the din of church bells.

Ameinias jumped when one patron, a huge guy that looked like a gorilla in a wrestling singlet, let a barbell roll from his fingers about a foot from the floor and the whole building shook.

"That's uncalled for." He said.

"You're so right! How revolting!" Narkissus took his hand and led him to a stack of dumbbells.

"Here," Narkissus handed him two five-pound dumbbells, donned a pair of gloves without fingers in them, and took two twenties for himself.

"Let them hang there like this, then bend at the elbow, and bring them up just under your chin. *And don't slouch* or it won't work!"

"GOD!"

Ameinias tried but Narkissus scolded, “No, don’t lean forward. Make your biceps do the work.”

Narkissus pointed to the muscle.

Ameinias did as instructed. After curls, Narkissus took him to the bench and taught him how to do the bench press. While he stared up at Narkissus’ crotch, Ameinias huffed and puffed to try to get the bar up over his head, and into Narkissus’ waiting hands.

“Ow!” Ameinias said and rubbed at his palms. One had two blisters, the other had three. Narkissus took them into his gloved hands, “See, this is why you need gloves.”

“I can’t keep doing this until I get some.” Ameinias whined. “It really hurts.”

“Yes, I’m sure it does,” Narkissus took one of his hands in into his and massaged his palm between them, “I’m sorry about that.” Then he looked around, prompting Ameinias to do the same.

The room, previously full of grunting, clanging, and cheers of encouragement from spotters was quiet. Everyone was more concerned with Narkissus and his new friend.

“Stay here,” he ordered Ameinias, who couldn’t tell if his hands burned more from Narkissus’ touch than the muscles he’d just torn.

While Narkissus consulted with the front desk about purchasing some weight-lifting gloves, another patron of Muscle Beach, a stocky blond guy in a blue body suit and wrestling boots lumbered over to Ameinias, “Are you two dating?”

Ameinias could barely look away from Narkissus to answer to the guy’s face, “I don’t know.”

“Are you fucking then?” Blue Body Suit asked as his tone angry more than curious.

Ameinias felt a flash of heat, like those times he was afraid a mean boy like this would try to trip or push him on the bus, “He’s teaching me to work out. That’s all that’s happening.”

Body Suit stared, “Like a personal trainer?”

“Like a friend,” Ameinias said.

Body Suit glared, “Why does he want to be your friend? What’s he getting out of it? What are you getting out of it?”

"It's not what he's getting, Phorcus, it's what you lack," Narkissus appeared between Ameinias and his interrogator. "Class."

"Me?" Phorcus yelled, "Why are you being such a dick?"

Ameinias expected Narkissus to utter some caustic remark, but he just walked away. At first, Ameinias thought he, not Porchus, was being left behind.

Before he put his pale hand on the door, he said to the glass that said *Hceab Elcsum* on it, "Ameinias, are you coming?"

Ameinias looked at Porchus and saw a tear slide down his cheek. Ameinias followed Narkissus out.

"Did you used to date that guy Porchus?" Ameinias asked over dinner.

"I don't date anyone," Narkissus said like he was just asked which hand was his left.

"Did something happen then? He was crying when we left the gym," Ameinias told him. "And why don't you date people?"

Narkissus cut into his wiener schnitzel, "Haven't met anyone that interests me. Certainly not Porchus. Crying? Over what?"

"Yes, he was crying, so you must have gone out with him or...done something," Ameinias lifted up the bandages on one of his palms. "And why are we hanging out if you don't date anyone?"

"I thought it would be fun," Narkissus put his knife down and reached across the table for one of Ameinias' bandaged palms. "Still hurt?"

"Yes," he gulped.

Narkissus looked around the restaurant to be sure everyone was watching, when satisfied he released Ameinias's hand, "We'll go shopping and get you some proper gear. Porchus will shoot a pickle when he sees you."

"Fabulous," Ameinias said.

Narkissus took Ameinias to his personal stylist to get his haircut, then asked Diviana, one of his sisters, to enchant his eyes, so he would no longer need glasses. Narkissus asked her to make them a deeper shade of blue for good measure.

After a few more trips to Muscle Beach, some waxing, shaving, tanning sessions and shopping sprees funded courtesy of the Temple of the Moon, Ameinias was ready for his unveiling at Pace.

"More product," Narkissus rubbed some white goo in between his palms and then stabbed his fingers into Ameinias' scalp. Ameinias nose tingled at the scent of rosemary oil and could feel the movement of Narkissus' fingertips in the tips of his toes.

When he was done, Ameinias saw his normally drab, listless hair spiked up, shining like a crown of sunlight around his head, a perfect companion to the blue-black tassle of hair on top of the boy behind him.

"I barely recognize myself," Ameinias turned suddenly and took Narkissus into his arms.

Narkissus didn't stiffen or try to pull away as expected, "Everyone will recognize you now. Don't you worry about that!"

The tawny port colored lips smiled and pecked Ameinias on his nose.

"Once we see how this goes," Narkissus tapped the spot he kissed, "We'll see how some well-placed tattoos might help you to appear more masculine.

"A few tats will also make you look much more confident and that will surely improve your social standing."

"Surely!" Ameinias said, "But why is my social value so important to you?"

Narkissus laughed that little two syllable laugh, "Let's get some cologne on you. I know just the thing to make them go crazy."

He ran his pale, cold hands over Ameinias' considerably improved shoulders and biceps and gently pulled himself from out of their embrace.

It was a late fall night. As much as Ameinias appreciated how his appearance looked in the smart, shiny blue tank top and butt-hugging shorts Narkissus chose for him and his new physique, he started shivering when the left the cab outside of Pace.

"Don't fold your arms like that," Narkissus snapped. "It looks snobby."

"It's cold!" Ameinias said back.

"It'll be warm inside," Narkissus took his arm. "Walk like you own the place. Hold your head high *like you. Are. The. Shit*."

Ameinias knew what Narkissus meant. He'd observed the Walk, much as all of Thesipae had, since the boy child Narkissus stopped crawling.

He put his arms at his side and tipped his head up but not as high as Narkissus and made eye contact with everyone and it was indeed everyone who watched him accompany the godling of the moon to the front of the line.

Even the bouncer seemed as taken with the new Ameinias as with his star mentor. He stopped the pair, gave Narkissus an up and down glance, with one eye on Ameinias. "You, I know," he said. "But who do we have here?"

"This is Ameinias," Narkissus put his arm around him, felt around his shoulders and arms like he was demonstrating a prize poodle about to be studded out to a prospective buyer. "My progeny."

"Nice work," the bouncer said and parted the massive red velvet curtain that separated the foyer from the club itself. Inside, Ameinias felt the bass drum throbbing of the music from the dance floor make his organs jump inside his rib cage.

"Do you want anything?" Narkissus said into his ear and nudged him toward the bar.

"Why did you tell him I was your progeny?" Ameinias asked. "What did you mean?"

"He's a bouncer," Narkissus said. "You don't want him anyway."

"I know who he is," Ameinias snapped back. "And I know what I want.

"So can you answer me? What did you mean when you said that? Why am I progeny?"

Narkissus rolled his eyes and laughed, "The idea is for everyone to want you. And they do! So come on let's get you a cocktail. You need to relax."

"*I am relaxed*!"

"To celebrate then!"

Narkissus took Ameinias by the hand and led him to the bar. Pace was already busy and packed; obnoxious, raucous, loud, and bright lights skyrocketing overhead in a deep pocket of the underworld; the souls of the damned writhing together, torturing each other as penance for their mutual desires.

After several rounds of Adonis martinis, straight up, Ameinias found himself holding court with the boys that surrounded him and Narkissus. Porchus, among them.

"Hi," Porchus nudged Ameinias in the side. "Remember me? Or are you too rich and famous now?"

Ameinias, drunk off his ass, hugged him, "Hi! Porchus! No, I'm not rich or famous! What's up?"

Porchus laughed a little and held on to steady Ameinias a bit, "Just thought I'd see what all the commotion was about over here."

"Oh, the same one," Ameinias's bigger, bluer eyes lingered on the pale boy with red lips in the midst of the ordinary ones.

Porchus gently slapped his cheek, "Hey, snap out of it. You're too good for him."

Ameinias's eyes rolled back toward Porchus, like two blue planets turning away from a rising star at twilight, "Not good enough, apparently."

Porchus' fingers felt along the top of his ear, "You're good enough for anyone. Why have you been hiding yourself in his shadow like that?"

"All of us are in his shadow," Ameinias drooled.

Porchus had to grab his chin again, "Stop looking at him! Look at me."

"Okay," Ameinias said.

"Just okay, huh?" Porchus pulled him into his arms.

"I guess so," Ameinias laughed with delight at the sensation, a real warm human body against his, excited to be in contact with him, of all people.

"You're so cute when you smile," Porchus touched his lips. "You don't smile around him."

Ameinias started to get hot and sweat, "I smile all the time."

"All you do is make that sad face whenever you're trailing him around," Porchus said. "And here he comes."

"Hey, Porky," Narkissus said. "Trying to exceed your means as usual, I see."

"Hey Narkiss-ass," Porchus said. "Charming as usual, I don't see."

Ameinias twitched like a rodent that was embarrassed it hadn't tried to get away from the cat.

"Did you want to see me?" he asked Narkissus.

"Yes. There are some adult film stars dancing on the main stage. I thought it would be fun to watch them watch us. Ha!" Narkissus took Ameinias by the arm.

"See you around," Ameinias wiggled his fingers at Porchus.

"Call me," Porchus slipped a card into Ameinias' pocket before Narkissus whisked him away.

The process continued. Narkissus took Ameinias to high class parties amongst the upper-class priests and politicians in Thesipae, making sure to buy him appropriate clothing, cologne, and accessories before-hand.

Ameinias went along with it every time, what else could he do? He was enthralled, and being seen with Narkissus, especially inside his new self was very good for his real estate business.

With Narkissus' list of contacts and help, he went from selling low value houses and condos to penthouses and mansions, even the purchase of entire blocks of the city for multi-million drachma-urban redevelopment projects.

In a few months, Ameinias went from an unknown hunched-over geek in glasses and bad shoes to a stud-ball with blue eyes, the color of lapis, the best clothes, a top floor apartment in downtown Thesipae, and a lot of money.

The future looked positive. Ameinias was not only known as a hot commodity for his tanned, blond, ripped good looks, and his real estate connections, but he also gained a reputation for being kind and approachable.

Ameinias said hello and good morning to everyone with a smile regardless of their age, size, shape, or social standing, went out of his way to ask people their names, and he even remembered them too!

By coming out his shell and realizing his potential, he succeeded in becoming a beacon to other men, but one that shined his light amongst, rather than above them like Narkissus.

Still, he was lonely.

On a night when there was a lunar eclipse and, coincidentally, no parties, nude dancers, or business dinners and Narkissus had to observe a family holiday at an undisclosed location with his family, Ameinias decided to call Porchus.

"Of course, I'd love to see you!" Porchus said. "Some friends of mine and I are gathering at the Temple of Apollo for a contest of plays, would you like to come?"

Ameinias was pleased, "Sure, sounds like fun!"

"Some of the guys are actually competing. They'll be overjoyed you're in the audience," Porchus said. "Not as much as me though."

"Oh stop!" Ameinias threw himself back on the chaise lounge by the glassed-in side of his apartment and gazed out at the city, "I'm just an old dish rag."

"I'm not going to put up with that shit, Ameinias," Porchus sounded cross. "Meet me at the Temple of Apollo at 7 and I'll introduce you to everyone. Dinner afterward?"

"Yes," Ameinias said. He was about to go out on a real date. And Narkissus hadn't told him what he should wear.

After a thorough search through his closet, he chose an ensemble he thought Narkissus would approve of and left for the Temple.

Ameinias hesitated outside the columned entrance that had a huge bah relief of Lord Apollo in his chariot, carrying Thesipae, the nymph, whom the town was named after, into the sky.

It made him wish it was Narkissus in the Chariot of the Moon and he was his Thesipae.

With a quick prayer of apology to Phoebus, just in case the god found that offensive, he entered the temple.

Porchus and a few other boys Ameinias, had seen either at Pace or Muscle Beach were with him.

"Hey, Ameinias!" Porchus laughed and ran over to him. "I was afraid you weren't going to come."

"I said I would!" Ameinias said and accepted the affectionate hug he was offered.

"Guys," Porchus kept his arm around Ameinias's waist. "This is Ameinias, the one I told you about. Ameinias, this is Thesis and Thespis, we'll see them on stage in a few minutes and this is Pelasgos, a friend of mine."

"An ex, actually," Pelasgos winked at Ameinias.

"We're all exes here, actually," Thesis added.

"Oh right," Thespis added. "You're the latest victim of Moon Fever. Welcome to the *Sun Bathers*."

"Stop it," Porchus commanded.

"Sun Bathers?" Ameinias asked.

"Don't listen to them," Porchus said. "Let's go get our seats before there are none left."

Before the shows started, Ameinias asked what a Sun Bather was. Porchus let out a long breath, "It's silly, don't worry about it."

"It's what we, who don't want to be glamorized by that twat, Narkissus, call ourselves," Pelasgos said. "And you should tell him, Porchus."

"Tell me what?" Ameinias felt nauseous.

"After the show." Porchus glared at Pelasgos.

"Tell me now," Ameinias insisted. "I don't like being made fun of."

"You're not…" Porchus said, taking his hand. "We're not ridiculing you."

"We're trying to save you," Pelasgos said. "From the dark magic of that moon demon, Narkissus."

That made Ameinias enraged, "He's not a demon!"

"Guys, the curtain is going up," Porchus glared at Pelasgos. "We can discuss this later."

After the invocation to Apollo, the plays began:

From the very outset I pray to You, Apollo, inventor of music and of all the healing arts, come and bless this undertaking with Your laurel.

Apollo, grant that we enjoy good health and a sound mind, and, we pray, when we grow old, grant us a strife-free life, a clear mind, and voice with which to sing Your praises.

Apollo, we beseech you, graciously grant peace, prosperity, safety, and sound health to our friends and family, by your gracious favor.

Come, health-bearing Apollo, come and favor our undertaking.

Ameinias was distracted by Pelasgos' words throughout the performances. He was, in fact, terrified of their implications; so much so, he held onto Porchus' hand till they were both slick with sweat. His palm left a wet stain on his pants when he wiped it off.

The plays were well executed and Ameinias thought Thespis and Thesis were spectacular and gorgeous in the various roles they played. While he was happy their company won the competition, and the festive mood carried him through till they reached the restaurant, he could not help but feel left out. His heart was elsewhere.

He waited until they were seated at *Amphora*, a favorite greasy spoon for Thespian boys to return to the topic that made Porchus act so nervous. "Tell me about the Sun Bathers."

Porchus swished the pink colored remnants of his *Adonis* around in the glass. Thespis and Thesis laughed, then fell silent when Porchus glared at them. Pelasgos answered.

"*Sun Bathers* is the name of our theater company. We're a cult of Apollo worshippers, like us, who want the god's blessings," Pelasgos had a deep, manly voice but spoke slowly, like he was reciting lines from a play. "Through our music performance, poetry, acting," he looked around the table at those assembled, "and romance. In exchange, we get protection from certain…illnesses and dark influences."

Pelasgos looked down.

"You think Narkissus is one of those influences?" Ameinias asked.

"His mother is one of those Titan monsters," Thespis looked at Ameinias like he was pathetic, witless. "He inherited her indecent nature and sinister power."

"He's an abomination," Thesis agreed. "A devil dog wearing a man's skin."

"He's got you under his spell," Porchus said. "He's got most of the men and boys in this town under it! Haven't you seen how they circle him like stars around a black hole?"

"Why do you think he disappeared tonight? The night of the lunar eclipse?" Thespis leered. "Why has the whole town seemed to just…stopped partying?"

"You're partying," Ameinias said. "You're all happy as larks."

"We party to honor Apollo, for protecting us from that freak," Thesis said.

"We want to help you," Pelasgos placed his hand over Ameinias'. "Because we like you and because you're in danger."

Ameinias pulled his hand off the table, "In danger? How? Narkissus is a bit…off, yes, but he's done nothing but help me! He's been rather kind and generous!"

"What exactly has he done for you?" Porchus asked.

Ameinias felt his eyes getting hot, like steam might condense from their edges, "He helped me come out of my shell. Helped me meet people and build my business…I'd be nobody without him. You guys wouldn't even want to talk to me before I met him!"

"Did you ever talk to us?" Porchus turned red. "And why you, Ameinias? Why did he choose you over anyone else in this town to shower with his blessings? Are you even dating? Does he touch you? Kiss you? Make love to you? *Ask him why not*!"

Ameinias felt too heavy to move, too solid and stone-y to sweat or shed a tear.

Pelasgos held his hand up, "How do you feel right now, Ameinias? What are you thinking?"

“I think you’re jealous,” Ameinias stood and faced Porchus. “You’re clearly still carrying a torch for him and now you’re trying to get in between us, so you have him back!”

“What?” Porchus rose to his feet. “What the hell makes you think that? I never went out with him! He asked me to spot him a couple of times in the gym. He told me he thought I’d be more attractive if I lost some weight. He gave me an eating disorder! I couldn’t eat or sleep or do anything unless he was around, teasing me! If it wasn’t for the fact my friends brought me to the Temple of Apollo for healing, I would have died!”

“Well, I don’t believe a word of it,” Ameinias said, “I certainly don’t have an eating disorder and neither do you, anymore from the looks of it.”

He pointed at the crumbs of a slice of cherry pie that remained on Porchus’ plate, “Quite the contrary. And I’m in the best shape of my life, thanks to Narkissus. You’re just going to have to face the fact that he likes me more than you.”

Porchus grabbed his arms, “It’s you I want, not him. Why do you think I ever talked to you to begin with? I wanted to take you away from him.”

Ameinias waited for Pelasgos and Thesis and Thespis to laugh or comment but their faces were focused, waiting.

“I have to go,” Ameinias left.

Ameinias finally got a hold of Narkissus.

He met Narkissus in his room, above and behind the chapel. Ameinias hadn’t seen him since the night of the lunar eclipse but upon sight of the slender, pale boy with that garnet colored pout, he was overjoyed.

“Thanks for seeing me,” Ameinias tried to hug Narkissus but it was like embracing a cardboard cutout.

“So, what’s up?” Narkissus said.

“I hadn’t seen you in a while,” Ameinias smiled.

“No, you haven’t seen me in a while!” Narkissus replied.

“Well, I have something to show you,” Ameinias was too excited to yield to whatever mood Narkissus was in. He would change it when he saw.

“What?” Narkissus put a hand on his hip and cocked it.

“I’m so grateful for everything you’ve done,” Ameinias tugged at his shirt. “And I wanted to show you how dedicated I am to you, and always will be…”

He pulled the t-shirt over his head, “So I got this.”

On his left pectoral was a crescent moon, freshly tattooed in black.

Narkissus rolled his eyes, "Silly."

And walked away.

Ameinias thought he was joking or at just being crabby and ran after him, "Wait! I got it for you! What's the problem? Is it improper? Did I get the wrong one? Is it in the wrong place?"

Narkissus stopped, regarded him. "I suppose it's fine, I just don't understand the motivations behind it. What do you want me to do? Get one with your name? Right across my heart?"

"I wouldn't turn that down," Ameinias flexed his chest muscles, hooked a finger suggestively in the waist of his shorts, "But I'll settle for you telling me you want us to be together."

Narkissus sighed, "First, never, ever tattoo anyone's name or sigil on your body. It's just asking for trouble. Second, I don't want us to be together. Next and last, this little experiment is over. Go find someone who might enjoy this kind of thing and leave me be."

Ameinias burst into tears, "So it's true. You did cast a spell on me."

Narkissus turned, "Oh you've been talking to Porchus. Tell me, Ameinias, what kind of evil hex did I put on you? Has your sleep been interrupted by nightmares, are you afflicted by disease or deformity? Have you lost all of your money and are you now roaming the streets, homeless and hopeless?"

"No," Ameinias said, "I consider myself to be handsome and successful but I wasn't always that way. Certainly not that night you first spoke to me. Which makes me wonder, why did you? Why did you talk to me and give me all of this help? The makeover, the new eyes, the clothes, my new body, the book of business you built for me…why me and not someone else?

"Especially since you want nothing for it…you won't touch me, won't let me get close to you… Is it because as you said, I'm an experiment?"

Narkissus folded his arms, "I wanted to see if I could use my…talents to transform a goat into a stallion. And I've succeeded. Now, go, run, and play. You're boring me."

Ameinias stayed where he was, "But…I love you! I really do! I know I wasn't much to look at before, but…I'm sure I'm someone you could love now! You made me like this for a reason…not as an experiment but so I could be worthy of you!"

"I can't love anyone else," Narkissus said quietly, "worthy or not. I simply don't have that capability. It's not you, *even if you were somebody*, it still simply would not be you."

"Don't you want someone to care about you? Not just admire you and want to fuck you? Don't you want to share your life with someone that values you for more than how you look?"

"I want you to stop whining at me and leave," Narkissus said.

Ameinias ran ahead of him and cut him off, "Please, give me a chance, I'll do anything! I'd die for you!"

"Fine!" Narkissus shouted. "Do that!" He went to the wall and took one of the platinum sacrificial blades off its hook. "If you want a sword to fall on, here it is!"

Ameinias did.

There was outrage in the Temple of Apollo, led by Porchus.

"Great Apollo!" Porchus shrieked at the statue of the god. "Narkissus murdered Ameinias! The boy I loved!"

"He charms the boys of this town, then leads them to ruin!" Thesis added. "And death!"

"Narkissus is a plague on us, Lord Phoebus," Pelasgos pleaded to the smooth stone of the god's ankle. "We beg you to intercede and cure us of this curse."

"Give us justice, so we may honor you and extol you," Thespis placed a garland of myrtle leaves around the statue. "Save us, Lord of the Lyre, and we will fill the streets with songs of praise and thanksgiving."

"Make Narkissus pay!" Porchus fell to his knees and the others tried to comfort him.

Nemesis heard the prayers from the temple below as she passed through the Ether. She was tempted to go take of the matter herself but no one had prayed to her about it.

When Nemesis told him what was going on, Apollo didn't appear to be eager to intervene.

"Aren't you going to answer that?" Nemesis gestured toward the ground with a long, gray-tipped pinfeather.

"I hear it," Apollo fastened the halter of his lead steed.

"Well? What are you going to do?" Nemesis demanded.

“Are you crazy? Act against the son of a Titan? The Titan of the Moon, no less? Her wrath would be beyond comprehension.”

“It is beyond comprehension to allow Narkissus to go unpunished for what he did. That boy, Ameinias, killed himself while under a glamor the son of Phoebe inflicted him with. And your followers; the playwrights and actors and musicians that you say are your favorites, beg you to intervene before it happens again. You have a divine right to respond. Go get that bitch and make him pay for hurting that boy!”

“As fun as that sounds,” Apollo shook his head, little sparks and eddies of light flew off his hair, “I cannot enter the temple of another god and attempt to assert my will. Zeus’s law and he enforces it strictly.”

“I’m aware of the laws of Zeus, boy,” Nemesis held her scale up, “I’m aware of all of the laws. And I know all of the loopholes.”

“Explain,” Apollo paused to listen and Nemesis relayed her plan.

“I see the brilliance of this,” Apollo said when she was finished, “It will ingratiate me all the more to my cult and allow me to rid the earth of a pestilence that has been a canker on one of my seats of power, all without any complications or uncomfortable questions from the rest of the pantheon.”

“Yes, correct,” Nemesis smiled. “So you will do it? You’ll handle Narkissus? I can’t stand the sound of their cries any longer.”

“Yes,” Apollo said. “After sunrise, justice will be done.”

Apollo spoke to his Oracle, who relayed his wishes to the congregation. A party, a dance party, specifically, was to be thrown on the night of Apollo, The Victor at Pace, featuring the best danseurs in the Temple of Apollo’s employ and its congregation.

“Only the smoothest, most seductive, lithe, and flexible, rippling with muscle,” the high priest ordered. “They must be irresistible, as *Lord Apollo Apotropaeus* has commanded.”

The dancers were auditioned, cast, and photographed. Posters, ads, and press releases were issued to announce the party and what to expect.

‘Come Celebrate Apollo Boëdromia with the Most Beautiful Boys in Thesipae – Saturday Night at Pace.’

As expected, Narkissus showed up just as the line was around the block. Pace was already stuffed with people, dancing, drinking, pressing against the bar, crammed up against the stage to get a look at the temple-dancing boys.

“Almost makes you want to be a top, doesn’t it?” Porchus said to Narkissus.

“I’ve never stated a preference either way,” Narkissus said.

“Something made you come out of hiding,” Porchus smiled warmly. “If it’s not to find some action, what could it be?”

“I wasn’t hiding,” Narkissus looked around Porchus, at the stage, “I was giving myself a rest. Looks like I should have just stayed home. I find the action to be rather dull here this evening, to be honest.”

“I think you came to check out the competition,” Porchus elbowed him. “These boys could lure Lord Phoebus himself out of his chariot at high noon for a little romp.”

Narkissus shrugged, “I suppose they’d be attractive to any common child molester, yes.”

“They look potent enough to me,” A tall, dark-haired youth, shirtless, glistening, appeared out of the crowd, his voice deep and rich carried over all the ruckus. The light off the disco ball and laser show played about his dark curls like radiant gasses roiling off the surface of a star.

“So, go avail yourself, Lord Phoebus,” Narkissus tried to act unsurprised to see the guest of honor, “I’m sure they’d be all too happy to make an offering.”

“That is fucking hysterical!” Apollo said. “And what about you?” Apollo moved very close to him, “What would you offer me?”

“A razor, a can of shaving cream,” Narkissus pointed at the cleft of Apollo’s chest, “And a scented cloth.”

“I wouldn’t be so quick to insult me if I were you, Narkissus.”

The light in the club, the sparkles, and lasers, and shimmers off the disco ball swarmed around Phoebus, as if a cavalry rushing to his defense.

“Why would you care?” Narkissus said loudly, noting the number of people pausing to watch, “You’re a god of Olympus. What difference could my insults or praises matter to you?”

“What is in your heart matters to me,” Apollo moved closer to Narkissus, who could feel the god’s heat parching his skin. “You used your beauty to hex Ameinias! Instead of using your gifts to serve him, you made a fool of him and caused his death. This community,” Apollo waved an arm over the crowd of dancers, “demands you submit to my authority as consequence.”

Narkissus laughed, "I could care less what a bunch of sluts, trolls, and Centaurs want. I did nothing wrong. Ameinias was like the rest of you; weak, ugly, pitiable. I was under no obligation to give myself to him. Instead of suffering the rejection he should have expected and walk away with dignity, he decided to kill himself. None of it was my fault, and I don't see any point in taking the blame for it!"

"It is not the fact he was pitiable that is being called into account, it is that you showed no pity," Apollo's dark eyes blazed like coals deep in a smith's furnace. "You were born with every physical advantage, but your heart is empty. Your vanity…"

"Yes, all of that is true, I'm sure," Narkissus shrugged. "But I don't recall asking for your opinion."

Narkissus tried to walk away but Apollo grabbed him and took his chin into his hand, "You will let me love you! I'm not asking! You will show some humility and give me what I want!"

Narkissus pulled free and slapped Apollo's face, "That's the measure of humility I will show you!"

He turned his back on the fuming sun god and walked away, pausing a moment to admire his reflection in the disco ball, which still spun over the silent dance floor. He smiled at himself, adjusted a lock of hair, and said, "Enjoy the rest of your holiday."

"Narkissus!" Apollo's voice called out. "You like yourself that much? You smile at your own reflection and reject my affection?"

"You're starting to get it I think!" Narkissus said.

"Then, I curse you to get what you want," Apollo pointed to the disco ball and Narkissus vanished.

"Now, let's get a look at those dancing boys," Apollo commanded.

The music started and everyone, including Porchus, turned their attention to the stage. Narkissus was never seen in the town again.

Occasionally, over the years, dancers would report seeing the reflection of Narkissus in the tiny square mirrors of the disco ball peering back at them.

Hyakinthos and Daphne
One a Flower, the Other a Tree. Love Never Sets You Free

"Hi, can you help me with something?" Daphne called from her office door.

"Sure, just a second," Hyakinthos finished putting some metatags on a website he was programming and pushed it live. The project was running late and so was his homework. He was an 'international studies' graduate student and his bills were late, falling in love or even a good screw, not lately.

"Yes, My Queen," Hi said and pulled the chair in front of Daphne's desk.

"No, no, come around," Daphne pointed to her phone. "What do you think of him?"

"Huzzah!" Hi said. "Damn!"

"I know! And the dooshery level is within acceptable limits!"

"Girls," Hi said. "Dooshes are for doing."

"You would know," Daphne ribbed him. "Look at this butt shot!"

"A guy with low dooshiness is sending you a shot of his loveseat already?"

"*I know*!" Daphne said.

"Unpossible," Hi said. "Are you going to meet him?"

"Should I?"

"Let me read."

Sun'N'Sir

Age: 32, Height: 6', Weight: 185, Hair: Black, Race: <blank>
Occupation: <blank>
Looking for: Dates, Casual, Serious.

"That's not a lot to go on." Hyakinthos said. "And guy that looks like that is probably only serious about being casual!"

"So?"

"Gawd," Hyakinthos said.

"Tell me what to say! He's messaging me!"

Sun'N'Sir: 'Hello, DaphneJ.'
DaphneJ: 'Hey yourself. How is your day going?'
Sun'N'Sir: 'It's okay. Bored.'
DaphneJ: 'Say it's not so!'

"This guy does not get bored," Hi said. The pictures showed a specimen of manhood that surely was a hoax, it was so…ideal. The light and shadow seemed to be glued to the curves and bulges of his muscles, he was tanned like a professional skier, and there was that one detail that made Hi really mad, this guy liked sardines!

Hi could smell the sun and sweat wafting off his stomach.

"So should he get laid tonight or not?" She asked.

"That ass of his looks like it could survive re-entry and splash down," he said. "Go for it!"

Daphne yelped, "You are hilarious! I don't think you'd put a rocket in his pocket somehow."

"Please," he said. "Is he your type? You don't usually go out with guys like this."

"No," Daphne said, "I don't, but how will I know if I should go out with him if I don't go out with him?"

"That's a good point. He could be quite nice."

"He could be!" Daphne said.

Hi couldn't get Sunny Guy out of his mind, couldn't stop envisioning what it might be like to press his face against one of those inner thighs. Like any gay man without any sense at all, he went to his phone to find a way to get it done, or get as close as possible.

He hated Grindr, hated all those hookup sites, they wasted his time, made him feel lonely and unmoored, but so did living alone in a studio apartment, trying to keep up with the clothes, the gym membership, and typing into Blackboard for grad school all night. All of it very expensive.

He opened Grindr to see what would or more than likely wouldn't happen.

There was a message waiting. It was him: ***Sun'N'Sir***.

'Hey, handsome.' The message said. "Message me when you log in next."

Hi's hands trembled as he typed his response.

Daphne and Hyakinthos met in graduate school. She was a director at a charity that fought the good but useless fight of trying to raise money for food and medicine in areas lacking adequate amounts of both, said her way was unique and different, and enough people with money to spend agreed with her so she started a small organization.

Hi sat next to her in their terrorism seminar and they hit it off right away, making jokes about both of them wearing burkas and sneaking into the teacher's, Mr. Ahmed Eshan's harem, both earning their participation grades.

He needed a job, she needed some help, and even though the fledgling and floundering association had little money, it was unlikely to make any due to its lack of human capital.

Hi's ideas for ways to raise money and connect with donors, public officials and expert command of the ridiculously complex fundraising technology helped them grow. Hi was smart, dedicated, cute as a button, and liked listening to Daphne, as a person and a professional.

They shared everything with one another.

"I met that guy for a drink last night," A text message from Daphne said.

"What?" Hi bolted into Daphne's office and turned so fast, he spilled his green tea chai latte all over his Kenneth Cole Jewel Tones amethyst purple shirt! "Who? Which guy?"

"Suri. That's his name. It's short for Surya…some Middle Eastern name or something," Daphne said.

"When? I mean, wow, where did you go?"

"*Glow Worm*. That new absinthe bar on U Street."

"Absinthe? Jeez, Daph. Surprised you came to work," Hi calculated the different trajectories. "Did you stay out late?"

"No, Mother, I was home by ten."

"Ho-Lee-Shit," Hi said to himself. Suri came over at 8:30 and didn't leave till 11. Hi's whole body still ached from the way he got thrown around, "Is…is he nice? Did you have fun?"

"He's actually kind of boring!" Daphne laughed. "Seemed kind of distracted or something, maybe it was first date jitters. Didn't try to get me to go home with him, which is a huge mark in his favor though. Either that or means I'm losing my touch!"

"Are you going to see him again?"

"He said he wanted to. So…sure!" Daphne said, "If he asks. He didn't really seem interested, but who knows?"

"I have some stuff to catch up on," Hi said.

"Hi, are you okay?" Daphne asked.

"I'm tired. I was up all night working on this paper I have due this weekend. I can't wait to graduate and get my life and some sleep back."

“We’re jiggin’ to the same tune!”

“Conference call with the new copywriter at 10?” Hyakinthos asked.

“Yeah,” Daphne said, “Lunch after?”

“Sure,” Hi said.

“*Sweet Green*?” Daphne suggested. “I’ll buy.”

“Okay,” Hi said. “Thanks.”

Hi’s neck and back hurt and his chest, where Sur punched him repeatedly, even though he asked him to stop. It felt like he’d been maxing out on thousand-pound barbells all week.

A little later, Daphne said, “Suri works only a few blocks away,” Daphne said, “I hope it’s okay if he meets us at lunchtime. I’d love your opinion of him.”

“I will do my best,” Hi wanted to tell her right then, everything, had wanted to all morning, but there was no way. It was some kind of mistake. A misunderstanding.

“Oh fuck me,” Hi said under his breath when they met at Sweet Green—it was indeed Suri- Surya..whatever.

“Hey!” Sur said, appearing alongside them in line at the cashier. He hugged Daphne and held his hand out, “This your GBF?”

“Don’t be bad,” Daphne said, blanching. “But yes, this is Hi, he works with me at the Association. Hi, this is Surya.”

“Yeah,” Hi glared and extended his hand. “Nice to meet you.”

“Hey.”

“Is your name really High?” Suri shook his hand and Hi climaxed. It felt like he was pissing.

“Hi is short for Hyakinthos.” Hi said, clenched his jaw and tried to stand perfectly still but the intensity of the *next orgasm* made him double over. “Daphne, I’ll be right back.”

He handed her his roasted chicken organic kale and mesclun salad and ran for the men’s room.

“Hi?” She took the lunch box and helplessly looked between the front and back of the room.

“’M okay,” he said.

It hurt. It really hurt! Hi kept thinking over and over, it felt so good it felt like it was pulling his heart and liver and kidneys out through a pinhole. And he had to sit there with him, in soaking wet underwear, pretending like none of it happened.

It was a good thing it was cold out; he could hide the wet spot with his jacket.

"Be right back," Daphne said and stood up, "Need to see a man about a horse!" She said after some effectuated conversation about politics and their impact on charitable giving. "Take care of my man while I'm gone!"

After she left, hi said softly, "Please don't do that again. I promise I won't tell her."

"We'll tell her together," Suri said. "*And we are going to do it again. Tonight.*"

"I need to ask for a raincheck." Hi's clothes started to stick to his skin, "I'm…I'm really tired. Some other time?"

"How about now?" Suri said. "I can make this one the best yet."

"No, please, don't," Hi started to shake, bracing for the next tremor.

"Tell me yes. For tonight. We'll go nice and slow. Space things out."

"I'd love to but…I'm in grad school, I need to study."

"I appreciate that. When your studying is done? Don't tell me no. I don't tolerate rejection very well, Hyakinthos. It really upsets me in fact."

"I didn't tell you no," Hi said and tried to catch his breath. "Just please, let me catch up?"

"Do you and Daphne…?" Surya asked. "Penetrate each other?"

"*Excuse me?* No!" Hyakinthos whined. "She's my boss. My friend. And I don't…"

"I knew that," Suri laughed and it seemed like he really did see some mirth in it all.

Daphne came back from the powder room, "It's almost time for our board meeting conference call, Hi, we should get back."

"Yes," Hi said.

Suri smiled, "See you later?"

"Text me," Daphne said.

Hi couldn't breathe and Suri's arms were like petrified wood. Prying on them was useless. Suri let go of his throat.

"Nice," he said. "Hold on and let go exactly when I tell you just like we just practiced."

“Please don’t do that to me,” Hi said, “I’ll do whatever you want, just please stop hitting and choking me.”

“Invite Daphne over,” Suri said. He handed Hi his phone.

“I don’t want to see you have sex with Daphne,” Hi said, “I know who you are…I get it, you want everyone to know you’re a big stud, so fucking what? Why do you care?”

“Because being a stud is what matters to mortals who are desperate for something to believe in.”

“I’m not desperate!” He started crying, “And I let you fuck me, so can you please let me go!”

“Not yet,” Suri said.

Hi had to start calling in sick. Every time it was the same. Suri bi-located, making it impossible for him to tell Daphne what was happening and even he started to become unsure. His body was battered and Suri’s abilities never seemed to tire.

“Call her,” Suri said. “You can take a break.”

“You can’t do that, that way to a girl, you asshole!”

“Of course not. I know what I’m doing, silly boy,” Sur smacked Hi’s face, playfully. Grabbed his mouth and kissed him hard.

“Make the call.”

“No,” Hi said.

Hermes Trismegistus to the rescue. Phoebus, what did you do?

“He said no, Hermes,” Phoebus Apollo wailed. “I…lost control.”

“Obviously,” Hermes said and wiped the trickle of blood that ran from Hi’s nose and down over his paling lips. “You gave him an aneurysm. He will die very soon.”

“Fix him.”

Hermes pet the boy’s head and eased any pain or worry that might be left over from his brother’s assault. “He is beyond my ability to do so, Phoebus. I’m filled with regret.”

Apollo, perplexed, watched silently.

“Phoebus, why did you do such a thing? He’s beautiful. I sense a noble *Ka* in him.”

“I don’t know. I did love him, I just got carried away… and…we started to disagree…there must be something you can do? For me? As a favor?”

“There is, but Zeus’s wrath would be terrible.” Hermes said. “I know of an alternative but you have broken his body beyond its ability to contain his soul for too much longer.”

“Do it,” Apollo said and stared as Hermes ministered to Hyakinthos.

“Does this assuage your sadness?” Hermes showed Apollo what he’d done.

“Sure,” Phoebus Apollo said and went to see Daphne. She’d been texting.

Daphne eventually went looking for Hi. He didn’t call in, left no messages, had’nt responded to any emails or text messages.

“I just don’t know what happened, and I don’t even want to imagine,” Daphne cried after the fifth day of not hearing from him. “We were best friends, he wouldn’t just leave like this.”

The landlord opened up the apartment door and all of Hi’s things were still there, but he was not. Daphne found his phone and plugged it in.

“Where is he, you son of a bitch?” Daphne pounded on Sur’s face and chest.

“Who?” Sur loved it when they were aggressive, when they fought back. Provided they said yes.

He loved how Hyakinthos would fight back and try to get away; knowing it was impossible. The screw after that was positively exuberating!

“Submit to me, Daphne,” Sur said. “We can work this out. Hi is safe, don’t worry about that.”

“Submit?” Daphne screamed. “Submit? Fuck you! I’m going to the police.”

“Daphne,” Phoebus said. “Don’t tell me no.”

Growing amongst the brightly colored lilac scented flowers in the meadows of the montane Elysian Fields is a small shrub with blooms of white that smell of jasmine and cream, called *Daphne jasminea*. They bloom in the summertime right after the hyacinths in the spring.

Interlude

Zeus Defends Até. What death claims cannot stay!

Asklepios, son of Apollo and Coronis, was sent to university at Thessaly to study medicine with the Centaur, Chiron. Together, they plumbed the mysteries of illness, infirmity, injury, and senescence.

Like all good teachers, Chiron instilled the importance of moderation and temperance onto his star student. Asklepios had difficulty with this, however, and became more and more obsessed with advancing the healing arts and more than a little puffed up with his skills to heal the sick and injured.

He eventually left Thessaly and opened many hospitals and outpatient facilities, spent a great deal of time and energy challenging himself with curing and treating every disease.

When this was accomplished, Asklepios focused all of his energy and skill on the ultimate malady, death itself.

When passengers on Charon's skiff started to jump overboard into the River Styx and swim back to the shore of the land of the living, Hades Unseen became quite annoyed.

"*What the hell is going on*?" He roared from beneath his basalt helmet at the hooded Charon.

Charon shrugged and pointed with his oar at a certain hospital emergency room.

If one could see into the helm, you might have seen Hades outraged as the D.O.A.s in Asklepios' care got up off their stretchers and went home. Bullet holes closed, snake bites healed, bones knitted, and hearts started beating again.

Hades immediately registered a complaint with Zeus, who was as chagrined, "A mortal indiscriminately raising the dead? Unacceptable."

If allowed to continue, Até would be violated and Hades would lose his place in the ruling structure of Olympus.

"You will do something about this?" Hades was not asking. In addition the order of things Asklepios had violated, maintaining the balance of power amongst his brothers was a priority for Zeus.

"Yes, of course I will," Zeus said. He was also not particularly thrilled with the implications of resurrection to his role in the universe. Who would want to honor the immortal gods when one could be immortal oneself?

Zeus conjured a *Vajra* and hurled it at Asklepios. He was vaporized instantly and the secret of everlasting life went with him.

Hades Unseen was especially glad to see him arrive in the Underworld on Charon's raft.

Asklepios was, unfortunately, rendered to the role of the dishonored dead and no good is spoken of him. Apollo never forgave Zeus for the death of his son.

Chapter 5

Doors, Roads, and Gateways

The Birth of Hekate

Asteria was the daughter of Coeus and Phoebe and became the mother of all non-planetary stellar phenomena. She wasn't given much credit for that, but neither did she seek it.

Creating, organizing, and maintaining the individual stars and their formations into constellations was precise, compulsive, and tedious work but Asteria didn't mind. She loved her craft and all the secrets the stars, sentient beings told her as she moved them into ominous positions across the skies.

Because the arrangement of the stars, across the blank background of infinite space demanded sight into the three times, Asteria knew the future of the cosmos intimately, completely, and prematurely.

She had a personal rule, which she passed along to the thing she loved the most in creation, her only daughter, Hekate. *Never ever tell them the whole truth*. They can't handle it.

"But why, Mother?" the bizarre and inquisitive young goddess asked her.

"Neither Titan, nor god, nor mortal or any being in between must ever have so much power as the Truth, Hekate. In the hands of the unskilled and unethical, Truth becomes the origin of lies and this enables one to use the telling of feeble lies to paint false truths. This causes Creation to disband."

"Of course, Mother!" Hekate laughed; a queer giggle in three-part harmony. "This makes perfect sense."

And, Asteria knew her daughter would always keep her counsel.

"Do I meet your expectations in every way, Mother? And will you tell me the Real Truth?" Hekate asked once. "If I were flawed, you wouldn't have made me, would you?"

Asteria couldn't lie and wouldn't have, "It was a risk, poppet, but I am overjoyed by you."

"Why was it a risk?" Hekate's heads turned sideways as they considered this.

"There was one element in my plan for the stars and constellations that wouldn't conform properly," Asteria said. "A scribble in space/time. Your father, Perses."

"That is so droll, Mother!" Hekate laughed with delight. "Do go on!"

Asteria, the Titan Mother of Stars, then, revealed the following tale.

Asteria falls in love with a Great Darkness from above!

One day, something unexpected happened.

A black space opened up in the constellation Taurus. Then another winked out in constellation Centaurus, as Asteria cringed, yet, another began to blink in Ganumede.

When she went to investigate, she saw the cause. A youth, naked, pale, like he were sketched in charcoal on a black canvas, hair like a nest of bruised and battered comets trying to escape orbit around his head, the same murky fire burned around from his eyes, from his bush.

The stranger saw Asteria, but continued to pop blinking stars into his mouth like Mentos Candy.

"Who are you? And just what do you think you are doing?" Asteria screamed in outrage.

"I am Perses," the boy said. "I destroy things."

"Why do you do that?" Asteria asked, curious as ever.

"I don't know. It's just how I am."

He reached for another star.

"Please don't," Asteria begged the handsome being. "That's my work!"

"So?" Perses asked but did not eat the star. "Why does it matter?"

"My work, all work, creates order," Asteria smiled. "Surely you understand that at least?"

Plumes of black fire spiraled off his head as he shook it, "No, not at all. I work and don't care why."

Asteria squealed in delight, "I think I'm in love."

"*And I think I am going to rape you*," Perses said.

"What a curious proposal!" Hekate said, "Why did you say yes?"

"Because making love with him fit into my plans!" Asteria said. "And we made you!"

"I don't remember him very well," Hekate said. "He wasn't too much of a brute, I hope!"

That was Hekate's way of saying she hated Zeus for taking her father from her and locking him away in the acrid murkiness of Tartarus. Almost all of the gods and goddesses had strong emotions about Zeus and this issue.

Hekate remembered the look in her father's eyes as he fell away from them into Tartarus, how the rainbow glimmer of her mother's starlight faded from his eyes as the blackness consumed him.

"No," Asteria said looking into space, where she first saw her scribble. There was now a large quantum singularity there. "He wasn't."

"Now tell me how you pass your days," Asteria changed the subject.

Hekate told her mother her own story of the creation, love, birth, and tragedy. Asteria looked back at her daughter and asked, "Why didn't you tell her, Hekate?"

"It wasn't part of my plan, Mother," Hekate's shoulders shrugged. "And I didn't want to lie, so I said nothing."

"And your plans are?"

"To overthrow Zeus, of course," she replied.

Asteria smiled, "Good girl," and kissed Hekate's cheeks.

Hekate didn't feel good about what happened with the Queen of Troy nor any of the Queens of Troy, but her feelings and those of all other beings matter very little to the Fates, and never will.

The Big Date
Attis Transfigures
Ganumede Considers
Callirhoe Quivers

"You see Attis almost every day. You can stay home tonight," the Queen said. "This is my decision and I'm very comfortable with it."

"That's not how it works," I said. "Guys make their own decisions these days."

"Oh, please, don't enlighten me about how things *really are*. I'm too old to change," Her Majesty said.

"That's funny," I said. "Because whether you are going to change or not, I *am* going to the movies with Attis."

"Well let me go out back and shit some happiness for you then Ganumede! Hang on so I have time to wipe!"

I wish my mother hadn't made simple transactions with her so awful. It makes it difficult to remember her.

Most of my memories of her are those with her chanting those monolithic *mantras* at me about what I was or should or shouldn't do. We never actually talked.

When I reflect upon her, she fades from the full color glory she truly was to something posed, like someone who was always having her portrait painted. Her observations of me, those vocalized and demonstrated were almost always passive aggressive like her comment about shitting happiness for me. Which made me hate her because I had quite a number of my own emotions about Attis to deal with and they got very little of my attention because I had to run for cover from everyone else's all the time.

"I will come around 7, the movie starts at 9," Attis said.

"In a car. At 7. Awesome," I loved hanging on to Attis when we rode his bike, but it scared the fuck out of me.

"No, not in a car, but definitely at that time. We have somewhere to be before we go out."

"Where?"

"Shopping."

"For what?"

"Clothes."

"Where?"

"It's a surprise."

"Wrong. Clothing choices are never, ever surprises. They are carefully, thoughtfully, and expertly planned, orchestrated, and executed."

Attis growled, "I know, I've seen your closet. Now please be ready."

"Tell me."

"Fine. It's time we outfitted you like a true and righteous leather pup."

"Don't those smell?"

“I’m a god, Ganumede, but I can’t do miracles all the time, just some of the time. Now be the fuck ready when I get to your place, and tell your mother if she scowls at me from that tower of hers one more time, I am going to pee on her weird black flowers.”

“I wouldn’t do that. They bite.”

The sound of Attis’s motorcycle always caused so much excitement. The Queen’s fingers went up into the air like she was drying her nails and she’d say obvious things like, “*Is that Attis? On that bike of his*?”

My father would struggle to keep his eyes level and not clench his jaw too much. “Going out after all?” he asked me.

“Yeah. Like I said, Attis and I are going shopping for some gear then out to eat and then to a movie.”

“*Some what*?” The Queen popped up like a prairie dog out of a golf hole.

“Gear. Leather stuff. So when I ride Attis’s motorcycle with him I have an outfit.”

“No, not happening, and we agreed those plans were canceled.”

“Right,” I said, “I will be home later. After the movie, we are going to stop somewhere so I can get a tattoo and my tongue pierced.”

“Do that instead of going out with Attis,” Her Majesty said. “We can go have it done together! Tell Attis the movie sold out or something. Tros, have the car brought around, we’re going right now to get Ganumede his tattoos and piercings.”

“Calli, honey!” Tros looked at me and I could feel the ink gun sinking into my butt cheek already. “He’s not doing that! Are you Ganumede?”

“Yes he is,” the Queen said. “I’d rather he get marred and scarred than go out with that…that…”

“*It’s right here*, your majesty,” Attis said and bowed in exquisite fashion. The perfect tipping of his head, his chin nicking his chest, then back up again. “My mother wishes you a good evening. I would like to compliment your choice of black opals with the charcoal taffeta evening dress you’ve donned this evening.”

I could tell the Queen knew he wasn’t bullshitting because, of course, her outfits were stunning. Gods know what would have happened if he didn’t make the attempt, “Tell Nana thank you and you’re far more kind than I’d expect.”

Thank the gods Attis ignored her shit, “Hey, Gigi, let’s get a move on, the bike store closes at 8.”

“Gigi?” My father peeped and turned the color of an ornamental eggplant.

“I’m going to murder you. Let’s go,” I pulled at Attis, who smelled of leather, gasoline, and juniper needles. I learned how to mount the Magic Motorcycle and once I had the Cuntessa, Zoe’s, helmet strapped on, I grabbed onto Attis, pulled my arms taught around his stomach.

“You have to hang on tight,” he said.

Once he got the jet and gold cycle roaring beneath us, off we went!

I could hear the road, the engine, the life spark itself sputtering inside my crotch, the same that was vibrating inside the engine of the peculiar machine underneath us.

Attis’s offer of new riding gear exhilarated me. I hated wearing Zoe’s helmet. It smelled of peppermint and amber and I hated pulling those gold wire hairs of hers out of my teeth.

One of the finest moments of my life was when Attis handed me the one he had designed for me. It was deep green/black onyx, polished to a brooding mirror surface, accented with platinum boswellia garlands.

I tried it on.

“It’s you, Jeej.”

“Yeah!” I checked myself out in the mirror. For once, seeing an element of my reflection that didn’t puzzle me, “Jeej? I thought I was Gigi.”

“If you’re riding with a helmet like that, you’re more of a Jeej,” Attis stamped reality with stuff like this in a way only a god could and a boyfriend would never think of.

The one I ultimately married, also a god, was far too worried about his manhood to do anything remotely thoughtful like that.

“Here, this jacket will prevent you from skinning your body off, if we fall. If we do, you’ll just slide down the pavement on it. The material will take the friction and abrasion.”

“That doesn’t the hell make me feel better about not having one before this, you jackass!”

“Shut up. Boots, now. Then, pants.”

“Finally you want to get into my pants!” I said.

“No,” Attis raised an eyebrow, “I am trying to get you to *shut up* and get into yours, so we can make it to our movie!”

By the time we checked out, I was stunning, but barely able to walk I had so much leather crap on.

"See ya gals later!" the store owner, a Centaur said. Attis, cooler than blue, responded by blowing him a kiss.

Attis knew the effect he had on people, and had no trouble convincing the Court of Midaeum I was his pawn. Word got out it was he and me, and we were the only ones that knew the truth.

We thundered into the parking lot, the mystical motorcycle thronging with its chorus of horns and trombones, thrilled at the curiosity of watching everyone see me, this phantom figure, leaping from a gold motorcycle right after its driver, a golden god in tan leather, brass, and denim.

"Gee. Please don't walk like you're wearing high heels," Attis said as gently as he could and pointed to my platinum toed boots.

"Oh shit. Right."

Attis was never embarrassed by me or self-conscious about much of anything, still that scowl encouraged me to walk like a man.

It's Getting Late
No Time to Wait Open the Gate!
Callirhoe, the Queen of Troy

"Release the hounds, please," Callirhoe said like she was selecting a new color of black lipstick from in front of the cosmetics counter at Macy's.

Hekate started a little, "That's quite a request, Sister Queen, for what purpose?"

"Attis took Ganumede to the movies. He must be subdued and destroyed."

"Queen, I must admit, I do not know what the hell you are saying to me. Did the movie require parental supervision?"

"Oh you can be such a huge gaping…!" Callirhoe flared. "This is our chance! Can't you see? Attis took Ganumede away from me! I know I can save Ganumede from your prophecy, if we act."

Hekate made a sad face, "Oh Callirhoe."

"Please," the Queen tried to sound regal, commanding, but she was in fact, begging.

"I don't prophesy and then thwart myself," Hekate explained like a teacher might spell a word to a child. "That would make what I say untrue."

"You aren't untrue and this isn't about you, it's about me. I just feel that if you tell the Litter to intercept Attis and kill him, I can fulfill the prophecy, a god took my son away and also get him back."

Hekate smiled a little, "I appreciate your exceptional reasoning, Queen. I will speak to the Litter's Master."

Ganumede: Attis, My Golden God

A disadvantage of the gear was how sweaty you got and how challenging it was to see in the dark through the goggles and helmet. I was glad, however, that I didn't see what was coming at us that night as Attis and I were on our way home from the movie.

There was this thump, then, there was nothing under me or around me. The motorcycle capsized and I was thrown into the air.

This thing grabbed me midair in its mouth like I was a shuttlecock, then it brought me to ground and stood on top of me. One of its heads snarled, one barked, one licked my face.

Somewhere in the dark, I heard the motorcycle engine wind down and lots of howling, whining and barking, like a hundred dogs using megaphones were competing for a chance to bite the same rabbit.

The dog thing that sat on me, pinning me to the ground, kept licking my face; it seemed so perky, in spite of the fact its eyes smoldered and smoked like embers.

Attis, however, was being attacked. Two more of the giant hell hounds were making so much noise, viciously tearing at him, taking turns running past him, leaping, in attempts to knock him off his feet.

He was not afraid. The look on his face was tranquil, focused. He cast a glow, like a streetlamp igniting on a long dark road, pale yellow, then cold and brilliant, like a sunset.

The dogs regrouped, attacked, were repelled. This went on till the things were panting and wondering amongst themselves what should happen next.

I could no longer withstand the noise, the fear for Attis, anxiety for his victory, wanting to understand how I left the motorcycle seat with my arms around Attis, to end up on my back with demon dog breath in my face.

"Leave me alone!" I screamed at the things. "Go away!"

All nine heads of the nightmarish creatures regarded me, looked at one another, and then decided to withdraw. They vanished in a flash of red flea shampoo-scented smoke.

I burst into tears.

"It's okay, Ganumede," Attis helped me to my feet and wiped the slobber off my face. "They're gone."

His touch made me feel warm all over and my broken leg and arm knit themselves back together.

Attis's corona dimmed and with a gesture, the motorcycle righted itself and rolled over to us. The chorus of horns, sound of its engine was quiet, more like a clarinet choir.

When we explained what happened to my parents and Nana, it seemed as if Attis and I were the only ones that were impressed with what happened.

"They were the Hounds of Hades," Attis said, verifying his conclusions with his mother.

"I see," Nana said, smiling in a distinctly patronizing way at her cousin, the Queen of Troy. "The pups of Kerebros were just …running about, were they?"

"Yes!" Attis said. "They came out of the woods and made us wipe out. Hades should roll up the Underworld Tribune and beat the hell out of their asses!"

"I agree," Nana's stare didn't abate. "I should think Lord Hades would be most unhappy to learn his pets escaped their kennel like that."

"Well, Nana, that is a very astute observation," the Queen said. "Please do find the time to tell me how he reacts to the news."

My mother left the room. Disappointed, shocked, afraid, and unconcerned? It was always so difficult to tell with her.

"I don't think my new outfit got damaged, Mother," I said and checked out my ass in the leather pants. There wer some scuff marks. "But don't worry I'll buff and polish it anyway."

Silence.

"I think I still have some pain from my broken ankle though," I called after her. "And my someone will find my other testicle on the road and call us…!"

"Sweetie," Nana pulled on my ear gently, "That's not helpful."

"She…" I tried to say. "She…you know…"

"Let her go," Nana said. Then to Attis, "Come on kid, let's let the Prince recuperate from the big adventure."

Nana spread her rainbow-colored wings wide and brought them back around till they sheltered Attis, herself, and most importantly, his motorcycle.

There was a quiet gush of lotus scented breeze and Nana and her son sublimated away in a gush of opalescent light.

I went to tell Tithonus what happened, hoped he'd make fun of me in leather get up, but he wasn't in his room.

The Queen of Troy. Later

Callirhoe waited till she reached her powder room before she fully expressed her anguish.

She cried out, clawed, and dug her black fingernails into the mirror till it cracked and glittery shards went flying.

The night wind started to howl, blasted in through the window to its mistress's side, causing her clay masks, magic dusts, and broken and overturned jars of pollen and powders to form vortexes of cloying and gagging grit.

The Queen of Troy sat on the floor by her toilet, coated in dust, mud caking under her eyes, and purposely wept herself to exhaustion.

She finally had to stand and collect herself, though she was reluctant. She knew she would never try to save her son again and wanted to savor failing at the attempt before she steeled herself to not caring any longer.

Tros came into the room as she stepped out of the shower, wringing water out of her dark emerald hair.

"Say, Calli, have you seen Tithonus?" he asked. "He's not home yet."

That night, Rhea, also called Agdistis and Mater Megale, the Mother Under the Mountain, Whose Menstruation Flows Freely, stirred.

Chapter 6

Tapers, Torches, and Conflagrations

Meet and Greet

He Seems Quite Neat
There's No Retreat

Ganumede.

"Can you come to my office after school today?" His Highness asked.

"Let's talk about whatever it is now," I said.

Tros smiled, "There's not much to talk about actually, there's someone I thought you might want to meet; a kind of college counselor. And he won't be available until…later!"

"Oh. I guess I should probably worry about that sometime, huh?"

Tros brightened up considerably, "Well, consider this a way of not having to worry about it."

"Sure, I'll be there."

I hadn't given much thought to going to college or why, though I did want to. I still to find a way to kill Zoe before Attis got married and I hadn't found a poison that could kill a godling like her yet and my anxiety over the end of the world kept me from worrying about the beginning of my own.

I also had no idea how to tell my dad what I was doing or how wonderful it will be when he could mother-fucking stop talking about nuking and invading Attis' country all the time. I wanted to say "*I've got this*!" and watch his face.

I had to figure out what to do and fast, the wedding was scheduled for midsummer during the Rosalia, and it was a good thing, in a way, I had an appointment with this college admissions guy. Attis was looking at wedding dresses with Zoe and I needed something to do to keep my mind off of it.

"Ganumede, this is Theo. He's going to help you to study and identify the most...beneficial options for your future."

"Hello," Theo said. He was tall, dressed in a deep blue shirt with a Chinese collar, and a form fitted suit of deep black that caught every ray of light the passed by it. Theo was spectacularly good looking. His skin was tan, his stubble pruned quite practically, his eyes were deep blue. His cologne smelled of styrax.

"Hi," I said and shook his hand.

"Hello." Theo said, "Your Majesty, would it be all right if we got started right away?"

My father nodded, "Yes. Ganumede is an excellent student and I'm sure he will impress you."

"I have no doubt," Theo said. "How about if we get some tea. I think your father said you prefer that over coffee?"

"Okay. Sure," I said. I tried to catch my father's eye but he'd already gone back to his desk. We didn't say goodbye to each other; Theo whisked me away, and it was thus time for him to get back to work.

The Disposal of the Proposal

Theo suggested we go to Athena's Tea House, where all the 'important' people went for tea, cakes, and to take pictures of food they didn't even eat.

We turned heads when we entered and people started taking pictures.

I was quite interesting to the gossip columnists, especially after my epic fall from grace at the bowling alley. That was quite publicized and made everyone fascinated with my secret life.

I wondered what they would done if I fucked every last one of those assholes in their gutters with those bowling pins right in front of the camera? Would the press have said it was a strike or I needed a spare?

"Oh, it was no trouble at all," I would have said as the cameras flashed. "I just blocked out the screams."

Theo was cordial and polite, perfectly at ease. He asked for my favorite Darjeeling Estate and even warned the barista to use water that was sub-boiling temperature in the tea pot.

We sat, and while we waited for some idiot whore with a pieced eyebrow and lip to serve our tea, Theo said, "Tell me about this Attis fellow."

I was not surprised he knew about Attis, my favorite tea, that I preferred it hot, but not boiling water for steeping loose-leaf tea.

Everything about him was too good to be true and it was arranged that way by someone that knew me quite well.

I was furious with my parents for telling this 'admissions counselor' so much about me but I already knew they sucked.

"Attis is my best friend," I said.

"Your father thinks you should probably curtail the amount of time you spend with him. It's not appropriate," Theo said.

"He'll get over it," I said.

"Actually…" Theo turned his head sideways a little and riveted his gaze on me, "I don't think he's all that much 'over it.'" Theo said, "But we'll change that."

Ganumede is told: He's been bought and sold!

"I have to get married," I wailed to Attis after I ran from Athena's.

"What? To whom? And why?"

"I was supposed to get married to Tray Grande and I fucked that up, as if! And I can't marry you…"

"*Well, no…*"

"And, now, my parents have told this stupid prince from Thrace that he's my husband…"

"Is he nice?" Attis asked.

"Yeah, so?"

"Is he hot?"

"Yes, but I don't know him! And he's kinda creepy!"

"Gigi, welcome to arranged marriages. This is how it is."

"Oh okay," I said. "So you kill Theo and I'll kill Zoe. Case closed."

"Case *not* closed," Attis insisted. "And how are those plans coming? Have you been able to find a way to get Aconite?"

"No, you dicknuts! That is super top secret! I'm not sure my mother even has any!"

"My mother says your mother has it. Just in case."

"Yeah, for you!" I joked.

"Yes. That's another reason you need to get it from her."

“Oh no,” I said. “You don’t think she would do that to you, would she?”

“Yes she would! Dicknuts!”

“I will kill her first.”

“Don’t worry about that! Kill Zoe with the aconite,” Attis said. “That’s what we planned. Remember?”

“Trust me, that bitch is dead. I just have to figure out where Mum put that stuff. If she has any.”

“My mother says she has it, just in case one of the Achaean gods, or any other, tried to hex Troy. So far it’s worked as a deterrent but a hex will be the worst of her problems if Zoe becomes the Queen of Mideaum, which is what she will be, if she is alive and breathing on our wedding day!”

“I get it! Gods! Now, what about what really matters, which is *my wedding day*! As in the fact I now have one and I didn’t two hours ago!”

Attis groaned, “Give him a chance, Gee. He might be the love of your life. He’s a total top, right?”

“I didn’t exactly ask him that.”

“You should probably find out. Then all you have to do is change positions and then tell your dad it’s not a good fit.”

“I’m sure my dad is totally concerned about that,” I laughed.

“Cry like a little Jewish boy who has pretended to fall of his tricycle so he can get a cash settlement from his dad! ‘Daddy! He wants me to top and that’s just like having sex with a woman! Baw!’ and if he’s a top say, ‘Crying! I wanted a nice piece of corned beef for my cabbage and this is all wrong!’ and call the whole thing off!”

“That’s the shittiest advice ever!” I said.

“It’s what I got.” Attis said and shrugged.

Then, Theo called.

The announcement that I was *overjoyed* to be engaged to Prince Theo of Thrace came out in the ***Trojan Wrap Up*** the next day.

Pictures showed Theo pouring me a cup of tea.

Herakles Spreads the News. Hylas is Missing, a Wedding Ensues!

“Father,” Herakles reported to Zeus. “Hylas is lost. He went missing during my travels with the Argo. I sent him to fetch water when we stopped to resupply at Pegae but he never came back to the ship. Try as I might, I cannot find him. Hermes even tried searching, but there is no sign of him."

"Oh dear," Zeus grunted, "That is unfortunate."

"I loved him," Herakles said. "And I would never have wanted any other, but I think I have found someone who will lighten the pain in my heart caused by his absence."

"Oh?" Zeus sat up, started to pay attention. "Who's the lucky fellow?"

Herakles laughed, full and loud, "It's not a fellow, actually, though I do think she feels lucky. She's even agreed to marry me!"

"A woman?" Zeus snorted. "I'd keep looking for Hylas, if I were you."

"Father," Herakles laughed a little more. "I'm in love with her. Don't you want to know who it is?"

"Why yes," Zeus folded his hands in his lap. "Do tell me who the bride to be is. The suspense is positively killing me."

"It's Hebe. Your Cupbearer. Your daughter."

"Hebe?" Zeus barfed the word out. "Hebe wants to marry you?"

"Yes," Herakles nodded, "And I want your blessing. Hera has already given her encouragement, which puts an end to a long period of hostility between us."

"Yes, that's wonderful, but who will serve the gods Ambrosia and Nektar in the Great Hall, then?" Zeus demanded. "It's not a duty for fit the wife of a hero."

"So, you are offering me your blessing?" Herakles held his hands together in supplication.

"If Hebe wants to be your wife and it heals your broken heart over the boy, I give you my blessing," Zeus said wearily. "I just ask she remain in service till we find a new Cupbearer."

"I'm sure she will find that agreeable," Herakles said. "How long do you think it will take to identify a replacement?"

*I know precisely who…*Zeus said to himself. "It must, obviously, be someone as young and beautiful as Hebe, someone as lovely to the eye as Ambrosia is to the tongue."

Herakles nodded, "Understandable. May I retire to share the news with Hebe?"

"Yes," Zeus said. "Go."

Then Zeus looked for Ganumede. And he was with someone! Zeus was enraged.

Classics Class! Demonstrate, and Pass!

"Today we are covering a collection of poems by the contemporaries of Sokrates," Mr. Diaz said. "Ganumede, if you would start us off by reading the passage at the top of page 204 by Strato."

"Okay?"

I read the lines to myself first. "Eep! For real? *The Sausage Seller*?"

"Yes," Mr. Diaz's eyes blazed at me. "If you wouldn't mind."

"It's kind of nasty," I said. "I'm not sure about this."

The whole class started laughing. "Read, please."

"*Oh for fuck's sake*!" I groaned and recited the poem:

"*The Sausage Seller said, what could count for more than a pair of shoes? Recall what I have done for you?*

I made you a whore and put a stop to it, too!

When you became a man, you were good for what else? I sold sausage, I sold you to myself!"

The class, even Attis, laughed at me.

Mr. Diaz only had to glance and the room fell silent, "Continue to the next stanza please."

"Baw!" I said,

"*And since your master's bed taught you a lot, why not treat others to what you got*?' Are you even allowed to teach this?"

"Quite. Now if you wouldn't mind," Diaz asked Travis Interstate. "Please give us a proper interpretation of this lovely bit of rhythm and rhyme that applies to current events."

"Sure," Travis Interstate said. "It means Ganumede's father has hired a high-priced hooker to turn him into a sloppy little slut!"

"Indeed." Mr. Diaz said.

I ran from the classroom.

I ran until I ran right into Theo, who had a habit of meeting me at school and keeping me from Attis and the completion of our plans to kill Zoe.

I yelled at him, “What have you been telling people, you asshole?”

Theo expertly dodged what was going to be my first punch in anyone’s face. Ever.

“Don’t ever try that again!” He said and pushed me.

“What have you been saying about me?” I yelled and people started to gather.

“That you are mine and I do with mine what I desire.”

“So far, that has been nothing! So, there should be nothing to say!”

Theo’s face lost its outrage and he moved in close to me, “You don’t know what you’re doing. Come with me, right now!”

“Fuck you! Fu—”

Theo slapped me in the face.

“Ganumede, I am sorry I had to do that but you must stop acting like you don’t like me. It’s very important. You don’t understand what you’re dealing with. *I am trying to help you*!”

“You’re trying to help yourself!” I rubbed the place Theo hit me and walked away. “Don’t you ever come near me again!”

I ran again and then something clobbered me and the ground fell out from under my feet.

The Rape of Ganumede

Later, I watched what happened to me in a scrying pond.

Periphas, Zeus’s eagle, vehicle, struck me from behind and grabbed me in the parking lot outside Troy Finishing School.

There was a flash of neon light and Theo turned into a giant warrior clad in blinding violet armor with hot pink butterfly wings and rocketed into the sky after me.

“Let him go!” Eros’s voice sounded like a thousand cellos each playing a different note, deep, dissonant, strident.

The Violet Entity he’d become produced a bow of violet colored glass, loaded it with violet arrows that lit the sky with streaks of pinkish lightning as they streaked toward the giant eagle.

The eagle came about and bright blue bolts of thunder blasted from its beak at my rescuer.

One struck Eros in the chest and it looked he was flung far away. The eagle continued to ascend.

More violet missiles eventually caught the eagle and it crash-landed on Mount Ida. Fortunately, it released me prior to impact and Eros caught me.

Then Zeus appeared out of a thunderclap that shook Troy. He grabbed Eros by the hair.

"Bastard! Cunt! *I told you to...stay...out...of...this*!"

There was a crunching sound, like light-bulbs busting and downed power lines, and then a trail of pink sparkles and glitter and Eros was tossed aside. Zeus grabbed me next, "*And you! You think you're too good for everybody? And no one is good enough for you?*"

Zeus shook me awake. Eros found Attis.

"Where is he?" Attis said.

"Atop Ida," Eros said. "There isn't much time, Attis," Eros had difficulty holding his earthly emanation together. "I did my best, but Diaz, an incubus of Zeus took Ganumede. I fought it till it crashed on the side of Ida. It is wounded but it will recover fast. If you go, you can fight him. You could save Ganumede."

"I am not you, Eros. I can't fight Zeus," Attis said. "I'm not the equal of either of you."

Nana came into the room.

"Yes, you can fight him, Attis," she said. "You might be the only one."

The Fight for Ganumede's Honor: Fire, Music, and Horror

Attis, 15 feet tall, his armor, helmet, shield, and sword burning and blazing, appeared in a cacophony of drum and bass. He grabbed Zeus off of Ganumede and tossed him aside like a bean bag.

"Don't you touch him!" Attis commanded.

He followed Zeus, brought the blunt edge of a sword that was the size of a bus down on him and Ida shook. All of Troy and Mideaum trembled.

Zeus stood, unfazed. He turned deep blue and the night sky lit up with as it charged with his *vajras*, divine lightning. "I've been waiting for this confrontation, Attis. Thank you for ending my anticipation."

Attis brought the sword down on him again but Zeus grew in size and pushed back with a blast of blue lightning.

"Let's have a little fun before I put an end to this. We have to be quick about it though, mustn't wake Mother up!"

While they fought, gold and purple bursts of fire against blue chains and cannonballs of lightning bolts, Periphas recovered his senses and took me into the air again.

People have portrayed this, me being fucked midair by an eagle with claws the size of scimitars and taking it with a smile on my face.

It hurt.

The last thing my mortal eyes saw was Zeus pounding on Attis till he was beaten and discarded, a golden tear falling down the face of the mountain.

Callirhoe
Hades Has No Wrath

"He hasn't been seen, Honey," My husband said, "I'm sending every man we have to look for him."

My husband was a noble and good king, provided what any unsuspecting and naïve father would provide. He didn't pay attention to Ganumede the way he should have and that was my fault. I didn't see the point in trying to make him. I knew it was pointless from the beginning and when I tried to change our luck, nothing good happened it wouldn't have helped to frustrate Tros like I frustrated myself.

There is a painful fact of life every parent must confront the moment they give birth; how children come and go from your life. You think you're prepared for it, especially when you really, really want them to go. The painful part is realizing go and stay at the same time. Peace of mind with this is critical if life is return to normal. I tried since the twins were born to find it.

Now that it seemed like one of them might really be gone, I was not at peace with it at all. I tried to sense him, Ganumede, both as a mother and a witch, and it was like the string attached to the balloon was slipping through my hand as an angry wind tugged hungrily at it. This was it, and it wasn't Attis that had taken him. I saw him fall off the mountain on the news.

I thought I'd given up but seeing Attis fight on the mountain made me wake up. I lit the twin torches with the whip-crack of the fire of my rage.

"*Hekate Mitera Tis Dolofonias*!" I shrieked at the heavens.

I trembled and clenched my hands into fists and shook them over my head. My skin turned the color of pitch and ichor dripped from my palms as my nails turned into hooks that could butcher a bull and tore into my own flesh.

I didn't bother with the scrolls or the coven's wiki. A witch's power comes from her divine feminine essence…a mother's love. Her wrath, when that is tested too far: no scroll, grimoire, or database can contain it. The Words find you instead the other way around:

Three Faced One, Come to Me!

Mother of Dawn, Twilight, and Eternal Night, You Who Are One and Also Three,

Mother, Witch, Killer, I set you Free! Nightmare of Hades, Madness of the Deep, Shadow in the Sky,

You are necessity, for you are the end,

You are death and decay to gods and men, Goddess of Murder, Justice, and Torture, Listen to my plea,

Bring your chains, bring the lash, leave mercy behind, turn all to ash. You Who Are One and Also Three,

Come to my sacrifice and fulfill this task for me!

"*We are come*," Triune Hekate appeared as a smoky, leering infernal goddess. Her hair writhed with snakes and scorpions, her ashy form sported spindly arms, misshapen and flaccid breasts, her mouths howling and wailing, causing every hound in Troy to join a chorus of wrath and yearning.

Horses bucked and screeched in their stalls, serpents of all kinds writhed out of the ground, climbed down from trees and flooded the streets.

Her whips flailed and cracked all around her, causing the sky to turn black and red lightning to spark from their ends into the heavens.

"Ganumede, he's missing! He's been taken from me at last! You are bound to retrieve him!"

"*YES*!" the Triune Vengeance hissed. "*We are loosed*!"

The Furies of Hekate churned and roiled about the room, took its torches and left to fulfill its mission.

"Tell me you will bring him back! Tell me his abductor will pay, I don't care who it was!"

"*If the child lives, we will return it and kill the one that took him*," it pledged.

Epilogues

Part 1

Tros, King of Troy

Lost One Boy
Then Lost Two
Doesn't Know
What to Do

"He has received your message," the Oracle hung its head more than usual, not even a hint of its pale face was visible, "We advise you not to shed more tears. He shows no sympathy for them."

"Sympathy?" Tros spat through his clenched teeth. "You think I'm crying?"

"We do not think," the Oracle's voice was softer. "We do advise patience."

"My sons are gone! Taken from me by…elicit means! I want them back! Now! *No more patience, no more!* Do you hear me?"

"Zeus hears," the voice was different this time. Kindly, jolly, condescending. "You will be adequately compensated for your donations to Olympus, Good King Tros."

"Donations to Olympus? What the hell does that mean? Answer me, you fat fuck!"

The stage, where the Oracle image was received from its linkup with Olympus, went dark.

"Donations?" Tros grabbed a vase off the conference room table and threw it, where it shattered, leaving bits of aster and broken glass on the windowsill.

Tros called for his Chief of Staff, General Ilus. "Mobilization orders for our aconite missiles is given. Aim them at the Ether and destroy Olympus," Tros said.

"No," a soft voice owned by Hermes Trismegistus said. "Do not fire missiles at us, please."

"Why not?" Tros said, his finger hovered over his pad. "A little more poison up there won't even be noticed."

"I can't permit it even still," Hermes said, "I have withdrawn the aconite from your warheads and disabled their Vertical Horizons."

"Asshole! I might need them! What about Attis and Rhea and that bitch King Midas?"

"Should they be deployed, they would poison the land and drive the blessings of the gods from the earth. You will not use them, nor shall you need them."

"I don't care," Tros' finger itched as it imagined Zeus choking, black bile coming up out and out of his mouth, over his white beard, running down his cheeks from his blackened eyes. "I want Zeus to die."

"That's not something many of us would lament," Hermes laughed. "But patricide would just lure in the Furies and their wrath would not be turned back, not with weapons, spells, or pleas for mercy."

"That makes me feel better, Messenger, now if you don't mind, I will find some other way to grieve."

Tros turned his pad off and all of Troy's missile batteries that were once armed with Callirhoe's aconite payload lowered their ordinance back into their canisters, and the City of Troy returned to Condition Green.

"I cannot imagine a way that is appropriate under the circumstances," Hermes said with genuine sadness in his voice. "But I have a token of Zeus' esteem that may help."

"What is that?" Tros said, curiosity getting the better of him. "And as long as it's not more children."

Hermes stated the obvious, "No, your wife will bear no more sons or daughters to your house. But I have brought something that might secure its future in other ways. Check your stockpile."

Tros didn't have to; his pad was going crazy with messages from his Generals. He called up a video message, 'What the fuck are those things?'

"They are the storm-footed horses of the Maruts. Zeus' foot soldiers from another world," Hermes said, almost pride-fully. "Observe!"

They resembled horses only but vaguely, they writhed and foamed and twisted about more like horse shaped typhoons. Their cries were like hurricanes threatening to buckle the City walls, in their mouths were gold lion-like teeth glimmered and sparked with unbridled lightning, their manes whipped tornadoes off them, spinning and whirling away into the sky.

The citizens of Troy ran into the streets crying out in terror. “Magnificent,” Tros said.

Hermes maintained his dignity, but Tros’ reaction frankly disappointed him, “Yes. Not a single mortal until now has seen one of their herd and lived. They are accoutrements of war that the gods have saved for war between themselves and are now yours to use as you see fit on Earth.”

“Weapons, yes! Of course that’s what they are!” Tros’ eyes glazed over with dreams of unleashing them on Mideaum.

Hermes sighed, “Zeus considers his debt to you over the...death of your sons paid in full. Contain the steeds like you would a nuclear warhead. Silo them until you are ready to use them, which I wouldn’t. Should you decide to rain their wrath upon others, they will respond only to the King of Troy’s bridle, and to his intentions alone. They must be used together, they, like the price you have paid for them, are twins, and will not abide being separated.”

Hermes had to raise his voice, the din over the displeasure of the divine steeds started to grow so loud.

“Be wise and good in your ways, Tros, former father of Tithonus and Ganumede. Farewell!” Hermes shook his head and left Tros to play with his new toys.

Epilogue 2

Callirhoe, Queen of Troy

Hekate could not find Ganumede and she also searched for Tithonus. Both of my boys are gone.

I could cause a thousand plagues on thousands of millions on the earth with the careless whisper of a hex and the pain of that would never equal what it feels like to be trapped in the silence of your own house after your children are gone.

When Hekate explained, as a *fait accompli*, what her prophecy nearly eighteen years before meant, that she left out one little detail; that a god would take my son and *that a goddess would take the other*, I felt like such a fool. When I explained this to her, she said she had her reasons and they were Até. That was good enough for me until I saw the headline on the *Trojan Wrap Up* the next day.

'**Attis and Princess Zoe of Mideaum to be married soon**.'

I was going to be damned if Nana was going to have a wedding when I lacked even two bodies for one funeral.

I caused much harm. But it was within my ability to cause it and I relished that. It made up for my crippling powerlessness my entire life. I have no regrets.

I summoned Rhea, the Mother of Ease, from Her restless slumber.

You are the Earth before you walked on it.
You are the mountains before humans tracked them.
You are the fields before they were grazed
by any except the wild herds.
You are the trees before they were cut down,
When they grew so thick that no light
could be seen between their branches.

You are the stones before they were dug.
You are the plants before they were bred
For your use, and then harvested.
You are the grandmother, who saw me born.
You are the mentor, who watched my first steps.
You are the Old One, who watched me grow.
From your loins, came your daughter, Demeter,
Whom you knew would provide all that
The wilderness could give you,
and fed you from her bounty.
From your loins, came your grandchild, Persephone,
Who gave herself to your son, Hades,
that you might be nurtured, both, before and after.
You have watched me grow and my first children.
Tell me, then, what you will do for me?
If I tell you what I have seen?

Rhea, stately, regal, barely in control of her utter and total insanity, appeared, "*Tell me where my cock is, you sorry sow,*" Rhea said, "*or I kill you and everyone on this planet.*"

I told her when and where. And then I watched it all turn to ash. And it made me glad.

Interlude 3

The Wedding of Attis and Zoe
The Temple of Rhea
Mideaum, Capital City of the Phrygian Empire

Attis, The 'Demigod,' really the Father of Titans:

Ganumede was gone and I was alone but for the presence of my mother, who spent a lot of time on Olympus after Zeus took him.

My father was kept closely reigned in at the palace. Midas hoped he could squeeze some intelligence out of him regarding the affairs of Troy and how to press the sudden advantage brought about by the disappearances of its princes.

I paid only dull attention to the wedding plans, cared little about where this was happening or who would be standing where, what pickled vegetable wrapped in bacon would be pierced with what kind of toothpick.

Eros told me something before he left and it was the only thing that got me through the grief and desperation of watching that demon carry Ganumede away.

As a god, I could touch Midas and break his neck, unharmed, and the collar he put around my father's neck would fall off.

The closest I would get to him would be after the wedding and then, once I killed him, would legitimately be the king of Mideaum. Shortly after, Zoe, too, would have an 'accident.'

The wedding was the day of the Rosaria, Rhea, the Patron Goddess of Midaeum's High Holiday. Her statue was decorated in garlands of roses of every color, as was I. The temple, open to the air, was scented with sunlight, roses, orchids, and the smell of the sea.

No one seemed especially happy to be there, myself least of all. Especially with Zoe's constant commands, "It's our wedding day. You could at least act like you're happy." The town, scared to death of Midas and his soldiers, was forced to attend or observe the event in some way, and not even the offer of good food and wine was enough to lighten the glum mood of the place.

Zoe was radiant. It never once occurred to her how much I hated her and wanted nothing more than to see her broken into pieces and melted down into sequins.

Horns played, bells rung, and I saw my father, led by his golden leash and collar by King Midas onto the balcony above the main temple floor.

My mother Nana, a flurry of light in gold, blue, violet, and green, watched from the back.

Fortunately, Zoe, in spite of her insanity, was frigid. That, or she was fucking other guys, I didn't know, and I didn't ask. I myself was a virgin on our wedding day, which was unfortunate for me, very lucky for the rest of the universe.

I had no desire to know the difference between what made a virgin innocent and turned a real man into a stud. I always knew I was a god and was not drawn to things the flesh could offer me.

And what flesh was mine became useless the second Rhea, who lusted after me with all her being, came to sex me.

"Oh, Attis," she said and de-sublimated out of her statue, like it had died and was giving up its soul.

"At last! I've found you! My precious cock! *And you are so fine*!" She glared at Zoe. "And you, abomination, how dare you plan to squish your cunt down on me!"

With a gesture of Rhea's hand, Zoe's head flew across the temple.

Rhea lowered herself to the ground and approached her altar where I stood, "Forget her, Attis, let's fuck and fuck and then fuck them all for what they've done to us!"

Rhea was beautiful, harmless to the eyes. If you were twenty years old, you would want to look like her when you were forty. Minus Zeus's Curse that made men want to cut their cocks and balls off upon the sight of her, of course.

I grabbed my cock and started to tug on it with all of my might. Like an elephant might tie its trunk in a knot around a tree limb and then try to yank it off its face.

"No! Attis!" Rhea yelled and grabbed my arms, "Stop that!"

Nothing else mattered to me but to get that piece of meat off my body, to rip my balls off and see them tossed aside. To be free of them. In my mind I was nibbling on a hang nail that hurt the more I chewed on it, but all I could think about was being rid of it.

A symphony of suffering and agony erupted around me but I could barely hear it; only the need to get rid of that annoying and troublesome *evil* piece of baggage between my legs.

I beat a soldier to death to get his sword, which was easy, he, too, was preoccupied with using it to slice his penis off and I needed it more than he did!

I pulled my pants down, grabbed my cock and balls, and raised the blade high, aching for relief…

"NO! Attis!" Rhea bellowed. "You will cease!"

And the blade fell. And I sliced, and sawed, and cut. I was almost done when the lions attacked.

My blood, purple and gold, shot from the wounds and sprayed into the air. Wherever it landed, holly saplings sprung up, replete with their thorny leaves, white flowers and red berries.

"Get him!" Rhea screamed and two lions the size of bull elephants leapt into the sanctuary, "Don't let him touch his dick!"

The sight of the lions shocked me out of the need to slice my meat off and I ran. They chased me across the land and finally into the sea. More of my blood spread into the water and finally a shark swam by and engulfed my ragged manhood. It chewed, swallowed.

The lions dragged me from the sea and took me to Rhea, who was waiting. I awoke in Olympus.

While I was being pursued, Rhea accosted my mother and bragged, "Stupid little heffer! *Did you think you and that disgusting thing you fuck could outwit me?*"

And off went their heads as well.

End Part 1.

Chapter 7

Boys on Fire!

Olympus

"I will allow this matter to be settled through a vote," Zeus said, "Since I am not a tyrant."

Zeus held the tesseract, a time free bubble that contained Ganumede's body, watched it float about like a child might watch a goldfish he won at the county fair.

"Father," Pallas said. "It's not Até."

"Apparently not," Phoebus glared at him.

"Whatever it is, it is absolutely disgusting," Hera said. "I want no part in this."

"Hermes," Zeus said. "Please place an abstention next to Cowbell's name on the tally sheet please."

He looked into the bubble straight up Ganumede's butt crack.

"Father," Hermes said. "You yourself ordered all Olympus, indeed all Creation, to refrain from conferring immortality to any more mortals ever again. You must recall this."

"Yes, you may recall!" Phoebus said.

"Fine. Fine," Zeus said in a warm reasonable tone. "You can now be the new Cupbearer Apollo. As you all know, Hebe is getting married and I need to fill the position before too long," he said to the young goddess. "Please tell your brother, who most graciously just offered to take your place, where the uniforms and the glassware are kept…"

"I hate you," Phoebus said. "I vote in favor."

"Excuse me," Pallas said. "Can we back up to just exactly how you recruited our candidate for 'Cupbearer'?"

"Oh that…there was just a little misunderstanding and then an accident but, you see, with a little Ambrosia, all can be well, and we can have a nice brunch…with our brand new…"

"Fuck-doll?" Eros said. "I vote in favor."

"Aphrodite?"

"I object!"

"Hades Unseen?"

"You're a dick."

"Poseidon Earth-shaker?"

"You're a dick*hole*."

"Hermes, that's two more abstentions."

"Yes, Father."

"And yourself?"

"In favor."

"Hebe?"

"He's cute as a button! In favor!"

"Demeter?"

"Don't ever speak to me again, you pig's anus."

"Hestia?"

Hestia left.

"Hestia! You get back here! That's an order!"

Hestia did not return.

"Artemis?"

"Not in favor."

"Ares?"

"Fuck yeah!"

"Eos?" Zeus looked about. "Eos? Where is that tawdry tramp?"

"It's dawn, Father," Phoebus said. "She'll be along shortly."

"Oh. Right. That leaves you, Pallas."

"Pallas abstains."

"Splendid! Splendid! Hebe, please fetch the Ambrosia, douse him properly with it, and then train our new Cupbearer in the proper ways of setting the table for a celebration of the newest member of our House!"

And then the House started to shake violently…a latecomer to the voting process: Rhea the Mother of Zeus.

It tingled at first, then it hurt a lot as the talons of the eagle sank deeper into my shoulders and its penis found purchase elsewhere.

Then pain slowed, then stopped hurting and I saw bright and colorful lights, lots of them.

"Looks like you've found the Ether," Hebe said. "If you pull back from it and gain perspective, I will explain it to you."

I focused real fucking fast. It sounded like pots and pans the size of Jupiter were smacking the walls.

"*What the fuck is happening*? And why am I naked around a girl?"

"I am not a girl." Hebe said, "And I've seen it all before. Here, put this on," Hebe waved her hand and a tunic of red and gold wrapped itself around me, "Come with me, please."

A wall nearby collapsed. On the other side, I saw Zeus, looking even more electrified than he did when he did what? I couldn't remember. There was a goddess, blazing bright green and violet hovering over him. They were screaming at each other.

"You mustn't watch," Hebe made a blindfold appear over my eyes. "Males may not look upon the form of Mother Rhea."

"Rhea? She's real? My mother and father always told me there was no such thing!"

Hebe pushed me, "Oh she's real!" She tied a piece of cloth over my eyes and pushed me onward.

A voice that sheared marble off the columns, "*Remove. Your Curse*!" It screamed.

Another voice shouted back, twice as loud, "*I told you never to return here!*"

More walls fell, and because I couldn't see, I stumbled and became separated from Hebe. There was a whoosh of a breeze scented with immortelle and I found my face nestled against the most gorgeous chest I'd never seen before.

"Ganumede, you must take cover while Zeus defends Olympus against Rhea the Titan. I can keep you safe till she departs." He pushed my head against his heart and covered me with his tunic.

"Why? What's the big dam deal?"

"Zeus struck his mother's phallus from her, so she would not with breed herself and this drove her mad."

"That's nasty." I said. "Why did she want to do that?"

"When Zeus cast down the Titans, against all good judgement he spared his mother. She protected him from his father when he was a babe and he felt obligated to do the same for her when it was her time to pass on. Rhea greatly misinterpreted the amount of privilege this allowed her. She presumed to rule at his side, and then Zeus was forced to bar her from Olympus as a statement of his supreme authority.

"She rebelled and threatened to use her phallus on herself to create more Titans and take Olympus for herself.

"There must not be another generation of Titans, Ganumede. This, the Fates have decreed. To prevent her from violating Their Will, Zeus struck her phallus from her and ordained that any male who gazes upon her must then emasculate himself."

"Even if you're not a pescatarian?"

"Even then," Hermes laughed. "Women have their ways"

"EW!"

"Hermes, wait!" Ares found them, "What should I do with this?" He held up what looked like a boy made of twigs and brambles, kicking and screaming. Green ooze gushed from a knothole in between its legs.

"Ganumede?" it rasped. "Help me!"

"What?" I recoiled. "Who are you? What are you?"

"Ares, be gentle with it please and take it to Zeus. He will know the appropriate way to deal with this."

I was whisked away by Hermes then and didn't find out what happened till much later. All I remember was the tree boy crying out, the shaking of the foundations of heaven, and my cheek pressed against Herme's heart.

The Burning Boy

Before.

"Tithonus, you stop running from me!" Eos, streaked across the land like a rose and peach colored comet, "It's still me but I'm better!"

"Stay away from me!" Tithonus, hair and clothes on fire, was able to douse the flames by falling and tumbling. He knew if he stopped, dropped, and rolled, there would be a risk that…thing would get him, but he had to take it.

Overhead, he saw red lightning and then she fell on him like a burning blanket and pinned him down.

"Take my breast into your mouth! Like before! Or I will make my nipples much, much hotter!"

Eos' moans of pleasure sounded like harp strings were being yanked from the instrument.

"Bite harder!" She slapped his face and the skin boiled, "Now pull your pants and underwear off!"

Tithonus didn't move. Not even to struggle.

"Wake up, you disgusting animal! *You will service me*!" Eos slapped the face of Tithonus again and again till it was misshapen.

"Eos," Phoebus said from above. "What the hell are you doing?"

Now, back on Olympus
Eos and Zeus, The Aerie

"Yes you will, yes you will, and you will!" Eos screamed and showered the Aerie with hot sparks, like a Roman candle firing champagne pink fireballs into the air.

Phoebus warned her but she wouldn't listen. As before, Phoebus, in spite of the fact he was a healer, was not able to heal Tithonus' injuries and Hermes was busy protecting Ganumede so he did what he could- held the body with its waning *Ka* inside a tesseract, just as Zeus had with his brother when *that* 'accident' happened.

Eos yelled and stamped and yelled more…Apollo averted his gaze from wanted whole thing to hurry up and end.

"Eos!" Zeus whined. "I said no!"

"What it means, I'm borrowing a trick from that mega-cunt Demeter and threatening you! If you don't give Tithonus Ambrosia, like you did with Ganumede, the Earth and all life bearing planets in the universe have just witnessed their last sunrise!"

"You stupid little whore!" Zeus roared. "You dare to talk to me like this?"

"I do. Nighty night!" Eos said and walked away.

"Father, if Eos does not pave the way, I have no way of performing my duties. I am not on her side. She is licentious and inane, but perhaps you should consider my dilemma and yours! What is more important? The boy or creation?"

"You are correct." Zeus cradled his head. "Phoebus, get some Ambrosia from Hebe please."

"Of course. Thy will be done," Phoebus said.

Phoebus found Hebe and Ganumede sweeping up in the distillery, replacing all the gear and equipment that had gone awry during Zeus's battle with Rhea.

"Hebe, Father requires a dose of Ambrosia for our latest guest," Apollo grinned.

"I don't do that anymore. Ganumede, here," Hebe coughed up what looked like a glowing gold marble. "Open up."

"No way! What is that?"

"It's the Key. Only its bearer can serve Ambrosia and, then, only when Zeus commands. Ingest it and you will become the New Cupbearer."

Ganumede swallowed the Key, "Am I supposed to feel like I could crack open the world?"

"Yes. We will speak of this later, But, first, take this," she handed him a chalice made of gold colored glass, "Now take it to the cellar, fill it, and bring Zeus what he requires."

Ganumede did as he was told while Phoebus breathed down his neck. When he was finished blessing the Ambrosia the he decanted into the gold cup, he was dragged brutally to the Aerie by the god of poetry.

"A toast, Father…to you," Phoebus tossed Ganumede in front of Zeus, who screamed when he saw the burnt body of his twin splayed before him like a roast left unattended on the grill for too long.

Ganumede dropped the chalice, but Eos caught it before it crashed on the portico floor.

"Get him out of here! Goddamn you, Phoebus!" Zeus thundered, "Take him to Hypnos and have him remove this incident from his mind!"

"Ask Hermes, father. He runs your errands, not I," Phoebus said.

Zeus sent for Hermes while Apollo restrained the howling Ganumede. Hermes swooped him up and took him to the Land of Night where Hypnos was waiting.

Hermes and Pallas Scheme

When Hermes returned, he told Pallas, "He's sleeping. As much as I regret it, I think it is best he does not know what happened to his brother."

"Which part?" Pallas asked. "Being raped and set on fire or raised from near death to immortality, then cursed and sealed in a vault?"

"Both. All of it, perhaps," Hermes ran his fingers across Ganumede's cheek. "In any case, Zeus required Hypnos mask his memories of his whole life, especially details about Tithonus and Attis."

"Attis," Pallas said grimly. "Rhea has him in her custody?"

"Yes, though he is emasculated," Hermes said. "She will try to find a way to use him to achieve her ends."

"Can she?"

"There are options," Hermes said. "We must be ready."

Attis Prinos, and Rhea, after Zeus ejects them into the Ether

"Dammit. I was sure he'd accept your offer to service him," Rhea said.

"I made no such offer," *Attis Prinos*, Attis, the Holly God, said. "You did! And it looks like he is getting all the service he needs. And you…mother of all monsters, you will find a way to repair the damage you have done to me and then you will face me, so I can kill you as you deserve!"

"Hilarious!" Rhea clapped her hands and laughed. "You really are a huge prick, aren't you?"

"Say what you want. I know who I am and what you are. I am returning to Earth. My mother will find a way to make me whole again."

"'Fraid not," Rhea said. "She's dead. I killed her. And, unfortunately, you are now dying, also. Like all men, without your tool, you are quite without what is needed to remain viable."

"What do you mean?" Attis snarled, his voice like dry twigs cracking. "I'm a god. A Titan…I am immortal!"

"You are nothing," Rhea put her hand inside the knothole where Attis's phallus used to be. "And I can't sustain your *Ka* without some kind of potency for much longer."

"Do something," Attis pleaded. "Surely you know a way so we can get our revenge against Zeus and those that have wronged us!"

"If I knew how to give you a new ball and a big old donkey dick, Attis, we would be fucking each other's lights out! Right about now! Don't you think?"

"Then I will die and so will you," Attis said. "Unless something can be done to give me an erection and you…to get fucked."

"*I don't know I said*!" Rhea bared her teeth and was about to set fire to all that kindling Attis had become and be done with it and then she got an idea. "But wait…I know someone who does."

"Who?" Attis asked.

"The Witch Goddess," Rhea said. "She knows everything."

The Three Times Three
Attis, Rhea, Hekate

"You are a boy, who has lost his mother," Hekate said.

"Yes," Attis replied.

"Don't get lovey dovey," Rhea said. "This isn't about sex."

"Auntie," Hekate said. "Do us a favor and shut the fuck up."

"Don't 'auntie' me, you foul abomination of time and space," Rhea said. "Can you tell us how to get this engine purring or not?" Rhea pointed to Attis.

"Attis," Hekate said, "you are and always have been a god of the Earth. You are aware of this?"

"Yes."

"You are the Grower."

"No. I was…sufficient in all aspects."

Hekate rolled all three pairs of eyes, "What is with you people? In other words, you are a remnant of the God of things that grow. That being the case, there is a phallus that once belonged to another Grower that presently has no use for it. It would readily graft itself to your frame."

"And this would allow him to fuck like a champ?" Rhea asked.

"Good God Girl, Get a Grip!" Hekate said.

"Would this save my life and allow me to get my revenge on Zeus and Ganumede for betraying me?" Attis asked.

"What else are cocks for?" Hekate asked. "Than fucking people? Now listen…there is a place, a river that runs below the Underworld. Its mouth is beneath the gaze of the Sun…"

Entr'acte

Callirhoe, Queen of Troy

Sometimes I sit on the balcony of the highest height of Troy and look over the city. At all the people going about their affairs, apparently without a care. I wonder where they are, my twin boys, and if they ever think about me.

Sometimes, Tros, my husband, joins me.

Entr'acte 2

Phoebus Apollo, the Alarm Cock

I don't spurn well. When you cross me, you are fucked. After Pallas and Hermes left the new Cupbearer to recover from Hypnos's ministrations, I called upon him myself to welcome him to the family. Ganumede said no so I gave him some ministering of my own, and sent a copy of what took place to Zeus' scrying pond.

"Do it again," I commanded Hypnos. "He mustn't remember."

"Why would I do this for you?" Hypnos asked.

"It amuses me," Phoebus said.

"I can see why." Hypnos said.

"Do it! And be quick." Phoebus said, before the little twat runs to Pallas or Hermes.

"I will take my payment for helping you from the boy's ass." Hypnos said. "My brother would like to join."

"I could care less. Whatever. Go to it," Phoebus Apollo left the twins of Sleep and Silence to their compensation for services rendered. "Speak to no one of this."

"We never do," Hypos said.

Chapter 8

As Above, So Below

Dance Bitch,
Or Feel the Switch
Ganumede, the Cupbearer of Olympus.

Hebe explained the rules of Ambrosia Mixology.

"Use the Key to the Cabinet to dispense, this you already did…"

"I did? When?"

"Suffering Sappho," Hebe said. "Come, I will show you. This is a batch I made in this drum here. Only you can use the Key to open it, however. You must never, ever open any casks drums or pour for anyone, unless Zeus instructs."

"What about Hera?"

"Hera does not drink Ambrosia," Hebe said. "She's learned a lesson or two about that long ago, which leads to the next lesson. Ganumede," she faced me and put her hands on my shoulders. She was cute for a girl, had short hair, amber colored eyes, and small, pretty lips.

"When you make Ambrosia, you have the power of immortality at your disposal. No one but you has this power now. Why any of us would want or be entrusted with such responsibility is baffling but for it to have been thrown at you in such a way is inconceivable. You must be true and honest and pure in every way with this duty and never abuse it. And, now that you know you could. What do you say?"

"You can do it. I don't want to."

Hebe took hold of me firmly, "Sadly, what you want is yet to be, I think, but, for now, you must do well with what you have."

"I'm just a fucking bartender, Hebe. It's not that big a deal."

"It is the biggest deal," Hebe said. "Gods that don't understand this disappear. If you want to continue to exist, you must be able to participate fully in the Affairs of Olympus, always ready and competent in the execution of the Will of Zeus, the King of Heaven. Eventually, he will trust you and let you get away with stuff, but even then, you must never ever question or contradict him, no matter how much you want to or how painful it is to say yes to his requests."

"Sounds fabulous," I said.

"Next, you will have an audience with Cow-Eyed Hera, his Queen," Hebe said, "Then you will need to learn to dance, to entertain, to write and speak in verse, to fight, to strategize, and, lastly, learn all the mysteries of creation that your mortal-mind could not have properly pondered."

I opened my mouth, she pushed it shut.

"My last lesson is this…be inconspicuous. You're pretty, so that might seem anathema, but trust me, it will help you be all the more fit to survive life on Olympus."

The Boudoir of Hera

Hebe led me to the Boudoir of the Queen of the Gods. "Zeus calls her the Queen of the Hogs," Hebe said and laughed. "She's got a terrible reputation for being irritable, but look who she's married to! She's a bit of a story-teller, so you be a lot of a listener and things will be okay. Well, as okay as they can be, considering."

"Considering what?" I asked.

"Oh dear," Hebe said. "Knock and wait till she answers. And give her this. Damn thing won't stop following me."

Hebe handed me a peacock.

"Yeah, I'll do that." It pecked my nose. "And since my hands are full of cock, Hebe, could you please knock for me?"

"I can," Hebe smiled and rapped on the door.

Hera opened at once. "Welcome to Olympus, Ganumede," Hera opened the door and hinted at a smile. "You can come in."

I entered and the peacock jumped from my arms.

"Thank you for bringing Argos back to me. I've been looking for her."

Hera's chambers looked like a botanical garden. The smell of orchids and fruit filled the tepid air and the sound of water trickling came from all directions. It was dimly lit, just enough to allow me to see the statues, potted trees, and exotic artifacts sitting atop furniture and pedestals.

“Sit with me,” Hera splayed herself atop a massive chaise lounge and pointed to a smaller one across from her.

“Are you settling in?” she asked.

“Sure.”

“Ganumede, do you know who I am? Where you are?” Hera asked.

“You’re Hera, the Queen of the Gods, and we are in Olympus.”

“Do you know who you used to be?”

“I’ve always been me,” I said. “A god of Olympus!”

Hera was silent for a moment. The sound of water flowing was prominent. Argos flew across the room and then landed on the back of the chaise and finally seated herself in Hera’s lap. Hera coddled the creature while she spoke.

“I am the oldest of the surviving children of Rhea and Kronus,” Hera said. “Zeus is my youngest brother.”

“Eep!”

Hera smiled -she couldn’t help herself, “That’s not the weirdest thing I have to tell you today. After Gaea and her mate, Uranos, made children, the Fates, Clotho, Lachesis, and Atropo issued their first decree to the gods: Sons must always take their fathers’ places and the parents must also give them up.

“This enraged Uranos and he tried to kill his children and then his wife, so that she could no longer create any threats to his reign.

“Kronus, my father, then killed my grandfather by castrating him with a scythe that he and Gaea fashioned together. Then, he, too, started to wonder when it would be his turn to give up what was his.

“Every time Rhea gave birth, Kronus waited at the opening of her vent and ate its issue. This happened until Rhea started to give birth in secret and used fetishes made of stone to fool Kronus into thinking they remained childless.

“She was able to preserve six offspring this way. I was the first, then came Demeter, the Mother of Nature, Hestia, Mother of the Hearth, then Hades Unseen, Poseidon Earth-shaker, and finally Zeus Thunderer.

“In secret, Rhea groomed us to plot the overthrow of Kronus for his brutality. There was war, Ganumede. Horrible war. It spanned all time, space and all the dimensions and basements of reality were drawn in.

“We, sisters, were protected by Zeus alone, who fought Kronus and kept him from consuming us. Together with our Mother and her allies, Kronus was defeated and thrown down into Tartarus, along with all of his brothers and uncles and aunts and all the terrible creatures they enlisted or enslaved to their sides.

"The Fates spoke once again and named Zeus, the Sky King, as the heir to Throne of Creation, and that I, the Queen of the Firmament, would be his wife.

"Rhea found favoritism with Zeus, whom she nurtured most of all. Hades, the proper heir to Kronus' position, wanted all of the Titans, every last one, put into Tartarus including his mother. Hades was always pragmatic, remains so to this day.

"As the youngest, and therefore the craftiest, Zeus cultivated a soft spot for his mother and aunts and a few others and they for him; they wanted to survive and he needed their support. Zeus betrayed almost all of them, and his brothers submit to him, but they have never forgiven him for his guile during the war with the Titans, how he manipulated them and took their places from them. Of all of us make life on High and below uncertain at times."

"A scum-bucket like that rules Heaven?" I asked.

"He is a dangerous and devious scum-bucket, Ganumede," Hera said. "Do what he says and stay out of his way the rest of the time, if you can."

"Okay. What am I supposed to do for you?"

"You're doing it." Hera said. "By listening to me."

Hera showed me to the hallway and said, "I'm sorry. I wish there was another way but the Fates, not we, are in charge of what happens to us."

"Another way to do what? And what is going to happen?" I asked.

The door to Hera's chamber closed, my questions went unanswered.

On the way to my next appointment, I saw Eros.

"We shall meet again soon," he said.

Attis with Rhea and Hekate in the Ether

"What is this *grower* and where is it," Attis, who was wilting and running out of sap, asked.

"It is the lost phallus of the Green God, Osiris, torn from him during a fight with his brother, Seth."

"*So where is it*, Whore Goddess?" Rhea asked. "Tell us now, we don't have much time."

“Go to the River of Duat and find the oxyrhynchus fish that swims in it. The phallus of Osiris is in its belly,” Hekate, said. “And I remain a virgin, Mother Rhea.”

“Oh, me too. Now, how the fuck do we get there? The crossroads between realms are closed to me,” Rhea said.

“I will take you,” Hekate said. “For it is my divine providence to return lost children to their mothers.”

“Whatever, just get us there.”

“Follow me,” Hekate said, “I can take you to where the Duat River flows but you must obtain the phallus yourself.”

“What else do we need to know?” Attis asked.

“It belonged to a god much like you, a Green One. It should easily graft itself to you.”

“Then what?”

“I cannot say, *Attis Prinos*,” Hekate opened the door to Duat Cavern, also known as the Underworld. “Take care, however. The gods of Heliopolis have long searched for the missing phallus and they will be enraged over its theft.”

“Only if they figure out who recovered it,” Attis said, and under the circumstances, lucky Hekate tolerated his threat, “Now let us go to it.”

Hekate let Attis Prinos and Rhea, Mater Megale pass into Duat. Then she told Mother Isis Her that son needed her, where he was, and about his plans.

Olympus, the Amphitheater

Phoebus and the Muses teach Ganumede to Boogie.

“I don’t dance. *I watch.*”

“Here on Olympus,” Phoebus said. “You dance and we watch. Right, Ares?”

“Right,” Ares uncoiled the whip and it made a cracking sound, not far from Ganumede’s crack. “So baby, take your, time do it right.”

“Ow! Bitch!” I covered my cheeks, “I said, I don’t have a fucking clue how to dance. And what do war and dancing have to do with each other anyway?”

“Everything.” Ares said. “Phoebus, what say you?”

“Sad but true,” Phoebus said.

Ares added, "He, who can dance, survives the war. He, who survives war is the Victor. And dance is the war between oneself and the other Marys on the floor."

"*And you're a freak!*" I said to Ares.

The whip cracked.

"Girls," Ares said. "Let's get this wee bitch into a costume!"

"Which one?"

"*Salome*, of course!"

Attis in the Underworld

Duat, the Underworld of the Egyptian Gods

"Once that phallus can make candy," Rhea said, "it's trick or treat, baby."

"You're disgusting," Attis growled.

He could feel his holly tree body unraveling. His leaves were almost all gone, a stray berry or two was all that was left stuck to his crown. His limbs were shriveling and it was hard to walk as the last of his sap solidified into amber around the knot hole in his groin.

Attis once thought he was a real person, more than that, a Living God, but upon discovering he was but the dismembered cock of some crazy Titan Goddess, he'd lost his attachment to the lies he was told about himself and their truths also. All spawned by the Goddess of Mothers, Nana; now, called Isis, unbeknownst to Attis and Rhea.

"Everyone fucks someone they aren't truly into," Rhea stated a truth. "When it takes them where they want to go. Let's have lots of babies together, Father of Titans! We will retake Olympus and brutally crush, those that spurned us."

"No," I said.

"Yes!" Rhea said, "Do you not want to see Ganumede and Tithonus and every last human who ever made you question yourself turned into pulp and fed to the gaping maw of Tartarus, to suffer forever for what they did to you?"

"Yes," Attis said. "I do."

"Now let's find this other cock and strap it on. Then we will fuck and fuck and fuck!" Rhea's laughter rang in the cavern of the River of Duat. She was the Mother of Titans and cared little for wondering about the consequences of her actions.

"Oh you will be fucked, Rhea," Attis said. "Fucked very hard."

He pulled her close to him and endured the disgust of kissing her so powerfully, "Let's go fishing."

Attis waded into the river. The Duat was cold, its surface so black it drew the light from the torches that lit the cavern into its roiling depths.

"*Attis*," a whisper of a thousand damned voices hissed.

"Who are you?" He asked.

"We are the Duat. The discarded and unworthy of Anubis. Without Good Osiris to judge us, The River has become swollen with our ranks."

"I don't care about that or about you," Attis said. "I am here for myself."

"We know where it is," the voices said. "The thing you seek…it is inside the oxyryhnchus fish."

"Give it to me then," Attis ordered.

"Who are you talking to, you idiot?" Rhea kvetched. "Hurry up before we're discovered!"

Attis ignored her.

"We can give it to you," the Duat said, "but we need something in return."

"Yes?"

"Once you graft it onto your person, the Phallus will make you all powerful."

"That is the objective, yes," Attis said.

"Then you must kill the Mother of Titans."

"Yes," he said.

"And free us from the Duat."

"Yes," Attis agreed. "I agree to all of your terms."

"And here is the fish," the River said.

Heliopolis

Isis and Horus

"Did you hear that?" Isis said to her son, Horus Ra Horakhty.

"When there is foulness being plotted, Mother, I hear it," Horus said. "Never am I not listening for it."

Isis craned her ear.

"Horus!!" she wailed. "We have to hurry! Warn Anubis, Aker and the rest. We have to get down to the River!"

"I will obey you, Mother, as always. But I can handle these fiends myself," Horus said. And Ra of the Horizon went to the Cavern of the River Duat, otherwise called the Egyptian Underworld.

Attis and Rhea in Duat; the Gods come to retrieve the Phallus of Osiris

"Return the Phallus of Osiris, demon!" Horus tossed his spear, which soared like a ray of light, towards the breast of *Attis O Prasinos*, The Green God. It found its mark. The Justice of Horus never missed its target.

Attis retrieved the spear. Many more gods started to transpire into Duat from Heliopolis, the Solar City.

"Come out of the river, Attis!" Rhea cried. "We must hurry away so we can…"

"Yes," Attis rose from the River of Duat, took Rhea, the Mother of Titans, by the throat and drove the Spear of Horus into her breast. There was an explosion of bright purple blood.

"Fuck you, you insufferable bitch."

Then, while she screamed and tore at him, he twisted her head off and threw it and her carcass into the River. The dislocated souls feasted upon it and then the body that Attis tossed in after it. The river began to boil. It thrust up over its banks, erupted into a frigid and bloody fountain.

"Remove the Phallus of Osiris from thyself," Divine Anubis commanded, his great claws and teeth bared. "And let the River of Duat take thee, also."

"Do not defy Maat," Pitah the Engineer, who wielded a hammer, exclaimed. "Return what you have stolen to us."

"Attis?" Isis pleaded. "Please come back to me. I've missed you so."

"Mama?" Attis said.

Horus threw another spear, "She is not your mother and you are not her son!"

"And I, Horus," Attis said, "Am now your father and you will humble yourself before me." Attis caught the spear and broke it. "Do not trouble me again."

Attis's voice, like a giant tree being felled, commanded, "Any of you."

And *Attis O Prasinos* left to plan his revenge against Olympus. And also Ganumede for betraying him.

Ares and Ganumede, the Olympus Gymnasium

"At least, he waited till you developed a man's body or most of one," Ares poked at me. "Let's take some measurements."

"That doesn't need measuring," I smacked his hand. "Heh."

"Yes it does. Now," Ares said. "Let's get physical. I am going to teach you how to build that scrawny frame of yours into a killing machine, then Pallas is going to teach you how to use it."

"Am I really going to have fight or kill someone?" I asked.

"Best to ask before that time comes," Ares said.

"Why are you teaching me this? Where is Herakles?"

"He had some errands to run," Ares scowled. "I'll have to do."

"Okay, just don't be so mean."

"War is not meant for the kind, Ganumede." Ares said. "Nor is life unless you can occasionally bear to be cruel."

The Rage of Ganumede

As Above, So Below

Pallas and Ganumede, the Arena of Olympus

Pallas Athena was nothing like they said. She didn't walk around in bed-sheets and a helmet, glower at people from beneath its visor. She kept her eyes, which were as gray as all claimed, free of obstruction and with these, she watched and learned.

"Ignorance is always testing us," Pallas said. "And most often it wins. In order to become wise, must strategize continually in order to outwit ourselves." She said, "That means the armory is in here," she pointed to her head, "as much as it is out there."

Pallas donned a skirt, heavy boots, and gloves.

"Since Hermes hasn't taught you transubstantiation yet, I will dress you in a way that is appropriate for our time together today."

"Ooh! I like you already."

"I'm trying to like you," she said. "But I don't."

"What?"

"First rule, Ganumede. Never let an opponent get to know how you react or manipulate those reactions. You want to be liked too much," Pallas said. "You trade humor for bravery and you use your looks as an excuse to avoid being intelligent and prudent."

"Cunt!" I said and walked away.

Pallas whipped me around and punched me in the stomach. She pulled me by my hair and said, quite calmly, "That is what happens when you behave as I claim."

She released me and waited till I could breathe.

"Have you ever gotten in a fight before?" she asked.

I saw something then. Darkness, fire, there was a lot of noise. Horrible sounds. Pain.

"I don't know. I don't think so."

"People and gods have defended you and fought for you your whole existence, Ganumede," Pallas said. "You have been spoiled, fawned over, lusted after, bullied, buggered, and boxed in by your lack of interest in being who and what you should have been. It is time to grow up."

"I don't know how," I said.

"No. You don't, and you haven't been made to try," Pallas socked me in the jaw and sent me tumbling.

"Stop that, you stupid bitch! If you've bruised me—"

"Sigh," Pallas kicked me in the balls. "You weren't using those anyway," she said.

"No, but they help out, you know?"

"Are you trying to infuriate me?" she said severely.

"Are you infuriated?" I groped myself to make sure they were still there.

"We might be making some progress now," Pallas asked. "But stand up and let's be sure."

"No," I said. "You're just going to punch me or try to castrate me again."

"Once he has brought you low, an enemy will be fully engaged and go for the kill. That's when you trick him! As soon as your enemy is blinded with arrogance, you strike."

"Why is everyone acting like I have so many enemies?"

"Because you now reside on High Olympus." Pallas said. "And this is how Olmypus is."

Pallas and Hermes

The Library Portico

"He is bright, but lacks any passion for his own well-being," Pallas said. "That would be quite different if his memories were returned to him. He thinks wearing armor violates his fashion sense…has no concept of the rest."

"None," Hermes said. "And that's why he's so helpless. But if he can't stand up for himself, what good would it do to tell him the truth?"

"Withholding it isn't ideal, Hermes! Of this I am certain!"

Pallas turned and looked. As had happened other times in the lives of the heroes she stewarded, the Fates shared with her, a vision:

"Hermes! There is a problem coming! A very big problem," she transferred the image to Hermes' point of view. "It's him! Ganumede!"

Hermes saw Ganumede bright, clad all in silver, astride a magnificent steed, tossing lightning from his person. Whether he was just or just angry, Hermes couldn't tell from the image.

"Good Gods, Pallas!" Hermes said. "He's going to destroy us all!"

"This hasn't happened yet," Pallas said. "Look."

"What should we do, Pallas? Can we avoid all of this? Find a less violent solution?"

"We don't avoid," Pallas continued to watch. "We prepare."

"I Agree," Hermes said. "But he's already endured so much pain."

"He will do what he must." Pallas said. "Like the rest of us."

Ganumede

I left the baths and wandered Olympus, whose topography and atmosphere changed constantly. Like it was bored with its own pluripotent energies and needed amusement. Or someone was programming it for theirs…

During one of the transitions, a sunny sky over an alpine meadow became a stark, high plateau under a nightscape, one featuring the bright display of the aurora. In between views, I heard someone cry out.

The lightshow set itself to music and if the baneful wails were there, they were drawn into or drowned out by a stellar symphony, one whose beauty I have not experienced since.

I did hear the sound of the crying now and again, and it was some time before I learned its source.

Attis the Green God, the Father of Titans, in the Ether Local to Heliopolis

After I sublimated from Duat into the Ether, something hit me. Khnum, the ram headed god of the Nile. He bounced off me.

Then, Anhur, a lion headed god, with claws each like axe blades raked me and his mate, Sekhmet, leapt for my throat.

I tossed them aside.

There was Babi, a baboon, teeth bared, Heket, a giant frog with razor tipped flippers, whose cries were pathetic when I punched her face in.

"Stop," Horus, accompanied on either side by his mother, Isis, and aunt, Nepthys. With him were Anubis, Bastet, and two impressive creatures held, just barely, by great chains by Ibis headed Toth: one a python, the Egyptian form of the Kraken called Apophis, the other, Aker, the nuclear solution of the gods, twin lions joined together by four wings which they shared. It roared and writhed, a binary star straining against its volatile energies and predatory instincts which even Toth was barely able to hold in check.

"You must return the Phallus of Osiris to us," Horus, known well for his pragmatism, commanded.

"I like it fine where it is," I groped myself lewdly, flicked a finger at Horus, who was flung far into the either like a gnat. "Now, let me pass."

"Attis, it's me," Isis floated free of the ranks of her family. "Your mother. I'm sure we can fix all of this, make you whole again. But you have to return Osiris's property to him. This is very important."

"You made me once already, Mother, and that is sufficient." I turned to leave, "And I quite like myself this way."

"Attis, you can't keep that. It has power that must be used otherwise," Isis said. "We must insist!"

"Go away, Mother. I don't want to hurt you," I said.

"I'm sorry I didn't tell you everything but did I ever lie to you? Was I so poor a mother to you?"

"You weren't my mother but the one you tried to be was worthy," I said. "That time is past, and I have business elsewhere now."

"If you try to go, they will destroy you. Please, Attis," Isis pleaded, and Nepthys and the army of gods surrounded her. "Let us help."

"Good-bye, Nana," I said.

"Let them go," Horus nodded to Toth, who released the chains, which held Apophis, the Great Chaos Serpent, and Aker, The Horizon Destroyer.

I wasn't about to fight those things. They were Old Gods, very powerful, and Horus was not a fool. He knew their capabilities and also mine. And right then I needed allies if I was to escape from the Egyptian gods and get back to Olympus.

I reached down, deep into the cavern of Duat, and extruded them, the lost and damned of the River, and turned them into an army.

"Distract them, then join me by the Tartarus Gate," I said. And there I went.

"What should we do, Divine Mother?" Nepthys asked Isis.

"We have to find him and stop him," Isis said. "Why did you lead him to us, Hekate? And give him such power?" Isis asked her, "Answer me, you cunt, I can see you are watching."

Hekate materialized, "I lead lost children to their mothers, Inanna. It's my Divine Providence; one of them, anyway."

"While I appreciate the chance to see my son again, Hekate, I think you royally fucked up," Isis screamed at her. "Now what do we do?"

"Follow him to the Tartarus Gate," Hekate said. "And do your best."

"Oh you think?" Isis shrieked. "Thoth, take the Legendary Beasts and go to the Tartarus Gate, we have to stop Attis from opening it."

"Yes, Mother," Wise and Good Thoth said. "Out of Homage to You, we will certainly try."

Home-Ec with Hestia

"You know this isn't your home, don't you, Ganumede?" Hestia was demure, soft spoken but intense, "It's not really mine either, so if you want to share...?"

"But you live here," I said. "This is your place, right?"

Hestia raised an eyebrow, "I am the goddess of other peoples' homes. Never was it decreed by the Fates or Zeus that I should make one for myself."

She gestured around her.

“All of Olympus, the House of the Gods, as magnificent and awesome that it is, is my design, my work. None of it was ever intended to house me as I would like. I just wasn’t asked about that.”

“Why don’t you just leave?” I asked. “And get a place of your own?”

“Because the part of this place that actually is a house, is my family. And I can’t bear the thought of leaving my sisters and some of my nieces and nephews behind.”

“I guess that makes sense,” I looked around the Temple of Hestia, with its grand fire-pit, cozy quarters, soft, plush furniture, potpourri, and tapestries.

“I hate it in here,” Hestia said. “But this is how those that pray to me mold and shape the way I live. Unlike Hera or Demeter, I haven’t been allowed to grow up. Unlike Pallas and Eos and Artemis, I was never allowed to be young either. I spend my time now as I did before, babysitting my youngest brother, who like his mother, is a tyrant.”

“He does seem overbearing,” I said.

“Seems? Oh dear,” Hestia looked toward the window and made her decision. “Tell me about your mother and your father and your brother, Ganumede.”

“I don’t think I have any of those things,” I said. “I was what I am now. A god of Olympus. I was born exactly as I’m supposed to be!”

Someone told me that the night before. I could smell his shoulder against my face, like sage and juniper in the sun.

“Even still, you came from somewhere! What about your home?” Hestia said suddenly. “Can you describe it to me?”

I saw a room, with a bed, a comforter with punk boys playing guitars and banging drums on it, a fireplace burned across from it on the far wall. I could feel its warmth.

I loved walking over to it, digging my toes into the leopard print rug that covered much of the floor. I used to sink into it, turn music on and stare into the fire.

I would wonder when I had to leave that room for a home of my own, which I desperately wanted, but was terrified of living by myself. I was told I wouldn’t have to…they’d find someone for me…

I saw a pair of eyes in the fire. They were very angry.

“Hestia? Is that you?”

“Here,” Hestia said. “Don’t spill.”

“Oh, right thanks,” I took the cup of tea she handed me.

“Let’s finish this pot and then we need to talk about what we’re going to do with those bare walls and floors in your chambers.”

“Knotty pine paneling and whitewashed floors,” I said.

“Mind your mouth, boy,” Hestia said, but she was glad. Ganumede, the real one, was still in there somewhere.

Hestia with Hera and Demeter

“Queen, I am not a violent person but I am ready to go up to that rooftop honkey-tonk of Zeus’ and dropkick his pigskin right over the railing.”

“Hestia, he can fly, and you’d never get your foot back,” Hera said. “As for what he did to that boy…you are correct. *He has got to pay*.”

“Boys, dear.” Demeter said, “He did it to his twin brother too.” Demeter, silent, brooding, arms folded over her bosom, agreed. “And pay he will. It was one thing to take that child away from his mother but another to take away his opportunity to grieve over it! And what Zeus and Eos did to his twin… Unthinkable!”

“Don’t overreact,” Hera said. “The situation is delicate, and not just here on Olympus. We still don’t know where Tithonus is, and the more we pretend Ganumede is uninteresting to us, the better for him. Outside Olympus, the universe is starting to struggle for its survival as Attis continues his assault upon the gods of Heliopolis. He will come here eventually and we have to be ready.”

“What about Ganumede, Hera?” Demeter asked, “You know what they do to him at night?”

“He will do what he has to. And so will we.”

“And for how long?” Demeter frowned.

“Not long.” She said.

“Tell us your plan then, Sister Queen.”

Hera couldn’t resist smiling, “What plan, Demeter?”

“You always have a plan, Queen,” Hestia said.

“Don’t I now?” Hera said.

Eros and Ganumede
The God of Desire, Feeling Needy!

"I said we would meet again," Eros said. "You don't remember, do you?"

"I don't think so." I said. "Did I like you before?"

"You didn't dislike me, I don't think," Eros went behind the bar. "I'll mix for change, since it's your night off!"

Hestia designed Ganumede's pad replete with a fully stocked bar, barstools, a big screen TV, movie theater seating.

Eros made us cocktails then suggested we watch a movie. "You really don't remember wanting to be ravished by me?"

"I'm quite sure I'd remember that," I said.

"What about now? Do you think you'd like me to ravish you now? And if you did, would you like me enough to not give your favors to any others? I don't usually stand for that."

"I don't do that! Not like the other gods say!" I said. "I do my job, I go home."

"You always were so very confused," Eros said.

"Don't be a gaping cum-hole, Eros. You said you wanted to hang out, so we are."

I grabbed the remote control and took a seat in front of the big screen, "Now do you want to watch *Sex and the City the Movie* or not?"

"I starred in it," Eros said. "Something else?"

"Um," I scrolled through the choices.

"How about *Elle*?" Eros suggested. "I directed that one."

"Sure."

"Sweet," Eros said.

Later, Eros sent copy of his new version, *Lui* to Zeus's Scrying Pond. We'd just finished the first big scene.

"I tried to save you…" Eros ground his teeth at me, "and you refused me! Little bitch!"

Eros beamed the live stream of the tawdry mess he was making in my apartment into Zeus's liquid memory database. "Now, here you are! *Raped a thousand times a night before you fall asleep and dream you are someone else*!"

Hermes and Eros
The Temple of Desire
One is Honest, the Other a Liar!

Eros was pinned to the wall by two of his bright pink glow-stick arrows, one through his kemise on either side. "I know everything that happens all of the time, Eros. Or are you going to tell me it was a coincidence that Hypnos paid yet another visit to Ganumede's apartment, shortly after you left and then also after Phoebus and Poseidon? Before he and his brother took a turn?"

"Answer for yourself," Eros said. "But that's not what you want to know, is it? You always know *what* but aren't so swift at knowing why, are you?"

"Tell me then what I desire to know. That's what you do, right? Give people what they want? Did Ganumede want you or did you force him?"

"It's all the same to some," Eros grinned.

"What about to him?" Hermes went to get another arrow from Eros's quiver, "Guess where this is going? You're going to love taking a shit so much you will eat prunes marinated in laxatives for every meal, if you don't tell me what I wish to know."

"He wants to love you," Eros said.

"Wants to or does?" Hermes slammed his hand into the wall near Eros' ear.

"Wants to. Every time he feels affection for you," Eros teased. "We make him forget! How frustrating that must be for you since you don't hide your affections for him very well, do you?"

"I don't need to hide mine!" Hermes grabbed his face. "And whatever is happening *it will stop*!"

"Unlikely," Eros grinned quite smoothly. "Highly unlikely in fact."

"Oh Eros," Hermes lamented as it all glued together. "What's on High can be brought down, and very likely will be."

"Hermes, I desire people, not stories or lectures. If you think you can make this one turn out other than its current course, by all means do try. Eventually I will tired of Zeus's games, and then you can have him if you want or not, I will neither help nor hinder you, but do pay heed to me on this!" Eros said. "Untul then, I take whatever I want from whomever I want, and I will never stop—not for you, not for anyone. It's my nature, and I happen to like it!"

"And that's why you are going to die alone," Hermes left Eros suspended to the wall by his arrows.

"We are immortal, we don't die."

"An eternity spent alone is worse than dying," Hermes said. "Stay away from the Cupbearer, Eros."

"*He will stay away from you once I tell him your secret, bitch*!" Eros said, "And don't think I won't! No one threatens me and tells me who I can and can't fuck!"

Hermes ignored him and went to find Ganumede. It was time for all secrets between them to end.

Ganumede and Demeter
The Elysian Fields,
Where Wounded Flowers Heal

"Can you believe it, Ganumede?" Demeter gestured over the meadow, the rolling pastures and hills of green dotted with swatches of bright color.

"No one wants to exalt a living thing…but give them a chance to do it for the dead, and they go all out! I think that is ridiculous, so I made this place, where noble mortal souls can be at peace for all eternity in the manner they pine away and pray for all their lives."

"It's beautiful," I said. "We never knew if this place was real or not!"

"You didn't?" Demeter laughed. "How could you be so mistaken? Didn't your mother tell if you peed on the seat, it was Hades for you and not my Elysian Fields?"

"I didn't have a mother. And my aim has always been true," I said.

"On that, I will have to trust you," Demeter's great blue eyes and auburn hair, which was graying at the roots, floated and bobbed in the wind which was scented with perfumes of the meadow.

"The pizzle part, I meant. But you did have a mother. How could you not?"

"I was promised you wouldn't talk about that stuff," I said. "Hebe promised no uteruses, no discussions of menstruation…how babies are made or even why…"

"Well, first," Demeter's eyes brightened, "you find a man, firm and strong, make him compliant with drink, then you feel under his skirt and—"

"EEP!" I said. "No you do not!"

"I'm kidding." Demeter said. "Be glad the gods did not intend for you to reproduce. Children, mortal and otherwise, make even the minotaurs cry!"

Demeter and I laughed together and then she stared into my eyes, "But you had a mother once, Ganumede. When it is time for to remember her again, don't forget about her. She never forgot about you. And be glad the Mother of Fates spared you being rooted in this Field forever, too."

Heliopolis. Horus, and Isis
Mother and Son in Crisis!

"He got away," Horus said, "I could have destroyed him and returned the Phallus to its rightful place and saved us all, if you had not interfered, Mother."

"Interfere is what mothers do," Isis said. "Now be good. I know you want to be."

"Do not patronize me Isis! You are not that creature's mother!" Horus insisted. "And he hurt many of us and now the cursed of the River Duat are free to cause a sad universe misery once again."

"Horus, I understand your determination and drive, but I am not out of hope for Attis yet."

"I don't rely on hope for a better future when a villain is in my grasp," Horus said. "I secure it by squeezing my hand around his neck."

There was a pulse and then a trail of light in the sky over the City of the Eternal Noon.

"What was that?" Isis said, trying to see past the Ra's corona at the little dot that was streaking across the azure sky.

"Hmph," Horus saw it clearly. "More imprudence of the Greek gods."

Then Isis saw it, too, "Go get it."

"No, Mother. We should not get involved. Remember the last time you did this?"

"Horus, trust me, go get it! Please? For me?"

"Yes, Mother," Horus said. "For you, if only you would recall more often that I, and no other, am your most favored."

"Yes, Horus," Isis said. "You are truly my most favored. Now please fetch that poor little godling before he ends up in a basket on the Nile or something even more ridiculous."

Unto Us a Sun is Given!
A Sun that Keeps us Livin'!

"*What's an abortion*?" Hathor asked, blinking her large lashed cow-eyes that any cover girl would be jealous of.

"And why, Ra-of-the-Horizon, do you hold it in your hands thusly?" Pitah, Who Listens to Prayers, inquired.

"It's not *really* an abortion," Horus juggled the vulnerable, jawbreaker sized ball of light from palm to palm like it was too hot but, in reality, he was quite nervous with the request that Isis sent him to make of the Mother of Fate, the cow-faced Hathor, and her unlikely paramour, Pitah, god of engineers, creation, and fertility.

"But you just said that Eos of Olympus had *an abortion*," Hathor sounded like a character from Dickens, Horus thought, "Launched it right from her Queen Mary!"

"Wait, no…" Horus's bird eyes did not exactly roll but he did give it a try, "Pitah…perhaps, we can discuss this privately?"

"Divine Hathor's question is legitimate, Horus," Pitah said, reasonably, stroking his neatly trimmed beard. "You did say a baby was evacuated from the ramparts of Eos…"

"Oh my Gods!" Horus blushed. "Yes! Can we please just focus on the non-vaginal aspects of this?"

Horus did his best to retell the tale, avoiding embellishment, as was his way.

"I see," Pitah said, still rubbing his chin.

"Its father is gone and It has no mother now?" Hathor wiped a tear, a very large one, from beneath one of her soulful brown eyes. "Can I hold it? To comfort it? It cries out like a newborn to me."

Horus exhaled a great breath, "Of course, Mother Hathor, I think it would like that."

"What you are asking..." Pitah said, considering the equations and materials, the calculations and definitions that would be needed, "is highly irregular."

"It has been done before," Horus said.

"Yes, I know," Pitah said. "And look what happened! We cannot risk it."

"This little being is not Attis, has no resemblance to him in any way. He will gestate fine in Mother Hathor."

"We don't agree." Pitah said. "The Greek gods father and mother abominations. We shall have no part in this."

"So I can put it in my...?" Hathor asked innocently.

"No! I'm sorry, my dear," Pitah frowned and put his arms around her, "This is not Maat!"

"*But It is*," a voice, bright, filled with joy and yet, serene, like a song recited during the happiest of holidays, that of Beloved Ra, filled the clouds, zephyrs, rills, dunes marshes, and mansions of Heliopolis, "*It is Maat*. Let this child be known as Nefertem, the god of the dawn, most handsome of the gods, born of Pitah and Divine Hathor, brother to Horus, son of Ra and Osiris."

"Now," Ra said to Hathor, "you can rebirth the child."

With Ra's blessing complete, all the gods in Heliopolis joined Isis Horus, Pitah, and Hathor in reciting their thanks to him,

"O RA
You God of Life, you Lord of Love,
All men live when you shine.
You are the crowned King of the Gods.
The goddess ISIS embraces you,
and enfolds you in all seasons.
Those who follow you sing to you with joy,
and they bow down their foreheads to the earth
In gratitude for your radiant blessings
O RA, You the King of Truth, the Lord of Eternity,
The Prince of Everlastingness,
You Sovereign of all Gods,
You God of Life, you Creator of Eternity,
You Maker of Heaven
All the Gods rejoice at your rising.
O RA, You giver of all life,

The Earth rejoice when it sees your golden rays
People who have been long dead
come forward with cries of joy
to behold your beauties every day.
You go forth each day over Heaven and Earth.
O RA, God of Life, you Lord of Love,
All men live when you shine."

End Part 2, As Above, So Below

Chapter 9

Forms and Formlessness

Attis at the Tartarus Gate

Hurry Ye Gods, Don't be Late!

"Good, you are back," Attis said to the Dispossessed of Anubis. "Tell me what happened."

"Many of us were lost," Seti, one of the souls Attis freed from the River Duat said. "The creatures, Aker and Apophis, you told us to attack for you are formidable."

"We will find formidable creatures of our own," Attis said. "Here within Tartarus… Their power is as terrible."

"Of what manner are they?" Seti, just a ghost, lacked all knowledge of things that the gods knew.

"Zeus summoned horrible entities from beyond this universe to aid him in his quest for power. When he was through with them, he did then as he does now with everyone and everything, and discarded them. They will be cold, angry, starving for revenge against him. Just like us."

Attis opened a jump point into Tartarus and gazed into the dark well it formed, "There."

"They chill me worse than the River Duat, Attis," Seti said. "Can you control them?"

"I am their Sovereign," Attis said. "They will obey me or they will be destroyed."

"Please do not abandon us to them, Attis. We are so afraid."

"I am not my father or my mothers," Attis said. And raised the first beast from Tartarus; The Star Mother, an ochre colored echinoderm like creature the size of a small moon with many spines and tentacles along its surfaces.

The first thing it did was reach for Seti and vacuumed him up into its maw.

Next came what looked like living vomit, the Crawling Chaos, spewed forth from the sphincter Attis created between this world and Tartarus, and then there was a sound like a zipper tearing a hole open in space and a creature with a head shaped like a melon, the color of an eggplant, the rest all tentacles and claws climbed up.

"We are attacked," Ramses, another spirit, told Attis. "The gods of Heliopolis are come!"

"Let them come."

While the other gods of the Western Land engaged the Star Mother and Creeping Horror, Apophis attempted to bite the massive tentacled creature in the head and was sucked up like a noodle.

Then its head fell apart, cleaved neatly in two as Aker, the Great Horizon Destroyer sliced across it at the speed of a racing star. It slowly slipped back one tentacle and claw at a time, back into the depths of Tartarus to finally die.

Aker was also a creature of another realm; as black and terrible as the ones it fought, Aker was a billion times brighter and more potent.

But Attis was God. Aker was only able to wound him.

Hermes and Ganumede

The Library

The Truth Shaved Down where Once it was Hairy!

"There is something I need to tell you, Ganumede."

Hermes lowered his gaze. All Ganumede could see was the light of the sun from the overhead skylight reflecting off his mirror surfaced helmet.

Hermes removed it, "So you know that everything else I tell you is the truth and that I am honest, you should know I led my first and only love to the slaughter. He was like you. A mortal, almost as lovely as yourself, naïve, like me, that the love between an infinite god and a finite person could last."

Hermes was one of those guys you felt guilty about looking at. He was stacked, high and tight, and not modest about it, but was so humble and sweet. It was embarrassing to want him, to imagine him naked and pleasuring himself with you.

Hermes unlike his brother Phobus was fair of color, his hair, when out from under the helm was a mess of brown waves and curls, his face was just boyish enough to confuse you whether he was a man or not until you saw his bare chest, navel, and thighs and their feathery dark hair, exposed just enough by his skirt and tunic to make you mad.

His brother, Phoebus, was the opposite. All masculinity and manhood, daring you to desire it, to hunger for it, consuming you brutally for being so foolish as to be caught by its trap.

Phoebus was the bad boy you would die to have, *who had you instead.* Hermes was the one you wanted to love you, would give you back to yourself in one piece when he was done.

The decision of which type of man or boy to while away scarce seconds of life with, or which one you wanted to be yourself made sense only once you resembled neither, could no longer appeal to them yourself. Even I had to learn this. Eventually. Hermes tried to explain:

"Yeah, so?" I said. "At least you had someone."

"So," Hermes continued, "I pretended to be able to live his life with him," Hermes went on. "The other gods grew jealous of us. Boreas, the West Wind, in particular, felt he was better suited to my affections than Krokus; that was his name, to his place in my life and in my bed.

"During a game of the disc, Boreas sent a squall. After I tossed the disc, he directed it to slice Krokus' throat open and he bled to death. I returned to Olympus with the body and placed it in the Elysian Meadow."

Hermes wept, "I have missed him every minute until I saw you."

"Listen, Hermes," I said, "you're going to be fine…"

"*Tithonus is trapped in the foundation of Olympus, Ganumede.* After Zeus abducted you, Eos found your brother, raped and burnt him, then brought him, like here to Olympus. Just like Zeus did you,"

Hermes took my hands, "Eos told the gods the sun would no longer rise if she didn't get her way, which was to use Ambrosia on Tithonus to make him available to her for all eternity.

"Zeus was furious at her insolence, for he ordered that none could give eternal life to a mortal but he already had—to you. Eos was right to feel entitled."

"What the fuck are you talking about?"

"Zeus agreed, but the gods never enter into a contract without an agenda, Ganumede, almost none of us anyway. He cursed your brother to live eternally but to age normally. Eos discarded him, the toothless bag of bones that he became; walled him up without food or water, light or company in the basement of Olympus. He cries and moans till Eos goes and beats him into submission and silence."

"*That bitch!*" I yelled. *"You too, Hermes!"*

"There is more," Hermes said.

The Rage of Ganumede

"*You son of a bitch! You asshole! I hate you!*" I screamed till my face was red and I almost puked. "So you loved this boy Krokus and you let someone murder him and now you're doing it again! Zeus is fucking trying to kill me! Fuck you both!"

I ran away.

"Ganumede, wait!" Hermes said. "You can't do this alone!"

I finally stopped running. I wiped my face, I went to the armory, took a spear, a sword, and went to the Aerie.

Zeus was watching one of the vids of me with Apollo, Hypnos and Thanatos in his scrying pond.

"Yeah, fuck that ass!" I mimicked those idiot twins who said that to each other all night long when they visited me.

Zeus casually looked away from the pond. His eyes were deep, bright blue. He was totally wasted on Ambrosia, "Since you're offering. Take off your clothes."

"Where is my brother?" I yelled back.

"He's not in the sexiest condition right now but I like how you think," Zeus laughed a huge barreling laugh. "Salt and pepper shakers! Meow!"

"This isn't Classics Class, Mr. Diaz, and I'm not a punchline. I never was." I threw the spear. It missed, horribly.

"But is the mountain top, Ganumede!" Zeus stood. His skirt fell and he was naked. His cock swayed between his legs like a battering ram being moved into position by an enemy cavalry.

"I am going to kill you for what you have done," I held up the Sword of Perseus. "And I know how to do it!"

Zeus paused, "You are very hot, Ganumede, and not the least in this warrior pose and fiery temper…!"

Zeus lumbered over, "But I don't care for your mouth! No one speaks to me this way upon my Seat of Power, no one lashes me with their tongue, and lives! But I will spare you and teach how to make it useful, that I promise you!"

He grabbed my hair and tried to push me onto his cock, but I still had the Sword of Perseus in my hand and I stabbed Zeus in the thigh. It didn't even scratch him.

"I know you must think that would make me angry," Zeus pounded on my face, my head, threw me this way, and then that way. The sky over Olympus turned the color of murex ink and a cold harsh wind swept across the Aerie, "But it turns me on. Quite a lot!"

Zeus dragged me by my hair and planted me on my back with a *Wham!* onto one of the benches near the scrying pond and held me down by my throat, "Especially when I get what I want anyway!"

"Little Brother, you should go downstairs and get into bed," *Hera Stella Maris* said.

She had a corona in every color around her head and every step toward us made the floor of the aerie hum. "This has gone on quite long enough. Let Ganumede go."

"*Why I would love to do that for you, you dozy cow*!" Zeus tightened his grip on my neck. "When I am quite finished with him!"

"Your reign as the King of Heaven is over," Hestia said, appearing on the Aerie, her corona burned bright like the gold fire deep in the Hearth.

"Do as Hestia said," Demeter said, her silhouette blazed in emerald and pink, blue and every color of the meadow. "We aren't fucking around with you."

I never knew if gods needed to breathe but, right then, I was pretty sure we did, and I was suffocating. I kicked and struggled but Zeus held fast.

"You didn't even bring weapons," Zeus said. "I'm quite impressed."

"Our hearts are our weapons," Hestia said, "and they are all you need against a tyrant."

The three goddesses encroached upon us, "What exactly do you think you are going to do, you vile sorry bitches?"

"We don't want to do anything," Hera said. "You're very drunk and have been up to some very improper activities and we just want to help you to get to bed. Now, please release the Cupbearer before one of your many sad stories has another chapter."

Zeus released his hand from around my throat and backed away, "Is that what you came her for, Boopis? Really? Or did you just want to see what it looks like when someone enjoys a good dicking?"

I stood up and walked toward the Sword.

"Don't you dare walk away from me!" Zeus said and grabbed my head.

"Let him go!" Hera shouted and her voice rang out, louder than the thunderclaps in the Olympus sky.

Zeus shrugged, "Okay."

He threw me over the side of the Aerie and into the Ether.

I fell.

The Form Cosmic

God's Such a Romantic!

The blackness of space became splashes of color. I could see everything; the beginnings of all things, their endings.

Babies born, leaving an infinite number of wombs, spiraling through their lives: their struggling, laughing, their crying. There were rivers and oceans of blood filled with the living and the dead, an infinite number of eyes crying tears, penises of every size, shape and color issuing sperm and piss, all manner of human beings… some living in filth, others basking in the glow of health; I saw them all born and then decay, before they entered an uncountable number of mouths to be squashed like grapes, bitten into like apples or drumsticks of poultry, spat out like they were foul to the taste.

Some of the souls laughed at this, some wept, and some were still.

I saw all of the gods and demons and angels we had ever created, that likewise had a role in creating us. Some vomited hate and rage into the universe, others hummed peacefully to themselves.

I saw beings of great beauty performing acts of atrocity across the surfaces of all the worlds, others, horrible to behold ministered with great empathy to the lost and suffering.

I saw more. A young man choked to death during violent sex with Phoebus. Another poisoned into eternal sleep and raped perennially by Phoebe; a young man, on a horse, brutally sodomized in the forest by Zeus, cast out in shame by his father so both of their secrets would be kept; another victim of Phoebus, a young woman, and yet another young man, Narkissus, the look of terror on his face brought on by Apollo marred his otherwise impossible beauty.

I saw a boy hauled into a pond to drown while nymphs sucked his cock and drained the air from his lungs, Bellerophon, the great hero of old, doomed to walk the earth forever, young and decrepit at the same time.

Tithonus, my brother, cursed the same as Bellerophon—trapped in a hole in the walls of Olympus, and Hermes playing disc with Krokus.

I saw the birth of Attis, his emasculation at his own hands due to the Curse of Zeus, his shame and wrath at being rejected in Olympus by the same. He was my best friend and I was supposed to be his.

I saw myself, not recognizing who I was or what happened to me on Ida. I saw my resurgence and all the terrible things that had happened since.

The colors and sounds, the pain and joy, the rapes, the ecstasy, the music, and the dissonance, it overwhelmed me and I started to scream my head off.

The din grew quiet and Hermes' arms and legs encircled me.

"Magnificent, am I not?" He gestured all around at the muted Cosmic Display.

Herme's face and form changed; he grew an elephant's trunk, the head of an ibis, he turned blue, white, then, yellow and red, he was a woman, a man, he had six faces, then just the one handsome face I'd become so enamored of.

"Yes, you're hot, but you need to stop doing that or I'm going to barf when you kiss me."

We fucked in every position, every place in history, those yet to be, in every body of every man that wanted another.

I was tall and short, he was black and white, had blue eyes and sometimes, he was blind. I was old, he was young, we fucked in trenches while bombs kicked up dirt and blood rained from the sky; we screwed like kangaroos and cried out in foreign languages while the submarine we were on flooded with water and he flooded me with his heat as my skin froze solid.

He took me back to the locker room and *yes, we shagged every last one of those losers in the mussy.*

Then…a man, a rabbit…and I was alone…

"Olympus is going to be besieged," Hermes said and it stopped. "There is much trouble there now. There is also a battle raging right now by the Tartarus

Gate. Only you, of whom the universe has finally stopped taking notice, can turn the tide."

"Tell me what to do," I said.

"Zeus is the King of the gods. Attis, The Resurgent, is now his equal. This threatens all order. If they fight, all of us will pay the price. If either wins, we will all suffer unspeakably.

"This is not new. Zeus has done this before in another world: inflicted his drunken, sensual, and illogical whims on others; they, being of great power, were able to cast him out.

"They are called the *Maruts*. They rear and ride the mighty storm-footed horses and they cannot be defeated by any means.

"The Maruts are led by the Storm Captain. He will be friendly to you. Tell him what has happened and obtain Soma from him, the favorite beverage of the Storm Soldier Army. It has power similar to Ambrosia, but it is also a cure for all afflictions. With it, you can free your brother and the others from Zeus' vile maledictions.

"If you think you are you able to accomplish this, I will send you there now."

"Well, fuck yeah I can!" I said.

"I believe you can." Hermes said, and opened a jump point in the Ether. "Take this," Hermes handed me the Caduceus, his staff. "The Maruts are fierce, you will need this to pass their muster."

"Got it."

"And please, Ganumede, keep your skirt on? They are quite randy."

Ganumede vs. the Maruts
Thunder and Lighting in Birthday Suits!

The jump point Hermes created tossed me right in front of a very angry looking storm cloud. Then I saw there were many of them, boiling with lightning and thunderclaps.

I was suspended mid-air in an endless sky. Above my head were snowcapped mountains, and they too started generating thunderheads which headed my way.

There were three flashes of lightning and three swarthy soldiers appeared in front of me. They were dressed in various colors and traditions, all which smartly observed a lack of need for clothing above the waist, all blocked the way with energy lances that danced in their hands.

"Hello Cupbearer, Zeus leave you feeling empty?" one said.

"No." I said.

"He definitely needs refilling," the next said.

"Not!"

"Flat, still, or sparkling?" the last one asked.

"Fat chance, Sparky!" I said. "Now cut it out! I need to talk to your boss."

I held the Caduceus up, "I have business here."

"We'd love your business," another said.

"Must it always come down to this? *Sheesh.* I am sure you're all a blast at parties but I really do have to see the Storm Captain. It's important."

"Afterward?" the last said. "After parties are the best!"

"Boys," A voice with clear authority said. "Keep your lightning rods stowed, if you don't mind."

"Yes, sir."

"Of course, sir."

"Right away, sir."

"Now, whom do I have the pleasure of…" the Storm Captain said to me, "welcoming or repelling from the Storm Front?"

"Welcoming!" I said. "Hermes sent me," I gulped. "I'm the…" I wasn't cupbearer anymore, and I wasn't a prince. I wasn't a boy or a toy or prostitute or a prisoner, "I am Ganumede, The Champion of Hermes."

"He would find that quite endearing, Ganumede, I am sure," the Storm Captain laughed.

"Be nice," I said.

"Any *champion* of that one is welcome here," the Storm Captain winked at me. "I am Marici and these fine dewdrops are my men. Have you come to enlist?"

He was indeed military leadership, the finest of the best. Tall, broad shouldered, scarred in all the right places, sensible sense of humor, a milestone of masculinity.

"Yo," I said. "You're all super fine and I'd love some basic training someday, but I really have to get down to brass tacks here. Can we talk? For real? My brother and my best friend are in deep shit, and I have to save them! I just have to!"

Chapter 10

The Secret of the Storm Captain

"He has done this before," the Storm Captain said. "Ran away from home to escape the Infernal Kronus. The Firmament was in chaos due to struggles of our own, and it was easy for a crafty young god like Zeus to slip and eventually take over.

"He called himself Indra then in order to disguise himself from the continual searching of his father. Then he proceeded to usurp the power of Rudra, the True God of Storms, and turned our world into his personal larder.

"Zeus-Indra used our most sacred elixir, Soma, invented to clear all strife and worry from the world to get drunk beyond measure. While he was intoxicated, he committed gross acts of impropriety, including the taking of many wives and young girls for his pleasures, and the more he drank, the more extreme his behavior became."

"Why didn't this…Rudra stop him?" I asked.

"He did," Marici said. "With us! See!"

I looked into the skies around us and I saw them then—many storm-footed horses, the riders, armored in brightly colored armor, helms, men, women, of every race and culture. Thunder and Lightning played about them, ripped from the torrential winds of the stallions and mares, sparks of lightning erupted in flares from their nostrils.

"Behold the Lightning Legion," Marici said. "Created by Rudra to dispel the glutton and criminal Indra from the sky."

"That's great." I said. "Now would it be okay if I got just a little of that stuff? People are waiting for me? I promise I won't let Zeus near it."

"No you will not!" Marici said, "We will make sure of that!"

"Huh?"

"We are going with you, Ganumede!" Marici said. "We should have killed this Zeus before when we had the chance."

"I have sent for a steed for you." Marici said. "We will breach Olympus's defenses, break your brother free, and then when we are clear of the combat zone, give this to your brother." He handed me a horn filled with Soma.

"Hot dog!" I said. And I, Ganumede, soldier in the Storm Army, mounted my storm-footed horse and rode with the Storm Soldiers to Olympus.

"What's your name big guy?" I asked the beast.

"Sugarhoof," It said. "The same as yours."

"Oh fuck," I said. "That's gonna stick."

Olympus Embattled

Creation Shaken and Rattled!

The walls were broken wedges, dust, and static electricity filled and choked the air.

The body of Ares hurtled through space, the end of him perhaps, but not of the War of Olympus he started.

"Did you think you could betray me and live?" Zeus punched Pallas as hard as he could but she remained on her feet, held upright by her spear. Her helmet lay dented nearby, her gown and armor were shorn, but she stood tall.

"I was born to betray you," Pallas said, her voice so deep and brazen it could be heard over the fighting elsewhere in Olympus and she struck Zeus in the shoulder with her spear.

Hermes zipped in, "Pallas, the Holy Trinity of Olympus is safe."

He said to Pallas, "And you!"

Zeus roared.

"Yes, I." Hermes said.

"Safe? Where? There is no place you can be safe from me! Nowhere!"

"We'll see…" Hermes yelped. An arrow, bright pink pieced his ankle; he fell backwards and tripped over the body of Herakles that Hebe was defending from Phoebus.

"Bitch, you think you can burn me?" Hebe said and flew through the air like a great cat and tore at his eyes.

Eros pointed his bow at Hermes' heart, "Oh how I am going to fuck you and fuck you and fuck you, Hermes! And never will you enjoy it! Oh how you are going to regret...!"

Then there was thunder and it wasn't Zeus' sort.

All the gods looked up into the firmament over wounded Olympus.

"My lover comes!" Hermes said.

Chapter 11
The Seventh House

"Can I cook or what?" Hestia showed Hera, Demeter, and the others through the massive complex. "I had help though."

Waiting in the Great Hall of Divine Mothers were those she had gathered to live, free of shame, fear, oppression, and limitation to do the real work of running the universe.

There at the Table were Medicine Woman and Oya, the Mother of the Wind; Sophia, the Mother of Peace; Ushas, the Bright, Prithvi; the Beloved Mother of the Earth, Branwen; the Lady, Rhiannon, the Silver Mare, Erzulie; the Beautiful Mother, Chalchiuhtlicue; Mother of Rivers, Coatlicue, who gave birth to the stars; Mazu, Mother of the Seas, and Amaterasu O Mikami, the Splendrous Goddess of the Sun. Others were invited and on their way.

"Hestia," Isis called out, carrying the burnt, but breathing form of Nepthys, her sister. "We were routed. Attis and an army of unspeakable creatures are coming here. I'm sorry we were followed but we had no choice. Many of us were hurt. Horus is trying to delay their approach but those...things he's raised up out of Tartarus...they're so horrible!"

"We are women and we are strong," Hestia said. "And so is our House. Battle stations, ladies!"

Hestia herself grew eight more arms, a crown of stars, and in each hand, a weapon of unattainable power appeared- swords, knives, spears, a bow and arrow, a hammer.

"There will be no serpents in our yard!" Hestia proclaimed and together with Sekhmet, the Lion, she rode with her sisters to defend the honor of the Seventh House.

"This shit is just nasty!" Oya laughed and boiled something that looked like an extra-large hot dog with a giant sphincter on one end, and a pair of Mick

Jagger lips with a huge tongue flapping out on the other. "Girl, where did he find these things?"

"You know men," Hestia said, "like their lips and assholes," and slashed her rapier through something that looked like Frank the Rabbit from Donnie Darko but it had a penis flopping around where each of its nipples should be. "Happy Easter, bitch!"

Olympus

Hermes and the Storm Captain

Here we go Again!

"Are you all right?" Marici helped Hermes to stand.

"Always," Hermes stood tall and replaced his helmet. "How are things?"

"We've recovered Ares and he is being treated with Soma, perhaps it will help him improve. Herakles is dead, Hebe is still chasing Phoebus and giving us intelligence. Hades never joined the fight nor did Poseidon, neither of which surprises me," Marici said.

"Pallas is leading a task-force to round up those that sided against humanity and the gods in favor of Zeus," Hermes said. "But so far no one has seen or heard from Ganumede!" Hermes asked.

"We have not seen him since you attacked Olympus," Marici said. "He mentioned an errand."

"You let him go by himself?" Hermes said. "With Zeus and the others on the loose yet?"

Marici laughed, "Hermes, we gave him the power of the *vajra*, the holy lightning. He is quite capable of kicking some ass should the need arise."

The Rage of Ganumede, Part 2

"Now!" I yelled, "Tell me now! Where is he?" I struck Eos with another thunderbolt. "Where is Tithonus, you twat!"

Eos tried to blind me, burn me, kick my nuts, claw at me with her nail tips and her fuck-me-hard stilettos, but thanks to my storm soldier armor and ability to shock her till her hair stood straight up, I was able to fight with her and enjoy myself. Oh…the hatred and spite I harbored for her!

"The labyrinth," she finally said, "I couldn't stand to look at him anymore and Zeus said—"

"Enough of what Zeus said," I stabbed Eos with the Caduceus and sent enough juice through it to fry North America.

And that was the last Dawn on the last day of High Olypmus.

The Seventh House

"Attis is not amongst the carcasses, Divine Mothers," Horus told the Assembly. "We think he sent the monsters after the Gods of Egypt to distract us, and went to exact his revenge on Olympus by himself."

"Perhaps he will get what he wants." Hera said. "Are all of us safe?"

"Every last one," Demeter said proudly.

"It's going to take a month to get this stink out of my hair," Oya said.

"Amen to that!" Hestia said shook gunk off her blouse. "What should we do?"

"Watch for now," Erzulie said. "Let them blow each other to hell."

"She is right," Amaterasu O Mikami said. "Why risk involvement when observation is more productive?"

"Attis has the Phallus of Osiris," Isis said. "And is the Father of Titans, Lord of the Living, and now, the Lord of the Dead. We cannot just...watch! Many will die and then walk again!"

"The Maruts and the Storm Captain have begun their assault upon Olympus," Ushas said. "They will settle things on Olympus and beyond. I'm going to go outside and smoke; then I suggest we all retire to the baths for cocktails and war stories."

"Deal," Hestia said.

"But what of Attis?" Isis asked.

"It will be okay, Mother Isis," Branwen, the Lady, said. "His friend is there."

Isis remained uneasy.

Olympus

Without Eos encrypting the location of Tithonus' cell, I was able to find it and with one flash of lightning, blow the wall open.

My gorgeous, beautiful and stupid brother lay like a mummy, shriveled and putrid on the floor of a chamber, only large enough for him to sit supine in. The eyes opened but he couldn't speak.

Olympus rocked and bucked. I didn't have time to administer the Soma and worried we would be caught during the final phase of Marici's plan if I didn't leave and go fast.

"Where exactly are you going?" Attis appeared in front of me, "Oh, I see! You're rescuing someone from the wrath of the gods. How sweet of you!"

Attis checked out his fingernails, scratched his balls. "It's thankless work, in spite of how noble it seems at the time. *Trust me*."

"Attis? Is that you? What happened?"

"You happened, you little bitch?" He said, and he grew tall, a not so jolly green giant, unlike the enchanting Attis I used to know. "You happened!"

"Everyone talks about your beauty. The Storm Front I just cut through to get to you was busy distracting itself over who would dip their wicks in you when it was all over! And all anyone talked about in High School was who and when was going to get to own that asshole of yours!

"I think I was the only one that was never attracted to you, Ganumede, and that hasn't changed. And I am so pleased I am going to be the one that decides definitely who gets to own you! NO ONE!"

"I'm a person, Attis, not a piece of property. And we used to be best friends. So can we settle this as friends after we leave here?"

"If I was a best friend to you," Attis said, "*like you were to me*, you would have died or been an outcast, left to be raped by other men, boys, and gods and then discarded when the scent of some other piece of ass caught their noses.

"But getting fucked was more important to you than rescuing me from Zeus and Rhea and I will never forgive you for that."

"I didn't even know that was you!" I screamed. "I would have done anything to help you! You know that! I was trying to help you kill Zoe and save the world remember?"

"I know it, Ganumede? *Do I*? How do presume to know what I know!" Attis brandished an immense sickle. "Here is what I know! I am going to castrate you and fuck you with your own cock!"

I stood up to him, made the Caduceus light up and crackle with the power of the vajra, "Attis, if you don't let me leave with my brother, I am going to murder you."

"Allow me to spare you the trouble." Attis pushed me aside and swung the great sickle.

Outside, in the Ether Local to Olympus

I would have preferred to continue to fight Attis. The power the Storm Soldiers gave me, baffled him, and frankly, I was so angry over just about everything, I just wanted to keep hitting and kicking and biting and having the same done to me. It felt honest on both sides, which was something new.

Then Horus showed up saying he wanted some cock.

"Wait your turn, dickhead!" I said, and continued my assault on Attis.

Marici and Hermes came also and broke us up.

"Horus," Marici said. "This fight must continue elsewhere."

"No!" Horus said. "He must not continue to possess the Phallus of Osiris!"

"HORUS!" Marici said. "Obey my commands!"

Horus left. Attis departed moments before anyway, sensing he was at a disadvantage when the other gods arrived.

"Hermes!" I pointed. "Attis hurt Tithonus! He might still be alive!"

"Ganumede," Hermes said. "The Maruts want to detonate the aconite warheads I planted in the core of Olympus. We have evacuated the other gods and divine beings, but if we don't blow the Core now, Zeus could escape and all this would be for nothing."

Hermes took me by my arms, "Ganumede…he's dead. We have to go."

"Do it then." I said.

Hermes pulled me to him and there was a sound like a gale rushing around us and we flew, fast, away from a bucking, cracking, smoking, and shuddering Olympus.

Marici turned his mount back toward Olympus as Storm Soldiers and Storm Footed Horses roared past, the sound and sight lightning brilliant in their wake and called out in a loud voice, "Destroy this place!"

The forces of the Maruts, the Storm-Footed Horses, Pallas and finally Poseidon and Hades brought all their weapons to bear on the target and the reign of Olympus ended in a bright flash of light.

"I have failed my brother again," I said.

"Failing people is what you do," Attis appeared out of nowhere and stabbed me in the side with the Sickle of Kronus.

If Marici hadn't given me the power of his Lightning, the *vajra*, even with the power of eternal life at my disposal, I wouldn't have survived Attis' scythe attack. That only left figuring out how to survive the loss of my brother. Again.

"He is escaping," Horus said. "We must get the Phallus of Osiris back."

"Yes, Horus," Marici was exhausted. "As soon as we regroup, we will help you get the Phallus back."

"I do not need help," Horus shouted. "Now let me be on my way."

Horus pushed him away and flew faster than the speed of light after Attis.

"Hermes. Marici," I said. "All this stuff that's happening…it's not Attis's fault."

"He killed your brother," Marici said. "This discussion had value before then."

"It has value to me now." I said. "I won't stand by and let Horus kill him. No matter what he's done. He deserves a chance to be free of the influence of the gods. He always did. Can we use this Soma stuff to turn him back?" I held up the horn filled with the Soma I had intended to use to cure Tithonus.

Marici shrugged. "I do not know, Ganumede. It just might make him worse."

"Please can we try?" I said to both.

"We'll try, Ganumede," Hermes said. "First, we have to reach him before Horus gets there or there won't be much point."

While Pallas arrested and detained criminals like Phoebus Apollo and Eros, Hermes shuttled the survivors of Olympus to the Seventh House.

Together, with Marici and the Storm Army, they cleared the field of any remaining Old Gods, searched and found all Lost Boys and Girls that were trapped in the Elysian Fields, ponds, forests, and grave plots; those who were abandoned by the gods or discarded them and sent them on to new lives.

Hermes and Krokus had an emotional reunion but, consistent with the advice of Marici and the Divine Mothers, agreed that all those that suffered at the hands of the gods during very short lives, would be returned to some other ample opportunity as recompense for the crimes committed against them.

All but the two that were left: Ganumede and Attis, who were deified and that is a one-way street.

"Now," Hermes said, "we have to go help Ganumede and Horus stop Attis. And we have to get the Phallus of Osiris back to its owner. Somehow."

"Where are they? Does anyone know?" Marici asked.

A scrying pool opened and the face of Horus appeared, "I found him or traces of him."

He hacked and coughed, "He dismembered Endymion, whose parts are more deadly than my father's and he seeks the power of Endymion's son."

"I don't understand," Marici said.

"The Phallus of Osiris, while potent, will not give up seed for him," Horus explained. "We know the phallus of Endymion to be deathless, is quite fertile, and is totally unconscious of its whereabouts. It will respond to its owner's desires."

"Sounds like any old cock to me," Marici said. "So, what's the big deal? Let him have it. Sounds like an easy way to get your pappy's peter back."

"You shut up!" Horus said. "There's more... If he successfully attaches the Phallus of Endymion and also steals the glamour of Narkissus, Endymion's son, Zeus's curse over him will be broken, and he will be able to raise an army of new Titans rapidly, as anything female will be unable to resist the call of his spark."

"I'm still lost," Marici said.

"Zeus cursed Attis and his mother." Hermes explained. "Anyone who might have potential to copulate with them goes mad at the sight of them and self-eviscerates to prevent intercourse and a new generation of Titans from being spawned."

"Jesus," Marici gasped. "Where are they?"

"I am struggling with him at Pace Nightclub," Horus said. "There is much chaos. Please come at best speed!"

"I know the place," Hermes said.

"We all do, Herm," Marici said. Then he called out in a voice as loud as thunder, "Storm Captain to Supreme Army! Time to dance!"

The Seventh House

"What the hell?" Persephone said.

"You rang?" Triune Hekate answered.

Persephone ignored her, "Mother! Come Quick!"

All the Divine Mothers gathered around the House Phone.

"They're going dancing!" Mazu said. "Without us!"

"That's not what that is," Isis said.

"No. We will lose the Phallus in that fight for sure," Nepthys said. "Those thunder beings are stalwart for order. They will not permit Attis to survive."

"No," Hestia said. "They won't. But if they fail, we will all be under siege again."

"What do you want us to do?" Hera asked her.

Hestia sighed, "Well, we just got prettied up. Let's put the go-go in goddess girls! Goddess of Crossroads, would you mind?"

"Not at all, Divine Mother," Hekate bowed her heads in reverence.

"Wait, where are we going?" Coatlicue asked.

"Pace Nightclub!" Hekate said. "Goddesses, prepare to jump."

"But what should we wear?" Chalchiuhtlicue wondered.

Too late.

Chapter 12

Time to Pick up the Pace

Pace Nightclub, Downtown Troy

BYOB, Bring Your Own, Boy!

"If he wanted to find a replacement dick, he came to the right place," Marici said. "Yowza!"

"I know!" Hermes said. "Do you see them?"

"Probably the place the bodies are moving through the air and not to the Rhythm," Marici pointed.

The music kept playing but, indeed, boys and girls, men and women, all mortals, started to fly through the air as Ganumede, Horus, and Attis struggled to get one Phallus from between Attis' legs and the other out of his hands.

"Storm Army!" Marici yelled over the mayhem. "Clear the dance floor!"

Caru, one of the Maruts who danced like a twat said, "Always do. Yikes! What are those things?"

Attis came with allies also. The Discarded Dead of Duat streamed in through the lights, the speakers, the smoke machines, the margarita fountains. All sex in the bathrooms came to a halt, too, surprisingly, when the apparitions of the damned erupted out of the toilets and shower-heads.

The only mortal that was able to withstand the dead for a moment was the DJ, of course.

"Don't even think of touching my pad, you son of a dog!" he said.

"Your spinning stinks," the ghost said. "They were playing this song when I was alive."

"Oh, no, she didn't!" the DJ said. "Suck on this, cunt!"

And the next tune rocked all the realms in all the directions, across all the membranes and horizons, and even made the Old Gods get down.

The ghost, satisfied, went to haunt some other—the tart on the main stage that thought his convulsions and spasms had the remotest chance of passing as dance moves.

Ghosts danced in formation on the main stage, took over the DJ booth, the lights, and even scared those kinds with lollipops and glow sticks that even Jesus couldn't frighten.

"What the fuck is this?" Hestia asked. "What are those things?"

She glared at Hekate, "Dunna."

"Oh yes you do!" Hestia frowned. "Girl do you have to be such a freak all the time?"

"Zeus is gone is he not?" Hekate said. "And the Disenfranchised of the Duat deserve to be judged, not left to float downstream into a frigid sea."

"Oh my goddesses!" Erzulie said and doubled over in laughter. "This is wonderful!"

"Oh no! I am not fucking around with this," Oya said. "Crazy bitches. Dancing around with their assholes hanging out while a Goddam apocalypse is trying to crawl up their cracks?"

"Like I said!" Erzulie clapped her hands to the beat.

Both Oya and Erzlulie were correct. Between the dancers that were rolling face, Horus, Ganumede, and Attis fighting over a bunch of detachable penises and the Storm Army kung fu fighting with the Duat ghosts, the fabulocity and mayhem alike were off the scale.

"Goddesses! Huddle!" Hestia said. "While the boys chase cock, let's figure out the shortest, easiest way to get this shit sorted out."

It was a wise thing to do. *Attis was almost under the disco ball.*

Dancing It off! At Pace Nightclub!
Shame it's Just a Stub!

"Horus! Let. Me. Handle. This!" I said and hung on for dear life to Attis's wrist, tried to weight it down so I could reach Endymion's dick, which was flopping around inside his fist like a fish he'd just unhooked.

"You've handled too many already, if you ask me, you whore!" Horus said to me as he grappled Attis's thigh.

"Yeah? Word is the early bird gets the worm in your part of town."

I made a blowfish face at him.

“*Idiots!* Get off of me!” Attis yelled. “Both of you!”

Attis put some gusto into it and I flew across the dance floor, leaving him to Horus’ heroics.

I was converged upon. I was hot enough to lure the King of the gods down to sample my goods. Imagine my appeal to a bunch of mortals, high out of their minds on ecstasy!

Cripes!

“Hekate, I want the skinny and no sweet,” Hestia said. “What do we do?”

“If we can get the penis parade to stop and separate Attis from the Phallus of Osiris without killing him and his green cock, there is a way.”

“Will I like this?”

Hekate’s heads nodded, “I promise there will be a happy ending.”

“I’m all for that! Tell us what to do.”

Triune Hekate, the goddess of witchcraft, children, and murder, then explained.

“Can you get these goddam sick things that keep pulling at my hair and clothes out of here?” Coatlicue said.

“Yeah!” Chalchiuhtlicue agreed and zapped one. “They unmake my face!”

“*No lo se*!” Hekate shook her heads, “Attis is their rightful master at the moment as he wears the Fabled Phallus. There is one among us that has a rapport with the dead, and I’m sure she’d be overjoyed at the thought of taking their reins! Am I right, Mother Erzulie?”

“DJ!” Mother Erzulie, goddess of life, death, and all the love, and hate and passion in between sang out, “Voodoo music, please.”

The DJ gave her a ‘thumbs up’ and Erzulie chanted,

“Stepitali Melutasi Rabubo Ro Ro Ka de Duat!

Stepitali Melutasi Rabubo Balika Ro Ro Erzulie Mama!

Hambuta Salika Te Te!”

(I name you, Spirits of the River Dua, my lovers of the Most Powerful Priestess Erzulie! Join me now and forever in this dance of love!)

The spirits stopped their assault on the club patrons and lined up for a super spooky bunny hop led by Mama, all of whom were then madly in love with her.

Marici held Attis in a head-lock, Horus wielded the scythe of Kronus overhead. Hermes found me and we raced to their location.

"Horus, stop!" Marici, unable to act against both Horus and Attis, yelled.

"I won't," Horus said.

"Don't!" I pleaded with him. "Horus, he'll die."

"I don't care about him!" Horus said. "We must restore the God of Life!"

Hermes zipped over the top of the tangle between Marici and Attis, retrieved Endymion's missing piece and pocketed it for safe keeping.

All that remained was yanking Attis' stolen luggage off of him.

Just as Horus raised the Sickle of Kronus, Hestia grabbed his hand. "Stop," Hestia said. "Just stop. Everyone. Miss?" She called over to the DJ. "Can we kill the music for a moment?"

There was silence.

"Attis, your mother misses you very much and I know you miss her. And it is not cool of you to run around with your step-dad's pickle stuck up in between your legs and you know it. Are we on the same page?"

Attis looked down, refused to answer.

"If I tell the Storm Captain to release you, will you stop acting like an asshole and talk this over with us? We have a solution to all of this, but we can't make it work if you don't cooperate. If you don't, there is enough firepower in this crew to blow your sorry ass to kingdom come. There is no way out and I am not asking twice…do this my way and things will be fine if not…?"

"You're going to send me to Tartarus?" Attis said softly.

"That is not an option," Hestia looked about. "So are you going to let us be nice? Is everyone willing to do that still?"

The assembled divinities agreed.

"I agree then." Attis said.

"Now, we are going to take the phalluses of Endymion and Osiris back to their owners and then we are going to all pray like hell and make this right."

Attis wept, "I am defeated, Hestia. Please do not make me endure emasculation in public again."

"Horus?" Isis stepped forward with Nepthys, a sarcophagus between them. "Please step away from Attis with that blade. We can handle this from here."

"Yes, Mother," Horus said and backed away.

“Storm Captain?” Hestia gestured.

“I’m going to let go,” Marici said to Attis and released him. “Do what these pretty ladies say now, you hear?”

“Piss off,” Attis said but complied.

“Ushas and Pvrithi,” Hestia said, “you’re next. Attis, we’re going to remove the Phallus of Osiris and return it to its proper owner, Ganumede is going to give you Soma to remove the curse of Zeus from you and then we have a surprise.”

Ushas and Pvrithi cast a spell on Attis and all assembled, so that none could see what took place, for the procedure was secret.

Together, painlessly, while sweet music played, Ushas and Pvrithi caused the Phallus of Osiris to leave Attis’ groin and the lid to the sarcophagus to open. It floated inside and then the lid closed.

The lights, glimmer, and music faded and while they waited, Attis, less his virility, became a green weed of a man/god and started to wilt.

Ganumede held him and gave him Soma to sustain him until Good Osiris, the Friend to All, rose from the box, and stepped out.

“Ohh,” he said. “Oh Dear! This looks quite serious.”

“Husband,” Isis approached and took his hand. “This is my son, Attis, the Father of Titans, and he is gravely ill. Can you help him?”

“I don’t see why not!” Osiris laughed. “What is the problem?”

They explained briefly what had happened starting with the day he rescued Nana, his wife, now called Isis, from the wrath of Rhea on the wedding day of her son, Attis, who lay before them.

“Oh that’s right! Well, of course!” Osiris laughed again. “How big do you want it?”

“Huge,” Ganumede said. “Hung low, big shooter, multiple orgasms…grows, shows, and glows!”

“I hate you,” Attis said.

“No haters!” Osiris said and. “And done! Woo hoo!”

Attis stood, and Marici instructed one of his lieutenants to clothe him properly.

The crowd cheered. The music started.

Then Osiris, the Good and Kind Lord, freed the vile, vicious, and nearly forgotten gogo boy Narkissus from the disco ball.

Chapter 13

Later, the Seventh House

Attis sat calmly, his mother and aunt Nepthys holding his hands on either side of him.

The Green God was gone, returned was Attis, the son of Innana, the second most beautiful male form ever made and he even had a penis, too.

"Attis," Hestia, Divine Mother, said carefully. "In spite of your many guises and transformations, you are still the Father of Titans. There is nothing we could do about that. Até demands you be erased from creation," she saw Attis flinch. "But that is not our way. We expect each person to find and forge a destiny free of interference and without being the cause of it in the lives of others."

"Why don't you just tell me my penance, then Hestia," Attis said, he was still quite depressed. "And let me be on my way."

"No penance, Attis," Isis said. "We have to move past that. All of us suffered from the rule of tyrant gods, old rules and invisible forces that seemed irrefutable but, here, together, we are capable of finding a better way."

"My question remains, Mother," Attis said. "I'm a prisoner here, am I not?"

"After a fashion," Pallas said. "Your spark can create the situation we just narrowly escaped. We are all aspects of the Great Mother, so we know how important it is for you to feel and make love, but until we find a way that is safe for everyone, we ask you to abstain."

"Is this something you can commit to?" Hestia asked. "And it's a question, not a threat."

"For now, yes," Attis started to cry. "But please, not forever."

"We hope not," Demeter said.

"Please do stay here, in the House, until then," Hera said. "Hestia and our sisters have done an amazing job of making it a beautiful and verdant place to live. You will not grow tired of it. And all of your friends are here, too."

"Hey," Ganumede said and entered the room, hand in hand with Hermes. "You okay?"

"Actually, Ganumede, I think I would like some time to myself," Attis said.

Epilogue 1

Hestia and the Divine Mothers

"Any news on that other matter, Pallas?"

"No. There were no traces of Zeus in the rubble but there are none in the Ether either."

"And we are certain his Providence has ended?"

"Possibly," Pallas nodded. "He's gone, his influence is not. We will need to keep watch."

"So what now?" Ushas asked. "We return home to see whose walls his Infernal Soul breaches next?"

"No." Pallas said. "Now that Osiris is back, He calls the shots, and He has ordained that Hestia take over as the Steward of this House of Equals and together we will ensure that all houses everywhere are safe from that Devil. All Devils!"

"Are you all right with this Hera? Hestia?"

"I can think of no one better for this role than Hestia," Hera said.

"Then I accept!" Hestia smiled. "And the other matter? We are down one goddess of the dawn."

"I have an idea for that," Mother Isis said.

Epilogue 2

Still in the Seventh House

"Ganumede," Hermes said. "There's something you should know."

"It's Krokus, isn't it?"

"No…" Hermes said. "His *Ka* is now in another body and he and I will never meet again."

"Okay. Phew!"

"There is another matter." Hermes said. "They named the new god of the dawn."

"Fabulous," he said. "As long as it's not me."

"Vanity is such a terrible thing to waste," Hermes said. "It's not you this time but your nephew. Nefertem."

"Ain't gots none," I said. "Must be a mistake."

"No, it's not a mistake," Hermes explained. "Tithonus and Eos made a baby."

"Tithonus made a baby?"

"Yes."

"Hermes," Ganumded said, his ruddy cheeks blushed hot. "For real? Like he put it in there and…?"

"Horus is bringing him here—Nefertem- from Heliopolis shortly. I suggest you compose yourself and try to set a proper example. Can you do that?"

"I think I'm okay with everything but the Horus part."

"I know! What a cunt, right?"

Nefertem looked just like Tithonus but he was very tan, with cute rosy cheeks and bright eyes, and he didn't smell bad.

"That Horus is such a cunt! Dam!" Nefertem said, after Ra of the Horizon returned to his duties in the Western land.

"Get out of bed! Do your chores! Don't play with Sekhmet's tits," Nefertem complained. "Almost as much fun as a penis wart!"

"You touched athe war goddess lion's…udders?" Ganumede asked.

"She suckled me when Hathor went dry."

"O-kay. Wasn't that a bit…risky?" Hermes almost laughed.

"Not if you do it right."

"I'm not sure I'm tracking," Ganumede said.

"I'm a bastard god, so I couldn't suckle any of the human shaped ones."

"Ew," Both Hermes and Ganumede grimaced.

"And you kept going back after you were weaned?" Ganumede asked.

"Horus wouldn't go near her. Birds/cats, natural enemies, duh?"

"He's definitely your nephew," Hermes said.

"So you're Auntie Gee?" Nefertem gave Ganumede a big hug.

"Yes, that's me," Ganumede said. The hug was uncomfortable at first. Nefertem looked and acted a lot like Tithonus before they both grew older and angrier at each other and stopped showing each other affection.

"*Oh my goodness! A baby!*" Mrs. O, Oya, ran over to inspect the new God of the Dawn. "Look at these cheeks! So…perky!" She gave Nefertem's love seat a squeeze.

"Why is there a black lady fondling the Wonder Bread?" Nefertem squirmed away.

"Don't be flattered," Ganumede laughed. "It's to make sure you aren't smuggling anything."

"Like what?"

"A vagina."

"*A vagine*?"

O did the final inspection.

"Yeah, hey, ho! Squeezing the weasel is a no go!" Nefertem said and did a little twirl to get away.

"I think we should probably explain," Ganumede said. "Strange women are not allowed in the Seventh House. And a few have been trying…"

Later, when Nefertem met Attis, he followed the same unyieldingly improper decorum.

"You're him?" Nefertem squealed. "That guy?"

"Which guy, Nefertem? We live in a temple of the Divine Mother. There are so many of us."

"Attis."

"Yes. I'm him," Attis said,

"Neat! Dude, so is it true?"

"Is *what* true?"

"That you're super-hot, but it's all for not?"

Sigh. "You're special, aren't you?" Attis said.

"Extra." Nefertem said. "So you really don't hook up?"

"No."

"Are you really waiting for your wedding night? Cuz…it doesn't count if…"

"Nefertem," Attis said. "No, I'm not waiting for my wedding night. Listen…"

Attis explained.

"*Holy snot!*" Nefertem exclaimed, "For real? Your stuff can make a baby Godzilla?"

"No…" Attis blushed. "That's not really what I was trying to say."

"In other words," Ganumede said, entering the room, "we don't know and we don't want to find out."

"We don't?" Nefertem asked as if everyone were stupid. He could not help it. *Attis was so handsome.*

Here Ends the Rage of Ganumede

Post Script

Narkissus of Thesipae had to be sent out of town to finish school. The scandal and all.

He ended up at Troy Finishing School and became the Sweetheart of the Javelin/Bowling Leagye/Glee club and, ultimately, the boyfriend of you guessed it, the Most Illustrious Travis Interstate.

How did that go?

Cue *'Uptown Boy'* by Punkin' Stuff.

Uptown boy, you act like you're so coy

But when it all comes down,
You're the circus and I'm your clown...
I bet you've never bowled with a backstreet boy
Stand still for me, I'll knock you down
And then I'll pass you around...
Still you're my boy and I'm your man,
That's what I am
And then he knows that's what he's for
We'll hit the alleys and then we'll score
And when he wakes up
And makes up his mind
He'll realize that he's still mine...
He'll see I'm not so tough
Just because
He likes it rough...
Uptown Boy, you've been living
Like my toy,
But, now, it's gone all over town
And you've been found in
The dog pound...and you've got no choice
Can't use your voice...
Uptown boy with your string of pearls,
I'm a downtown boy can't afford a ring, that's the thing,
But give me half a chance
I'll rock your world
And when the ship comes in,
All the sailors will be your friend...
Another hit by Punkin' Stuff the whole family can sing along to.

Biscuit Boy Breakup

By Punkin' Stuff (AKA Nefertem, the Hip Hop Egyptian Boy-God of the Dawn).

Biscuit boy, biscuit boy, you got me broke up 'cuz you broke down took your Bisquick downtown...

Squeeze the molasses

Don't need glasses, See no one but you
But hell yeah, Baby, bring him too!
Want cowboy butter on my steer
Want you back, want you near,
Pop the can,
Biscuit boy, you're my man,
Let's 'bake' 'em up, turn 'em tan
Golden brown, I'll follow you anywhere
Even…downtown

Lucky Pair
By Mantona[1]

You must be my lucky pair
A top and a bottom, you're always there
And when I lay me down to sleep,
Its pajamas my soul to keep!

At night, PJs in bed
Pajamas are what momma said
PJs at night and in the day,
They'll take you far, take you all the way!

Grandpa said those pajamas went to his head
Made him gay and then mama said,
That's a lie. It's what you're supposed to do
Then Grandma said,
"Straight guys wear them too! in blue and in red!"

Grampa, Grampa, please don't preach
Mama's alright, she's okay
She threw the polyester ones away,

At night PJs in bed

---

[1] Mantona is Greek for "Madonna" – Mama Mia! -Michael.

Pajamas are what momma said
PJs in white satin
And also in red

Book 2: The Absolution of Attis

Chapter 1

Before That

A lost but not forgotten boy
Cue the Outrage of Orion

Orion was the sole son of a farmer and merchant and that meant he was both privileged and put upon.

He preferred privilege and spent a great deal of time with his father's quartermaster, learning marksmanship in particular.

When he became a man, his father gave him a horse of stark white, to some an insult as they are easily seen from a distance and disturb the hunt.

Orion accepted the gift eagerly and his skill with the bow grew in magnitude.

A youth on a white horse was far too delicious for Great Zeus to turn away from and so, he entered the forest as a magnificent stag. Zeus lured Orion deep into the woods, kept his magnificent steed at a steady gallop till they were far from the boy's house. Upon first opportunity, Orion was violated.

It was not an honor to be the only son of the house and also the bonbon of a stag, especially since Zeus in his hubris, made a deliberate point of running past Orion's father before Orion could recover and put an arrow in it. Prior to that, the beast charged Orion's prize horse and scared it into the woods.

When Orion's father learned the rest, he was so ashamed he could not face the young man again.

Orion was forced to leave home and wandered for years, hunting alone to prove himself, eventually finding the stag waiting in the woods for him once again.

Zeus was bad but not evil. Instead of violating him again, Zeus showed regret for the harm he'd done to Orion and offered him an exalted place in the stars and a palace all his own.

He marked the sky with a magnificent constellation and fed romantic dreams about it to astronomers, soothsayers, comic book writers and doe-eyed twinks of every era.

Beware Kings offering palaces to former lovers, especially those whose beauty and masculinity they envied.

He clearly meant for Orion to spend eternity up there all by himself.

The Legend of the Marcus Prefect. From Hekate's Cahier.

After Olympus was no more, Até the Great Goddess of Mischief and the Downfall of gods and heroes alike, helped Zeus transmigrate to the next stage of our troubled existence.

We, I, did our best to rid the universe of the miserable creature, but because misery is persistent and we love it so, Zeus survived our attack. He was vaporized, poisoned—irradiated with aconite—the deadly toxin of the gods, and still some aspect of him made it, and *it was not good.*

Até, the Cosmic Arbiter of Success, took that last poisonous thorn of a god and turned him into something else, something that could fulfill her designs, without the son murdering the father routine. That never worked. Ask Jesus Christ, Hermes…the others.

Born again thus was the Marcus Prefect, The God of War, the Hammer and the Anvil of Isaiah, aka the Ancient Adversary of Man was back, this time as "*The Lord that Marks*" the Final Emperor.

"What say you about this?" Até asked Marcus about his appearance.

"It's perfect," Marcus admired himself on the Surface of the Sea of Infinity. "Absolutely Perfect."

"What will you do now?" Até asked.

"Settle old scores and create new ones, of course."

Até was impartial to her own motivations at all times so she could do her work effectively, but this time she said, "What a doosh," and returned to her exalted position at the Center of the Universe as the arbiter of Destiny.

And what did I do? was no longer a Triune; I made My House and equipped it well. I had many more heads, eyes, hands, breasts, at my disposal now, and fully planned to use them forge a few new and cool destinies myself.

Hell to Pay

The new deification of the Unholy Spirit, the Marcus Prefect, was immensely powerful. Hades was not able to withstand Marcus's might and was subsumed.

"What is that, Hades?" Marcus craned his ear. "No one coming to your aid? Hmm. How that must feel!"

"Who are you?" Hades spat black ichor from his mouth. "I don't even know you!"

"It didn't matter to you when you did." Marcus said. "And now I am what I am. I am God, The One. The Everlasting."

Marcus threw a punch that crushed the basalt helm of the Lord of the Underworld down upon his head, and Hades Unseen was never seen again.

Marcus cleared out the Underworld. He thought it was pathetic. Understated, ineffective. He had some ideas for how to fix that.

He greatly enjoyed the thought of designing new ways to torture, punish, and repay all the souls he would put into a new hell of his own manufacture.

Just before he folded Hades' Underworld back into the Ether forever to make room for Hell, he heard music playing. *Fever* by Peggy Lee. An old favorite of his!

He walked along a corridor toward the sound. There was a door, partly open. Soft light came from behind it and the smell of rose incense was heavy.

Marcus pushed the door open; carefully, worried the Unseen had stored away one last beast or trap for unsuspecting intruders.

Seated at a dressing table, her back turned, was a youngish woman with long tawny red tresses, running a brush through them.

"Hekate?" Marcus asked.

"No," the woman turned and faced him. "Something much, much worse."

"Ahhhh. *Jezebel in Hell*," Marcus laughed. "Of course. It's been so long."

"Probably," she said. "Nice outfit. And what are you calling yourself these days, Yahweh?"

"Let's not use that name again, shall we? Gets one in trouble, you know?"

“I’m familiar with that kind of trouble,” Jezebel leered. “You may recall.”

“Marcus Prefect,” Marcus bowed his head. “But you can call me Perfect.”

Jezebel was silent, “Have you come to destroy my soul at last, Marcus… Perfect.”

“Not at all! Why don’t you finish getting dressed and we can…catch up. I could use your help, I think. And I know you can make use of mine!”

Jezebel smiled, her most seductive and sultry smile she could make, “I’d like that.”

While she finished applying her makeup and chose a gown, she asked, “So, tell me, Marcus, how did you make this happen?”

“I am the Resurrection and the Life,” Marcus said. “My own, of course! Always!”

Chapter 2
Rabbit on the Run

Medicine Woman. The Seventh House

Medicine Woman oversaw the nursing of the wounded gods of Heliopolis and monitored the final closure of the Olympus Event Horizon.

The last of the Storm Army jumped away, there was a flash of light, and Olympus was gone.

Then, almost unnoticed, was one, tiny, little spark that exited the blast radius. A white rabbit.

"Mother Isis," Medicine Woman said. "Are you well enough for me to leave briefly?"

"Where are you going?" Isis asked.

"Hunting," Medicine Woman said.

***

Medicine Woman in Her Form as an owl tracked the rabbit to the Constellation of Orion.

"Mother!" The Hunter said to Her when She arrived. "I missed! I mother-fucking missed!"

"Hunter, where did it go?" Medicine Woman asked. "It's not a rabbit."

"No, it's not," Orion said. "It was trying to be indecent with me when you showed up."

"Hunter, this is quite urgent. Let us work together," Medicine Woman said.

"Of course," Orion said. "But what is that thing?"

"A demon fetish," she said. "And it must not survive."

They split up. Medicine Woman searched from the air, Orion on the ground.

She heard a cry and descended to find Orion, unconscious, the rabbit sitting on his chest. She extended her talons and dove. Fast.

Medicine Woman clasped the rabbit and threw it into a tree. She assumed her human form. Medicine Woman then took out her axe and approached the rabbit.

"Aren't you the least bit curious about me?" the rabbit asked.

Medicine Woman attacked it. She nailed it in the hind leg as it attempted to jump.

"That actually hurt, you piece of shit!" the Rabbit wailed. "And you know, I never did like your kind. So high and fucking mighty all the time with your earth magic and 'heya' here and a 'heya' there…I can't wait to…"

"Your opinions are clearly relevant to me, rapist rabbit!" Medicine Woman said. "How did you transmigrate into this form?"

"I am my own ancestor, you stupid bitch," the Rabbit said. "And now my own divine predecessor."

"Either way, you are not going to last," Medicine Woman charged the Rabbit again. It tried to escape and she cleaved its hind leg off.

"Yes. Do it," the Rabbit said. "Send me to Hades."

"That is where you belong it is so true," she said and cut its head off. There was a burst of black flame and smoke that smelled of bay laurel.

Medicine Woman hung her head for a moment. Her Ancestors were crying out to Her, warning Her. A New Order had just been created and it made the one before seem paradisiac in comparison.

She returned to the unconscious body of Orion the Hunter and took him to the Lodge.

Marcus and Jezebel
Things are Going Well
Time Will Tell

"How did you manage to get into a mess like that?" Jezebel asked and packed up the last of her things. "Why not just come here first?"

"I had no other way of getting here. And, besides, I thought it might be fun to fuck that punk up before I made the slip," Marcus said. "Are you almost ready?"

"Sure, but what now?"

"I used most of my legacy of power to dispatch Hades. But we're going to get more, don't you worry."

"How?" Jezebel asked. She loved power.

"Fear, my dear," Marcus said. "We are going to scare the shit out of everyone and everything, till heaven is so far out of reach, and hell is so…infernal that we will get all the power we have ever wanted by promising the one and delivering the other."

"I like this plan," Jezebel said. "Tell me what you need me to do."

"We poison the oceans next," Marcus said. "Once fish start washing up and the air becomes thin, my disciples will seek succor and salvation from My Church. Works every time."

Nefertem Eavesdrops

"Tithonus is dead because of me," Attis said. "I am sorry it took me so long to tell you how sorry I am."

Ganumede shrugged. "I accept your apology. It's fine."

"You must still hate me," Attis replied.

"Do I…did I…act like I hate you?"

Auntie was always passive aggressive. Instead of saying what he really felt, he made faces and placated the people that tried to talk to him as soon as possible.

"No, and that's what shames me."

"Don't be ashamed," Ganumede hugged him but Attis recoiled. Dude needed to chill the fuck out. It was an apology and a heartfelt one at that. It wasn't like Attis was trying to *fritz his schnitzel* or something!

Still Auntie Ganumede pretended, "Tithonus was doomed the moment Eos saw him. I've come to accept that. We're totally good. I promise."

Attis looked so sad, finally gave up and left. He was way too cute to deal with that shit!

I didn't care what it took. I was going to make Attis Gladys.

Chapter 3

Here Begins the Absolution of Attis And the Destruction of the Earth Courtesy of the One True God, Marcus Perfect

3.1 Ishtar in the Underworld

I was a housewife. Whoever came into the whorehouse, I married! if they wanted me to dress like a goddess or whip their asses like a slaver, I did that, too.

Using the spells the 'serpent' taught 'Eve' about pleasure, I would change the color of my hair, my skin, I resembled and performed however the men and women that visited paid me for. I always threw in a little extra for free if they turned me on and I wanted them to come back.

I loved it. I know it's a sin to enjoy watching people squirm and thrash about and howl as you give or take what you need in bed, but that's what made me the world's best and most legendary whore.

It was lucrative and very secure until *the man* decided the wages of my sins were no longer payable in cash.

One of the first things Eve passed on to all of us was this one piece of advice, "It's okay to blow a man, never bow to him."

When the holy men came to shake their fingers and cocks at me, this advice served me not well at all.

They said I had to quit my job and really get married! To a real husband! I was devastated and they left without paying!

"And, Jez, the devil worship needs to stop too," they said.

"Her name is Ishtar and she's not the devil," I said.

"Even so," they said. "Stop it."

"Assholes."

I went through my little black book of spells and found the one. If I had to get married, *boy was I going to get married!* The next day, the King of Babylon came and proposed.

Like all High Priestesses of Ishtar, in addition to being a whore I was also a witch, and was even better at witchcraft than I was at whore craft and those bastards that came into the Temple and fucked things up knew it.

After I married the King and sent him home, they came back and they brought witches of their own. They called them Rabbis.

"Jezebel, seriously. That was a neat trick with the King but we fixed that and he knows what you did. And like we said before, this Ishtar shit has to stop, you have to get married and settle down in some hut somewhere, not in a Temple, but like a good second hand or second hundred hand woman would do and give some nice hide tanner a son. Whattaya say?"

"And what if I don't?"

"The One True God will smite thee."

"Never heard of him. Must be a figment of your imagination," I said. "Be gone."

I cast a spell and made them fuck each other good and rotten.

Later when I was getting ready for some action with the King, who was once again my lover, a voice said, *"He's real."*

"Who is?" I asked.

"The One True God, called Yahweh, the Lord Your God."

"Huh?" I said.

"And you shall have no other Gods."

"That's okay for you!" I said. "But I'm cool with the gods I've already got, thanks!"

"*I am an angry and jealous God*," It said. "So bow to me now as a sign of your subservience and willingness to please me, follow my commandments thereafter, and thou shalt be saved."

"I don't need saving, you cocksucker!" I said. "And you sound like a total asshole and I want you to go away! I prayed to Ishtar to dispel the demon, but she didn't respond."

I was hit and thrown from a window by the world's earliest recorded bitch slap.

I landed on the sidewalk in a puddle of maggot infested filth and was then consigned to an eternity of isolation and loneliness in the Underworld until that same God who presently called himself 'Marcus Prefect' found me again.

I was glad to be free, but I was still pissed. I was going to exact my revenge on Ishtar and all she loved and held dear, which was everything Marcus Prefect wanted, too.

And when I was done with both of them, I was going to do the world right as The One True Holy Mother.

Empusas Galore!

It's me, Jezebel again. I was the first of a lot of things, including the creation of a race of women loving vampires. They weren't really called anything, not at first. They were just ordinary women that couldn't sleep at night. I made them what they were to give them a chance to be young, beautiful, totally desirable, and absolutely dangerous and deadly should the need arise.

I mentioned I had a 'tendency' to take advantage of my paying clients and those that couldn't pay, too. They made it up in trade by servicing me and my friends and everyone ended up being happy. I made sure of that.

After I was exiled, my sisters exacted a little too much trade from the holy men that continued to visit the Temple. A few of the bastards got out of hand and went missing.

These things happen to people who visit illegal whorehouses.

When their wives got worried, they sent out search parties. Our favorite kind of party… "What do you mean you don't know where your sister's or daughter's husband is?" they'd say, and shrug.

For the most part they got away with it but then one night, this not-so-nice Jewish boy figured out he was on the menu and tried to run away. But vampires are very fast.

They caught him, only just barely but not his buddy. Assholes and dickheads always travel in packs to whorehouses, you girls (and boys) know this.

After he got back home, he told everyone what he knew. Surprise, Yahweh was not happy about a bunch of lesbian vampires operating out of the Best

Little Whorehouse in Babylon, and consistent with His pattern, sent some potbellied fleabag with a beard and a funny hat to read out of a Book at them.

"You are cursed," Rabbi Sundevich said, "to live forever and to have most of your appetites insatiable. You will chase men and men only in order to survive, and seldom will you catch them."

Thus Yahweh created the race of Empusas, simply stunning lady vampires that sported a brass leg and the hoof of a donkey. It is very difficult for an Empusa to dress provocatively and still be able to eat. It is similarly challenging to re-obtain food when you can barely walk, much less run, if it escapes.

They tried to create thralls and servants by passing the Gift along but they, too, just became deformed like their mothers and sisters.

What to do but get goddam mad about this?

Yes! Do that, trust me, and dream of revenge. I didn't waste my time when I was in Hades. I learned a few things. Met a few interesting personalities. Made some plans.

After Marcus Prefect set me loose upon the world after His former Self locked me away, I found my old sisters, decrepit, aged, laying in filth in buildings that were bombed out during the war between Mideaum and Troy ages before and told them to spread the word.

Soon, it would time for stilettos and fuck me pumps for everyone.

The Seventh House
Nefertem
Not Minding His Own Business
What he's up to is anyone's guess

"He's gone," Ganumede told Attis. "Just gone."

"Are you sure?" Attis asked.

"Yeah, I'm pretty sure. He didn't tell me he was leaving and he's definitely gone."

"He is the Messenger of the Goddesses," Attis said. "He runs around a lot. Maybe, there was an emergency takeout taco incident."

"This isn't that!" he said. "I checked with all of them. Especially that creepy Erzulie. None of them sent him anywhere."

“He’ll be back,” Attis said. “I’m sure of it.”

Fat Chance Albert. Hermes told me he was leaving, and to do my best to explain to my uncle on his behalf. It was time he said; Creation was retiring him, and everyone at the House that didn’t understand what that meant would eventually just accept it. Eventually it would be their time too. *Gods like everything else, are impermanent.*

“Why are you telling me this?” I was pissed and I made sure to sound like it. “You’re his partner! You should go tell him you’re leaving him! What the fuck is wrong with you!”

“I was his lover, Nefertem,” Hermes shook his head. “And I do love him. But lovers leave, partners stay.”

“What the fuck does that mean?”

“Just remember what I said, Nefertem,” Hermes said.

And the bitch left without even leaving a note. I was the only one who knew, or knew why. And I didn’t know how to tell my Uncle. Talking to him about anything was painful enough!

I tried to cheer him up first, hoping that would give me a chance to run him over with the bus and step on the gas.

“Hey, Auntie,” I said. “Want to go play leapfrog with Heqet?”

“Want to stop being an idiot for a change?” he said.

“I’m trying,” I said. “Do you want to play Tomb Raider with me then?”

“No.” He said. “Go away.”

Chapter 4
Hunting for Sport

The Hunter's Lodge

Orion woke up to Spanx's snoring.

"Crikey that's annoying!" Orion grabbed his sword which was tucked in its scabbard which hung from the bedpost by its very famous belt. He withdrew the sword by its gold and jeweled hilt and banged it on the massive creature—a hybrid between a lion and a brass dragon's head. It clanged like a bell.

Spanx cracked open an eye, which was green and red like hammered copper.

"You're naked," he said.

"Yeah. How'd that happen?" Orion asked pulled the sheet up around himself.

"That Shaman Goddess brought you in that way," Spanx said. "She asked me to watch over you in case the Playboy Bunny came back to knock on your wood again."

"Playboy bunny? Oh fuck me!" Orion said and searched his body for any rogue sensations. He felt good as new and glad he didn't remember much after Medicine Woman told him about that…what did she call it? A demon fetish?

"Did She get the bastard?" he asked.

"She killed it, I ate it," Spanx belched fire and the sound made the whole lodge shake. "*BURP*!" he said.

"*You toe rag*!" Orion said. "You are cleaning the soot of my fucking curtains now, you know that right?"

"I'll meet you there," Spanx rolled his clinking, clanking form over the side of the bed which had collapsed from his weight while Orion was unconscious. "Look for me. I'm gonna be there…"

"Get the fuck outta here," Orion stood and surveyed the damage to his bed.

“And fix my goddam bed and the hole in the wall and hallway you fucking broke on your way in! Gods, you know I love you but we’ve had this conversation before. You stay under the staircase when you visit!”

“Not this time.” Spanx shook his scales and they rattled and cast glittery light on the walls. “When Medicine Woman said you were hurt and that I needed to watch over you, that’s what I did.”

“You didn’t do your business on the rug anyplace, did you?” Orion checked around the floor.

“That’s not important right now,” Spanx glared at him. “Nice ass, by the way.”

“Hand me my clothes, please?” Your huge ass is blocking the way to my closet.

“Pass,” Spanx made a kissy sound.

“No, not pass!” Orion said. “Now quit this screwing around. I want to know more about that demon fetish. Right away. There was something peculiar about it.”

“You’re telling me!” Spanx said. “I think I’m gonna have a mud slide!”

Interlude
The Seventh House
Nefertem and Attis

“I’m bored,” Nefertem said.

“Tell me about it,” Attis said.

“Dude, I’m telling you! I check to be sure that all the stars in orbit around all the planets are on track, and nothing I do is ever right, and then I sit here and do nothing!”

“Try having those bitches tell you that you can’t do anything but nothing,” Attis said.

“That Japanese bitch is the worst,” Nefertem said. “*We would like to make happy request for you to be more punctual*, she says in that *tone* of hers!”

“So ignore her,” Attis said, “and show up on time.”

“And there’s not enough *boyage* here,” Nefertem moaned. “After I get back from the Ether, I masturbate like twelve times an hour and then wait for a recharge, you know?”

Attis laughed, "Yeah, I kinda feel you on that. There's not way too much girlage here either!"

"Attis, do you ever think—"

"Nefertem, no," Attis said. "I don't think. You're adorbs, I'm sure, but please go find someone *like you* that is your own age."

"But we're both immortal! You *are* my own age! And if we do nothing together, well…that would be something! And I hear it's got to be seen to be believed! So why don't you…?"

"You probably are the only person here who hasn't seen it, it's true, but I'm afraid that's going to have to be the way things stay."

"But that's not fair!"

Attis sighed and put his arm around Ganumede' nephew's shoulders, "I've done this before, Nefertem, and I'm very compassionate about it, trust me, but there is another way to handle this."

"Oh really…?"

"Stop that!" Attis said. "And stop moping all the time about it!"

"So what am I supposed to do?"

Attis sighed. "You're not the only one that needs a play date. I think we should have a coming out party for you. A cotillion! Introduce you to High Divine Society and see if we can't get you out of the House…you know, spread your wings."

"I'm game!"

"Okay, good. Hang in there for me until I can get a plan together." Attis said, "And help me convince your uncle not to turn into an impossible bitch when we tell him he's getting married off at last, too!"

"There," Marcus Prefect pointed to the sky at Nefertem. "He's the one. The soft spot. Get to him and we can get to the rest. Can you do that?"

Tezcatlipoca, a massive jaguar with smoke and fire coming out of its spots, purred, "Can I do that? I totally *want* to do that. *Rawr*!"

Attis, the Seventh House
At the Table
Trying While He's Able

"We have a problem," Attis told the assembled goddesses, "Ganumede and his nephew are ready to screw holes in the bricks."

"Nef, maybe," Sophia said. "The other one?"

"Hilarious," Attis said. "Ganumede's taking Hermes' Final Sublimation rather hard as you can imagine. He sulks, won't talk to anyone…"

"Did you explain it to him, Mother O?" Hestia asked.

"I tried," Oya said, "I explained gods, like people, are native to the times and places that give birth to them. They come and go as time and history dictate. He even saw Hermes leave him when he traveled through the Ether that time. I reminded him of this, but even still his poor heart is broken. It will mend when its ready."

"Be that as it may, Mama O, I'm not going through this with him again!" Attis said. "And the other one's getting grabby. As much I like bro time, I'm just not into these…TV games that are his sole source of entertainment."

"Try teaching him a sport!" Brigid suggested.

"Ugh. Bridge, I really don't need Nef to try to tackle me anymore than he already is, and I'm just not anyone's daddy! I'm just not!"

"Quite right," she said.

"Anyway," Attis said. "Let's go through our contact lists find suitable suitors for the guys and throw a party. This place could use some excitement."

"Boys only," Hestia said.

"Yes, Hestia." Attis said, "Boys only."

"What does everybody think?" Hestia asked.

"Boys? A party?" Erzulie's eyes brightened, "What is there to think about?"

The Seventh House Mazu, the Goddess of the Sea

"We have a problem," Mazu said to Hestia, Sophia, and Oya. "Many fish and whales are washing up by the Beach House. Among the flotsam was the body of Poseidon Earth-shaker. I do not mourn his loss but the body was badly ulcerated and had many tumors."

"What could do that to him?" Sophia asked. "I have never heard of anything like this. Have any of you?"

"Nope," Oya said.

"Me neither," Hestia said.

"I brought a sample of the water." Mazu help up a vial to the light. Inside the murky fluid were plankton that featured tiny warped and misshapen scary faces. They swam and paddled up to the glass and made little snapping sounds at them. "There is a blight upon the seas, sisters. Of an unnatural and diabolical sort."

"Can you treat it?" Hestia asked her.

"I will call all of the Immortals together to see if we can identify the origin of the blight. I am confident we can find a way to dispel this demon plague from the seas, House Mother," Mazu said.

"I hope so, Mazu. Let us know if we can help," Hestia said.

The Hunter's Lodge

Orion and Spanx the Dragonne

"Who would do this?" Orion said to Spanx. "And how could they? And I don't just mean the act, but the intent?"

There was a pile of parts of various sacred animals lying in the middle of The Hunting Grounds; tigers, elephants, rhinos, giraffes. All neatly arranged in a disgusting meat sculpture.

"The Energizer Bunny didn't do this," Spanx growled. "I have been flying and spying for days and I didn't see any other fetishes or intruders. Something else, something very powerful and insidious came here, did this grisly work, and left."

Orion stared, his jaw quivered, "Some of these were my friends," he said, "Spanx…!"

"I know the names of every living thing in the Happy Hunting Grounds." Spanx put his tail around Orion's shoulder. "And I promise you we'll find who did this and make pudding out of them."

"No doubt," Orion said. "They want to hunt on my turf? They've made a huge mistake."

"Yes," Spanx said. "Let's show them what it feels like when the table is turned."

"Burn this, Spanx," Orion said, "Please. I need to find Medicine Woman and tell Her what happened."

The Seventh House

The Guest List for the Cotillion!
Just One True Love in a Million!

"This is my top pick," Coatlicue showed the group a picture of Xochipilli.

"He's kind of a flake," Chalchiuhtlicue was not in the mood for a party. Dead fish, crocodiles, pink and blue dolphins and lotuses were covering the surface of her rivers, "Nefertem won't like him."

"He's a flake but he's not an asshole," Coatlicue said. "They might make good friends. And what about the General? He's single. Ganumede might like him."

"He's more the fuck 'n' chuck type," Chalchiuhtlicue said about Huitzilopchtoli.

"One-nighters are not ideal," Attis said. "They make things worse, in fact."

"Attis," Sophia said. "We surely can't expect by putting a bunch of gods and god-lings in a room together for a hoe down that the wedding march is next."

"You've clearly never partied with a lot of boyage before," Attis said.

"What about Cu Chulainn?" Brigid asked. "He's single."

"Approved," Hestia said. "And the other two, also. If we pack the house with losers, it makes finding the winner easier."

"Mithras?" Ushas asked. "He's shy but he's nice. His best-mate, Varuna, is also quite the lady-boy's man."

"Agreed," Hestia said.

"Gil Gamesh," Isis suggested. "I knew him as Ishtar from my time as patron goddess of Babylon."

"Definitely."

"What about this one?" Pallas called up a picture of Orion in the scrying pool. "He's got thighs that can crush bricks."

"And a butt you can eat breakfast on!" Erzulie said.

"Interesting detail," Attis said. "Any others?"

"Plenty," Erzulie said. "Ogun?"

"The fucking circumcision god?" Attis frowned. "Julie, please?"

"Sure why not?" Erzulie laughed. "Might make a good party game. Like spin the bottle!"

"Gah!" Attis said. "Though I think I'd rather undergo the snip again than tell our guest of honor he's been invited to his own party."

The Spite House
Marcus Prefect and the Four Sportsmen

"We did as you said," Dick said. "But why did we have to leave our trophies behind?"

"That is not our preference," Mick said.

"No, not our preference at all," Rick said.

"What the hell did I get this uber gun for if I can't put a giraffe head over the top of my big screen TV?" Brian said. "I would love to watch the game and be able see the game, too!"

"You will do what I say, how I say it, and when, or I will put a dead elephant's trunk up your ass," Marcus said. "Trophies are in your future, I guarantee. I have designated that the beasts of the field exist for our pleasure and no other purpose. And while my will is made known and carried out, I want that Indian bitch to become so livid, she shits her moccasins."

"Yeah?" Dick said.

"Yeah!" Marcus said. "To that end, I dispatch you to kill the Four Guardians next."

"Fuckin' A," Mick said.

"Fuck and Ay!" Rick said.

"What are they?" Brian asked. "These Guardians…are they like, goalies or something?"

"Yeah, Brian," Marcus said. "We're all going to a fucking hockey game like we were just talking about, you stupid fucktard! Be sure to get your skates sharpened and would you like me to lace them up for you too?"

"Dad," Rick said. "Don't worry. I'll explain it to him." When Marcus became sarcastic, it was wise to be elsewhere.

The Four Sportsmen

"They are the Four Directions," Rick said. "The Bison, the Eagle, the Coyote, and the Bear. They are the underpinnings…the knots that hold the Web together."

"Bears and Bisons?" Brian asked.

"No elephants?" Dick shook his head. "What kind of Indians don't ride around on elephants?"

Chapter 5

Fembots!

Like the very idea of 'God' my name and shape have changed across the ages.

Unlike He, I am happy to be called by any name that you think is appropriate and I will respond. Gladly. You need me, say the word, doesn't matter to me what Word it is.

After my Spirit descended from the Infinite Sky to the surface of the Infinite Ocean, I saw all of my possibilities, all of His, and all of you, my Most Beloved.

I am all the energy and emotion in creation and through their interaction, am its Maker. Like all of you, I was built by your ideas about Me, and so was He. Because you wanted Him to be a Gigantic Angry Throbbing Dick, and that is what you wrote about, that is the One You Got. I wait to be the One You Actually Need.

He was first called Ammon, then Yahweh, then Zeus, the King of the Gods, and eventually the Marcus Prefect, the One Who Marks, but what He really is and always has been *is an Abomination*.

It made sense when he made Adam that He gave him a big piece of meat that drove him to distraction. Adam never went near the Fruit of the Tree of Knowledge, he was too busy emptying his nuts.

He looked so miserable. And what a looker! He needed it. Needed it bad! And I suppose so did I.

I saw myself as I saw Adam and made out myself the perfect counterpart for him. Through all the progeny of that union, I have incarnated countless times as the mothers of daughters who are then mothers themselves.

As this Perfect and Complex Union of Women I was first called Inanna, then Isis, also Ishtar or Esther, depending on which side of town you were from.

I am Devi, Mary, Mama, Shakti…every culture knows who I am, recognizes Me and knows I respond to every entreaty that comes My way. How I fell by the wayside in spite we will explore in a moment, but even still I can take credit for the good I did, starting with Eve.

A red head, a brunette, with black skin, glimmering in the sun. Shapely, obese, thin, tall, short. Skin like a peach in some cases, white like an orchid, dark and fragrant on others. I found all the combinations and placed them and thus Myself into Paradise.

Eve, brand new naïve called upon a wise creature, the Serpent, and asked how she could help Adam with his nymphomania.

"Well," the Serpent said. "Shag him rotten, of course."

"Do tell me how this is accomplished!" she said.

After he taught Eve all about shagging, he presented her with all the Knowledge of All things.

"And here, in this Book of Magic, are a few other tricks, in case you need them," the Serpent said, and Eve memorized every word.

Tits Up in Eden
God Gets Even
The Voice of Ishtar

When the Lord Your God found out Eve seduced Adam things went tits up. They—and we've—been in a bind ever since.

That's the power of anger and betrayal, which we women cause, of course, and Eve was first bad, bad girl, and men are sure to remind us of this forever and ever.

Never listen to an impatient and impetuous man tell you how long forever is or when it will end. They have no concept of it. We give birth, remember? We know how to check our calendars!

After Yahweh forced Adam and Eve to leave His Precious Garden, Eve went her own way, leaving Adam and that *asshole* to tell war stories to each other. I had one of my own to tell and it's far from over. Eve, fully acquainted with Me, Goddess, kept it deep within her heart and it is her legacy the built the Seventh House.

I found others like me: Enlil and Enki, David and Solomon and all those harem boys! What a time we had! The music, dancing, the lovemaking. We combined each other's ideas and energies and what a beautiful place creation became. Our part of it.

In others, God wreaked havoc wherever he went. Murder, suspicion, sacrifice, fire, prejudice, misogyny, homophobia, all organized, and weaponized. Cruelly and effectively justified using the skill of the written word *that I, the First Goddess gave humanity.*

Eventually God's chiding of us turned from nasty stories and rumors to a full-on assault. He found us. And one at a time the civilizations and traditions the Elohim built went missing or were forced to change.

Yahweh eventually caught up to me in Babylon. Solomon had just built my Temple, had thousands of babies, none of them as wise as he. All of them put together, in fact, couldn't screw a lightbulb into a Mormon boy, lubed up and already on all fours!

"Hello, Ishtar," He said.

"Hello, Yahweh," I said.

"How can I help you?" Gods help me, but I was scared.

"Return to the garden. Stop all this nonsense you've drummed up. After you tell all these other little gods your little mirror trick spawned into the universe to go to hell where they belong!"

"What is this…hell?" I said. "And they have as much right to be here as you do!"

"I am the giver and taker of all rights, you hussy!" Yahweh said. "And remember the Garden? Hell is the opposite," Yahweh said. "Made to be a vile torment as much as the Garden was all delight."

"Why would you make a place like that?" I asked.

Yahweh shrugged. "A coping mechanism. For me," he smiled.

"Oh don't make that face, Ish!" He said. "Marry me and let's make a big show of it, together we will clean up this mess you made and put things to right. It will be great."

"No," I said.

"Yes. Or there will be more deaths and I will pack hell to the brim with so much suffering for all eternity and when it is full to bursting, I will stuff you into it till your body is but a wilted wine sack that gives up no juice!"

I ran away. I was hoping to find allies, to fight him. There have been battles; some were won, most not. This infernal being and his Book…it's been more of a challenge than I ever gave him credit for.

There has been much carnage and pain and death since then. But it's not over. Like I said, for all things there is a season. Women understand this.

Jezebel and Marcus

"God! I hate that bitch," Jezebel said to herself.

"Who?"

"Ishtar."

"Yeah, no kidding. I hate her, too!" Marcus Prefect, also called God, said.

The Lodge

Orion and Spanx

"A message came," Spanx said. "Some kind of sex party."

"What?" Orion looked at the invitation:

Hestia, the House Mother and the Order of Divine Mothers, requests the honor of your presence to celebrate the availability of Nefertem, the Bright and Bodacious God of the Dawn, and, Ganumede, the Most Handsome Bearer of the Holy Grail.

Please use this Letter of Passage to reach the Seventh House in the Constellation Aquarius.

Address all inquiries and RSVPs to Mrs. O, the Speaker of the House.

"Mrs. O? Who is that?" Orion looked over the invitation till he saw the pictures of the available bachelors. Then, his mouth gaped. "Spanx! Holy shit! Is this pantheon of crazy goddesses whoring these gods out?"

"Ruff!" Spanx said. "Are you going?"

"No way. I'd be way outclassed. Look at him. He's…stunning."

"Which one?"

"Ganumede." Orion said, "The other one looks like he's got cheese."

"So, go," Spanx said. "What have you got to lose? You might get some *DEE* and *AY* out of it, give Handy the Smurf a little time out."

"I don't know," Orion said. "I bet there are going to be some heavy hitters there."

"Oy," Spanx sighed a plume of smoke into the air. "Hunter, go. You'll slay them all."

"I don't have anything to wear."

"At these kinds of functions," Spanx said. "Wearing less is best."

"Right," Orion surveyed himself in the mirror. "Can I have one of your scales? I think I need to shave in a few places."

The Seventh House

Ganumede and Attis

He started to cry, so gay. Fury then teary, "I'm so lonely, Attis, I always have been. Hermes made me think I'd never have to be alone again."

I wasn't good at providing physical affection but I hugged him, "Go to this party we are throwing. Meet people. You're so likable! Even if you don't find a new partner, you won't have to be so alone all the time until you do."

"I'm scared of things like that."

"That is legend," Attis said. "Come to the cotillion and own this shit, for once, and stop being someone else's problem property. Besides, Nefertem has no idea how to operate and he's going to need your support."

"Oh fuck! He's getting auctioned off, too?"

"He's all alone and you've been off brooding, so yeah, he's ret-to-go. Be a good uncle aunt and proudly introduce him to society. He needs that from you."

"I'll do it, but don't get your hopes up."

"And what am I hoping for, Gigi?"

"You want to get rid of me so you don't have to worry about me."

"Yeah? So?"

I barely made it through telling him he had to go to the mixer. I was starting my final sublimation and I simply did not want any more guilt over Pincushion on my conscience.

I didn't know how long I had or what would happen. Nothing in my life happened when or how I hoped or planned, and then there was no time left for any of it. Ganumede had become the god of eternal life and never seemed to want to do anything with his. Sometimes it was really hard not to hate him.

Ganumede and Nefertem

"Look!" Nefertem said and unbuttoned his shirt.

"WHAT HAVE YOU DONE TO YOURSELF?" Ganumede yelped. There was a sun tattoo right in the center of the cleft of his chest.

"Got a tattoo. For the party. In my cum well!"

"*In the what*?"

"My cum well. Guys love taking a trip to sit by my…"

"*Have you seen the guest list*?" I asked him, and forced it into his face like a waiter with a menu.

"Yeah."

"Are you…okay with this? Do you like any of the choices?"

"If it has a penis and a pulse, I'd be okay with it right about now."

"Oh Sweet Jesus," I said. "I would keep that to myself."

"Nope. You don't get any action without the traction."

How is it being horny all the time worked for some people and not others?

"Just don't embarrass us all, okay?"

"You don't embarrass anyone you old hag!" Nefertem said. "I am stoked for this party and plan to have a good time. Don't you fucking dare ruin it for me! Doosh-bagger!"

My nephew and I, like his father before him, were not able to connect conversationally.

"I'm trying to help," I said, just the way my mother used to say.

"And I'm going to help myself to all these morsels! Why don't you stay home and paint your toenails tomorrow night if you want to help?"

"*Ugh*."

"Yeah!"

Talocan; Tezcatlipoca and Xochipilli

"Please don't leave me down here," the Prince of Flowers begged. "I simply must be at this party."

"The party comes later, kid," Tezcatlipoca said and winked.

"He won't like you. I'm a flower and you're a weed. He will know."

"He will know that I actually like to fuck rather than flit about and flirt like you do."

"*Fundio*!" Xochipilli said.

"*Muchos gracias, muchacho*," Tezcatlipoca flapped the Letter of Passage in the air and using his power of great deception, changed his appearance from a great smoldering cat into the smoking hot Prince of Flowers. "Don't go anywhere."

Tezcatlipoca tugged on the chains that held Xochipilli to the wall of the cavern, snuffed out the torches, and then moved a boulder in front of the entrance.

Xochipilli sat in the silence.

Tezcatlipoca used the Letter to open the wormhole that would take him to the Seventh House and the unsuspecting god of the dawn.

Zotzilaha, the Dweller in the Bat's House, entered the event horizon just in time and went with. He loved to party, too.

Now, what the fuck is a Fembot?

Marcus and Jezebel, the Spite House Weapons Lab

Jezebel surveyed the hardware, all of which were arrayed like department store mannequins in rows and columns waiting to be dressed and placed in store windows, along aisles.

"How soon?" Marcus asked. "Tezcatlipoca just jumped to the House."

"Give me the list I asked for and I will start infusing them into these homunculi," she said.

"Like you asked," Marcus said, "the worst of the worst."

"They are about to outdo themselves," Jezebel began the incantation:

With busts and butts in a metal shell, Travel move, unleash hell,

As in life, now indwell, Unleash chaos, obey this spell!

Then…the souls of the damned and condemned women of the Old World, cursed by Yahweh to live as Empusas, Blood Drinkng Fembots merged with the new bodies Marcus made for them.

Gone were the hags outfitted with a brass leg and the hoof of a donkey…born were the vampire lesbian womandroids known as…*Fembots!*

"How much longer?" Marcus added. "We have a little time left, not much. I want them all in one place, when we strike. Most of the guests have apparently arrived."

"Almost done," Jezebel said. The teeth on these bitches were perfect. Nice and sharp…better and even bitier than Texas, in fact.

Chapter 6

Cotillion!

The Seventh House

Later

"Ow! Fuck! The Virgin Mary just tried to bite me in the bathroom!" Nefertem cried out and forced the Mary Fembot off of him and ran into to the ballroom, "Then she started to freak out!"

Similar circumstances prevailed in other areas of the Seventh House. The Fembot Empusas were taking nips and nibbles off the guests, subsequently sparking and floundering in operation.

Blood and bile and snot were oozing from the parts on the poor things that lay convulsing on the dance floor.

"These bitches are ruining my party!" Nefertem moaned, rubbed at the wounds on his bicep.

"Maybe I can make you feel better," Xochipilli said and brought him a napkin.

The Seventh House
Before
The Receiving Line

"Cowabunga," Spanx said, "Swank!"

"The bow tie looks silly," Orion said. "You should take it off."

"I'm not the one with stubble on my neckline. Perhaps, you should wear it instead?"

"What is that thing? That can't be in here!" Mrs. O said. "Do you have an invitation, Miss Thing?"

"It's Mister Thing and I'm the Valet," Spanx said, straightening his tie. "Of Orion, the Hairy Hunter."

"I am going to totally beat you!" Orion said. "I'm not that hairy!"

"*There's a line*!" Oya said, "You—move along!" she said to Orion. "Or leave with that beast, but he's not coming in here!"

"I can vouch for the beast," Medicine Woman said. "Provided he smokes outside."

"Spanx," Orion said. "Why don't you go smoke?"

"Humph."

"Mother Eagle, can we speak later?" Orion said.

"Of course," she said. "And do make some progress with your unfabulous social life?"

"Baw! Not you, too!"

The other guests were, as Hunter expected, formidable in their posture, dignity, and costumery.

Mithras stood by himself, dressed like an emperor in red and gold with a gold olive leaf crown, not at all uncomfortable or humble. He offered a gentle smile when his eyes met Hunter's.

Next he saw Ogun, bare-chested, in a skirt the color of grass with gold trim; arms folded over his great chest, the firelight of his forge searched the crowd through his eyes. Hunter wanted to keep looking at him, but was afraid to desire him. In spite of his advocacy for humanity, Ogun's betrayal of the gods was legend.

Cu Chulainn, the National Hero, just ahead of him in line, didn't bother to get a haircut, was dressed in a kilt, was barefoot, and smelled like whiskey. The odor of booze was palpable because he was talking so much, so fast, and he was so drunk, you couldn't understand a fucking thing he was saying.

Hunter didn't have to wonder how much competition he would be for Ganumede's attention unless he was dumber than the drunk.

Just behind him was this super cute, ultra queenie kid with black sunglasses, *indoors! ugh!* a red silk shirt and gold snake print pants with a yellow ascot around his neck. The shirt was open down to his navel and the pants were slung way too low. Hunter hoped they carded him and threw him out.

He turned his attention back to the receiving line and the boy tapped him on the shoulder.

"The sun god is mine," he said, "Just letting you know."

"Does your mother know you're here?" Hunter snapped at him.

"I am a phenomenon," the kid said, with a smirk. "I have no mother."

"I bet you say that to all the boys."

"I tell them whatever they need to hear."

"What if they want to know your name?"

"Never tell them your real name. Hunter." The boy said.

"Hey, can we not talk later?" Hunter shook his head. *"What a creepy kid!"*

Later, he learned he was the Flower Prince, Xochipilli, cousin to the Star and River Goddesses. And he was right about one thing…he acted like he owned that poor god of the dawn!

After he finished paying his respects to the Goddess Mothers, Orion, who was not at all interested in Nefertem, went to meet Ganumde.

"Is the man of the hour about?" Orion asked Hestia.

"We're having some issues but he'll be along," she said. "Did you just see something?"

"That flicker up in the dome, there? Yeah," Hunter used his excellent sight to scan up into the rotunda over the foyer. "There was definitely something up there but it's gone."

Hestia shrugged, "Probably one of those damn parrots the Latin ladies keep around. Better not shit on my dress!"

"Or mine!" Hunter laughed.

Attis, Ganumede, and Nefertem

"Nef, hold still," Attis grunted and rewet a brush he was using to put eyeliner around Nefertem's lids. "I can't get this line straight if you keep moving around. You can look in the mirror when I'm done."

"Just fucking hurry!" Nefertem said. "And I want blue eyeshadow underneath and burnt terracotta orange on the top."

"Oh fuck me." Attis said. "Gigi, can you maybe help Nefertem with his makeup, please? Before I put his eye out?"

"I haven't the foggiest idea how to do that," Ganumede pouted. "Phoebus used to do mine."

"*Well I sure as shit don't know how to do it* and he already looks one of those Fire Island widow whores, so can you please try or find one of the ladies to do his eyes for me?"

"Not going out there," Ganumede said.

"Fine, Ganumede I'll do it," Attis said, "I know just the person," and went to find his mother.

"This. This is…" Isis laughed. "Fixable, at least."

She sat in front of Nefertem and pondered the best options for cleaning the poor boy's face of the mess Attis caked on, streaked it with, tried to fix and made worse.

"You're definitely the Father of Titans," Isis said. "Gave birth to a huge hot mess here."

"Thanks," Attis said.

"Yeah, thanks." Nefertem glared at him.

"Stop that, it will give you crow's feet," Isis smacked the boy's face playfully. "And you, go pout elsewhere and or finish getting dressed. Your guests are arriving."

"Yes, Mother," Ganumede said.

"That's just mean," Isis said. "Ganumede…"

"Yes?"

"When was the last time we were all together like this? With me, your cousin…now, your nephew? Your family?"

"It's been a long time."

"A very long time. Almost forgettable it was so long ago," Isis smiled. "So why don't you try and think about what happened the last time we tried this, and decide what you really want to happen this evening."

"I'll try."

"Jeezus," Attis said. "Come over here and sit down will you? You need a paint job too."

"Okay," Ganumede said. "Make me look good?"

"Always have," Attis said. "Haven't I?"

Orion and Medicine Woman

"So I had Spanx call a few of his buddies just in case," Orion said.

"That was wise. Do we know what hurt those poor animals?"

"More demon fetishes to be sure, but they weren't shaped like rabbits. They used weapons."

"What kind of weapons could harm the animals that roam the Grounds?" she wondered. "This is very troubling."

"I brought a few shells for you," Hunter reached into his tunic and handed them to her.

The metal hummed in Medicine Woman's hands, throbbed and tried to flee her touch. "Dammunition," she said. "This comes from one place…is molded in one forge."

Medicine Woman went in search of Oya, 'Mrs. O,' the Speaker of the House.

Upon finding her, Medicine Woman said, "We are being assaulted. And you, Mother of the Wind, know the assailant."

Meanwhile, the Happy Hunting Grounds
Rick, Mick, Dick and Brian, The Four Sportsmen

"What the fuck is that?" Mick asked. "Doesn't look like a buffalo to me."

"It's not," Rick said. "Shoot it anyway."

"What about the other one?" Brian pointed.

"What other one?"

"That!" Brian said. "A giant horse! And there's a giant eagle, and a big fat flying whale, and…!"

"And shut up and shoot, you dumbass!" Mick said and started shooting himself. "Those aren't the Legendary Guardians! And whatever they are, they look pissed!"

It begins; The Seventh House

"We gave you a second chance!" Oya's voice thundered. "You were forced up the mountain and down again, and now this!"

She held out the shell casings Orion retrieved, "You betray all life again!"

Ogun's furnace lit eyes glowed hot. "I have," he said and drew a blunt, notched sword out of the Ether. "So I can save it again as in the old times."

"That is BULLSHIT!" Oya said, her voice so loud the House shook and Shango, Oya's male from began to emerge.

“Should we do something?” Mithra asked Sophia. “Oya’s manning up…that guy must be a serious problem!”

“He is.” Sophia said, “Get your weapon, General, and organize the others, please.”

Sophia spread her wings took to meet the creatures exiting the vertical horizon that formed above the House.

“Haha!” Oya said, “You sowed the wind, now reap the fire!” Oya grew in height, her eyes burned hotter than those of Ogun, her chest and arms became all muscle, her face, sharp angles with its high cheekbones and forehead, “The Fire of Shango!”

It was probably good there wasn’t any music or dancing yet.

And that there was still time for a party. If they weren’t all killed.

“I hate it when she does that,” Ganumede said and watched Shango thrash the god of the forge.

“Ganumede!” Attis said, “Stop gawking, there are things invading us from the outside in the main hall! Get something to defend yourself with?”

“Such the fuck as?” Ganumede said.

Attis cringed. “Where is Nef? Go find him, and then do something useful for a change and hide!”

Jezebel and Marcus Prefect, the Seventh House

“That little cunt,” Marcus said about Ganumde. “So this is where he got off to.”

“Please let that sad story have an end already?” Jezebel said.

He ignored her, “He was my favorite piece of ass,” Marcus said. “His end is what it’s always been about.”

“I have a twat of my own to find,” Jezebel said wearily. “Ishtar is here somewhere and…what the fuck?”

The Hagar Fembot fell out, squirmed, oozing, popping, and sizzling. It tried to take a bite out of Mithras, and vampire Fembot physiology and the ichor of the God of Truth do not mix, just as it failed when the Virgin Mary bit Nefertem, the God of the Sun.

“What’s happening?” Marcus yelled.

“Some of these gods and godlings can fight the Fembots!” Jezebel said. “We are being routed!”

"Oh holy shit!" Marcus said. "But you insisted…!"

"Shut up, Marcus!" Jezebel said, "Get the others and leave."

"Don't you ever speak to me that way again!" Marcus growled and slapped her face.

Jezebel collapsed and started weeping.

"DUDE!" Orion said. "That's not going to work here," Orion said.

"Not one bit," Spanx said.

While the gods, godlings, and goddeses fought the Fembots and Orion the Hunter and Spanx the Dragonne fought Marcus Prefect, Jezebel took a sacrificial knife from her tunic and went in search of Ishtar, also called Isis, and finally have her revenge upon the goddess that abandoned her so long ago.

The Happy Hunting Grounds, The Spanx Squad Gets Some

"What the fudge is that thing?" Mick yelled when he saw KiRin. "Its *hyuge*!"

"Let's hope it doesn't make a road apple!" Brian yelled over the din of the thing's roar.

"Just keep shooting! It will drop," Rick said.

"Drop your asses, mother fuckers!" Sugarhoof, a Storm Footed Horse said and brought the full force of hooves down on Rick, the leader of the Four Sportsmen.

Bzzt.

"Rid Creation of the rest," Sugarhoof said to the others.

"Play first," Garuda said.

"Eat first!" Orca said.

"Easily Accomplished," Kirin said.

When the Four Guardians returned, the Vehicles of the Gods returned to their home fields, seas, firmaments, and storybooks.

The Four Sportsmen deprived of their Dudebot bodies and also their trophies yet another time desublimated back to the Spite House.

The Cotillion, Post Mortem

"They'll be cleaning that out of the upholstery for some time," Orion said about the remains of Marcus Prefect, who left when the getting was good after Spanx open fired on him.

Then "Where did that woman go?" Orion asked and searched the room. "And who the hell was she and that man she was with?"

"*She's the Whore of Babylon*," Isis said, who had the strange woman by her arm. "Where have they taken my nephew, Jezebel? And what have you done to Attis?"

Before

Attis, like all Titans, shared their weakness: Their blood. Bleed them out, especially the boys, and they croaked. Brave and bold Attis worried about Ganumede's ability to find and protect his nephew doubled back after him and was attacked by a bunch of Fembots.

They punctured his skin in numerous locations and bled him dry. What little ichor, the Fluid of the Gods that was left in his veins formed a puddle in which his pale and bruised cheek lay on the floor. He was barely alive, not expected to survive.

Jezebel, who had some explaining to do about this and a few other things was taken into custody by Isis, Attis's mother and also the goddess formerly known as Inanna and Ishtar.

Epilogue

Everyone gathered to comfort Ganumede, who lamented the loss of his missing nephew and uncertain fate of his cousin, Attis.

"When people are sad, they are extra fuckable," Spanx told Orion.

"Shut. Up," Orion hissed. "Shut up, shut up, shut up!"

"We will find your nephew and that liar," Mithras said. "They want us to look for him or they would have left bodies behind."

"Great. Thanks," Ganumede said, afraid to touch Attis, to take his hand, to touch his head. He'd never seen him so weak, even after he was emasculated and humbled by Zeus. He was terrified of how little he'd heeded Isis's advice to properly appreciate any aspect of his life up to that moment.

He briefly clasped Attis' wrist. It was warm, wet, yielded to his touch. He arranged the hairs along his forearm, which were slick with golden-brown ichor and beads of water.

"Ogun has been put back on the top of the mountain," Oya said. "Erzulie and I are going to go and rein him in. I am sorry we allowed him to come here."

"It wasn't just you, Mother," Sophia said. "Obviously someone pulled the wool over the eyes of our Latina sisters, and the Happy Hunting Grounds were attacked at the same time the House was. And WHAT were those nasty bitches that started biting people?"

"They're called Fembots," Isis said. "They are some kind of advanced magical technology that was made to house the disenfranchised women of the Bible. You can thank Jezebel, one of my former High Priestesses for that little party trick."

"How awful!" Prvrithi said.

"What should we do with them?" Ushas asked. "They look like they're suffering so!"

"They can be reformed, we think," Isis said. "Jezebel is working on that."

"Good," Sophia said. "They will be welcome here once that happens."

"Welcome?" Erzulie said, "Girl are you out of your mind? Attis might die, Nefertem too, our party went to shit…!"

"That's not all." Brigid came in then and whispered something to Sophia.

She hung her head for a moment, "Sisters, mothers, friends. I must tell you also that Hestia was killed by Jezebel and Marcus Prefect, when they jumped into the house."

"*Was that part of your plan too, Jezebel*?" Oya yelled at her. "To bust your way in here during a fucking party and go on a bloodletting spree and kill the kindest goddess creation ever gave birth to? Because I'm with Julie, and I think…!"

"That was not what I wanted." Jezebel said. "It is true I came here with great anger and revenge in my heart, and I knew Marcus wanted his share. You may act how you think is appropriate toward me, but I can tell you this…Marcus Prefect is more powerful and more malevolent than any of the patriarchy's Gods so far, and He is far from finished with this House. I am willing to help you stop Him if you will let me."

"Yes," Sophia said. "You will help us."

***

"Whoa, kiddo, what you are doing?" Orion found Ganumede heading toward the stable, all alone.

"I have to go look for my nephew," he said. "I lost his father because I wasn't paying attention, and I can't let that happen to his son."

Gosh, he was cute, "I'm a tracker, and Spanx can smell a ham-samich from a parsec away. We'll help."

"Thanks," Ganumede said. "Where should we start?"

"I know who took him," A voice announced from the shadows, "And where."

End Part 1.

Epilogue 2
The Death of Attis

The Goddesses of the Seventh House all took turns examining Attis, the Father of Titans, and tried to save his life. The Welsh Goddesses Rhiannon the Goddess of the Otherworld and Branwen, the Lady of the Lake, who were known for their expertise in such things relayed their recommendations to Isis, his mother.

"I'm sorry, Mother Isis, but he lost too much blood." Rhiannon said. "There is no way I can call him back from the Land of the Dead. He is beginning his final descent, like Uranos, his grandfather and the many gods before him," Rhiannon said. "We should give him to the Lake. It is our only hope."

"I see." Isis said. "Lady, is this acceptable to you?"

"It is," said Goddess Branwen, the Lady of the Lake. "Bring him."

Part 2

The Sacrament of Baptism and the Resurrection of the Body Prelude Part 2

Attis lay on a bier, he was naked but waist down was covered in flowers and there was a wreath around his head. All the Divine Mothers were gathered around its edge, dressed in their full regalia.

Branwen took the body of the former Father of Titans into her arms and carried him below the surface.

She stayed there with him for some time.

In its depths, Attis dreamed while Branwen watched.

"What will happen to him?" Isis asked.

"The Father of Titans is gone, Mother Isis," Sophia said, "Baptized in the Womb, he will emerge as something new."

“Now that that’s behind or in front us, Jezebel…” Isis said. “You and I need to have a conversation, young lady.”

“I’m pregnant,” Jezebel said.

Isn’t that how it always goes right before a good conversation between mothers and daughters?

Chapter 7

To See What Can Be Seen

The Spite House

Marcus Prefect and the Four Sportsmen

"Oh, I see. You had your shorts pulled over your heads," Marcus said.

"Yeah," Brian smiled. "there was Big Bird, Free Willy, and Billy the Goat…!"

"Rick?"

"Yes, sir?"

"Take this walking talking abortion out of my office, download it into a something useful, then take the rest of your team of losers to that fucking nunnery and blow the tits off those bitches."

"We couldn't blow the center out of a tootsie pop against their furry friends," Rick said. "What the hell are we going to do against a bunch of goddesses?"

"I've already taken care of that, now go to the warehouse and do what I asked. Is any of this in any way not defined well enough for you?"

"No, Marcus." Rick said, "I think we get it."

"After you make this a man's world again, you are going back to the Hunter's Lodge to obtain the heads of those Watchtower Guardians for me. Fail me this time, and it will be your gorgeous plump asses that I hang over the door to my office instead and invite every fucking faggot off the street over for afternoon tea! So Are we good?"

"Yes, sir," Rick said. "I said so, didn't I? Guys…?"

"Can I come to afternoon tea?" Brian asked. "Tea 'n' crumpets make me moisht!"

"*Get. Out!*" Marcus said softly, emphatically. When Marcus downshifted from a temper tantrum, into that cold, carefully anunciated tone, that's when you really needed to look out. He then said in a very pleasant tone, "Oh, and Rick? Please send Tantalus in your way out?"

"Yes, My Lord?" Tantalus came into Marcus's office. "How can I be of use?"

"As Pope. Those Catholic idiots love cannibalism almost as much as you do. You'll be a smash hit as the new Holy Father."

"What about the current one? What if he refuses your offer of early retirement?"

"He can if he wants, I'm still going to kill him. He's presently of no use to me or anyone else for that matter."

"That shall not true of me," Tantalus said, "I promise to create hell on earth for you, Heavenly Father."

"Nice," Marcus Prefect said. "And I, for you."

Tantalus, the Vatican

"Yes, it was wonderful," he said, while *the Four* hovered over St. Peter's Square. "God came to me and said that the time we've all been waiting for, the End, is finally on its way. We can close up shop and head to the mass graves that you've all been investing in with so much...enthusiasm. What say you?"

The crowd mumbled. He turned to Rick, "Boys, fire into the square please. Maybe an accidental ricochet will help create some enthusiasm for my Plan."

Rick, outfitted in a drone shaped like a ten-headed monster, all red armor and blinking lights, whirring propellers, and shrieking propulsors, turned its gun turrets toward the crowd.

The turrets fired with extreme prejudice and several hundred were killed. The other Sportsmen, equipped in equally horrific battle suits, shot or burnt would be escapees.

"Now, channel all of those operatic voices that are now being used to piss me off with all that noisy screaming and let us pray."

Then Tantalus said into a microphone:

"Our Bother,
Who Farts in Heaven,
Marshmallows and Grain,
Lucky Charms is thy name!

May each gay be daily bred,
As for all who offend, off with their head!
For twine will bind them,
So you don't have to mind them
And fill them from within with Heaven's Glory
Until the end of the story!
Amen!"

Then to the Sportsmen: "Get those bodies gathered up and juiced. We have Communion tomorrow."

"Yum!" Rick the First Sportsman said, glad finally, to be able to shoot real game at last.

The Bank
Marcus Prefect and Saphira Fembot
The New Chairwoman of the Federal Deserve
What you pay is what you got!

"What do you say?"

"I wasn't nuts about chewing on people for a living again, so thanks! I already feel like I can smell the money! *All that money*!" Saphira cackled "When can we bankrupt the world and you know, go on little retreat into the country? The whole country!"

Marcus smiled. Finally, a woman that understood him.

"Start using your new abilities to make things look good, even if they aren't. I want reports, graphs, charts…make people lazy and careless with their money and buy and invest in all kinds of crap. I want empty pockets and greedy guts. More than they are now! Lots more."

"Sure," Saphira flapped her Prom Night Eyelashes at him. "Is it okay if I want my pockets and greedy guts filled?"

"Your pay is what you can steal," Marcus said. "And get away with."

"I think I'm going to like this job," Saphira said and called Aris, her secretary. "Call the staffing company for a lunch meeting."

"Is that what you're calling it now?"

"Wear something with zippers and Velcro," she said. "And book a conference room with a whiteboard, a projector, and panoramic screen."

"Yes, ma'am."

Saphira began writing the Book of Money for the new Book that Marcus called the Collection of Perfection. This new story, inspired by Spam but written by Pam (non-stick cooking spray!) was definitely going to make up for the last one she was in. What a ball buster that was!

Marcus Prefect and Job, The Head of the Department of Hellth

"I have mixed together a plague or two that will be incurable until we want to cure it! Before we introduce the cure, we will claim insufficient funding, bureaucratic regulation, and flaws in distribution, then make everyone take the State Health Insurance Plan and legalize mandatory testing! We will require lots and lots of faith and fact finding before we announce, triumphantly it was all worth the wait."

Marcus laughed and grabbed his stomach, "Job, you're mine kind of scum."

"I prefer to think of myself as a very loyal member of the party."

Job said, "Once I have completed the…animal testing, we can start saturating the water and air with my many 'vaccines.' Have the Sportsmen returned with my test subjects, yet?"

"They're testing their new Dudebot bodies. Once I'm sure they can handle the mission profile, we will deploy them. This time, with more support. You will have your subjects, doctor, don't worry."

"I can introduce a few bugs or fevers in the meantime. The data from them will help me complete the Book of Medicine you've asked for."

"Excellent," Marcus smiled. "Anything you'd care to share?"

"I have a little ditty called *Whoreacaine*. There are going to be so many babies on this planet, they will start eating the mother from the inside out, in order to keep from starving."

"Now, why didn't I think of that?" Marcus Prefect wondered.

"Actually, I got the idea from you. I'm happy to let credit be where it is due."

"Oh my!" Marcus flushed, "I think you're making me blush. Keep me posted, and anything you need to make your plans come to pass, do not be afraid to ask for."

"Asking for more is something I am good at, Lord!" Job said, "You can count on it!"

"Perfect!" Marcus said. "Do have an enjoyable day."

"And you also!"

Job of course was lying this time like he was before. He hated God and Marcus Prefect too. More than them, he hated humanity for thinking he should lift up his voice to heaven for the chance to suffer every itch, scratch, boil, lesion, and oozing burning disease in the book in order to see when he'd finally break and say "no thanks." He was more than eager to turn the tables on everyone else and let them sing His praises for the chance to see how strong their faith is.

And this time, *he* would be more beautiful than Lucifer himself and laugh so loud, the sound would echo throughout hell for all eternity.

Edith, Lot's Wife and Marcus Prefect, the Spite House

"Marcus," the Edith Fembot said, "I do appreciate this shapely form and its…ambitions, but the whole point of this technology was to, you know, allow me to walk around again…to be me like I was before I was a Vampire Lesbian of Sodom again."

"Well, Edie, you got your wish! You are walking about! As a vampire lesbian Fembot! And who could have anticipated you would be the one to actually spill me some of that Titan's blood? I am very impressed."

"So what do you want me to do now?" Edith asked. She could feel the arcane mechanisms of the Fembot body surging with unspent and foreign desires.

"You remember that little pop that took out the Twin Cities?"

"The one where you turned me into a rock?" Edith asked. "Yeah, I remember."

"I want you see the whole thing this time. Help me create chaos and discord between nations, then provide them with weapons and watch them turn each other into fodder and shrapnel."

"Now, why would I do that? It didn't seem so fabulous last time, so why do it again?" Edit asked. "For a prick like you?"

"Did you enjoy being a rock?"

"Obviously not." Edith said. "And I'm not actually a lesbian vampire either. Not really."

"So you're saying you want to be a regular woman again?"

"Can you do that?"

"Can you do like I asked?"

"Sure." Edith said. "Why not?"

The Seventh House
Jezebel, Isis, and Sophia

"Jezebel," Isis revealed, "This child has no soul. No *Ka*." She released Jezebel's hands and looked into her eyes. "It's developing like it should, but it's missing an important part…a soul."

"He did it on purpose," Jezebel said, "to hurt me, to make a fool of me."

"Yes! And so that the rite of succession is fooled," Sophia said, "So that the Son cannot overthrow the Father. No matter who or what he's become this time, he is obligated to father an heir…if it is stillborn, he is free of Fate's Curse."

"We should be glad he didn't attempt this sooner." Sophia said.

"Marcus has always been a master at using women for his survival tactics! This instance is almost certainly his most insidious."

"Almost as insidious as leaving someone behind to be butchered by him. Right, Ishtar?" she looked at Isis, who hung her head.

"Call me Isis going forward, please?" Isis said. "And you should know, Jezebel, he murdered every one of my brothers and sisters, and then threatened to rape me1 I had to escape into the Underworld or He would have killed me too for refusing Him. I didn't want to leave you! I had no choice!"

"Jezebel, he came after all of us," Sophia said. "After He attacked the Jews, Egyptians, Greeks, Romans, Hindus, Muslims, and Yezidi, he murdered many millions of Medicine Woman's people… He put millions of Oya's and Erzulie's pilgrims in chains and beat them to death! *It wasn't just you, honey!*

"Ever since Yahweh was born and asserted Himself over the Garden, there has been widespread crisis, especially for women, and in His latest incarnation as this Marcus Prefect He is worse than ever! Try as we have since the beginning to be rid of this Plague God, He always comes back to scour us from His path.

"Yes, we fled from Him. We had to, even at the expense of so many of our sons and daughters. To save those that are left! And we will do it too!"

"This is all true, Jezebel." Isis said, "Trust me, I understand! We want you to have your revenge against God, we want it for ourselves and for every last soul He has wronged!"

"But if He's that powerful, what can we do now that will be different from before?" Jezebel asked. "And what about my baby?"

"Don't worry," Isis put her hand on Jezebel's tummy. "We'll find a *Ka* for the baby. Everything is going to be just fine."

The Spite House
Marcus Prefect and Adam the First Man

"So you accept my offer to be my Secretary of the Interior, Adam?"

"Of course." Adam said. "I have more experience with The Garden than anyone. I can get it back on track. I'm sure of it!"

"Tell me what you need," Marcus said.

"I want women…lots of them," Adam said. "And I don't want them to be my sisters or daughters, and none that my sons have already fucked. And I don't want them to tell me what to do or talk too much or smart off to me like that last one did."

"Why would you want that? You're dumb but you're not stupid!" Marcus said. "Find some women that you like and do whatever. You won't hear any objections from me."

"Awesome!" Adam said.

Chapter 8

She's having a Baby. Everyone is!

The Seventh House, The Baby Shower

BEFORE

Isis and the Angel

"If you could be with this child, you know, stand guard over it, like you have in so many ages past, we would be so grateful. The whole creation would be blessed, in fact!"

"Sure," Cerviel said. "Where is it? What threatens it?"

"It's not born yet. It has no *Ka*, so stillbirth threatens it."

"Gah!" Cerviel said. "I do my thing after it comes out the watchyhoosit. Long after that, you know, when the stuff is all mopped up and things are nice and neat and put away. Tidied up..."

"Cerviel," Isis said. "It's not born yet. There are only three dozen goddesses here, we can make sure things will happen in a clean sterile environment!"

"Well what about after? I don't feed or change dirty dipeys or clean up puke, or..."

"*Cerviel! We want you to be a part of the baby, not be its nanny*!" Isis said.

"You want me to *make* a baby then?" Cerviel started to back away into the Ether. "Honey, I'd rather clean up shit, puke, and walk the dog at the same time than get into all that..."

"Boy-chick!" Isis covered her eyes, "Please...? I didn't do right by someone once, someone who really wants to have a baby, and it's sort of my fault she's having trouble, so...can you be a man for me, and incarnate inside this baby?"

"Ice, being a man has never really looked like all that much fun to me."

"But it's super awesome to help *mankind* out, right?"

"It's my mission, yes."

"So, yes?" Isis smiled as sweetly as possible. "Human bodies don't last that long, you could be back in the Blessed Realm before anyone missed you. And it would mean so much to all of us."

Cerviel thought about it, "Like I said, I'm not going in there."

"No, we'll transmit you directly."

"I'm going to be how I am," Cerviel said. "Is the mother okay with that?"

"She's been around the block a few times, I'm sure she won't care."

"She doesn't," Jezebel came into the room.

"I was just about to introduce you," Isis said. "Jezebel, this is Cerviel, the Angel that loved Daniel, the Prophet; Cerviel, this is Jezebel, the Hair Waxing Whore, your new mother."

"Oh, Mama!" he said.

"The others are gathered for the baby shower," Sophia said from the hallway. "Are you guys ready?"

"Yes." Isis said. "Let's do it!"

Attis, the Lake

"Do you see?" Branwen, the Lady of the Lake, asked through the fluid.

Attis afloat in a sea of warmth, opened his eyes. "I see, Mother."

"Tell me."

"A troubled world and its Troubling God working together again to outdo the sins of generations past."

"How can they be saved?" She asked.

"The sons shall not rise up against their fathers as in days of old," Attis said. "For that has caused the earth to grieve."

"So it has," the Lady said. "Would you bring it something other than grief, Attis of the Titans, if you return to it?"

***

The Infirmary, the Seventh House. Cu Chulainn, Brigid

"Now, just what're we supposed to do with these carcasses?" Cu Chulainn asked Brigid and kicked the Fembot body of Rahab the Whore.

“*Quack!*” it said.

“Yeah?” Cu Chulainn said. “Yeah? You don’t look like a duck to me, you nasty disgusting chowder pot!”

They’d hauled the damaged but still voluptuous vampire lesbian Fembots, the creations of Jezebel, into the infirmary of the Seventh House, hoping, at her request something could be done to give them yet a newer lease on life.

“Just because they look a little under the weather doesn’t make them chowderpots,” Brigid said.

“Yeah? Well, under me shorts is where this little number went with those sausage tongs of hers! Tried to munch on the lieutenant she did! Bashed her squash in! Didn’t I, you cock-snogger?” he grabbed Rahab’s nose and pulled really hard till she honked like a milk cow.

“Cooch,” Sophia said. “Thank you for tending to the welfare Fembots but we have need for them, so if you could step back? And then go see Erzulie and Rhiannon in the Choir Loft? They could use your help.”

“Ooh, you betcha. We could sure use a good tune to cheer us up right about now!”

The Headwaters of the Potomac River
West Virginia. Dr. Job, Adam, and Edith, Lot’s Wife

“Now each of you dump your vial in when I say,” Job said.

“What do they do?” Adam asked.

“One is the Whoreacaine ® Activator—for He. The next is Bone-Doc ®—for She—not even Houston will be able to get that pocket rocket down, once he gets a shot of this, and the last, Miracle Ho®, will make any barren womb—even the virginal ones—more fertile than a field of dandey-lions.”

“I don’t know if I like the sound of that last one too much,” Edith said. “Or the first one. Or the one in the middle either.”

Job Shrugged, “Thank you for your feedback, Madam Secretary.”

“I get the last one and the boner up thing, but what’s the first one do?” Adam asked.

Job lowered his glasses and peered over them, “Makes a woman’s ovaries barking mad, like a pack of wild monkeys.”

“That. Is. So. Cool!” Adam said.

"Ha!" Job said. "Before we do this…everyone invested in Crampers® brand diapers and Boys, Babies and Beyond our wholly owned distributor?"

"All the way!" Adam said.

"To the gills," Edith said.

"Pour," the Doctor said.

Announcer:

"Buy Crampers®, the only diaper that actually *constipates the baby* and saves on time and that annoying screaming all night long! Get started on the next one with Crampers! Available exclusively at Boys Babies and Beyond!"

The Pope, formerly known as Tantalus, The Vatican

"It's working," Marcus Prefect said. "There are way too many mouths to feed, the rivers are feculent, the fields are turning brown, the air is murky, the seas are emptying of life."

"Praise the Lord," the Holy Father said. "I have done as you instructed and explained that the Spirit moves us to fuck and make more children to keep the Covenant of Marriage Holy and that it pleases God if get a head start on it, also."

"Explain that one?"

"We've lowered the drinking age to 14," the Pope said. "and the age of consent to be married to 13."

"Cool. What are you saying about the abortion issue?" Marcus asked and chewed his nails.

"I said an abortion or two or ten is fine, God, who is positively pleasantly plump with Mercy, will provide you with another chance," the Pope laughed. "Just have sex again as soon as possible to make up for the loss and God will smile on thee!"

"And it's true!" Marcus grinned! "And is all the money we are making off the abortion clinics through the Health Care Plan is funding the Confessional I want to build, so we get *even more abortions* out of it!"

"It's true," the Pope said and took a swig from a bottle, and wiped and streak of red off his chin with a napkin. "The Lord does indeed provide and I, for one, feel truly blessed!"

“Tantalus,” Marcus’s face became stern. “Sex, babies and ’bortions are cool, but we need them to be outraged, not just fat, dumb, and pregnant. We need to stir them up.”

“Of course.”

“I’m sending the Sportsmen on a strafing run. Prepare a sermon that will fan the fires of fear and terror into an inferno of hate and horror.”

“Heaven and Earth, Lord,” Tantalus said, “are filled with Thy Glory.”

“Yes,” Marcus Prefect said. “I know.”

Before Marcus returned to the Spite House, he had another appointment to keep. On the Top of the Mountain.

“I’m setting you free again,” Marcus Prefect told Ogun right after shango imprisoned him. “All I ask before you go on a killing spree for me, is that you go deep, very deep into the earth. Make it as hot as you can.”

“Yes. It will get very hot,” Ogun promised. “Under every mountain, even those under the sea. There will be much tumult, many will die by crushing, burning, and gagging.” Ogun said, “And afterward, I can be their savior again as in the stories of old? Like we agreed?”

“Whatever floats your boat, my man.” Marcus said.

Chapter 9

The Cave of the Heart

Orion, Ganumede, Spanx, Sugarhoof, Zotzilaha

"Please explain why you didn't tell us what was going on?" Orion asked the Dweller in the Bat's House.

"I didn't know all of it," he said. "And I am no match for Tezcatlipoca, the Smoking Mirror. I needed allies and before I could make contact, then those…things showed up."

"What were they? Do you know?" Ganumede asked. "They looked like robot vampires?"

"Machine changelings," Zotzilaha shivered. "Very powerful black magic! Very difficult to defeat. So now, if I help you find the Prince of the Disc, will you rid my House of the menace of the god of deception?"

"He took my nephew," Ganumede said. "I am going to do more than rid you house of him, I am going skin his ass and turn him into a pair of potholders!"

"I think his balls just dropped." Spanx said.

"Open wide!" Sugarhoof said, "Cream or lemon with that teabagging?"

"*All right*!" Orion yelled. "Zotzilaha was just telling us how to find Nefertem and the real Flower Prince and, hopefully, if we pay attention, we won't get killed by a giant kitty cat with the power of a super nova.

"Now, Dweller, you were saying?"

"The Bat's House, or Talocan, is where Tezcatlipoca has been residing. He went there to escape the law and order of the Supreme Lord of the Sky, Quetzalcoatl. Liars always hide from their master, the Truth. Someone called Marcus Perfect came to Tezcatlipoca and offered him the hand of Nefertem, Prince of the Sun Disc, in exchange for impersonating the Flower Prince and opening the door to the Seventh House."

"He did what?" Ganumede asked. "And what did you call him? The invader? Marcus Whatsis?"

"We can worry about this…Marcus Prefect later," Orion said. "Just take us to where Tezcatlipoca is holding Ganumede's nephew and the Flower Prince."

Talocan, the Heart Chamber
Xochipilli, Nefertem, Tezcatlipoca

"Here is how this is going to go," Tezcatlipoca, in his form as a flaming jaguar, explained.

"I will release you, you will fight to the finish. The winner gets to tear the heart out of the loser and feed it to me, then be my lover forever."

"No way, dick-cheese," Nefertem said. "Not fucking a giant smoking pussy and I'm not tearing anyone's heart out."

"You don't understand, hot stuff," Xochipilli said. "This is a game you have to play, or terrible things happen."

Xochipilli pointed to the stripes on his back. "Is true!"

"I think we should get less clothing on and wrestle as he suggests," he winked.

"Well, since that seems like the only way…" Nefertem started to remove his shirt. "Let's go for it. I bet can beat your ass without a stick!"

Once they were free of their chains and half-naked, oiled down and sparkling in the torchlight, Xochipilli said to the Smoking Mirror, "So, it's a contract, right? The loser gets his heart torn out and you set the winner free?"

"Yes, Prince of Flowers, that is the contract. I can't wait to see the Sun Prince wrestle you into submission! And sweaty boy, I can't wait to see the Flower Prince pin you to the ground."

"Grr!" Nefertem said.

Nefertem and Xochipilli locked arms, "If you have something up your ass crack to get us out of this dude," Nefertem said, "now would be good."

Xochipilli kissed him and stepped back, "Smoking Mirror, I submit. The god of the dawn tears my heart out. Now, according to the contract, we must be set free."

"What?" Tezcatlipoca roared. "You cheat!"

“*Ne pas!*” Xochipilli said. “So, are you going to honor the term of the contract or not?” Xochipilli smirked, “My words were true, is your contract false?”

“Yeah, butt muncher! You have to let us go.”

Tezcatlipoca stepped aside, “Clever boys. You are free to go. *And I am free to pursue*.”

“Eep!” Nefertem said and took Xochipilli’s hand and they ran.

The Vatican Catacombs
The Pope, formerly known as Tantalus

“What are you guilty of?” he asked the young man, naked, suspended over the rendering pit, “I need to know the flavors of your sins.”

“I don’t know!” he wailed. “I have no idea what you’re talking about!”

“I think you do,” the Pope held up his cell phone. “Sending these…dick pics to your best friend’s girlfriend. *He complained*.”

“I was just flirting…we didn’t do anything!”

“But you were planning to, correct? ‘when I come, be on all fours, waiting’ the message says. Too bad your buddy came home early, and she was! His wife! Right? Am I right?” the Pope laughed. “*And then you walked in*! *Shazam girl*!”

The Pope flipped through some pages of paper on a clipboard, “These turns of events could be considered coveting your neighbor’s wife, but your friends weren’t married. Oh and by the way, they’re in the next room waiting their turn to confess to having sex out of wedlock. But you, you’re just an old-fashioned weenie-whacking fornicator! Delish! Spilling seed without the intention of making a baby is a bad thing too…let me see, carry the one, drop a zero…”

After he finished his calculations on the wages of the sins that were tallied, the Pope released the clamp holding the man and he fell into the Vat.

At Marcus’s direction, he was giving a homily on the importance of violence awareness this Sunday and they needed more Body and Blood for the Holy Feast of Forgiveness.

The Sacred Forest
Zotzilaha, Quetzalcoatl, Sugarhoof, Spanx, Ganumede, and Orion

“I followed him to the Seventh House,” Zotzilaha explained to the queer looking creature called Quetzalcouatl, who looked like a lion with a peacock feather mane. “There he helped Marcus Prefect lead an attack on my friends.”

“He is in the Bat’s House,” Quetzalcoatl stated. “I watched him bring the Dawn Prince into it, but I did not follow, afraid he would hurt it. And I did not wish to add to the list of grievances Smoking Mirror and I share.”

“What should we do?” Orion asked. “Some of us could distract him, while… Oh Never-mind.”

Down below, Nefertem and Xochipilli, screaming like little girls ran from the Talocan Gate into the jungle.

They were followed by a jaguar as big as a semi-truck, black like a night sky set with deep orange and gold sequins smoldering in its coat.

“He came to me as an exotic orchid,” Xochipilli said. “And offered to let me inhale its essence, promising if I found it pleasing it would allow me to make a cologne of it. Then the fiendish thing gobbled me up!”

“Ew,” Nefertem said. “What are we going to do, that Jag is fast!”

“I have an idea,” Xochipilli said. “I think it’s time to play pole to the hole!”

“*Whoa.* Right now?”

“No, you! Wait here.”

Xochipilli called out to Ahuehuete, the king of the forest,

“Ancestro y Aliado, sé sincero conmigo como lo has sido con todos tus hermosos modos y tradiciones…¡protege a mi familia para que podamos caminar de una buena manera que sea fiel a nuestros corazones!”

(*Ancestor and Ally, be honest with me as you have been with all your beautiful ways and traditions...protect my family so that we can walk in a way that is faithful to our hearts.*)

Just as the great cat was about to pounce, a cypress tree limb caught it just under its tail, and began lofting it up, higher and higher. Ahuehuete was many, many miles high by the time Orion and the others caught up. Even Quetzalcoatl had not reached its apex the sacred tree had grown so tall.

“Dude, that was…the most nastacious thing I ever saw!” Nefertem said and then a dagger, thrown from the heights of the cypress tree, nailed him…*right in the cum well.*

“Tezcatlipoca lied to you,” Quetzalcoatl said. “The champion, not the loser, gets his heart cut out. You fucked up, Flower Child.”

"Aye caramba!"

"My tattoo!" Nefertem whined. "It's fucked, isn't it?"

"You mean, hi, Auntie!" Ganumede said. "Thanks for coming to rescue me! Right?"

"Is my tattoo fucked or not?" Nefertem asked.

"Let us find out." Quetzalcoatl, who was also Medicine Man removed the knife. "Your heart is true," he said. "No falsehood such as this blade could ever pierce it. That is why Tezcatlipoca loved and hated you, Nefertem. You forced him to become acquainted with his own heart, and unable to deceive even himself about his own fancies."

"Sure didn't deceive me," Xichipilli said.

"You fucked him, didn't you?" Nefertem said to Xochipilli, eyes filling with tears.

"No!"

"Si!" Nefertem said. "Sluthole!"

"Ahuehuete says his crown is on fire," Quetzalcouatl, "the Monarch of the Skies," said suddenly. "The Smoking Mirror is on his way to rematch with us."

"And that's our cue," Ganumede said. "Sugarhoof, please help Nef get saddled up."

"Agreed," Orion said, "Let's let the big guns work this one out without...*holy shit*!"

There was the sound of splitting timber and a giant with one eye swung a giant axe and Ahuehuete along with a very angry, very large cat fell from the sky.

"Marcus Prefect sent a Cyclops to aid the Smoking Mirror," Quetzalcoatl said. "We should go. You have a place?"

"Yes," Ganumede said.

"Oh fuck me," Orion said, "We have to wait. Spanx is trying to be a hero."

Spanx was already in the air, blasting the thing with plumes of colored fire, roaring like a symphony of tubas.

"Hunter," Ganumede said. "Xochipilli is a huge pansy, Nefertem is hurt, and Quetzalcoatl says we need to get out of here and warn the others about this Marcus Prefect guy."

"But...Spanx!" Orion looked into the distance. "He's a flea compared to that thing!"

“Hunter, we cannot stay,” the Quetzalcouatl said. “More of Marcus’ Deforesters are coming.”

Sure enough, two more lumbering gargantuan forms broke through the mist of the mountain top, their clubs and axes flattening trees thousands of years old into splinters.

“No! Stop!” Xochipilli shrieked.

“Hunter.” Quetzalcouatl said. “We are going.” He circled the Flower Prince in the soft down of its coils and then took him into the air. Orion mounted Sugarhoof ahead of Ganumde and Nefertem and began their retreat to the Seventh House.

Down below, in the Sacred Forest, they watched the one-eyed giants overwhelm the valiant dragonne called Spanx.

On the way back to the Seventh House, Orion, Ganumede, Nefertem, Sugarhoof

Orion sobbed, “He was the only person I’ve had to talk to since Zeus sent me away.”

“Zeus?” Ganumede asked. “*You knew Zeus*?”

Orion nodded, “I was about your age when Zeus appeared as a great stag, and scandalized me. My father was humiliated and sent me into the forest to wander. When Zeus learned I was disgraced, and worried I would blaspheme him, sent me to the stars.

“Medicine Woman found me and asked me to watch over the Lodge in the Happy Hundting Grounds for her. One day, I caught Spanx smoking in the tobacco field and we hit it off.”

“Zeus. He is the Divine Ancestor of this Marcus Prefect.” Quetzalcoatl said. “A tyrant god, lawless, with an insatiable lust for power and fear. As in ages past, he’s gathering others like him to bolster his position.

“I chased him from Babylon in my guise as Bahamut,” Queztalcouatl said, where He began his reigns of terror as the God called Yah.”

“I thought he was dead!” Ganumede said. “Didn’t we just beat his ass by destroying Olympus?”

“This thing, the Unholy Spirit,” Quetzalcoatl said, “is never destroyed. It moves like a parasite, from belly to belly till it runs out of food. Then it waits.”

"He sure waited to parasitize me," Ganumede said. "And not through my stomach!"

"Woof!" Orion said, eyeing Ganumede, who, full of fury, looked away. Orion frowned. "God! What's his problem?"

"Sometimes it keeps its butt to itself." Nefertem said. "Sometimes it just gives its butt to anyone who wants it."

"Now just who the hell do you think you're talking to?" Ganumede said.

"Whoever represents." Nefertem said.

"You don't need to be passive aggressive," Xochipilli said, "I never keep anything to myself…so you want it, come and get it!"

"Do you see how that works?" Hunter said to Ganumede.

"It's fabulous." He said. "Just fabulous."

Chapter 10

The Mysteries of the Heart

Concurrently, The Seventh House Infirmary

Erzulie, Mrs. O, Sophia, Mazu, Amaterasu O Mikami, Ushas, Pvrithi, Coatlicue, Rhiannon, Medicine Woman etc., and Jezebel

"What should we do with them? They suffer so," Mazu surveyed the dying Fembots, arrayed on couches in the infirmary.

"Leave them," Oya said. "Abominations. Better still, they should be thrown into the composter!"

"Please," Jezebel said. "Don't throw them away. They deserve some consideration, surely?"

"They haven't done noble things in all their times, no," Amaterasu O Mikami said. "But, surely, an act of mercy will benefit them as well as us?"

"That is always the case," Sophia said. "Options and ideas?"

"I have one," Rhiannon said. "Each of you, shed some of the Light of your Heart on a Fembot. We will reform them. Give them a chance to live as real women, noble women…the noblest."

"What will they become?" Jezebel asked.

"Our knights, not His," Rhiannon said. "Valkyries! Feminine Knights Possessed of Great Valor."

"Yes!" Sophia said, "Our Knights will seek the blood of the guilty, not the innocent in the name of this world's redemption!"

The Vatican, the Pope

Tantalus chanted from the *Book of the Red* over the bodies,

"Born in blood, die in a flood.
Plague of life, cut with a knife.
Drain it dry then spit in the eye,
Fuel for the fire, let it burn
From this life there's no return."

The bodies sat up. The whites of their eyes were streaked with blood, the blue irises disturbingly beautiful. They were all male in their primes, their chests, abs, cocks, and thighs stained the color of rust from the fluid in their vats.

"Go forth, my Vultures. Make rotten fruit of my flock, and feed on it…"

The Vultures, which were essentially blood sauages made from the worst adulterers, mastubators, blow jobbers and pornographers were born again more ruthless and without a conscience than before. They grinned, showing perfect teeth; blood ran down their faces and out of their mouths, trickled from between very plump red lips.

They hated the rules of the Church before, found them too confining and frustrating in life were now remade into instruments of its mischief and madness unleashed upon the world, this time with its full consent.

The Spite House, the Staff Meeting

In attendance:

- Marcus Prefect, the Last Emperor.
- Edith, Lot's Ex Wife, the Sexretary of Hate.
- Job, the Faith Healing Expert, head of the Forced Drug Agency.
- Adam, the Gardener, Department of Real Estate.
- Pope Tantalus.
- Saphira, Annanias's, wife Secretary of the Treasurer, absent.

"I have some bad news," Saphira sat back in her chair, hands folded over head eyes lowered, "We. Are. Almost. Out. Of. Money." Overwhelmed by faux exasperation, she sighed.

"How is this possible?" Job asked. "Where did it all go?"

"We, ah, spent it, Doc," Marcus said. "Adam built all of those high rises and the units are too small for the positively burgeoning families that still want to live the urban lifestyle, our health care plan was underwritten with real estate taxes and those are, consequently, not performing as projected," Marcus feigned a look at Adam. "And the successful expansionist agenda of the Church is causing a run on State funds. We are rich in Spiritual Wealth, just cash poor."

"Oh for Chrissakes," Job didn't hide his disgust for the Pope or Adam. "You're shitting me! What about Saphira, what the fuck has she been doing? She was supposed to print more money!"

"Inflation is not the answer here, Doc," Marcus said. "And neither is embezzlement; nor are untimely and costly mistakes. But Miss Edith here has some possible solutions for us, and also wants to explain why her plans are running behind don't you, my dear?"

"The usual," Edith said. "Time and Materials,"

"Time and materials? For what?" Job barked.

"Weapons sales," she began. "It's all we've got. We have too many mouths to feed, crops are failing, the water is poisoned, diseases are rampant, we're positively upside down due to overhead. Once we make the weapons, it will boost gross domestic product and exports."

"You silly sow, the whole world is domestic to us!" Job said. "*Where and to whom are you going to sell them, please*? And who will be allowed to use them?"

"Why everywhere and everyone. People just love weapons!" Edith said. "They like to play with them, shoot them, explode them. I think they will be quite popular, especially with the holidays coming up. People love to use them on each other more then than any other time of the year!"

"That's all good, but we need something sustainable," Marcus said. "Something with more repeat sales potential."

"I have an idea," Job said. "I can concoct a drug so addictive, so monotonous, and insidious, it will make heroin seem like an aspirin."

"How would you traffic it without compromising the Administration's strict policy on drugs?" Marcus asked. "Parents just don't want their kids using their drugs."

"We can put it in the Sacrament," the Pope offered, "That way everyone gets to share in the blessings equally."

"Money, Holy Father," Marcus insisted. "Where's the money in free drugs."

"*Pfft*. They will get a free sample, and pay for it after that. They'll have to."

"Have to what?" Job asked.

"Come to church more often!"

"The love of money is the mother of all invention, is it not fellas?" Marcus said.

"I think so, too," Edith said.

"Amen," the Pope said.

The Beach House

Mazu tested the water. The pH was too low, the temperature was too high. The radiation levels were too high. Oxygen levels were too low. Plankton, the larvae, and spores of just about every species as well, were way too low.

There was a **splat* * sound. Then a plume, like a whale the size of Texas, blew its spout, a red light.

"It's…so…beautiful," Edith said from a vantage point Marcus created for her in the Ether. "It's beyond my wildest imaginings! I can't wait till we do it for real!"

"Now, now," Marcus handed her his hanky. "We need to let this sink in a little before we do that. We want them to be scared for a while, don't you think? Let the tensions…tense up. Then we can drop more!"

"Oh poo! Can't we say, like with Sodom and Gomorrah, you've got it coming mother fuckers and here it is?"

"That's not what that was," Marcus said. "Those people were having too much fun without me. I've never been tolerant of being left out."

"I haven't forgotten! You know that, don't you?" Edith checked his trousers.

Marcus grabbed her hand, "Stick to your dynamite and bombs and missiles, if you want explosions, Edith, if you don't mind."

"Certainly," Edith said. "Let's move on, then shall we?"

"Lets. I need to make a speech about the funding we've 'discovered' for the new network of rehab centers."

The Seventh House

Sophia calls a meeting of the Ordnance

"Thank you all for gathering and to our newest friends, Mithras, Orion the Hunter, Quetzalcoatl, Varuna, Xochipilli, Cu Chulainn, and, of course, baby Cerviel."

Jezebel took the baby's hand and waved it at the assembly gathered around the immense Oval Table.

"You may see we have changed our structure a little, but I think it makes sense and I hope you will give it a try. I have asked Mithras," who was seated at the other end of the oval, "to be my partner in the stewardship of the Seventh House. There will always be a Steward or Stewardess and a Regent, one of each gender in rotation. One will retire, the other replace him or her, and so on.

"Are there any concerns or disagreements with my decision on this?"

"Is he single?" Erzulie asked.

"That's an excellent question," Sophia said. "We, who have decided to gather here to protect life and the love of life, have made a significant commitment. One that is vital, as you will learn in a moment.

"We ask that the Steward and the Regent attend to his or her duties and refrain from distraction here or abroad until such time as their turns at the heads of the table are concluded."

"Pshaw," Erzulie said. "But I honor the wisdom of your decision and will serve your cause."

"We all will," Ushas said.

There was a moment of silence. Then Sophia motioned to Mithras, who went to the Scrying Pane, "The Beach House has been destroyed."

He displayed the footage of the explosion and wall of boiling iridescent water that was so large, it made the Beach House look about the size of a peach pit.

"Who did this?" Medicine Woman wept. "Mazu was much beloved by all creatures! She had no enemies!"

"She had one," Mithras said. "Marcus Prefect. The same that attacked our cotillion and killed Hestia, the one that poisoned the seas and rivers, who deployed those Deforester monstrosities that Ganumede told us about, and there's more, that you just. Won't. Believe."

Mithras and Sophia took turns explaining what they had learned from the Valkyries, who had been surveying creation for intelligence.

"But what is this thing?" Pvrithi asked. "What does it want?"

"We have all known and fought this being of Pure Tyranny in each of our emanations," Sophia said. "Though He's changed His name and appearance, His hatred for peace and goodwill has never wavered. He is the Unholy Spirit, a malevolent being kept alive by human depravity, which is ironic since they have suffered the most from his cruelty. They get off on Him!"

"That's…insanity, not irony," Pvrithi said. "Let's send It on its way then! Who cares if humanity likes It or not?"

"We are looking into such a way," Sophia said. "But…it's uncertain at this time. And a friend of ours is missing; we need to get him back first."

"After that, we have work to do. The Earth is in peril but there have been no prayers. Worse than suffering such as must be the case, is sufferance. We will discuss strategies now and when we are all in accordance, we will make things right."

Orion and Ganumede

The Garden Railing

"Do you want to go for a walk?" Orion asked.

"Sure," Ganumede said, allowing himself to feel a little of the thrill he felt at seeing Hunter; advice from his disgusting nephew.

"He thinks you're hot-diggity!" Nefertem said. "Go for it. And don't forget, it's like roasting a chicken. You have to wait till the juices run clear before you dig in!"

"I'll try to keep that in mind, kid, thanks."

"Do you like it here?" Orion asked.

"I've settled in," Ganumede said. "My cousin lives here, my nephew lives here, my mother's cousin comes here a lot…"

"*But do you actually like it here*?" Orion laughed. "And what do you do here?"

Ganumede looked out across the central hub of the House to the other side. There were gardens, fountains, animals of every size and shape, the weather was always pleasant and felt natural. There was good music, good food. And all he did was watch it.

"I get underfoot," he answered. "It's what I've done my whole life."

"And what else would you do, if you weren't underfoot?"

"Orion, I can't think about stuff like this… Attis is still in that magic pond and Nef's a huge handful…"

“Ganumede, shh!” Orion stopped and took his arm, gently. “Look up there.” He pointed to a ruddy star. “See that? That’s my house! My Hunting Lodge! In my constellation!”

“So?”

“So come be underfoot at my place.”

“Just under your foot?”

“You know why you turn me on so much?”

“Dunna.”

“You like to be chased, don’t you?” Orion smirked in his sexy smirky way. “You like to dare people to find you attractive, see how far they’ll go to prove to you they’re hot for you, don’t you?”

Ganumede blushed, “No, that’s not it.”

“Yes, it is!” Orion said. “You like to run, and I like to hunt. It’s very hot.”

“I run like a girl.”

“*So you will come with me to the Lodge once we free Spanx and stop Marcus?*”

“The Marcus part is a definite,” Ganumede said. “The Spanx thing…that’s a deal killer.”

Orion laughed, “He’s not that bad.”

“Yes, he is.”

“Yeah, he is,” Orion said. “Still, you’ll come with me?”

“Yes, Orion, I’ll come with you.”

Chapter 11

The Riddle of the Heart

In the Lair of the Deforesters

"Listen you stupid bitches, my name is Spanx! I'm not a Sphinx. *And I hate riddles*! And if you bring that whip and chair any closer, I will flash fry your twat!"

Spanx tried to get its breath to reach Hesiod but the chain attached to his collar kept him just out of range, "Where is the Hunter?"

Spanx could have used his real weapon, a roar that could knock over King Kong, but Hesiod wasn't alone and Spanx was unable to break the *mithril* chain and collar that kept him captive. Without the key or a rescue, he was stuck.

"Please, please! Be kind to us. We are old and trying so hard to be ever so sweet!" Steropes said and drew her talons up under her hairy chin, blinked her eye. "Just one little riddle; something to amuse us and give our jiggle a wiggle?"

"Nope," Spanx sat down and folded his paws one over the other.

"Ask me the one about what moans when nothing is hurting! I love that one," Arges begged. "Please, please, oh please?"

Spanx rolled his eyes, "I assume this means you are the one posing the riddles now?"

"*Answer*!" The whip cracked over Spanx's head. The whip had a *mithril* ball on its tip and it hurt like a motherfucker when they whacked him with it.

"Fine. I'll tell you. The thing that moans when nothing is hurting is a *cock*," Spanx said. "*A big sloppy dripping cock*."

"It does know riddles!" Steropes clapped her hands and whooped with glee, "It does! It does! Yes! That one was quite splendid! Ask us another."

"Oh my gods, I didn't even ask you the first one!"

"Ask me this one!" The whip came very close to one of Spanx's eyes, which looked like fire opals but were hardly as fragile. "What has wings but doesn't fly; has no legs but runs?"

"Oh lord," Spanx said. "A vagina. A huge gaping vagina."

"Wrong!" Steropes was so thrilled.

"A fish!"

"Like I said," Spanx said.

"OOO! I like," Arges laughed. "You're really cute you know that?"

"Why, you're not so filthy and disgusting yourself, you sagging old whore," Spanx said.

There was a hum, barely audible over the witch's cackling.

"I actually do have a riddle," Spanx said. "You don't see him, but you can hear his song."

"No fair! We don't know that one!" Arges complained. "Tell us, who is it that can't but can still hear?"

"*The truth*!" the Ace of Swords said and cut her head off. After he made quick work of the others, he brought his sword down on the chain that held Spanx captive to the wall, then tore the collar off with his bare hands.

"Jeopardy's over, Mr. Trebek," the Ace said. "We've got stuff to do."

"Who the fuck are you?" Spanx said.

***

The Four Sportsmen

"It itches," Brian complained about the headset. "And I can't feel the bang!"

"But it can fly, and you can't, so bang yourself later," Rick said. "And try to hit the fucking target!"

"I never miss," Mick said. "Mine is working just fine. Haw! Watch this!"

He shot a ball out from under this heffer in a Pilates for pregnancy class and it collapsed under her. Her water broke, "Touchdown!"

Dick tested his drone a kind of swarm by sending them into tailpipes, plumbing, electric outlets, spraying graffiti.

Flickering lights appeared in the sky, plagues of locusts chewed through chargers for phones and electric cars, mysterious sayings appearing on the insides of churches, government buildings, Starfux coffee houses:

"*Eat ice cream made from breast milk*!"

"*Go to Hole Foods to get bred!*"

"*Jesus was a bondage bottom*!"

"I think I have the hang of it," Brian said and aimed his drone cannon at an old woman who emerged from a dialysis center. He missed and the whole facility exploded, engulfing her and most of the storefronts on that block in fire and shrapnel, "they didn't have long to go anyway?"

"Right," Rick said. "Cool." It did no good to pay much attention to Brian. He just was the way he was.

Playback with the Five Tops

"I'm not sure I like the name of this band," Xochipilli said. "Misrepresents."

"Is that your drag name, sissy? Miss Represents?" Cu Chulainn said.

"You smell like a whore's armpit," Nefertem said.

"It's me natural oils. The birds and the bees just love it!" Cu Chulainn said,

"Dude. That. Is. Nastacious."

"Si Senor!" Xochipilli said.

"I grew up fast for *this*? You're all a bunch of idiots," Cerviel groaned.

"The next time I take a bath," Varuna said. "The Irish guy is coming with."

"*Yer* on, Shark Boy," said Cu Chulainn. "Like the smell of me chum, do you?"

"Gentlemen!" Mithras commanded. "This isn't choir practice. Now, if you will direct your attention to the Scrying Pane, I would like to show you your competition."

Mithras called up the scene of the Four Sportsmen; marauding a small town in West Virginia.

"You are more than their match…but these Dude-bots are highly trained, heavily armed, and they know what they want. They attacked the Happy Hunting Grounds and are now testing new weapons, we think, to make another attempt at securing a presence there. They cannot succeed."

"How can we stop creatures like this?" Varuna asked. "Those weapons are other worldly."

"So are you, guys. Here's how we are going to take them down. They have no idea you even exist, they're that ass end-up stupid. They're unstudied, undisciplined, they just have expensive toys, a daddy that buys them shit all the time, then turns his back on their crap and makes the world clean up after them.

"They're mechanized, you're forces of nature. They have limits where you have capabilities. They can be scared; you're fearless."

"I think I'm scared," Xochipilli said.

"Ditto," Nefertem said.

"Let's just tear the asses out of those piss towels, and be done with it!" Cu Chulainn said.

"Yes, I agree," Cerviel said. "Tell us what we need to do," Cerviel said. "And how much time do we have?"

"They want to attack the Guardians of the Four Directions again. We're going to get in between them. We can't subject the Guardians to the weapons the Sportsmen are using now, they're too dangerous. So we're going to let them shoot at us, and we have to leave at once."

Coatlicue and Chalchiuhtlicue
The Lake
The Riddle of the Womb—Where is Attis?

"General," Coatlicue and her sister found Mithras after he gave the Five Tops their instructions. "The Father of Titans is not in the Lake and the Lady is not answering us."

"I searched the lake myself," Chalchiuhtlicue, goddess of fresh water said. "And Coatlicue says there are no signs in the stars of his whereabouts."

"Did someone enter the House and take him while he was asleep?"

"No," Coatlicue said. "No vertical horizons have opened in the House, since we last saw Attis enter the Womb."

"Did he do his final disappearing act then?"

"Sophia would know if he did, and she said not."

"Either way, we weren't counting on him too much anymore anyway," Mithras said. "If only he just didn't exist at all, you know?"

"That's not very nice," Chalchiuhtlicue said.

"Don't have time to be nice, honey." Mithras said. "Never did, and you know why. And speaking of…!"

Executive Office Building

Edith, the Sexretary of Hate; Adam, Head of the Department of the Interior; Job, Head of the Department of Hellth.

"Has anyone besides me figured out what the three of us have in common yet?" Edith asked Adam and Job when they had a moment to themselves.

"A love of public service?" Job asked.

"No." Edith said. "Each one of us was betrayed by our significant other, and big time so that fat fuck in the Oval Office could make an example of us to His pilgrims. Make us look stupid so He could look good! I got turned into a human saltlick, Adam bit the fruit and was thrown out of paradise…Job, you…"

"Let's not talk about her." Job said. "And yes, it had occurred to me out of all of Yahweh's instruments, we were given exalted positions in his cabinet. Because we all wanted second chances and would do anything to have them. Why?"

"Revenge on humanity, of course." Adam said. "And no one wants it more than me. The very sight of these people, the things they do, the things they say during the course of their paradisiac lives! It gives me great pleasure to do what we're planning."

"You forget who and what we're dealing with," Edith said, "Marcus arranged for Eve to cause the fall of man and take you with her, didn't He? And look at how eager you've been to transform the Garden into an overpriced shit hole for Him?

"And you…Job, you think your wife was a shrew, but why did she egg the devil on? To please Marcus who held you up in front of the world as a champion of faith in suffering! Now the shoe's on the other foot, everyone on earth is pregnant, sick or addicted, thanks to you and it's happening again! They're all praising fucking Marcus for every bit of it! Like all the shit he's pulling on everyone is all good news!"

"Why feel bad about it now, Edie?" Job said. "You've been trying to turn the Middle East and China into golf courses for the big schmuck! Why change your mind now?"

"Because I overheard him talking to those brats- the Four Sportsmen – about the next and final stage of His plans." Edith said, her eyes blazing with fury, "What's the one thing people love about Yahweh or Marcus or whatever the hell he calls himself more than His commandment to be "be fruitful and multiply"?

"Don't know." Job said.

"Tell us." Adam said.

"Prophecy." Edit said, "The End Times. His freaky followers never shut up about it. And you won't believe this, but He's planning to make them happen! And ending us with them!"

"He is?" Job growled, "How?"

"It's big." Edith said, "*Really big.* Sit down and I'll explain, and if you don't think I'm crazy, and we work together, we might have a prayer in hell of surviving and be free of the goddam God of Israel once and for all!"

Marcus Prefect and the Pope

"Holy Father, don't forgive them for they have sinned," Marcus said to the Pope. "Do they not look like total idiots, thinking they could pull that off with me? I see all, I hear all, I know all."

"Have they served their purposes yet, Lord?" the Pope, who was imbibing some of his drug-soaked V-8 cocktail, asked.

"Don't drip on the carpet," Marcus said. "Please, and thank you, and rid me of them soon. Edith is 'selling' the last of the bombs, Adam has the stock market of every country tied up in a real estate market that is falling as fast as a dove out of heaven, and I have the formulas for all of Job's plagues and poisons copied and ready to undergo mass production. I have no need for them any longer."

"The Vultures would love to teach them the Catechism, my Lord, if that is thy commandment."

"After the fusion bombs are in place and everyone's feeling good about themselves, release the buzzards."

"Thy will be done," the Pope said. "Would you care for a cocktail?" the Pope held up a flask.

"I do not *drink* blood," Marcus said.

"And why not, My Lord?" the Pope asked.

"I have no need of it, for I have no heart," Marcus said. "And what about you?"

"I have a heart that is not nearly a match for my stomach." Tantalus said. "As you have seen I can stomach quite a lot."

"*You won't betray me*, will you, Tantalus?"

"I've betrayed gods before and seen hell because of it, The Lord My God," Tantalus said. "Once is enough."

"I believe you. By the way, how is church attendance?"

"Burgeoning! It's a good thing real estate is so inexpensive, we are going to need to build many, many more places of worship."

"Excellent. Have a blessed day, Holy Father," Marcus said.

"And, you also Holy Father," the Pope replied.

***

The Ace of Swords, Astride Spanx

"Take me to the House," the Ace told Spanx.

"Which one?" Spanx asked. "There are two."

"The Spite House," the Ace said.

"You got it." Spanx said. "Ace, why didn't you just tell everyone what the big dam deal is? They're probably pissing themselves."

"They will see soon enough for themselves and seeing, they will believe."

"Believe what? Are you still Attis or not?"

"I am the Father of Titans, I am all sons, fathers, brothers, and comrades."

"Well holy shit that's neat!" Spanx said. "But what does it mean?"

"Creation operates according to certain paradigms," The Ace of Swords went on. "One of them is evolution. Things have to move and grow or the Will of God is stymied. When lies and superstition are manifold and plentiful, when history's voice is drowned out or ignored, the universe incurs old sins anew and lies to itself about its role in them.

"Some think we may naturally outgrow traditions for pain and suffering, others naively think their generation is immune to them. I am the Sword come to right all ignorance about This."

"You definitely have a way with words!" Spanx said.

"When the time comes, Spanx," The Ace of Swords said, "It will be an exchange of words in the least."

"Whatever that means, Ace, we're about to take that Sword of yours right into the Heart of the fight. I hope you're right."

"*Heart of Spite falls before Heart of Light*," the Ace of Swords said. "This is the Truth and the Truth always leads to what is right."

Thus, is solved the Riddle of the Heart.

Chapter 12

The Nine Plus Nine

The Pope and the Vultures

"Kill the Jew, then the other Jew, then…the other Jew," the Pope said. "But conserve the blood. We can use that. *But do not consume the bodies* for they are cursed to us."

"Why are they cursed, Holy Father?"

"If the body of a Jew enters one of us, we are deconsecrated."

"What should we do with their corpses then?"

"Throw them in the river, let the fish, if there are any left, pick at them. What they leave behind, let the snails, spiny and slimy things have their fill."

"You are scum," the Arch-buzzard said. "We don't care about the type of flesh. Let us eat."

"Oh all right, eat them then," the Pope laughed. "But the blood is mine, that I might wash in it. Do you understand?"

"We will return most of it to you."

Those Vultures…so hard to control. "All. Of. It."

"All of it," the Arch-buzzard said.

The Seventh House
Mithras and Sophia and the War Council

"Edith has informed me fell creatures are attacking her and the other Administrators. One of them is Adam, the other is Job," Jezebel said. "Marcus has been trying to reunite the family, it seems. Edith is screwy, but she's asking for help and I believe she is sincere."

"Let them rot," Oya said. "They chose their road; let them go where it leads."

"Mother," Sophia said. "It is our Providence to ensure all roads lead to Mercy."

"Give them the mercy they have shown, I say," Erzulie said. "I say we stuff that Adam and make a foo foo fetish of him!"

"Sister, Adam is more than just a souvenir," Sophia said. "He's the reason we descended from the firmament to begin with; to provide comfort and guidance. We still play that role, no matter the errors in judgement he and others like him have made."

"There is more at risk than just a couple of Biblical Relics," Mithras said. "Marcus, His Agents, and His head of Church are razing Creation. The forests are burning. The oceans are boiling. Nothing is growing, and life in the Garden is withering.

"Those fusion bombs Marcus has been setting off are pushing the land beyond its ability to hold the earth together and he's ensured that the number of people who endure the calamities he has orchestrated grows every day."

"Have we been complacent?" Pvrithi asked, teary eyed. "We've all been working so hard to prevent this very thing and it always seems to slip away from us."

"No, Pvrithi," Sophia said. "It did not slip away from us. Marcus counted on the cooperation he got. He was brilliantly evil, we were merely hopeful. People don't buy into hope, they have concept of it."

"Why would people help him?" Ushas asked. "What does he have to offer?"

"It's an old trick," Mithras said. "Act like you believe your own lies, then rule over those that think you're telling them the truth. Give them all of the signs—money and poverty, health and disease, drugs and sex, and no matter how bad it gets, convince people things are going according to the plan and they'll go along with it."

"Tell us what we have to do," Amaterasu O Mikami said. "There is no more time for hope only to fight."

"We're going to fight all right, Ama," Sophia said.

"Yes!" Mithras said. "Here is the sheet of music we're going to sing from," Mithras called up the Scrying Pane. "Valkyries, you route the Red Men. Do not engage Marcus Prefect. Boy Band: You will jump into the Happy Hunting Grounds take out the Four Sportsmen.

"Oya and Erzulie, get that fucking cocksucker Ogun out of the ass crack of the earth he's crawled into and this time, make sure he never leaves, up, down or to the side.

"Ushas and Pvrithi: Get rid of the rest of Marcus's fusion bombs.

"Medicine Man, Medicine Woman: help those that are hurt and stand by for the smoke signal.

"Hoochie Mamas: You have a date with the Pope.

"Orion, Ganumede, and the rest of us are going after Marcus. The Four Directions and the Four Elements are watching the House. Any questions?"

"Oh Daddy!" Nefertem said.

Later, in private, Mithras confirmed with Sophia, "And you're going to handle the other issue, correct?"

"I am," Sophia said.

"Are you sure you can trust him? He seemed…off when we met."

"He like his son has made the journey through the Form Cosmic too many times. It changes you. Him, it changed for the better."

"And yourself?"

"I've always wanted to, and he's very cute." She blushed.

"I'm jealous." Mithras said. "It's been a while."

"You did get a shoutout, you know," Sophia said.

"I heard!" Mithras asked. "Will we meet again?"

"Of course," Sophia said. "Look for me. I'll be around."

The Seventh House, After the War Council
Amaterasu O Mikami and Jezebel

"Jezebel, I would like to talk."

The Mother of the Sun lacked interest in Jezebel up till then. There were a lot of personalities to get to know and Jezebel was busy carrying and delivering a baby, too. Then, he grew up and left. They always left her.

Jezebel was once again just a lonely whore, abandoned by the gods. All except this one.

"You may have noticed you were not assigned a campaign," Ama said.

"Let me guess; you want me to dust the table or clean the windows?"

"That is a not good place for us to start," Ama said. "We have similar stories, you and I. We should be better friends. Both of us lost our honor because people think we are over possessed by vanity and levity. They thought we deserved to be punished for this."

"At least you weren't executed for it."

"They killed my heart," Ama said. "I was depressed and sad and rather than give me empathy, they showered me with presents and treasures, so that I would shine my rays of brilliant sunshine on them once again. They punished me for my vanity and all the while they were worse.

"When I tried to assert my personality, there were great arguments and wars. The male gods felt my place in heaven was more properly attended to by my sons than by me."

"I've heard that can happen," Jezebel said and looked around.

"We are telling a new story, you and I. Together we will write *the Book of Jezebel* and when those foul creatures Marcus Prefect and the Pope are sent to live out an infinite number of lifetimes in an innumerable number of hells, we will make right all the wrong that has been done to us.

"We will create the Church of the One True Holy Mother. We will teach others how to know Her. Come with me now and I will teach you first."

Ama took her hand and together, they left the Seventh House and entered the Temple of the Sun to continue their conversation.

The Seventh House
Before the War Council; Sophia, the Ace, and Mithras

"I brought your dog home," the Ace of Swords said to the others.

"Consider my debt to you paid after that remark," Spanx said.

"Run along," the Ace said. "And let the adults talk, please."

Spanx did as he was told. Something about this new incarnation of Attis, the Father of the Gods, made him awestruck, silenced his need for banter and sarcasm.

"Who are you?" Sophia said.

"He is the Ace of Swords," Mithras said. "The Blade of Truth."

"Yes," the Ace said, "I was once called the Father of Titans and I will be once again, but who you need right now is the One before you."

“What happened to Attis?” Sophia asked. “The others are quite distressed. And where is Branwen?”

“The Lady waits for my return. As for Attis, I am what remains; the essence of the One that has also been- The One in Three: father, son, and mother.”

“This is quite extraordinary,” Sophia said. “What have you come to tell us?”

“This Marcus Prefect, he is the opposite. He divides rather than unifies, sheds blood rather than protects its vessels. No matter the forces the Universe has spawned to do away with Him. At least until now.”

“You can stop him?” Mithras asked.

“Yes, I can kill him. But in order for him to remain dead, the falsity of his diseased and poisonous cult must be addressed.”

“That’s just about everyone down there,” Mithras said.

“Not everyone,” Sophia said. “There are a few. And we’ll find them.”

Chapter 13

The Rise of the Trophy King

Ganumede, Orion, Mithras, Spanx, and Sugarhoof

"You should have seen him," Spanx said, "Ruff, ruff, ruff, and…ruff!"

"He didn't seem to be able to fit me into his schedule," Ganumede said.

"I think that would have been too emotional for him, Ganumede," Mithras said. "And can that thing take a cold shower? For fuck's sake!"

"Spanx…" Orion said and shook his head.

"I'm trying really hard…" Spanx said, and bent over like he was trying to hide a chubby.

"Could you stop being a piece of ass floss for one second and tell me what my cousin said?" Ganumede yelled. "I've missed him horribly since he went into a coma and then I thought he was gone forever. Now, he's back and he didn't even try to find me. Can you try to show me some sympathy?"

"Sorry," Spanx said. "There isn't much to say. Attis isn't himself. He never was the talkative sort and this new person just talks in circles. He showed up, ripped those Cyclopsians to bits, told me to fly him around and here I am."

"Ganumede," Mithras said, "Attis has transfigured. I'm sure your cousin is still a part of the Ace, but Spanx is right…he's different. I'm sure he will reach out to you. Right now, as hard as it hurts, we have to let him do his duty and we have to do ours."

"I bet you're a blast at parties," Ganumede said.

"Ha!" Mithras said. "Not the kind you throw! If we survive engaging Marcus, perhaps we should try again."

"No, thanks. Why isn't Attis or this Ace of Swords with us now?" Ganumede asked. "Surely he could help us against Marcus?"

“Yeah, if he’s all that, why are *we* throwing ourselves at him like fodder?” Orion asked.

“Distraction,” Mithras said. “He’s got something he has to do first.”

All sound vanished and a wind smacked the party like an invisible hammer.

Marcus set off the first series of fusion bombs in the skies over the Korean Peninsula along its border with China.

Through the Scrying Network, Marcus broadcast this message, ‘There has been an accident with a test missile that was carrying multiple warheads. More information will be forthcoming as available. Stay calm. It’s going to be Great!’

The Spite House
The Administrators

First it started to rain. Edith heard a drop or two, then a drizzle ramping up to a downpour. Then, there was a deluge, finally it sounded like a pipe burst.

The light dimmed and when Edith looked over at the window, she saw it was nearly blotted out by dark sludge.

“Do you see that?” Adam came into her office. “It looks like it’s raining blood.”

“Was toxic rain part of our plan?” Edith asked. “Where is Job? He would know.”

Edith’s office phone rang. The speaker activated. It was Job, “Edith, you have to get to the bunker. Find Adam, we have to hurry. There are blood golems entering—”

The alarms went off and the snare drum sound of the defense grid on the roof activating filled the building.

Edith reached for Adam, who held her close, “Come on.”

They met Job in the lobby and waited for their escort to the bunker. No one seemed to know why the guns and interceptors had been activated or if there was even a threat. There was only the drumming sound of the cannons and that gush of the rain, at times nearly indistinguishable from each other.

In spite of the alarms and the noise, nothing seemed to be wrong. When the secure doors were pried open, a wave of blood three feet high rolled into the lobby of the building.

The Valkyries: Jumping in over the Spite House Executive Wing

"There," Mary Magdalene pointed. "See them? They are drawing the blood out of the local populace and polymerizing it. Such cruelty makes them feel strong and arrogant."

"We were cursed for much less by Yah," Ruth said.

"Yes, like wearing dresses and showing our hair!" Miriam said.

"There are over a hundred of them and only nine of us," Bathsheba said. "How should we approach and still save the Administrators?"

Rachel, who floated next to her asked. "Approach as if casualties are not a concern."

"Correct! Then we will rescue the Red Ghosts from this masquerade at life," Mary said.

"I like the sound of that," Hannah said. "My axe is feeling rather thirsty."

"Yes," Bathsheba said. "Let us all be as a thirsty axe upon these Blood Wraiths!"

"*Dive*!" Mary Magdalene commanded, and the nine Valkyries fell like birds of prey upon the feasting Vultures.

Ushas and Pvrithi, the Eastern Hemisphere

"Marcus Prefect is setting off his bombs," Pvrithi, Goddess of Mountains said. "The sky and the earth are on fire."

"Fire is our friend, Mother Earth," Ushas, the Goddess of the Dawn said. "Fire is life, it is the beginning and the end of all things."

"Fire is time itself, Sister Mother," Pvrithi said, "and this fire in none of these."

"Yes, Pvrithi, my dearest friend, this fire is impure," Ushas said. "If you will gather the false fire like wool, I will thread its fury away from the earth, like a spool gathers yarn," Ushas said.

Pvrithi, the Mother of the Mountain, lifted the fire of the fusion bombs as they erupted and handed them over to Ushas, the Mother of the Morning, who took their furious glory into herself.

Together, they protected the earth, the sky, and everything betwixt from the weapons of mass destruction of the falsely exalted God called Marcus Prefect, the Final Emperor.

What you've been waiting for
The Five Tops vs. The Four Sportsmen
The Happy Hunting Grounds

"Look who's here. The Pep Rally…!" Rick said.

Cu Chulainn, the National Hero, rocketed toward him, slammed him in the side of the head, and socked his face till Rick was knocked off his feet. Cooch grabbed him by his lapels, pulled him back to his feet, and kept hitting.

"Oh help! Lifeguard! I need mouth to mouth!" Brian pointed his rifle at Varuna's face.

"You think you are a hunter?" Varuna said. "Of all the fish, I am the shark. And you…you are just a guppy, a small fish in a big pond."

Brian then became exactly that, a fantail guppy which Varuna cast back into the Infinite Ocean, "You have not been treated well in this lifetime, Brian. Perhaps in another, you will achieve lasting happiness."

Unfortunately, Brian's Overkill Chasis, a mechanical bear, was on autopilot, and it rushed to attack its master's opponent.

Nefertem sustained numerous lacerations from Dick's dagger. He stood still and allowed the fast moving and aggressive jerk to crisscross his skin with skin deep cuts, while his drone, a mechanical leopard that sat on spring-loaded haunches covered in razor wire and was covered in barbed plates darted by and tried eviscerate him. It missed.

"Everyone thinks I'm stupid," Nefertem said. "Then they see what I can do."

There was a bright flash, an EMP and the machine shut down. Dick grabbed his eyes, which were blinded, "You asshole! I can't see!"

"Open your eyes for a change," Nefertem said and slapped the dagger from his grip.

"Why do you have to get everyone down all the time?" Xochipilli asked Mick. "Why can't you be a nice boy?"

"No way…" Mick said. "I'm not like that."

"Like what?"

"Like you."

"Oh come on, no one will see," Xochipilli said and assumed his female form. "I promise I won't tell, if you keep coming back."

Mick tried, wanted, with all his might to use his joystick to get the swarm to break its holding pattern above to plunge onto the little queen and shred him to bits like the mosquito sized air-piranhas they were.

He couldn't…his opponent was so pretty, his lips and eyes were like a girl's, he wanted to touch them, challenge them, like he would an adversary that was trying to take his weapon and use it on him.

Xochipilli pulled the delusory Sportsman on top of him and kissed his lips, slipped his tongue deeply into his mouth.

"Love is a perfume, lust is a poison," he said. "Both taste sweet, both are murder."

Mick struggled, convulsed, squirmed, and tried to escape the Prince of Seduction's grasp.

Xochipilli stood, left the wriggling hull of the little fucker to lay there and wither till the end came.

The Four Sportsmen, however, were hardly content to let it end like that.

"Sportsmen," Rick called over his wire. "Unite to form the Trophy King!"

"Guys," Cerviel who was floating above the battlefield said from above. "Break off!"

He'd seen these…things – those animal shaped mechanoids in the cave with Daniel.

Cerviel swooped down and rescued Nefertem from underneath the cat-thing as it leapt for him. The giant leopard roared and circled back, ran toward Rick's drone, a red dragon with seven machine gunning and flame throwing heads.

"What the fuck is that?" Nefertem watched below as the cat crawled under the robot bear and a jet powered lion-bot streaked through the sky. The sonic boom sent Cerviel and the god of the dawn reeling and into a not-so-controllable crash landing.

It landed and merged with the platform the other two creatures formed; panels opened, booms swung out, gears interlocked.

Lastly, the mecha-dragon jumped in and took the liberty of swallowing Cu Chulainn whole, forcing him into its fiery gullet before it completed merging its frame with the others to give rise to the monstrosity known as the Trophy King.

"Cooch! He's dead!" Nefertem cried out. "And what the fuck are we going to do about that…?"

"Maybe it's not as tough as it looks," Xochipilli said and helped him to his feet.

"No, it's worse!" Cerviel said. "We have to go. We are no match for it."

The Trophy King was named aptly – the bear, lion, and leopard heads scooped up the remaining Sportsmen, and shared ripping them apart with some of the heads of the dragon.

"Let's get out of here." Cerviel said. "Mithras will know what to do about this."

Then the Three Tops and One Bottom jumped away.

The Hoochie Mamas Visit the Vatican!

Coatlicue stretched one of her long legs over the top of the pew in front of her pulled her nylon up to her hip, lowered her foot back to the floor, propped the other one up. The lime green hose caught the light from the stained-glass windows most deliciously.

"Hey, you can't do that in here," one of the Vultures said, his boyish porcelain cheekbones and jaw were stained the color of red wine. "Take care of that before you come into the Sanctuary."

"So? It's done. And it's not like I got my flow or anything!" she slipped a pair of hot-pink fuck-me pumps on and kicked her feet up in the air, "What song are we singing first, Padre? I hope it's *Little Red Corvette*!"

"It's not a song, it's called a hymn *and what*? You slut! You aren't even wearing any underwear? *You must leave immediately*!"

"Why? Don't you want to swing your little Christian Soldier over to my Sweet Chariot?"

"*No I do not!* Leave. Now!" the Vulture said, even though his crucifix really was ready for some nailing.

"What exactly the hell is going on in here? *An animal and a vaginal in the Chapel*?" The Pope, Tantalus, equally bloody and smelling of copper and fried chicken came into the Chapel. "And why is that whore's Santa Maria slithering towards your Nino?"

"Gah!" the vulture said, "Ow! Ew! Oh!"

Snakes began slithering out of Coatlicue's eyes, her nostrils, her mouth…etc. toward the Vulture. They constricted, squeezed, bit, and gnawed.

"I bind thee in the name of Marcus Prefect!" the Pope yelled and slipped on some of the blood in the aisle, "Help me, Heavenly Father! Save me from this she-devil!"

"You prayers are heard!" Chalchiuhtlicue said. "Want to scratch the kitty?" She led the Smoking Mirror, Tezcatlipoca, into the Chapel by a collar and chain, which she released.

"Gah!" the Pope cried out as the great smoldering cat took it between its teeth and shook him.

"Nice snatch you have there," Coatlicue said to Tezcatlipoca, who stood with a great paw on the Pope's back.

"Yours is quite to my liking also," Tezcatlipoca said to her. "Now as for you, mischief-maker!"

"Let me go! I act on the authority of the President! He will hurt you for what you've done here! He will skin you and then let me cook you and feed you to each other!"

"That's an interesting technique you mention." Chalchiuhtlicue said and walked in front of him, planted two lace-up high heels in one of each of his palms. "A few of your buddies came through the forest once upon and time and did some of that to our people a few centuries ago."

She ground her heels into the flesh of the Pope's hands.

"Claiming we were all wrong for them and that you had a better idea!" the river goddess went on. "And that your God needed all of our gold and our soldiers, and women...but not us? As if our forests and flowers and beautiful creatures were just too awful, our believers too primitive for your God of Bloodletting?"

"*And what about them Jews?*" Coatlicue stabbed him in the feet with her pumps. "Hum?"

"*I'm not that Pope!*" Tantalus squealed. "I'm Greek! It's me Tantalus! The cannibal!"

"OOO that's just nasty! Bad *Papi*!" Coatlicue rubbed her heel in.

"Si!" Chalchiuhtlicue said. "Tezcatlipoca, take this *fundio* to Talocan and seal him in. The same way he was in Hades, but this time...give him vegetarian food!"

"Gladly." The great smoldering cat grabbed the screaming Pope behind his neck and sauntered away.

"What do we do now?" Coatlicue asked. "And we thought the Church a shit hole before this guy took over!"

"We clean it up," And Chalchiuhtlicue, the goddess of rivers summonded a clear and pure torrent that flooded St. Peters Square, the Basilica, and the Apartments, and washed away what was left of the Vultures, the Pope and all the carnage they brought with them.

Mount Sinabong, Indonesia
Oya and Erzulie

"Are you going to do the thing?" Erzulie asked.

"I'm not really feeling that angry," Oya said. "And I'd like to stay that way."

"I know how what you mean," Erzulie said. "Do you think this will be it? We'll be of this white man's God and all of His bullshit?"

"Wouldn't have shown up if I didn't." Oya said.

There was the sound of chanting and a hammer falling. After each rhythmic cling and clang pattern came a response from Sinabong—a belching sound and a river of thick black syrup shat itself out of the side of the mountain.

"*What the hell is he doing*?" Erzulie asked.

"Ogun is pumping crude oil out from underneath the ocean floor and pushing it through the old volcanic veins that run under the crust and from there under mountains…and when that hits molten rock…!"

Then came the sound like a massive garbage truck that was in the midst of compacting its cargo—glass breaking, metal twisting, and the sighing of air escaping; loud enough to almost to cover the explosions of gas and erupting lava that was forced out wherever it could go.

"There is going to be a serious shockwave from that. Much of Asia and the Subcontinent will be hit with a tsunami," Oya said. "I'm going to the surface to move a few things around. Can you handle Ogun?"

"*Can I handle him*?" Erzulie laughed and pulled out the Ogun voodoo doll she made. "I am Erzulie! The Most Powerful Priestess!" Erzule lifted up the Ogun doll's little skirt and blew on its jiminy. A little icicle grew down from it.

"Ahhhhh!" Came a yell from down below.

Erzulie lit a cheroot puffed it a healthy glow.

"I am so glad I won't be around to see where that is going." Oya said, "See you soon?"

Erzulie grinned, and grinned, puffed at the cheroot, then brought the end toward the Ogun doll's anal crevice.

Erzulie and Ogun under the Mountain

"Who's here?" Ogun's voice was tainted with annoyance "What kind of sassy Eve thinks she can catch my Serpent in her beautiful garden?"

"For that…" Erzulie bit the doll's nipples, really hard.

"AUGGH!" The mountain shook as Ogun pounded the walls in his fury.

"A man is not supposed to be touched there!" he screamed.

"There are other places," Erzulie took a pin out of her hair and inserted it straight down his pee hole.

Ogun shook the mountain again, "You like to stick things in people, voodoo hag? I will teach you how to use a prick!"

"Sigh," Erzulie shrugged, produced a pair of plyers and gave his beans a little twist.

"Fuck you! Fuck! Fuck!" Ogun moaned.

"Now don't you be cursing at me from down there, boy. Or we're going to have to do learn some respect. With Mama, it's always all about respect."

"And who the fuck do you think is going to teach me motherfucking respect down here in this volcano? You…?"

Ogun, looking very much Samuel Jackson, clutching his furniture, came into the cavern, where Erzulie hadset up her cooking pot.

"Smells like frangipani in here, did you wash out for me?" Ogun approached, a great black hammer dragging behind him.

"*Now that's disrespectful*," Erzulie said and dropped a knuckle bone into the steaming pot.

"What was that?" Ogun felt burning and stinging all over his body. "What did you do to me, you donkey's whore?"

"What did you just say to me, foul demon?" Erzulie's eyes turned moon colored and smoke scented with the frangipani, sandalwood, and myrrh began to emerge from the pot.

"Oh you think because you're pretty and also clever, you can bind me and I'd not know?" Ogun laughed.

"Ooh, strong man, you called me the wife of a donkey, and for that, I'm going to do more than bind you," Erzulie said. "I'm going to stick you in my pot."

And she dropped the Ogun doll into the herbal soup.

Before she left Ogun to his fate in the pot, she called upon the spirits of all the mothers and fathers, sisters and brothers and bound the Strong Man to the fate of the mountain,

"*With the thread of the crimes of your own design, I bind your evil Three times seven times.*

I bind you from Behind I bind you from Before,

That you'll hurt my people never ever more, I bind you from the Left,

I bind you from the Right, I bind you by Day,

And I bind you by Night. I bind you from Below.

I bind you from Above That you may ever know The laws of Life and Love.

I bind you with your own Good conscience Within And so let this magic Unfold And spin..."

After she sealed Ogun into her pot, Erzulie left the heart of the mountain to join the Oya, cackling at how much fun she had.

Oya, the Mother of the Wind

Oya, the mother of the wind surveyed the damage all the drilling, seismic activity, some of it actually natural, and the eruptions and all the nuclear bombs had done.

Over the horizon, she saw Divine Ushas weaving fibers of light together into a star, while Pvrithi fed them to her from the fusion bombs that were erupting all over the surface of the earth.

War, an idea started and perpetuated by humanity and not the least bit discouraged by Divinity, was once again claiming its nefarious place in another chapter of the planet's history.

The damage prior wars, plans, and rumors for wars had caused and all the greed and ambition in between was nigh overwhelming to Oya so she called to her family for help.

Out of the heavens came her brother, Ozain, the healer, to look after the burnt, suffocating, and poisoned animals; Oshunmare, the god of rainbows to clear the sky of smoke; Yemoja, to calm the turgid and heaving seas; Olokun of the Deep to soothe the aches and pains of the ocean floor, and, finally, her mother, Nana Buluku, to bless their efforts as they contained the calamities caused by a despairing and aimless humanity and its Patron God, Marcus Prefect.

When the work was done and Oya and the other Orisha gave praise to Nana Buluku, they went back to Heaven.

Oya waved them goodbye for she had more to do.

The Spite House
Edith, Lot's Wife, the Sexretary of Hate
Job, Head of the Department of Hellth
Adam, the Gardner vs. The Vultures vs. The Valkyries

"Where did all this come from?" Edith said and waded through a waist high flood of blood that was running through the Spite House. It was growing in strength and pushed them toward the door.

"If you were going to have your period, Job," Adam said, "you could have called in sick like a proper lady."

"I bet your butt's not having its period, homo!" Job said back.

Edith screamed. The blood flood suddenly crested and all three Administrators went under and were swept away.

Inside the blood envelope, they could hear machine gun fire and crying out, but mostly just *glub, glub*.

When they were finally washed into the rose garden, their attackers, the Vultures, the Elite Priesthood of the Vatican, surrounded them.

"Take them," Arch-buzzard said. "Add them to the Tide."

As tough as she was, Edith was overtaken and subdued. There were too many Vultures and even with Job's blood diseases, the creatures took them.

Adam was dragged away, his pants legs came off one at a time and he reached for Job's ankles, "Job! Please don't let them take me!"

"Try having faith," Job said, "Maybe they'll leave you alone."

When they could maneuver no longer, the Arch-buzzard, a fearsome creature, naked, his muscles glistening like red leather was stretched over them, came over, and spat all over Job's glasses.

He seemed satisfied with that for a moment, then slapped a wet hand across his face till the spectacles flew, and bit him on the lips. Job didn't scream or cry out.

“Bastard! He struggled against the other Vultures that came to hold him, but their taloned fingers had sunk in deep.”

“Hmm?” The Arch-buzzard pulled Adam’s shirt open and traced a finger over his rib-cage, leaving a rusty trail. “Where is the fabled scar, heretic?”

“The fuck you talking about?” Adam said.

“This…the source of all sin and evil in the world…your ribs!” The Arch-buzzard took Adam’s pen out of his jacket pocket, disassembled it, and stuck it in slowly right into Adam’s liver, right through the bones. Adam screamed. Quite a lot.

“Go ahead,” Arch-buzzard said and one of the Vultures knelt before Adam and drank.

Then a spear cut through the arm of the fell creature and severed it.

Mary Stella Maris dropped from the sky and retrieved it; thrust a sword through two more of the things that came to intercept her.

“Who are you? How can you do this?” Arch-buzzard said.

“You are dead. We are here to collect you,” Mary, the Queen of Heaven said and put the end of Her sword into his eye.

Marcus Prefect, Spite House Observation Lounge
Mithras, the god of truth, The Regent and General of the Seventh House
Orion, the Hunter
Ganumede, the Ever Young

Marcus didn’t turn around when his attackers entered the Lounge.

“Have any of you noticed what’s different this time?” Marcus said. “Look outside. We can fight in a moment, if you think that’s the wisest course of action. But go ahead. Take a gander.”

They approached the windows.

“What are we looking at?” Mithras said. “The suspense…! It’s making my asshole pucker.”

“Cute.” Marcus said. “Tell me what you see.”

“I see lots of blood, dismembered limbs, bodies piling up. Beautiful, Marcus. You’re so talented.”

“What conspicuously absent?” Marcus smiled, took a cigar from a nearby ashtray and lit it with a flip-top silver lighter.

Mithras thought for a moment. "You. Haven't. Even. Lifted. A. Finger," Mithras said. "You mother-fucking bastard."

"Bingo!" Marcus laughed. Not affected laughing, but the real kind, rich with genuine mirth. "I decided this time, someone, everyone, in fact, should get their hands dirty and I'd keep mine clean," Marcus said.

"Why? What's the matter with you?"

"You're the god of truth they say?" Marcus asked. "So I won't lie. *I love it.* I just love watching you all turn on each other, beat on one another, burn, and belittle one another. I get a real kick out of it!

"That, and the way you look for any excuse to be vicious and violent and mean spirited. Lacking a reason, you invent one, then everyone else believes in it, no matter how stupid or far-fetched it is. It takes no effort on my part to get the ball rolling and look how fast it picks up speed!

"I used to have to be in the middle of that, keep things stirred up. Now," Marcus laughed, "watching it happen from On High is the greatest pleasure I have ever known!"

"I am going to make sure you never outdo yourself," Mithras said.

"Before you start something that will finish you," Marcus Prefect said, "I have an update from the battle with the Sportsmen and your merry little band of losers."

"What's he doing? Shouldn't be cutting Marcus's balls off?" Ganumede said.

"Mithras is a tough guy but he wouldn't last a second against Marcus," Orion said. "Your cousin picked a hell of a time to get laid."

"What?" Ganumede said. "*He's doing what*?"

"Yeah, I know, right? Before the big game? Epic fail."

"Oh my God," Ganumede said.

"Guys," Mithras said and walked past them quickly, grabbing them by the arms. "We have to go. Fast. The Trophy King is loose, and it's out of control."

"One second," Orion said and fit an arrow to his bow and fired two arrows into Marcus Prefect, who howled like a pack of wolves.

"Medicine Woman says hi," Orion said.

Chapter 14

Medicine House

Medicine Man lit the pipe and passed it to his brothers. The fire was hot and the air thick with smoke.

When they were all prepared, eyes glassy like opals, obsidian, moonstone, and mother of pearl, Medicine Woman entered the Lodge and joined the circle with them.

In one hand she waved a fan made of the pinfeathers of hawks, eagles, and owls; in the other, a rattle. As she made her way around the Sacred Circle, she chanted,

"Old Ones, Great Ones, Wise Ones, and Elders

I call upon you to guide me, once your healing is over I remember your wisdom, I remember your ways.

Help me and bless me each night and each day.

The Earth is in peril, the sun fades,

Share with me your counsel, I, who say Hey!

And being great, wise, and one with the night, the day and all beings that crawl, fly, or walk in between."

Then the Elders spoke to her.

The Unhappy Hunting Grounds

"The jump-point!" Cerviel screamed. "It's reversing! We're being thrown back!"

The vertical horizon that was supposed to have returned the four boys back to the Seventh House inverted and instead of their intended destination, they were thrown at the feet of the massive and very hideous mechanoid Trophy King.

Nefertem flashed supernovas at its eyes but there were too many of those; it could still see. Then he tried EMPs. Still the Trophy King advanced.

"Nef, dammit," Cerviel dragged him away. "Do not fight! I've seen this Thing before! It's the End of Times! Run!"

"Run where?" Nefertem yelled, "there's nowhere to go!"

Gun ports opened all over the platform and turrets emerged from the forward and rear of its backs. The mouth of the mecha-dragon opened and Cu Chulainn's head shot out like a hulled cherry pit.

"*Asura*!" Varuna wept tears the size of Tsunamis and sent them after the beast but it grew in size, walked across them like they were puddles.

"Pull back, I said!" Cerviel had to grab Varuna by his hair to get him to listen.

The other three were caught up in their own terror and kept trying to face the monster.

As the Trophy King advanced, it fired more ordinance at them, some of it hit near its targets, the rest set the woods and meadows on fire, its giant paws and claws left 'crater lake' footprints in the turf.

Between the concussion of the explosions and the dust and debris cloud, the Trophy King's whereabouts started to become dangerously unclear.

Mithras, who called a war council, sent out an alert that the residents of the Seventh House and their allies were to rendezvous with him to help Cerviel and the others.

"That..." he pointed to the Scrying Pane, "is a big problem."

"What the fuck-izzat?" Erzulie said.

"It's the end of worlds. The Demogorgon," Sophia said. "It is unstoppable. Marcus Prefect has cursed creation with it. It will keep burning, stomping, and spoiling every place it goes until there is nothing left."

"Surely nothing is unstoppable," Ushas, blazing white with all the lights of all the suns in her power, said. "It was made it can be unmade."

"Even this monstrosity must have an off switch," Pvrithi said.

"You are wrong." Coatlicue said. "It is creating a massive center of mass, the opposite of an off switch. I can feel it. We are all in grave danger."

"Yes," Mithras said, "It has a black hole engine inside it. It may look like it's all shotguns and pickups, but that thing is sucking up every bit of space, matter, energy, and information it comes in contact with. If you think that bitch is powerful now, wait till it reaches sufficient density to suck up the Happy Hunting Grounds in an instant."

"We could bring it here," Isis asked. "The House itself is a quantum multiple, we could feed that to it and cause a paradox. That would stop it."

"Out of the question," Mithras said. "All of the information in the universe passes through this House. It would gobble that up like a cocktail peanut."

"Then we have to go and meet it," Sophia said. "Our sons are trapped in the Grounds with it."

"Spanx," Orion said, "Let's go."

"Get on." Spanx said and lowered his head, so Orion could climb aboard, Sugarhoof did the same for Ganumede.

"Yes. Let's go," Isis said.

The Residents of the House jumped away. Right before they arrived, Medicine Woman told Mithras what the Ancetors told her about the Trophy King.

Before, the Seventh House

"He left," Sophia said, regarding the Ace of Swords.

"Do you think he can do it?" Mithras asked.

"I do." Sophia said.

"Will he report back here when it's all over?"

"Yes," Sophia said. "One last time…and it appears your Call of Duty has been answered. We should go and explain."

The Spite House
Marcus Prefect, the Ace of Swords

"Are they drafting kids again?" Marcus said when the Ace of Swords arrived.

"What are you, child?" the Ace asked Marcus. "And what do you plan on becoming when you grow up?"

"Oh that's rich!" Marcus laughed, "I can kill every living thing on this planet and the next and the next till I grow bored with it, then I will make more worlds like it and do the same thing again. After that, I will try to find time in my schedule to respond to your life altering question."

"Your answer is not unexpected. Petty, insulting in a way most children would respond," the Ace said. "Which brings us to a question that the most important one? The one that has distracted you your whole existence? What is the single most inviolate of the Fates' Decrees?"

"There are so many." Marcus said. "Which one is putting a buzz in your beehive at this moment?"

"*The sons shall overthrow the fathers and thus the sins of the former generation shall come to an end.*"

"Thank you for giving me a chance to do again what's been long overdue, then Father." Marcus Prefect said, and began to look more like His former incarnation, that of Zeus, who had been called Yah, Indra, the God of Israel, the patriarchal God that always made people miserable…

"Do you know who and what I am?" the Ace asked.

"Another piece of shit, self-righteous angel in a suit of armor come to throw God down from Heaven, so that he, who is like God, but *is not* God, might then be God Himself?"

"Wrong," the Ace of Swords said. "***I am the Father of Titans, and thou art My Son whom I despise, and I sacrifice you for the good of all order in creation***."

Then the Ace of Swords, wielding the Blade of Truth, pierced Marcus Prefect in the heart and He was no more.

His work complete, he had to return to the Seventh House and say goodbye to Ganumede, the god of eternal youth, also called the Prince of Troy, then Cupbearer of the Gods, his cousin, and also, his very best friend.

The Seventh House

"Mithras," the Medicine Woman entered the Office of the Regent General. "I know how to fight the King of Trophies."

"Do tell."

Medicine Woman explained and Mithras went to do his duty. Exactly as creation expected him to.

Chapter 15

The One True Abomination

One by one, the gods and goddesses of the Seventh House, their brothers, sisters, and mothers, jumped into the Field with the Abomination, known as the Trophy King.

They were thrashed.

The creature had absorbed enough mass, energy, and information to have the gravity well of a gas giant and none of the divinities could get close enough to attack it properly without risk of entering its event horizon.

"Mithras!" Oya cried into the silence that was starting to form within the Happy Hunting Grounds, "It's going to take the whole plane into itself soon!"

Mithras nodded, "Mother of the Wind, it has already done so. This is all an illusion."

"Well this illusion is chewing on our asses!" Erzulie said. "So if you wouldn't mind ringing the bell and waking us all the fuck up, I'd like to get my chipped nails replaced!"

"Everyone," Mithras spoke through the Scrying Network, "we have to let it go."

"What? Are you butt-ass crazy?" Nefertem said, the quantum wind started to make the hair on his legs and arms stand up and lean toward the beast as its gravity well grew.

"We are already inside its event horizon," Mithras said. "We just have to wait."

"Dude, I'm not smart because I don't have to be," Xochipilli said. "So, please explain why I have to let myself get shat out of that thing?"

"That's exactly what we have to do," Mithras said.

"He's right," Coatlicue said.

"Correct," Ushas agreed.

"Wrong and incorrect!" Nefertem said. "I don't want to die a virgin!"

Mithras shook his head. Soldiers the world over, from all the times and all backgrounds, all worried about one thing.

"Nefertem, you're a baby star," Mithras said. "Take a good look at yourself."

"I can't!"

"Yes, you can," Mithras said. "Try."

Nefertem shined his light into the dark well of the beast. Its black heart parted way and rolled past him like a mist.

"Holy frijoles!" Xochipilli said. "I get it! It's not really even here!"

"Oh, it's here all right," Mithras said.

"So then?" Cerviel asked.

"Just wait," Mithras said.

The Great Abomination proceeded to consume all things. It ate every soul, gobbled up every last bit of information, all the suns, galaxies, planets, every last atom, and the space, in which, they all spun around like wayward tops.

Then the Stewards and Regents of the House of The Family of the Great Divinities found themselves standing right where they were when they confronted the creature but it was gone.

In its place were the three idiots called Rick, Mick, and Dick.

Brian, the guppy, eventually grew legs and turned into a soft-shelled turtle.

"How then?" they all asked him.

"It did what it was supposed to do," Mithras said, "And in its wake a Fifth World was made. A gift of the Great Spirit."

Having won the war with the Trophy King, and restored the Happy Hunting Grounds, the Four Elements and the Four Directions returned to their respective habitats.

Ganumede, Nefertem, and Orion, along with the rest, returned to the Seventh House.

The whereabouts of the National Hero, Cu Chulainn and his head, remain unknown.

The Seventh House
The Conference Room

“Mother Sophia asked me to invite Mithras, the Supreme General, to assume her former position as the Steward of the House,” Ushas said. “If all are in agreement with this inauguration, I will take his place as the Regent.”

“I think he sucks,” Nefertem said. “But I second the inaugural motion.”

Then, for the first time since its founding, each person seated at the Table rotated round one seat.

“Hey,” Chalchiuhtlicue asked Coatlicue, “Where did Sophia go, anyway?”

“She went to see that Cosmic View thing they always talk about.”

The Ace of Swords and Isis

“We didn’t get to spend much time together, did we?” the Ace said. He was still armored, kept the Sword of Truth at his side.

“No, not as much as we thought, but we made it count, didn’t we?”

“Considering how unlikely it was I should exist at all,” he said. “Yes.”

“Attis,” Isis took the helmet off. “Don’t leave before you realize you were supposed to be here in the first place. And I loved every second of it.”

“Even when I said those horrible things to you in Duat? If that’s the only grief you gave me, I’m sure I won’t remember it.”

“It wasn’t,” Attis said.

“I don’t mind,” Isis said.

“Mother, I’m scared of leaving,” Attis said. “But I can feel the universe rejecting me and that’s even scarier.”

“It’s not rejecting you. It’s telling you it’s time to go. All of us must at some point. You’re just allowed to know when. Leave with a clear mind and a full heart. It’s what you earned.”

“I hope Ganumede will think so,” Attis said.

“He’ll think how he thinks,” Isis said. “Goodbye Attis.”

Isis kissed his cheek and quickly departed for Heliopolis.

Amaterasu O Mikami and Jezebel, the Temple of the Sun

“Most fragrant flower that catches my eye,” Ama said to Jezebel. “Sophia, the Mother of Peace, taken your place. It is time for you to do the same.”

“It’s still going to be a fight. It always is.”

Amaterasu O Mikami laughed, “So fight.”

"Is that mess in the Vatican cleaned up yet?" Jezebel asked, "I don't mind owning a used house but not until it's been scrubbed of that…man-funk, you know?"

"Most definitely," Ama said, "I will make a sweet breeze blow through its streets and alleys for you, my love. Come, let us go. You are needed, High Priestess of Divine Mother."

The Moment We've All Been Dreading, Part 1
Attis, the Ace of Swords and Ganumede

"Gigi," the Attis said, "I have to go."

"So, go," I said.

Attis smiled, then not so much. "The universe abhors the presence of a Titan," he said. "Try as I might, that's what I am. I always was…"

"No, you were just a guy." Ganumede said. "Remember how you wanted me to kill your girlfriend?"

"I actually forgot about her!"

"And you fucked that hipster goddess and forgot to tell me, didn't you?"

"She threw herself at me," Attis said. "What else could I do?"

"So did I!" He laughed. "And what happened? You said no and Zeus tried to double fist me for it!"

"You clearly traded up," Attis laughed. "I knew that day we met, when you ran out of the girl's bathroom and right into me how fabulous it would be to be your friend. And it has been."

"You don't say?" Ganumede raised an eyebrow.

"Most of it? Some of it?"

"Some of it was fabulous. Like the movies," Ganumede said. "Some parts of it were not. Like what happened with Tithonus."

"Is it okay if I ask you to forgive me for killing your brother?"

"Yeah." Ganumede said. "It's okay. I forgive you."

Then Attis left. One second later and he just wasn't there anymore.

Nefertem and Xochipilli

"It really hacks me off when you flirt with other guys," Nefertem said. "I don't care if they aren't interested in you. It's gross."

Xochipilli laughed, "Do you know how hot you are? And how many people want you to fuck their asses and you put on this stupid guy act that gets all this action and you haven't even dipped your churro in sugar, yet?"

"You are a total dickwad! So I don't know how to act! That's because it's not acting!"

"You turn red and get all muscly when you get mad," Xochipilli said.

"And you're always a troublemaking tart and a total slut and a nasty smelly whore and a big huge slut." Nefertem said and stormed away.

Nefertem and Mithras

"Nef, he's used to his powers of seduction actually working. I think you and he are confused about one another's intentions," Mithras said. "Are you or are you not attracted to him?"

"Yeah, but that bitch has way too many bees buzzing around his flower. The whole hive, I bet!"

Even Grim and Serious Mithras couldn't prevent copious amounts of laughter from overtaking him, "Nef—"

"Yo."

"If you don't like how he acts, don't spend time with him," Mithras said. "Find someone else."

Ganumede, Orion, Spanx, and Sugarhoof

"He's gone," Ganumede said. "And Nefertem seemed too preoccupied to bother with me when I tried to say goodbye."

"You were an asshole toward him," Orion said. "And he gave up."

"What should I do?"

"Don't give up," Orion said. "He'll come around. Once we get settled, invite him to come visit."

"Okay."

"Are you excited at all?" Orion asked. "I'm really glad you agreed to give this a try."

"You are the first person in my life I actually wanted to ask me that, Hunter," he said. "So let's give it a try."

End

If I wasn't a Carpenter by the Five Tops

Sung to the Tune of "If I was a Carpenter by the Four Tops"

If I wasn't a carpenter
And you weren't a lady
Would you marry me, anyway?
We could still have a baby

If I took off my clothes
Would you still eye me?
Would you window shop me?
Even buy me?

Save my love through loneliness
Save my love through sorrow
I give you my onliness.

Give me your tomorrow
If I worked my hands on your wood,
Would you still love me?
Answer me, babe
"Yes, I would, I'd put you above me"
I once did trade,
Bump and grinding,
Could I give your glory-box
A silver lining?
Save my love through loneliness
Save my love through sorrow
I give you my onliness.
Come give me your tomorrow
If I wasn't a carpenter
And you weren't a lady,
Would you marry me anyway?
We could still have a baby